The Cubicle Next Door

Siri L. Mitchell

HARVEST HOUSE PUBLISHERS

EUGENE, OREGON

Published in association with the literary agency of Alive Communications, Inc., 7680 Goddard Street, Suite 200, Colorado Springs, CO 80920

Cover by Garborg Design Works, Minneapolis, Minnesota

Cover photos © Lisa Gagne /iStockphoto; Andreas Rodriquez / iStockphoto; Rainforest Agencies/ iStockphoto

THE CUBICLE NEXT DOOR
Copyright © 2006 by Siri L. Mitchell
Published by Harvest House Publishers
Eugene, Oregon 97402
www.harvesthousepublishers.com

Library of Congress Cataloging-in-Publication Data

Mitchell, Siri L., 1969-
The cubicle next door / Siri L. Mitchell.
p. cm.
  ISBN-13: 978-0-7369-1758-2 (pbk.)
  ISBN-10: 0-7369-1758-6
1. Computer technicians—Fiction. 2. Fighter pilots—Fiction. I. Title.
PS3613.I866C83 2006
813.'6—dc22
2006001666

Printed in the United States of America

06 07 08 09 10 11 12 13 14 / LB-CF / 10 9 8 7 6 5 4 3 2 1

To Tony
Without you, this book could not have been written.
Even more than the wind beneath my wings,
you are the rhythm of my heart.

Acknowledgments

Thanks to Carolyn McCready and Terry Glaspey, for being excited about this story. To Beth Jusino, for reminding me to write from the heart. To Kim Moore, for pointing out the places where I needed to give just a little more. To Tony Mitchell and Lanna Dickinson, my first readers; the depth in this book is due to both of you. To my father-in-law, Lynn Mitchell, for driving me around Colorado Springs and Manitou Springs and freely contributing his observations to this work. To Tim Scully, the A-Basin expert. To Marsha Scully, Tim Hayden, and Dorri Karolick, for educating me on the finer points of the interworkings of the Academy. To Dr. Dale Agner, for advising me on flight medicine. To Mike Hutson, who deepened my understanding of John 3:16. To the Bandas, who introduced me to Bollywood. And to those men and women of USAFA Class of '91, who embody their class motto: *Munus Primo, Semper Integritas.*

And to my sister, Heidi Hand, who grappled with difficult questions and made tough decisions with great courage. I'm proud of you.

One

****

So what do you think, Jackie?"

What do I think? Funny Joe should ask me. He's just finished reading my blog. He's just quoted me to myself. Or is it myself to me? Do I sound surreal, as if I'm living in parallel universes?

I am!

The blog—my blog—is all about Joe. And other topics that make me want to scream. But the clever thing is, I'm anonymous. When I'm blogging.

I'm Jackie, Joe's cubicle mate, when I'm not.

And that's the problem.

Joe is asking Jackie (me) what I think about the Anonymous Blogger (also me). And since I don't want Joe to know the blog is all about me and what I think of him, I can't tell him what I think about me.

My brain is starting to short-circuit.

If I can't tell him what I think about me, I certainly can't tell him what I think about him, so I'm going to have to pretend not to be me. Not me myself and not me The Cubicle Next Door blogger—TCND to my fans.

I have fans!

If I were clever I'd say something like "Look!" and point behind him and then duck out of the room when he turned around.

But there's so much computer equipment stacked by my desk and so many cables snaking around the floor that I'd probably break my neck if I tried to run away. So that option is out.

I could try pretending I didn't hear him. "What?"

"SUVs. What do you think about them?"

But then we'd basically end up where we started.

So how did I get myself into this mess?

It was all Joe's fault.

The year Joe came into my life, I'd been working the same job for ten years, doing the same things I'd always been doing when the department hired one too many people. Had I been working for a private company, it might not have been such a big deal, but I was working at the U.S. Air Force Academy as a civilian in a building classified as a National Historic Landmark. So it's not as though we could carve an extra office out of a closet or bump out a wall somewhere. At least not without 51 requests in triplicate, 32 meetings with the architect's office, and a project deadline scheduled for 17 years after the date of my death.

May God rest my miserable soul.

We could, however, order extra cubicle panels and subdivide an existing office as long as the panels didn't cost more than a specified number of dollars.

So that's what happened.

I should know.

I was the one who ordered them.

Unfortunately, no one bothered to tell me it was my office that was going to be subdivided.

Maybe I should have suspected. I mean, how long can a civilian GS-07 keep an average-sized dimly lit interior office to herself? It was only a matter of time, right?

I ordered the tallest panels I could find. And after they came, I called the casual status lieutenants to install them. They were freshly graduated Air Force Academy cadets who were hanging around the department until their real jobs came open. And when they came into my office, they asked the question that would change my life.

"Where are they going?"

"Where are what going?"

"The panels."

"I don't know. Don't you guys?"

"No. Who ordered them?"

"I did."

They stood there in front of my desk, all three of them in camouflage battle dress uniforms, arms crossed in front of them, ready to take on the world. "So...what do you want us to do?"

"Go find out who they're for." Duh. Double-duh.

They just stood there.

"Go ask Estelle."

That made them happy. Estelle was the department secretary. She knew everything—except how to use a computer.

That's what they'd hired me for.

They sauntered off down the hall, but they came right back two minutes later. "They're for you."

"No, they're not. I ordered them, but they're not for me."

"That's what Estelle says."

Estelle was usually right, but this might fall under the Scanning Software category of things in which she was completely mistaken.

The previous year, the colonel had asked me to install scanning software on her computer for the new scanner, and in between the time it took me to store the software disks in my cabinet and come back to show her how to use the program, she'd dropped a textbook on top of her keyboard, pressing all of the F-key functions at the same time.

Never, ever do that.

I snatched the book from her computer and contemplated hitting her on the head with it, but I dropped it onto her desk with a bang instead. "What are you doing?"

"Scanning. The colonel wanted me to scan the chart on page 137."

"You don't scan that way." It really killed me not to be able to kill her.

"But you just installed the software, so I held it up to the screen for it to see."

"The screen doesn't scan it; the scanner scans it."

So you see, the Scanning Software category was a gigantic catchall for tasks, both large and small, that Estelle just didn't and never would know how to do.

After we replaced her keyboard and reinstalled all of her software, the colonel made me the official scanner person for the department. Which gave me one more title to add to official digital camera person, official video camera person, official department website person, official overhead-slide-projector person, and kick-the-copier-in-just-the-right-spot-to-make-it-work person. That's why I needed all of my office space. It wasn't just me in there. It was the scanner, the cameras, the slide projectors, and assorted small appliances that didn't work anymore but might be useful if there were a nuclear explosion and technology devolved back to the Bronze Age.

I marched out of my office and down the hall. The lieutenants trailed me to the front office in perfect flight formation.

"Estelle?"

"Mmm?" She was rubbing lotion into her hands.

"Those cubicle panels are not for me."

"Of course they are. That's what the colonel said."

"When?"

"In the e-mail."

"What e-mail?"

"The one where he said we'd be getting one too many instructors, so we'd have to find a place to put him."

"And?"

"And so he said to make room for him. And I e-mailed back that I thought your office would be perfect."

It was. It was perfect for me.

"And someone was going to tell me about this when?"

"Um…no one told you?"

I shook my head.

"That's funny. Because I thought…" She began dragging her mouse around the screen, clicking at various folders in her Outlook program.

"See. Right there. It was in April. *Good idea. Lt. Col. Gallagher will share Jackie's office.*" She read further, mumbling words, running her finger across the computer screen and leaving behind a greasy streak. "Oh. Huh. I guess *I* was supposed to tell you. Sorry." She looked up from the computer and raised her eyebrows. Smiled.

"Is the colonel busy?"

"Let me see." She took a scheduling calendar from a stand on her desk and found the day's date. Consulted her watch. "Not right now."

I told the lieutenants I'd get in touch with them later, and then I stepped around Estelle's desk, walked about three steps, and knocked on the colonel's door. I peeked my head around the corner. "Sir?"

"Jackie? What can I do for you?" He stood up as I approached and fiddled with a pencil on his desk.

"I want my office back."

"Office?"

"The one you decided to subdivide in April? Because you hired one too many instructors?"

"Oh, yeah. Well, not really. Greg got the dean's extension, so he stays for another two years. If he'd gone, we'd have been right on target with the number of instructors. You know how it is."

"No, I don't. Your office is bigger than mine is. Why don't you subdivide yours?"

His eyebrows shot up into his hairline. People don't usually talk to colonels like that. But see, they couldn't fire me because nobody else knew how to kick the copier. And I was a civilian. And I was a woman. "We chose yours because it's the only office that will work. We don't have to reconfigure any overhead lights, there were enough outlets, enough telephone jacks. Space is at a premium in this building. You know that." He shrugged and sat down.

The interview was over.

Two

****

The talk with the colonel may have been over from his perspective, but it wasn't from mine.

Far from it.

It was, however, time for a cease-fire.

I walked outside and stalked around Fairchild Hall a couple of times. No mean feat. It's the single largest academic building in America, and its low, linear, 1950s architecture broadcast the Academy's no-nonsense approach to life.

This summer, like most summers, the brilliant blue skies had been tempered by the smoke of forest fires. But the sunlight still blazed down, unfiltered by the native trees.

Here at the outskirts of the city, cottonwood trees congregated around streams or dips in the landscape, offering shade to things that didn't need it. Pines marked the runoff patterns of the hills, ever alert for the next cloudburst.

Back behind the academic area, beyond the point where the 17 spires of the Academy Chapel pricked the sky, the foothills broke like rows of waves against the horizon. Their undulations were slow and lazy, like the motion of a gentle ocean.

The spectrum of the Colorado summer ran from the green-golds of earth and grass to the purpled hues of the mountains and the dazzling blue of the expansive sky.

I walked down toward the Aero Lab, leaned against the wall separating it from the wilds below, and was doused with sunshine. I watched the beginnings of clouds sneak across the sky, heading out toward the freedom of the open plains. They were starting to form into cute cotton ball puffs. Over the course of the next hour, I knew the random dots would congregate and associate to form drifts. By noon I would be witnessing the birth of thunderheads. Like clockwork they would gather strength and advance slowly out over town and then onto the plains. And if the weather reports held true, by the time I got ready to log off my computer, the afternoon clouds would have followed like a blanket, as if someone were spreading cotton candy over the sky.

I yawned. Stretched. Took a deep breath. Then I turned around and went inside.

If I were going to be subdivided, then I was going to draw the new boundaries. Two-thirds of the space for me and one-third of the space for Lt. Col. Gallagher. That seemed reasonable. Of course, that meant the door to the office would be on my side of the cubicle, but then I'd be able to see everyone who came in. On the other hand, they would also be able to see me. And only me. But that way, we could all just pretend the lieutenant colonel didn't exist.

While the lieutenants installed the new cubicle walls, I stayed busy rearranging my things. If I wasn't going to be allowed to keep my office, then the department was not going to be allowed to keep its stuff in my space.

"Which of you is the equipment custodian?"

There was a pause in the rhythm of the work. A silence of hesitation. And then an answer. "Me."

I rolled my eyes as I threw yet another outdated version of Microsoft Office onto a pile off to my right. Disks, books, box, and all. It hit the top and then skidded down to the bottom, an avalanche of computer disks following the trail it had blazed. "Me who?" The lieutenants had already installed half of the panels, and now they were hiding behind them.

A scuffing of combat boots along carpet, a metallic clink, a loud "Ow," and my inventory guy emerged from the new cubicle. Oh. Too bad. He was the one I liked best. Maybe I'd have to take him out to lunch. If he'd ever speak to me again.

"I have a project for you," I said, trying to smile, trying to think of how to make it sound enticing, but by then he'd already seen the pile of odds and ends I had accumulated. Cassette tape players, broken VCRs, an abandoned Dictaphone hemorrhaging wires. An industrial strength glue gun that had nearly been consumed by dried droplets of its own glue. A toaster oven. A microwave. "All of those need to be turned in."

Turned in. Such an innocent phrase, but one which meant many hours of tedious paperwork and coordination between three different offices to delete the items from the department's inventory.

His eyes opened wide, his mouth clamped shut, and his face turned red. One of the best and the brightest. Those are the kind of cadets they have at the Academy. For being a brand spanking new lieutenant, he was catching on quickly. He retreated behind the panels.

They banged and pushed and shoved for another half hour before they left.

So that's how I got subdivided. And how I got reorganized. And how, the next week, I came to be tacking up a giant poster of Che Guevara on my side of the cubicle wall in front of my desk. I had a soft spot in my heart for that bearded, beret-topped, Marxist Cuban guerilla leader. I'd probably get a black spot on my personnel folder; no chance at a secret clearance for me.

Too bad.

I didn't plan on the poster taking up permanent residence. I'd already decided to use the space as a soapbox for my struggle against the Establishment. I had the rotation schedule filed on my Palm. Next month I would feature a poster with a quote about ineptitude. The month after, demotivation. I'd found a great website called despair.com a few months ago while I was kicking around on the Internet at home.

Because I never do that at work.

Anyway, I figured that for a couple of weeks I could count on Che to make a statement about the communal sharing of property and which class of citizenry gets called upon to do all the sharing.

Call me a subversive. Call me an adolescent. One thing I'd learned after working for the government for ten years: If you don't say it when you feel it, you burn out or blow up.

"Nice poster. How old are you? Nineteen?"

Okay, that scared me, a voice coming out of nowhere, interrupting my thoughts. I took the remaining thumbtack from between my teeth and pushed it through a corner of the poster and into the cubicle wall. Leaned back and made sure it was straight. "Didn't your mother ever tell you it's not nice to sneak up on people?" I slid off my desk and turned around. "I'm thirty-one."

The voice belonged to a Caucasian male, 6'1," pilot. After working with the military for a decade, there are things you can tell just by looking. Who is and who is not a pilot is one of them. And it has nothing to do with the uniform because this guy wasn't even wearing one. He had on Levi's that looked as old as mine and a faded blue polo shirt. It was something about the way pilots stand. And the way they take in information. As if they're the ones who make all the decisions. It's not a fact until they decide it's a fact. Confident at best; cocky at worst. Pilots have to work extra hard to overcome my initial prejudices.

Usually, they don't succeed.

"Thirty-one? Are you sure?" He smiled. Teeth together. Gleaming. A smile so big his grin was lopsided. He was one of those 110 percent guys, smiling so hard it looked as though his nice solid jaw was clenched. Either that, or he was trying really hard not to laugh.

I couldn't blame him for asking the question. There was no uniform for civilians at the Air Force Academy, and keeping with Colorado culture, most of us were casual. Some of us, to a fault. I was wearing my standard summer uniform: jeans, T-shirt, and Converse low-tops. My standard winter uniform was a variation on that theme: jeans, T-shirt, wool sweater, and Converse low-tops. I buy Levi's 501s and shrink them to fit. And I buy men's extra large sweaters. I pick them up at thrift stores. Shetland wool are my favorites. No patterns, just solid colors. When I get them home, I throw them in the washing machine and shrink them too. Maybe some of them have shorter sleeves than wrist-length, but if you shove your sleeves up anyway, what does it matter?

Levi's, shrunken sweaters, and colorful Converse shoes. Did you know you can throw Converse low-tops in the washing machine too? That's why I buy them. I have them in every solid color ever made, plus the flame print. I couldn't resist. Converse shoes are my thing.

And they were my thing long before they became everybody else's thing.

Along with snide remarks and a dry sense of humor.

I bent down, picked up my backpack from under the desk, and grabbed my wallet. I fished out my driver's license and handed it to him.

He looked at it. Looked at me. Looked at the license again. "Jackie Pert Harrison. After Kennedy?"

"After Gleason."

He raised an eyebrow. "Was that nice?"

"No." But then leaving the decision of naming me up to Grandmother's best friend was not nice either. Adele's all-time favorite TV show was *The Honeymooners*. But my name had turned out to be a misnomer. Jackie Gleason was round and jolly. I am not, thank you, God. I'm small, dark, and intense. Which is appealing to trolls. And maybe muskrats.

"Pert, huh?" He handed it back to me with a shadow of that dazzling grin. Then he pulled his wallet out of his jeans and handed his license to me. It was of interest mostly because I'd never seen a driver's license from Idaho before. Potato boy. Figured. I almost forgot to look at his name before I handed it back. Glad I didn't. "Joseph Gallagher. You're Lt. Col. Gallagher."

Life as I had known it had ended. This was him. In the flesh.

His plane hadn't gone down on the way to Colorado Springs; his car hadn't been driven off the road. He hadn't gotten hit by a bus. How come God never answers my prayers? Isn't he supposed to know the thoughts we think in private?

He grinned again. Were those dimples? "I'm Joe. Thirty-seven." Joe, age 37, had clear blue eyes and curly auburn hair, cut Air Force short on the sides but left long enough on top to curl. See, that was another pilot thing. Pilots follow most of the rules most of the time, but in letter only. Never in spirit.

"Well, Joe, good for you. Your office is over there. On the other side of the wall."

"Hey. If you like Che, do you salsa?"

"Dance? No." Not unless someone's holding a gun to my head.

"Cuban food?"

"French."

"Cigars?"

"Only if you want it stuffed into your nostril."

"So you're one of those trendy Che fans?"

"No, I'm one of those political Che fans. I'm protesting the elitist distribution of resources. At least the kind that takes all its resources from the most impoverished of society."

His face went blank. He blinked. Thank goodness. It was a little unnerving to be stared at. "What elite distribution of resources?"

"The cubicles. This used to be an office and it used to all be mine."

"Oh." At least he didn't seem too put out. "So how did a nice communist girl like you end up working in a place like this?"

I blushed. Sat down in my chair. "Consider me a communist mercenary."

"Which is also an ideological impossibility. Either you're lying about being a communist or lying about being a mercenary."

"How would you know?"

"I did my graduate studies in Russian history."

"Oh. Well…I never said I was a communist."

"Ah." He turned around and walked over to his side of our space. I heard him opening and closing the drawers of his desk. "What do you have to do to get a decent pen around here?"

"Bring it from home."

I heard a snicker and looked over to find his face peering at me from around the side of the wall. "Spoken like a true government worker. As good a reason to foment revolution as I've ever heard."

Foment? He was a pilot, wasn't he? Pilots weren't smart enough to go around talking about "fomenting" revolutions.

He emerged from his cubicle and stood close to my chair. Too close. The hair on the back of my neck started to prickle. He glanced at his watch. "Hey, time for lunch. Let's go."

"I don't normally do lunch."

"And you don't normally have to share your cubicle—office—either, right? So it's my treat."

And before I could say yes or no, I found myself outside in the middle of the terrazzo.

"Aren't you supposed to be in uniform to be out here?"

He gave me a curious look. "I'm with you."

True.

The only people allowed on the terrazzo, the quadrangle bordered by the chapel to the west, Vandenberg Hall to the north, Sijan and Mitchell Halls to the south, and the academic areas to the east, were cadets and other military and civilians employed in that area of the base. I carried my civilian ID and Proximity card around my neck at all times.

They used to allow almost anyone on the terrazzo as long as they were escorted by a cadet, but 9/11 changed everything. So while Joe in uniform might have been welcomed to walk where he pleased, Joe in jeans was getting a few glances.

Joe paused once we stepped out of the shadow of Fairchild, his eyes sweeping across the static aircraft crouching at the four corners of the terrazzo. "The F-16, the F-105, F-15, and the—"

"F-4 Phantom."

"You know your planes."

Only that one. The one my father flew.

We walked north, past the airplane displays. We began the turn toward the edge of Harmon Hall's courtyard, but then Joe stopped and turned toward the chapel. "Just a second."

I followed behind him as he walked toward the chapel wall.

"Last time I was here, my class crest was front and center." The lower chapel wall displays the crest of each graduating class. The current senior class, the firsties, have their crest displayed in the middle.

"You haven't been back since you graduated?"

"It took a couple years after graduation for my guts to stop twisting when I thought of this place."

"So which one is yours?"

Joe pointed. "Class of '91. Bold Gold. *Munus Primo, Semper Integritas.* Duty first, integrity always." He stood there for a minute, staring at the crest, and then he turned and gestured toward Harmon Hall with his chin. "That was a place I never wanted to visit if I could help it. It was never a good thing to be called up to the superintendent's office."

It was a place I never wanted to visit if I could help it, either. Harmon Hall meant travel orders and travel vouchers. And since Estelle was so extraordinarily busy, I usually got to deliver them, by hand, to the travel office. Not, of course, that it couldn't be routed through the Academy mail system, but somehow officers had a habit of requesting travel orders at the very last minute.

We approached the back of Arnold Hall. I held my Prox card up to the automatic card reader. It clicked and I pushed the fence open. Repeated the procedure to open the door into the building.

We walked past the box office for the Academy theater, through a dining area, and into the food court.

"What sounds good? Taco Bell?" Joe had me standing in line before I'd even considered Subway or Anthony's Pizza.

He ordered some combination of tacos too numerous to count. I cast a longing glance at the other restaurants before ordering the latest greatest item being advertised.

I added a couple of packets of the hottest of the hot sauces to my tray.

He picked up a couple of straws and lids.

"Could you put those back?"

Joe turned toward me. "Did you pick up some already?"

"No, but we don't need them."

"Sure we do."

"No, we don't. Technically, you don't *need* a straw or a lid to drink from a cup. You only think you do."

"It's easier."

"It's lazier. If you can bring yourself to raise the cup all the way to your mouth, then the environment wins. Do you know how many straws Americans use and throw away each year? It'd be one thing if they were biodegradable, but most restaurants don't buy that kind."

"What would a straw have to be made of to be biodegradable?"

"Potato starch and corn starch."

He stood there looking at me for a moment. "That's just gross. And you're strange." He slid back toward the straw dispenser. "But I'm putting them back, see? Everything's going to be okay. You do realize that even if I don't use this straw, somebody else will. In the big picture of all the straws in America…"

"If you save a hundred straws a year and I save a hundred straws a year…"

"Then that's only two hundred straws. There are still millions left over."

"But the point is, you don't need one and I don't need one. And a huge straw industry has convinced us all that we do."

"You're not really a communist, are you? You're one of those conspiracy theory people."

"I'm one of those environmental people."

"Are you sure? Because those people drive me crazy."

"Don't worry. You can be reformed."

"Don't count on it."

We returned to the large dining area. Joe steered us toward a table in the middle of the room. "This okay?"

I nodded. If I were choosing, I'd select one of the small tables in the back corner. But normally I never ate lunch out. Today, for instance, I had a perfectly good grilled chicken breast and a container of tabbouleh waiting for me in the department refrigerator.

Joe grinned at me before attacking the first of his tacos. After he was finished, he wiped his mouth with a napkin, collected stray pieces of cheese and lettuce, and wrapped them into the next one. "So. Tell me about you."

"You already know my name."

"But I don't know…what you're really good at doing."

"Anything with computers. I'm a geek."

"Really?"

"Really. And I can make crêpes."

"So you're a good person to know if my computer ever gets disabled by a hungry Frenchman."

I smiled. Just to be polite. Took a drink.

"Tell me something you're not good at."

"Making snowflakes." I cannot now, nor have I ever been able to, make snowflakes. The ones you fold and cut with scissors in preschool. I have visions in my head of beautiful, geometric, shimmering flakes.

But when I unfold my creations, they fall apart. Literally. "And I can't cut my own hair." It's amazing how often I forget.

Right now, my black hair had been cut in a Christiane Amanpour I-have-better-things-to-do-than-fool-with-my-hair wedge. It dries by itself and mostly falls into place. Sometimes when my hair gets shaggy and if I know I'm going to be crawling on the floor stringing cables around the department, I put it up in ponytails. I save the rubber bands that hold bunches of herbs together in the grocery store. Most of the time they're blue. Most of the time I wear jeans. I figure everything matches well enough.

"Neither can I."

"So...you're a pilot, right?"

"I hope so."

"Then why are you here? What did you do? Wreck a plane?"

As he looked at me, his eyes went dark. "Wrecked my head. I started getting migraines. Haven't had one in two months, but I still have twenty-two months left until they'll consider putting me back on flight status."

Migraines? I doubted it. Lots of people said they had migraines and didn't really know what they were talking about. But I did. "Are you okay?"

"Just peachy...or I will be when I can start flying again." He tried to smile. "How long have you been working here?"

"Ten years. And I would really like to have the rest of my office back, but I'll let you stay on one condition."

He froze mid-chew and asked the question with his eyebrows.

"I'm the department's systems administrator. When you're working on your computer, could you not eat or drink at your desk?"

He swallowed the taco. Drank half of his liter of Coke. Smiled. "Sure."

Sure. That's what they all said.

"If you can do one thing for me."

"What?"

"In the morning, first thing, I like a strong cup of coffee. No milk or sugar. But it's got to be hot. I usually try to get to work around seven."

It was only the twinkle in his eye that kept me from flipping the contents of his tray onto his lap.

"Come on, Jackie. I'm not a cadet. I know how to take care of a computer. Relax. I'll be your best customer and your biggest fan. Trust me."

If only I'd known.

After lunch, I got him up and running on the network. Showed him all the important department folders, such as the events calendar which no one ever bothered to look at, and the FYI folder holding "important" information dating back to 1995.

"In case I might want to…?"

"…sign up for the 1995 First Annual Christmas Potluck?"

"Good idea. What should I bring?"

"Squeeze cheese?"

He glanced from the computer screen up to my eyes. "Squeeze cheese." His eyes flicked again to the computer screen. "No problem. It's my favorite. I'll bring two."

It's my favorite too. Not that I'd ever tell anyone.

I also like Bugles.

"Need anything else?"

"Nope." He was navigating his way through the department website. Clicking at a fast enough rate to make me dizzy.

"If you need anything—" I slipped away behind the wall and into my own cubicle. Immersed myself in work. If nothing else, he made for a quiet cubicle mate.

Several hours later, I almost jumped out of my skin when he poked his head around the wall.

"I'm heading out. You leaving?"

I shook my head, looking back toward the monitor.

"What's wrong?"

"Still backing up the system."

"Oh. Well, see you next week."

Next week? It was only Monday. I turned to look at him across my shoulder.

"I'm still on leave. House hunting."

Oh. "Good luck."

THE CUBICLE NEXT DOOR BLOG

Sad day on the cubicle farm

My office for one has been turned into cubicles for two. Of all the indignities of modern life, this is one of the worst. Not only have I been subjected to life contained between fake, padded "walls," not only has the original poorly designed air circulation system been blocked by those "walls," not only do I have to freeze in the winter and broil in the summer from the blockage, but now I also have to do it in the presence of someone else. And in a bizarre mathematical equation, dividing the space in two has made the injustice twice as bad.

The only appeal I have is to Che Guevara, champion of the oppressed and powerless masses. I have to wonder how my boss would look upon such an austere work environment. Whether or not, in fact, *he'd* like life as one of the proletariat. Office space should be allotted on the basis of who does the most work.

My new cubicle mate is not a bad guy, but he's not good either. Let's call him "John Smith." He's one of those types I've always secretly despised. One of those guys who's done such a good job of figuring life out that he wants to do it for everyone else too. Tall, confident. Good-looking. To some people, maybe.

Posted on June 5 in **The Cubicle Next Door | Permalink**

Comments

Amen, sister. Workers of the world, unite!

Posted by: **justluvmyjob | June 5 at 08:09 PM**

Not as bad as it might have been.

Posted by: **philosophie | June 5 at 07:30 AM**

CLOSE

Three

****

Joe cruised into work the next Monday with a large paper bag trailing cinnamon roll fumes and a superlarge cup of coffee.

He stopped suddenly, midway between our cubicles, and sent a raised eyebrow greeting as he held the paper bag between his teeth and the coffee in a hand while he zipped and unzipped various pockets on his flight suit.

"Ants in your pants? Oops, I forgot. My mistake. You're still wearing your pajamas."

He set the paper bag down on my desk. "Ha-ha." He wore a look of both offense and condescension. "These are not pajamas. I happen to be wearing my purse."

My lips turned up at the corners. I couldn't help myself; it was too early in the morning to exert the required level of self-control. To call the flight suit a uniform is a misnomer. Uniform implies that a person needs to exhibit some sort of grooming in order to wear it. Flight suits are the military equivalent of sweat suits. They never have to be ironed, never have to be starched. You could hypothetically just roll out of bed, hop into one, and zip it up. They look like something a garbage collector would wear. An olive green coverall garment with elastic at the back of the waist meant to protect whatever is worn underneath. In fact, pilots call the suits "bags."

And they are in every sense of the word.

When Joe said he was wearing his purse, he wasn't kidding. There are pockets of assorted sizes running up and down the suit. Pockets on the arms, on the chest, on the legs. People hide their hats in there.

Pens, pencils, wallets.

"I hate to tell you this, Joe, but it's summer. You might want to change purses. I'm thinking white. Then you could moonlight as a hazardous waste collector."

He sent a half smile in my direction before he rounded the cubicle wall into his office. I heard the paper bag thunk down onto his desk.

"I know you're not opening that bag anywhere near the computer."

"Yours or mine?"

You know, it's pretty disgusting to have to clean a keyboard. If people ever bothered to do it themselves, then I could almost guarantee they'd never eat hunched over their computer again.

If you really want to gross yourself out, take a computer mouse, the old kind with a tracking ball, open up the bottom and tap the ball into your hand. Yeah. That's what I'm talking about.

"Hey, your good luck wish worked. I found a house."

"Where?"

"Manitou Springs."

Luck or misfortune? Whatever it was, he had chosen my town to live in: Manitou Springs. With a population of 4500, we were practically neighbors.

"You can't live in Manitou Springs!" In thinking about Joe, not that I had done it very often, I had pegged him as a Gleneagle or Black Forest kind of guy. Gleneagle, one of the more prestigious and pricey neighborhoods north of Colorado Springs, seemed just his style. I would have guessed he'd have bought into one of the proliferating townhome projects that kept sliding down the hill, ever-closer to the interstate.

I heard his fingers pause on his keyboard. They began typing again. "Why not?"

Because it's my town! "Because."

"You're not my mother, so 'because I said so' is not an acceptable answer."

"You're not the type."

"What? I'm not tall, dark, and handsome? No, wait. I am."

"Manitou is eclectic. Artsy. It's a very tight-knit community." And

I don't want to have to worry I'll run into you every time I turn a corner.

"Then I'll just have to put on my beret and set up an easel in Memorial Park. Think I should buy a pipe too?"

"Not that kind of artsy. Hippie artsy."

I heard his chair wheels cross the plastic floor mat and then squeak across the carpet. Joe stuck his head around the wall. "You're talking tie-dye and Birkenstocks, not smoking jackets and Pavarotti?"

"Exactly. People who enjoy coffin races and public pajama parties and host festivals for professional bubble blowers. You don't want to hang out with people like that."

"Maybe I do…and maybe I don't. But I have to do something with myself for the next two years until I can get back on flight status. And the house needs a lot of work. Don't worry. I won't crash your little party."

Don't worry? "But there's all the New Age people, and crystal shops, and metaphysical bookstores. You don't seem like you're into that sort of thing."

He looked at me, the twinkle absent from his eyes. "Listen, if I have to be here, then at least I can try to have some fun. Besides, in Manitou, I can stroll through the middle of town, which from my place I can actually walk to, and get a latte, buy a dulcimer, or talk to my neighborhood shaman. What could be better than that?"

"That's it? That's your reason?"

He smiled. The dimples flared. "And I like to hike."

Okay. I could buy that. Divide was just up the road, and from there you could tramp, snowshoe, or cross-country ski in Mueller State Park.

His eyes were scanning my face. "So, am I in?"

"In what?"

"Your little club. Can I join the Residents of Manitou Springs, or is there some kind of probationary period?"

"You're in. Just stop by Hazel's Crystal Shop to pick up your broom. For ten bucks extra, you can get the wizard hat and cape set."

"What is it with you guys, always trying to make another buck? I had to pay through the nose for the house, and then I found out ghosts weren't even included."

"They're a dime a dozen in Manitou. In fact, here's how you can pay off your mortgage. Just start advertising yourself as the only house in Manitou without a ghost. You'll make a fortune."

He winked at me and then rolled back into his cubicle. "Thanks for the tip."

I worked through the morning in vague discomfort. I was sharing my office with Joe. Did I have to share my town with him too? Maybe it wouldn't be so bad. Maybe I wouldn't run into him. Maybe I could wear headphones at work and dark sunglasses when I was at home. And maybe if I closed my eyes and moved into a bubble, I could pretend he didn't exist.

As I was thinking all these thoughts, I had slouched down in my chair, rested my head on the back, and closed my eyes.

When I opened them, Joe was grinning down at me. "Time for lunch."

"I brought mine."

"So take it home at the end of the day and have it for dinner."

"Do you ever take no for an answer?"

"No. And I have to go to the uniform store, so we'll go to Burger King."

I just sat there staring up at him. I tried to figure out some way to relieve him of the idea that he was my personal social director. "Just because we share an office doesn't mean we have to do everything together."

"Do you want to eat lunch or don't you?"

"Ye—"

"Then let's go." He walked to the wall, slapping his flight cap against his thigh, looking as if there were no time to waste.

How do you tell someone you don't want to be their friend? The longer I looked at him, the more I realized it wasn't worth the effort. Once school started, he'd be much too busy to go out to lunch all the time. And then I could finally finish off my bowl of hummus and container of carrots.

We walked at a fast clip through Fairchild Hall and then rode the elevator down to the parking lot below.

He unzipped a pocket on his flight suit to fish out a set of keys. As he hit a button, a car ahead of us beeped to life.

No, not a car. An SUV.

I almost turned around and headed back toward the elevator.

I have this thing about people who drive vehicles that are bigger than they need to be. I really wanted to say something, but I kept the words stuffed in my chest and decided to spill it all out onto my blog later. I would never say anything to Joe himself. Or to the dozens of other people I know who drive SUVs. I try to hate the SUV and love the SUV owner. Everyone who moves to Colorado from out of state thinks they need some kind of Driving Machine to make it through the winter. Two words: Subaru and Saab. There are safer, more efficient ways to achieve the same result. And they don't involve squandering gas or terrorizing the local population.

At least the SUV was clean. Spotless.

He drove out of the parking lot and then navigated his way onto Academy Drive. We got an up close look at the steep Flat Iron, a barren inverted-V rock formation in the hills. Trails had been etched into the earth by the clambering feet of generations of cadets. At the moment, government-issue sheets had been twisted around the rocks to form "06," a reminder left by the class that had graduated the month before. I had no doubt that by August it would read "10," courtesy of the entering class of freshmen.

We twisted and turned, following the topography of the foothills. Black-eyed Susans were growing wild along the roadway. Out in the air in front of us, parachutists made colorful bubbles in the summer sky.

A car rounded the corner in the opposite direction and flashed his lights at us.

I touched Joe's arm. "That's the Academy signal for—"

"Deer. I know." He stepped on the brake as we turned the corner. And there, in the grasses along the road, were a doe and her fawn. The fawn was grazing, balanced on slender legs. In a maternal gesture of sacrifice, the doe placed herself between the road and her baby, unwilling to let danger approach the fawn unless it touched her first. We saw her head rise. She stared at us, ears tipped in our direction.

Joe stepped on the gas after we had passed them. "I had a room-mate once who rode a deer."

"How do you ride a deer?"

"First, you have to be drunk. Then you have to be able to sneak up behind one. He was a basketball player, so he had a great vertical jump."

"He just jumped on the back of a deer?"

"Basically. He tried to hold on, arms wrapped around its neck, but the deer bucked him off and kicked him in the head. Broke his jaw."

At the bottom of the hill, Joe turned left. He gunned the motor to get his SUV up the hill.

"There's usually a cop around here somewhere."

He lifted his foot from the accelerator and we lurched back into gear.

We crested the hill in-between the commissary grocery store and the Base Exchange department store, drove past, and then went in the far entrance of the Community Center. We patrolled the parking lot looking for an empty space and did a U-turn as the road bent around by the library.

"You're not going to find anything. We might as well take one back by the road."

"Something will open up."

Joe closed the loop we'd made around the parking lot and started another. And as he came even with the first breezeway entrance into the quadrangle of buildings, a car backed out right in front of us. He grinned at me.

I scowled at him.

"You want to stay here? I'll leave the AC on."

"I'll come with you." No need to waste the gas. We were experiencing one of Colorado's scorching summer heat waves. I didn't think I'd last in the car for five minutes, even with the air conditioner on. And I'd never been in the uniform store before. In fact, I'd never even been to the Community Center before. The base was full of services for the military and their dependents: the commissary, the BX, the gas station, the recreation center with ski rentals and discount tickets to places like Elitch's up in Denver and the Disney theme parks. But for civilians, there was nothing. Next to nothing.

We were allowed to use the base gym.

We turned left from the breezeway and walked up a short flight of steps. Joe held the door to the store open for me. Then he made a beeline toward the right wall, leaving me to wander.

I'm not sure what I expected in a uniform store, but this wasn't it. There were military books. Calendars. There were racks filled with blue uniforms: baby blue shirts, dark blue pants and jackets. There were Air Force Academy souvenirs. There was a section in the back for shoes: lace-up oxfords, low conservative heels, flats, and combat boots. There were purses and attaché cases. There were three or four aisles of shelves holding nothing but clothing: undershirts, socks, gloves, stocking caps, battle dress uniform pants, and camouflage blouses (even for the guys). There were toiletry kits and shirt garters. I picked up a package of the garters, interested to know how they worked, how they attached themselves to both your socks and the hem of your shirt. That's where Joe found me.

"Do you actually wear these?"

"When I wear blues."

I started laughing. Tried to picture him. But something happened when I mentally unzipped his flight suit and left him standing there in his underwear. I stopped laughing.

"Are you okay?"

"What? Oh. Yes. I just…I mean…they don't bother you? To wear them?"

He plucked the package from my hands and set it on top of the small box he was already carrying. "No more than it would bother me to keep tucking my shirt in all the time. Ready?" Joe walked to the cash register, flashed his ID, and scanned the front of the *Air Force Times* while the sale was rung up. He'd gotten new shoulder boards for his formal uniform, his mess dress. Dark blue with an oak leaf and two stripes, embellished with silver braid and embroidery.

He tucked the bag under his arm and was out the door before I could catch up. "I hate having to buy these things. I'll probably use them twice before I retire. And they were thirty-five dollars."

"But you're a pilot. You're supposed to be rich."

"Tell my bank account. And it's not about the money; it's about the principle. If they're going to require me to wear a uniform like this, that has to be changed every time I pin on a new rank, then at least it ought to be affordable. I've probably spent a hundred and fifty dollars on shoulder boards alone. And five hundred on the uniform."

"Versus the flight suit…?"

"Which is issued."

"Well, that's tough."

He laughed as he beeped the SUV doors open. Then he cut in front of me to open my door.

We retraced our route and turned this time between the commissary and the BX. Tucked beside the commissary was a Burger King.

And as always, during the lunch hour, it was packed. We waited in line for 20 minutes and then waited another 15 for our food. You'd think with so many uniformed personnel bunched up, staring at the counter, waiting for food, the staff would move a little faster. Especially when a pair of military cops with guns gets thrown into the mix.

They never do.

Finally, we slouched into a booth, sitting opposite each other. Joe swiveled, resting a knee on the bench and leaning up against the wall.

I hooked my finger around an onion ring and slipped it into my mouth.

Hot! I grabbed my Coke and took a swallow.

"You seem a little touchy about the ghost and goblin thing."

I shook the rest of the onion rings onto the paper tray liner to cool. "I'm not. Everyone else seems to be."

"Everyone else who?"

"All the Christians in town."

"So you're not one?"

"Christian? I am. But it doesn't mean I have to be afraid of people who aren't. People are people. Just because they don't believe the same things I do doesn't mean they're not worth knowing. Or living next to. Where *are* you living, anyway?"

His eyes changed hues. Seemed to lighten. He named a street which was just one street up and three blocks over from me. "We could carpool."

Yes, I'm wash-and-wear. Yes, I'm a zealous recycler and very big into reducing my impact on the environment, but I just couldn't bring myself to say yes. "No."

"We could meet on Saturday mornings downtown for breakfast."

"No."

"Or lunch."

"You mean like a standing date?"

"Yeah."

"No. I don't do dates." Something in his eyes made me want to take my words back. Maybe he didn't know anyone in town yet. "I also help Grandmother at the shop on Saturdays."

"Which one?"

There was no point in lying. Even if I told him Antique Bazaar or Canterbury Gifts, he'd still be able to figure it out. All he'd have to say is, "But Jackie told me her grandmother…" and he'd probably be escorted straight to the shop. "Alpen Ski."

"For cross-country skiing, right?"

Nordic, cross-country, XC, there wasn't any difference. I nodded. "*Only* for cross-country."

"Great! That's what I want to do this winter. Get a pair of cross-country skis and head to Mueller."

"Why don't you try snowshoeing? No lessons required; just strap them on and go. You'll have the trails all to yourself." Grandmother didn't sell snowshoes.

"I want something that will keep me in shape. You ski?"

"Not really. Not since I was in junior high. I used to ski with Grandmother."

"You liked it?"

"Yes." Grandmother and I skied at odd hours. If we got to Mueller by 5:30 AM, we could put in two good hours before we had to pack up and head home so she could open the shop. In the dead of winter, we could ski at least an hour before sunrise. It was magical, sliding through silent snow-shrouded forests, watching the darkness retreat until it was banished by the sun. I loved how blue puddles of night lay abandoned in the ridges of snow. How a handful of stars fought off the morning, glimmering in the lightening sky.

If the moon was full, or close to it, we would also ski at night. I always imagined myself as Lucy, walking through Narnia's frozen world with Mr. Tumnus by my side. Night skiing was extra exciting because it was illicit; I knew if I had been home, I would already have been in bed. I loved the clear moon-glazed nights. But sometimes we would have a full moon during the crossing of weather systems, when thin strands of clouds were being pulled across the moon. On those nights I always skied looking over my shoulder. Shadows flitted, and the darkness of the forest seemed to pulse.

"Want to go?"

"Where?"

"Skiing. This winter."

"I don't even know where my skis are anymore."

"Buy new ones. Maybe your grandmother would give you a discount."

I bit into the last onion ring. It had already gone soggy. "I'm not a very good teacher."

"Who says I need lessons?"

"Have you ever cross-countried before?"

"No, but I used to downhill all the time."

"Then you need lessons."

"If I take lessons, then will you ski with me?"

"I'm not the only person in town who skis."

Joe's hamburger had already disappeared. He chugged the last of his Coke and then pulled his chin into his neck to hide a burp. "That's true." He winked. "Maybe I should ask your grandmother."

THE CUBICLE NEXT DOOR BLOG

SUVs

John Smith wouldn't be so bad, except that he drives an SUV. A Socially Unsustainable Vehicle.

Why do people need so much space? Why don't they learn how to pack lighter? And why do they need to sit so high above the ground? It still doesn't allow them to see over an 18-wheeler! I bought the smallest car I could find, and I bought it used. Great gas mileage. And when it finally falls apart, I'll buy an electric car. Which creates its own set of conundrums because my city uses environmentally unfriendly ways to produce electricity.

But that's not what I was blogging about.

I hate SUVs. Their owners can't even reach the roof to wash them. They take up extra space in parking lots, they require so much gas they require *me* to pay more for *my* gas, and on top of that, they're trying to kill me! My little car doesn't stand a chance in a face-off against an SUV. It's the equivalent of modern day jousting. Or boxing without separating the athletes into weight classes.

And that's what John Smith drives.

Too bad.

I might have been able to like him.

Posted on June 12 in **The Cubicle Next Door | Permalink**

Comments

SUVs: Unsafe at any speed for humankind.

Posted by: **philosophie | June 12 at 10:22 PM**

Four

****

Later in the week I found myself in the middle of a traffic jam on my way home. Traffic on I-25 had stacked up at the Interquest exit. That was bad. I was only three miles into my commute. I still had seven miles to go until I could get off at the Garden of the Gods exit. I didn't have any other options.

I fiddled with the car radio, adjusting it from my morning talk-radio channel to NPR. Finally made it to the Garden of the Gods exit.

After turning south onto Thirtieth, I watched as Kissing Camels emerged from a background of striking red rocks. I imagined the camels to be bedding down for the evening, legs folded under them, humps in profile. Nuzzling each other before sleep.

I signaled and turned into the park.

Anyone who says rocks are inanimate has never visited Garden of the Gods. There, the rocks breathe life. They glow with energy. Flare with motion. Trees grow from them—roots exposed—using the formations as a dance floor. Birds build nests in them. Marmots and snakes scurry through their holes.

If Colorado Springs is built on the pathway to the plains, Manitou Springs is built on the trail to the mountains. Manitou marked the entrance to the land of dreams: gold and silver mines, ore fields. It was a leafy oasis on the journey to thin air, harsh landscapes, and frozen winter. Above the town, Pikes Peak projects up from the landscape like a fabled lone breaker at the ocean. The seventh wave. The big one.

I turned left off Manitou Avenue and climbed the hill toward home. Home is a turn-of-the-century two-story with an attic. Light blue with white trim. It has everything you'd imagine: a wide front porch overhung by a second-floor balcony and a cute dormer window in the attic. The house sits up from the street; the separated garage is on street level, burrowed into the hill. The front of the property is buttressed by a stone wall, with stone steps leading up into the front yard. And everything is surrounded by a white picket fence.

I pulled the parking brake and got out to push the garage door up. Then I inched the car in, rolled the garage door down, and locked it.

Grandmother was trolling the kitchen, looking for something to eat, when I came in through the back door.

"I have pork chops marinating in the fridge."

She pulled the refrigerator door open and bent over to verify that I was telling the truth. "Oh. I hadn't looked there yet. How was work today?"

I didn't say anything.

"That good?"

"I have a new cubicle mate."

"They come new every year, don't they?"

"In general. But this one's specific. He's sharing my space. How was your day?"

She didn't say anything.

"That bad?"

"No one wants the Rossis."

"Oh." Well, in the larger picture of things, it wasn't a big deal. No one had wanted the Rossis for the past ten years. Rossignol was her own personal favorite brand of skis. And since she didn't ski anymore, not since she broke her hip ten years ago, she tried to pawn them off on everyone else. The problem was that this particular pair of Rossis was just as old-fashioned as she was. In the nicest sort of way, of course. They used to be top-of-the-line, but technology had passed them by and she refused to mark them down. Which reminded me. "You could always mark them down."

"A pair of skis like that? I'd sooner let my only child run away to India." An inside joke.

"If you price them low enough, someone will buy them."

"They're not for just anyone. They have to be for someone who appreciates them." She sniffed and crossed her arms, leaned against the counter, and watched me prepare to cook.

I shrugged. And that was it. We'd had the same conversation every day for the past ten years. Except for Sundays. She never worked on Sundays. Not for any religious reason, but simply because most tourists were on their way out of town at the end of the weekend, making Sunday one of the slower days in the shop.

"Is he nice?"

"Who?"

"Your new guy."

"He's not my guy."

"Well, he is new, and until you tell me his name, I don't have anything else to call him."

Cranky, cranky. The weather must be starting to change. Her hip always ached when pressure systems shifted.

"Is he mean?"

"No."

"Well?"

"Joe. His name is Joe."

"Italian?"

"Irish."

"Humph."

My father had been of Irish ancestry. An O'Flaherty. Grandmother had nothing against my father, but everything against his family.

"He seems nice." It wasn't that I was defending Joe; it was only that he didn't deserve to be in Grandmother's bad graces just because his father had an Irish last name.

"Well then."

Well then. Well then, I'd just have to bide my time until Greg's extension ran out. And Joe left. Then I might get my office back.

I left Grandmother in the kitchen and let myself out the back door. I lit the hibachi out on the porch and then came inside to take the pork chops out of the refrigerator and make our salad. A can of black beans, a can of corn, a few snips of cilantro, and a couple heaping tablespoons of salsa. I took the pork chops outside with me and shook off the excess chipotle-lime marinade.

While the pork chops cooked, I went inside and opened all the windows. Like the vast majority of older houses in the Springs area, Grandmother's didn't have air-conditioning. There wasn't much of a breeze, but at least the open windows would exchange the stuffy inside air for stuffy outside air. I turned on the pedestal fans in our bedrooms, positioning them in front of our windows to coax the air inside.

While I was upstairs, I pulled off my shoes and socks and left them in my room. Then I went back outside, flipped the pork chops, and walked off the porch to make a quick tour of the yard. I loved feeling the heat of the flagstones against my bare feet. The yard is a xeriscape. I'd done the work when I'd returned from Boston ten years before, when I'd come back home.

Home, and my life, had always been odd. By the time I was born, Grandmother was done cutting sandwiches into triangles, baking cookies, and training roses to climb her trellis. She'd dealt with her share of household pets. And she had long before resigned from the PTA.

She was happy to make grilled cheese sandwiches or heat up store-bought lasagna, but I'd learned if I wanted anything fancy to eat, I'd have to make it myself. Same went for the yard. For many years, we were the only house on the block with artificial turf substituting for grass. And plastic tulips in the flower boxes.

Now that I'd moved back, we were the only house on the block with xeriscape. But then we were also the only house on the block with an affordable water bill.

Xeriscape used to mean lots of rocks and little tiny plants. Or cactus. But a little research goes a long way. We do have pebble and flagstone paths, but we also have ground-hugging sprays of magenta poppy mallow drooping down over the garage. Spiky fans of chives and dusk-shadowed purple sage. Rounded drifts of lavender, clumps of fuzzy lamb's ear, and square patches of spongy lemon thyme. I broke off a few leaves of lemon thyme and rubbed them between my fingers. Took a big whiff. Then walked back to the porch, took the pork chops off the grill, and went inside.

Grandmother was sitting at the table with a glass of ice water pressed against her forehead. "Let's eat outside."

We filled our plates and then took them out to the front porch and sat on the steps. Eating outside during summer heat waves had become a tradition, but we had never gotten around to buying furniture to sit on.

As we ate, we listened to the evening noises of Manitou Springs. Cars swishing past. Birds calling. Children shouting. The occasional parent yelling.

We were halfway through dinner when she said, "Your mother is fifty today."

Happy birthday, Mom.

I used to tell anyone who asked that my mother was dead. She might as well have been.

My mother had just finished her first year at Colorado College when she met my father. It was an interesting match: Vietnam War protester and Air Force Academy instructor. No worse than Romeo and Juliet. And it didn't turn out much better.

They had one summer of love and then he got sent to Vietnam. He died before my mother told him she was pregnant. His F-4 was shot down. She was inconsolable. Practically catatonic. I was born seven months after his death. When I was less than a day old, my mother walked out of the hospital and ran away to India.

My paternal grandparents denied my paternity, so I ended up living with Grandmother.

I wrote a letter to my mother when I was 13, asking all of the "why" questions I could think of. She wrote back once. Said she thought about me every day. Sent good thoughts my way.

And that was it. I'd rarely thought of her since.

She might as well be dead…except for one small ember of hope that stoked my heart no matter what I told myself. The hope that one day, someday, she'd come home. And then she'd tell me how much she loved me and that leaving me had been a huge mistake.

Crazy, wasn't it?

My church had a series of sermons on legacies right before I had stopped attending. It made me think long and hard about the legacy my mother had left me. And I'd decided then that her legacy was going to stop with me. I didn't want to curse anyone else with it, so I made the decision to remove myself from the gene pool.

I decided I would never fall in love with anyone.

I never wanted to care so deeply for someone, depend so completely on someone, that I would go off my head and end up messing up my entire life. And everyone else's.

As the product of premarital sex, I planned to stay as far away from temptation as I could. Because, as far as I could tell, losing your heart meant losing your mind. So I planned to do whatever it took to stay in control of mine.

I was not, God help me, going to be my mother's daughter.

Happy birthday, Mom. Love, joy, peace, and other groovy thoughts.

Five

****

We finished dinner in silence. Grandmother went to the living room with the newspaper to do her crossword puzzle while I cleaned up the dishes.

After I'd finished I hiked up the stairs and logged onto my computer. I knew from experience that trying to go to sleep before 1:00 AM in such hot weather would be a wasted effort. So I changed into the boxers and tank top I would eventually fall asleep in. I brushed my teeth and washed my face in our tiny closet-of-a-bathroom that has never recovered from its aquamarine-blue 1950s phase. I leaned over the sink and poured a glass of water over my head. Evaporation is the poor man's air-conditioning. I returned to my bedroom, shivering from the droplets of water making serpentine trails down my back. Repositioning the fan, I turned it to high and then sat down in front of the computer.

I needed to blog.

I've never been one for writing. Ask any of my English teachers. But blogging isn't really writing. It's thinking while you type, and I can do that. So the previous year I had started a blog. In place of those clever images people post, I took a digital picture of myself with a paper bag over my head.

Since it was mostly about work and the stupid things people do, I called it The Cubicle Next Door. I made sure there was no way anyone would ever trace it to me. And I always blogged at home.

Remember my theory about needing to vent regularly? The blog helped. Posting a blog was like screaming, yelling, and throwing a tantrum without having to utter one word. Same satisfaction, less energy required.

I blog nearly every day. There are predictable peaks of vehemence in my entries: around evaluation periods when I rant about the futility of overinflating everyone's performance appraisals and just after the release of new rules that sound efficient but only end up creating more work for everybody. But, generally, I'm a "part of the solution" kind of person.

That evening, though, I was looking forward to writing about one of my traditional pet peeves: Waste.

The department was gearing up again for the school year. The new department Snack-O, the designated snack bar stocker, had replenished the shelves that day with all manner of junk food, each sealed in its own shiny, plastic-wrapped package. Said package was quickly thrown into the garbage after the snack had been consumed. It was just wrong. For all sorts of ethical, moral, economic, and health reasons.

After I blogged, I felt much better. I surfed the Internet for a while, trying to kill time. Logged onto the message boards I frequented and chatted with those who were signed on. Glanced at the computer clock in the corner of my screen.

Sighed.

Three more hours. At least.

I adjusted the fan so it would hit the back of my neck, blowing my hair up and to the side. It didn't help much, so I picked it up and used it like a hair dryer, directing the air flow to different parts of my body. My arms and legs. The back of my knees.

Grandmother knocked on the door. "Goodnight." She nudged the door open. Saw me with the fan. "Can I have some?"

She took off her reading glasses, closed her eyes, and motioned with her hands toward her face. She stood there a full five minutes, basking in the air like a cat in the sun. Then she opened her eyes, kissed her palm, and pressed it to my forehead. She'd been doing that for 30 years. "Goodnight."

After she left I returned the fan to the floor and logged back onto my blog. I'd been meaning to jazz it up a little. All I had was time, so I went to work.

I played around with the colors. Played with background graphics and photos. Tinkered during those postmidnight hours when everything seemed like a good idea. Finally arrived at a combination I liked. Figured it would be a nice change for the ten people who read it every week. Over the course of six hours, I'd gone from having a no-frills black-and-white site to having graphics and color and a nifty background.

By that time it was 3:00.

I went to bed.

The next morning, heading out of town on Highway 24, I got honked at. After being stuck in the previous evening's commute and watching everyone else do something illegal or immoral on the highway, I was hypersensitive about my driving. And I am a good driver. Really. I've never gotten a ticket or been in an accident, knock on wood. I always drive with the traffic, even if it's ten miles above the speed limit, because statistics prove it's safest that way.

And someone was honking at *me*.

I'm a good Christian girl, so I don't give people the finger or roll down my window and scream at them, but I do begin to drive extra slowly, and somehow this always seems to block the honker from changing lanes or doing whatever it is he wants to do so badly.

Just trying to set a good example.

I moseyed down Highway 24 and got stuck at the stoplight at Twenty-sixth. And the honker came right up to my bumper and honked. Again. And of course he—I could assume it was a person of the male gender because women will usually just cut a person off instead of harass them—was in an SUV, so I couldn't actually see his face. Just his grill. A polite reminder that, should he wish to, he could roll over my car and squish me like a bug.

Driver's exams should include psychological profiles.

The light changed and I ever so slowly rolled through the intersection, but I needed to pick up speed. Eighth was just a block ahead, and I wanted to make the light. While I was switching gears, the SUV roared around me on the left and then jumped in my lane.

I took a deep breath and reminded myself that jerks were better off in front of me than behind me. Then I saw the person wave. And that's when I recognized the vehicle.

It was Joe.

Of course it was Joe.

He was the only person I knew awake enough in the morning to recognize a fellow commuter.

So I waved. What else was I supposed to do? And then I let him make the light while I fiddled with my stick shift. It's temperamental. And I didn't need to play cutesy-poo hopscotch all the way up I-25.

By the time I got to work, he was drinking a cup of coffee and chatting with Estelle as if he were her best friend.

He waved when he saw me walking down the hall and then continued talking.

I got my own cup of coffee from the break room—ceramic mug, not a Styrofoam cup—and took a sip. I walked back to my office and set it on the bookcase behind my desk, and then I sat in front of the computer and started my morning routine.

Checked e-mail. Deleted everything from Jimmy Pitts, department crackpot.

Opened and replied to everything from Lt. Col. Miller, deputy department head for personnel.

Left everything else alone until later.

I ran through my systems checks.

And then I visited gazette.com, the Internet home of Colorado Springs' newspaper. It's a good newspaper. And by reading it online, I saved at least half a tree every year. One small sacrifice for me, one small victory for the environment. It's little things, compounded over time, that add up to a big thing. I try to do my part. I figure it's the least I can do.

It really bothered me to see so many people in town trashing the planet. And I included myself in that group. Sometimes, even I was too lazy to collect my dead batteries and take them to the county waste collection site. Sometimes, even I throw old printer toner cartridges in the trash instead of taking them to the base waste collection site.

But I do collect bottles and cans. And I recycle plastics. How hard is that? They even come to your house around here and pick them up.

And I'm not an overly zealous recycler. I'm not an in-your-face environmentalist. Just a concerned citizen. Maybe I read my Bible wrong, but in my version it says God created the earth. And everything else. Sure, Adam and Eve screwed up and started the planet rolling downhill, but that doesn't mean we have to push it along. It's not very complicated. It only involves basic principles of etiquette. Share. Be nice. Use some common sense. The greatest mind in the universe created the earth and everything on it. Seems like we could show it a little more respect. But then, that's my other theory. I think Americans in general have stopped respecting the planet, each other, and even their bodies. And that's why I save my squeeze cheese and Bugles for special occasions only.

Like Fridays.

So I was alternating scanning my electronic version of the *Gazette* with sipping coffee at the bookshelf when Joe walked in.

"Did you know Estelle's son has cancer?"

"No." I tried to keep my visits to Estelle on an as-needed basis.

"It's not looking good. She might have to fly back to take care of him."

"When was he diagnosed?"

"March."

"Wow."

"Yeah."

Cancer. The thought of your body consuming itself from the inside was the worst sort of horror I could imagine. Much worse than the B-grade horror films Grandmother and her friends loved to watch. There were few things that truly terrified me.

Cancer was one.

Death was the other.

Not mine.

Grandmother's.

THE CUBICLE NEXT DOOR BLOG

Waste not

At least half of the environmental and health problems of America could be solved if Americans stopped snacking. Or if they started snacking properly. People eat what's readily available; I understand that. But why can't people take two seconds to throw a bag of carrots into their shopping cart and then take it into work with them to snack on? Why do they have to grab individually-sized packages of chips and candy? First of all, they end up paying more for the privilege than if they bought a family-sized bag and ate them a handful at a time. Because that's all there is in those tiny cellophane packages: a handful. Second, it's inefficient to wrap millions of tiny things instead of thousands of large things. It costs more money and takes more energy. Third, what happens to all of those tiny packages? I'll give you a hint: They don't get recycled. And yet those snacks still keep being made and the packaging still keeps being produced. Why? Here's my theory. The people who eat those kinds of things are fundamentally lazy. If they can't be bothered to make a wise economic choice—to buy a large portion of something and divvy it up themselves—then they certainly can't be bothered to make a wise environmental choice.

I've come to the conclusion we all practice our religion with the opening of our wallets...and we either worship ourselves and our own convenience or we worship something else.

Posted on June 15 in **The Cubicle Next Door | Permalink**

Comments

I couldn't care less about the environment, but I do care that I'm the one who usually has to clean up the mess in the break room.

Posted by: **justluvmyjob | June 16 at 07:33 AM**

We have to worship something other than ourselves, or we'll all turn into pigs. Wait—we already have!

Posted by: **philosophie | June 16 at 06:41 PM**

CLOSE

Six

****

The following day, Wednesday, was my birthday. It was also bridge night. All of Grandmother's friends came over to play. All three of them. I always tried to be around because I was the Designated Substitute. And I always tried to make them something to eat because for years I'd also been the Designated Taste Tester of dozens of batches of cookies made with secret ingredients, like ground-up popcorn, lemon-lime soda, and Snappy Tom tomato drink.

Knowledge is power.

The only cookies I eat now are the kind I buy from Wild Oats.

The ladies were all in their early-80s. And, amazingly, all of them lived alone. Two of them still drove, although they carpooled on Wednesdays.

None of them ate much. I think Grandmother was the healthiest of the bunch and even she picked at her food.

I baked things like banana or zucchini bread. Things they wouldn't feel too guilty about eating. That night, after dinner, I had made Fruit Cocktail Cake. A birthday cake they wouldn't feel bad about eating and that wouldn't send their blood sugar levels hurtling off the charts.

Grandmother kept me company in the kitchen while I baked and then cleaned the dishes. At 7:00, the doorbell rang. On any other evening, any of the women would have walked up the path and kept going until they reached the back door, which opened into the kitchen, but bridge night was special. They all dressed up and they all came in through the front door. It had been held at Grandmother's house for as long as I could remember.

Grandmother got to her feet and went to let the ladies in.

We'd already set up the card table and positioned four chairs around it. I gave them about ten minutes to get seated and then went in and took orders for drinks.

"Jackie! Good week?" Adele smiled up at me. She was my favorite. She had sparse tufts of carrot-orange hair she carefully fluffed over her scalp. She wore purple tracksuits and glasses on a chain around her neck. She is one of the nicest people I know.

"It's been fine. What would you like?"

"A tall glass of ice water will do."

Ice water had been "doing" for the last 20 years.

"Thelma?"

"Milk."

Thelma was a tank in every sense of the word.

"Betty? What can I get for you?"

"If you don't have any gin, I'll have to settle for water." Betty still thought she was 40. Still thought if she fluttered her eyelashes enough and dropped enough hints, she could have anything for the asking. Including men in a wide variety of ages. For an 80-year-old, she was extremely well-maintained.

I got the drinks, including a glass of milk for Grandmother, and passed them around.

The ladies insisted on singing "Happy Birthday" to me. Then they each gave me a present. I could tell, without opening, what each gift was. Adele's was bound to be something for my hope chest. It didn't seem to matter to her that I didn't have one. Betty's would be a compact of makeup or a vial of perfume; hope sprang eternal. Thelma's was always something useful, like a can of mace. Grandmother's would be a donation to one of my favorite charities.

I opened the gifts. Thanked the donors. Displayed them on the coffee table.

Then I went upstairs, changed clothes, and went to work on my blog. I'd thought of a few more changes to make. I was interrupted a few minutes later.

"Jackie? Jackie!" I could hear Grandmother's voice calling me from downstairs.

I yelled back from my room. "What?"

"Are you there?"

"What?"

"Jackie!"

"What!" Everything about Grandmother was aging gracefully except for her eardrums. They'd already pulled up stakes and headed to Arizona. I went to the top of the stairs where she could see me.

"You have a visitor."

"Who?"

"I don't know."

Odd. Grandmother knew everyone.

Adele crept up behind Grandmother, put a hand on her arm, and leaned toward the stairs, looking up at me. "It's a man!" She thought she was whispering, but she wasn't. And as soon as she said "man," I knew whom she meant.

Joe.

He was the only person in Manitou Springs Grandmother didn't know.

And he had to show up on bridge night.

I used to wonder what God would give me if he ever thought I needed a thorn in my side. Now I knew for sure: Joe.

"I'll be right down."

I went back to my room and pulled a T-shirt on over my tank top. Not that he was here for sightseeing, but...well...I don't know.

I went down the stairs, leaning on the railing as I went so the stairs wouldn't squeak. I wanted to see what Mr. Congeniality would do with a room full of geriatric belles.

I tiptoed across the front entry and peered around the corner. He was looking at pictures. Grandmother's friends had gotten out their wallets and were accosting him with the photos they'd stashed inside. I didn't have to see them to know what the pictures were. Their grand-daughters. They were shameless. All of them.

And I'd bet money Grandmother thought she had a leg up on the competition because her granddaughter was there, in person.

"A very pretty girl, Mrs. Robinson."

"Thelma. You can call me Thelma. Please."

Adele had put her glasses on. She shoved her wallet right on top of Thelma's. "This is my granddaughter, Lisa."

"She looks very nice."

Betty actually elbowed Adele in the ribs. And when Adele looked over at her, she took the opportunity to hold her wallet up as far as she could. It barely cleared Joe's elbow.

Grandmother spied me. "Jackie!" By the way she was smiling, I could tell I'd pegged her. She looked like a proud 4-H exhibitor at the State Fair.

Joe had taken Betty's wallet from her hand and was still looking at it. The photo was probably of her granddaughter, Nikki. She was one of those naturally blond and breezy California girls. And she was kind too. I'd met her the summer she divorced her third husband. She'd come out to Manitou for a break.

Joe looked over at me and grinned.

"Can I do something for you?" My plan was to get him to the kitchen and then scoot him out the door as quickly as possible.

"Yeah. Do you have a ladder I can borrow?"

The ladies' eyes were bouncing between us as if they were watching a tennis match. It was making me feel uncomfortable. "If you can come out to the garage…?"

"Ladies, it was nice to meet you."

They twittered and fluttered back toward the card table.

Joe paused. Then he turned back toward the table. "What are you playing?"

I started toward him, intending to grab his arm, kick him behind the kneecaps, club him over the head, do anything to make him leave.

Adele was the one who answered. "Bridge. Do you play? We're always looking for a substitute."

Liar! Maybe they had been ten years ago, when the other half of the original group of eight was still alive. But I was the only substitute they needed now.

"I play poker." He made it sound like a question. As if they might want to play. I could guarantee they wouldn't. Wednesday nights were sacred.

"Poker? What do you think?" Adele queried the group. Everyone nodded. She turned toward Joe. "You in?"

"I'm in. Is there an extra chair?"

Betty headed toward the dining room. She was probably planning on placing Joe's chair right next to her own. I really should have followed to carry the chair for her, but I was still gaping at the scene in horror. "You can't play poker! You play bridge!" What was happening here?

Grandmother frowned at me. "We know how to play poker too. That's what we played in the early days." The Early Days meant the 1960s, when their kids were graduating from high school.

"Joe can't play."

"Don't be rude. Of course he can."

Joe was casting long glances at both Grandmother and me. He cleared his throat. "I don't have to stay. All I wanted was a ladder. I'm painting my living room. I should probably go, anyway."

I braced my hands against the table and stood on tiptoe, speaking toward his ear. "It might be better. They've been playing bridge on Wednesday nights for years."

Thelma rapped my knuckles with a deck of cards. "Don't talk about us like we're not here. Joe stays."

"Ouch!" Well, that was that. When Thelma made up her mind, she made a mule seem even-tempered.

Betty was pulling a dining room chair through the front entry. She was bent nearly in half, grasping it by the seat.

"Let me do that for you!" Joe was beside her in two seconds. He set the chair down on all four legs and then took Betty's hand to help her regain her posture.

Faker! Her eyelashes fluttered and she placed an unsteady hand over her heart. "Thank you, Joe. You're so strong."

I didn't need that. I walked out of the living room and had almost rounded the corner to the stairs when Grandmother's voice stopped me. "Jackie? Aren't you going to play?"

I kept climbing the stairs. "No, thank you. Not tonight."

"Joe needs the ladder."

"Call me when you're done and I'll get it for him."

They did better than that. They sent him up to find me two hours later.

"Knock, knock."

If people aren't going to go to the trouble to knock on a door, then why do they say the words? It's one of those questions I'll ask when I get to heaven. If I don't kill Joe first and get disqualified.

"Yes?"

"Do you mind getting me the ladder? I really do need it."

I turned from the computer to look at him. He was standing with one arm propped above his head against the doorframe. He looked tired.

"Did they give you a hard time?"

"They beat me. Took me for fifty dollars!"

"Good for them." Maybe he wouldn't come around again. I pushed my chair away from the computer, rose to my feet, and looked around for some shoes. I opened the closet, picked up the closest pair of Converse I saw, and shoved my feet into them.

When I turned around I saw Joe, still standing in the doorway, casting nosy glances around my room. I marched past him, closed the door, and trotted down the stairs. I was in the kitchen before I realized he wasn't behind me. I retraced my steps and found him in the living room, saying his goodbyes.

Adele was counting the money she had won. "You'll have to come next Wednesday. You might be able to win your money back."

"Only if I can sit next to you again."

Grandmother stopped Joe as he turned to leave. "Do you have our phone number?"

He shook his head.

Grandmother wrote it on the tally sheet and then handed it to him. "Call if you can't make it."

Joe took the piece of paper, folded it, and tucked it into his wallet. "I'll put it on my calendar. Wednesday night with the card sharks."

They all giggled.

Honestly! How do you like that? They'd switched from bridge to poker. And I'd been replaced. They'd gotten a permanent substitute for their substitute.

He raised a hand. "Goodnight."

We walked through the kitchen and out the back door. There was a suggestion of stillness in the air. Night was settling around us. "Does your house have air-conditioning?"

"No."

"Do you have any fans?"

"Not yet."

Couldn't he do anything for himself? "Just a minute." I went into the house, unplugged the fan from the living room and started carrying it away.

"What do you think you're doing?" Grandmother used to add "young lady" to questions like those.

"Joe doesn't have any fans for his house yet."

Choruses of "poor boy" followed me back to the kitchen. They probably would have run out and gotten him a snowmaker if they'd had the means.

Joe was sitting on the back steps. I almost tripped over him.

He stood up and put a hand to my elbow to steady me.

I held the fan out between us. It wasn't a very big one, and it was at least 15 years old, but it was something.

Moonlight made his face glow. "Thanks. I'll return it to you as soon as I can get my own."

He put his hands out to take it from me, but they clasped around my own. I tried to move mine, he tried to move his, the fan teetered in the middle.

"Just let me carry it." I clutched it to my body.

"I can—"

I was already moving down the path toward the street.

Joe caught up with me while I was unlocking the garage. He stood right next to me, blocking the moonlight.

I fumbled with the key. "Do you mind?"

"No door opener?"

"Yes. It's called Jackie."

"Here. Let me."

He took the key from my hand, unlocked the door, and pushed it up.

I pointed to the ladder.

He pried it away from the wall without bumping the car. "Can you do without it until next week?"

"No hurry." I held out the fan. "Do you have enough hands for this?"

He hooked his arm through the ladder, hefted it to his shoulder, and then took the fan from me. "No problem. Thanks."

I stood there, watching him for a moment as he clanked down the street.

Seven

****

The ladies were standing in the kitchen arguing when I got back. It sounded bad, but it's only because they had to shout to make sure the others would hear them. They were arguing about me.

"She wasn't rude. She was shy." I could always count on Adele to stick up for me.

"Shy people don't say anything. She said things." And I could always count on Thelma to think the worst about me.

"So she said things. She's the one who lives here."

"She works with him all day. She knows him better than we do. Maybe she just doesn't like him." And Grandmother was rational, if nothing else.

"She likes him. I know how it is. She's sexually frustrated."

"I'm what!" I don't know why I was surprised at that statement. Betty always turned everything into something about sex.

They scattered like a flock of pigeons. A flock of very slow-moving pigeons.

Adele laid a hand on my arm. "We're concerned about you."

"Why?"

She exchanged glances with the other women.

"Why?"

"We just think it's time you found a man."

"Really."

"You are over thirty."

"And you're getting snappish."

"And chewing ice cubes."

"What has that got to do with anything?"

Betty squeezed my arm and whispered in a loud voice, "Chewing ice cubes means you're sexually frustrated, dear. It's okay. We've all been there." See? Everything into something about sex.

It was surreal. Getting advice on my love life from octogenarians! "I've always chewed ice cubes."

"I know." Betty's eyes blinked wide. "And you've never been with a man, have you?"

They were all staring at me.

"Have you?" Grandmother was the only one who looked as if she didn't want to hear the answer to the question.

"No."

"See, that's the problem. You should stop yelling at him, dear. He might start thinking you don't like him."

"But I don't!" Was this so difficult a concept to grasp?

"Of course you do."

"Of course I don't."

"Playing hard to get is fine for the young, but you don't have the luxury of youth, do you?"

Thank you, Betty. "Are you trying to marry me off?"

"Would it be so bad?"

"I'm perfectly happy on my own."

"No, you're not." Just because she wanted someone, she assumed everyone else did too.

"So you want me to throw myself on someone I've barely even met?"

They all stared at me.

"You do? Why?"

"Because you need someone, dear."

"Listen, I know this concept is foreign to your generation, but modern women don't need anyone. It's perfectly acceptable to go through life on your own these days."

They were shaking their heads. "But not for you."

I decided to play along, hoping it would allow me to get to bed earlier. Better yet, maybe I could shock them and they'd all just go home. "So what do you want me to do, sleep with him?"

"Yes. Well…maybe not. But you could at least make him think you want to."

If I hadn't loved her fuzzy head so much, I'd have strangled Adele. "What! You're supposed to be a moral example. And you want me to hop in someone's bed? Just like that?"

"We went through the war years."

"You mean the old 'sleep with me, I might die tomorrow' line works?"

"Only when you wanted it to."

I really, really hadn't wanted to know that about Adele.

"You just never knew which boys wouldn't be coming home. And sometimes, it wasn't practical to get married before they left…such a lot of good boys never came home…" You could tell Betty was flipping through her mental scrapbook of wartime flings.

"He's a nice boy and he likes you. Help him out a little." Adele patted me on the arm. "You can do that, can't you?"

He likes me? Really? "Did he say that?"

"We're not blind. Yet." Thelma always told the truth, no matter what. Tanks had eyes in the back of their heads. And turrets. I knew from experience.

Adele gave me a quick hug and a kiss. "Just think about it."

I went upstairs and got ready for bed. Joe's scent still lingered in the hall. Exactly how long had he stood there watching me before he'd bothered to "knock"? Just the thought gave me a funny feeling in my stomach. I stood there in the doorway, trying to see what he must have seen.

My bedspread from India, bought at a time when I was thinking charitable thoughts about my mother. Old challis shawls from a thrift store made into curtains.

The floor-to-ceiling gilt mirror I'd rescued from a dumpster behind an old boarding house. The frame was beautiful, but the mirror was useless, clouded with spots and streaks.

My prized *Bride and Prejudice* poster.

I'm a Bollywood fan. Along with millions of other people in the world. It's amazing to me that an Indian movie industry which produces more films and sells more tickets than Hollywood is still so unknown in the U.S.

I watched my first Bollywood movie just to see what it was like where my mother was living. Granted, after the first 15 minutes I knew it was an idealistic picture of India, but it had the illusion of the reality of daydreams. An Indian's daydreams. So it *was* India just the same. And gazing at the images swirling in front of me, I could believe my mother believed she was living in a better place than here. A world filled with family who cared enough to try to control your life. A family who loved you enough to feel as though they had a stake in every decision you were making. A world vibrant with color and motion. Who wouldn't want to live there?

Of course, the India that existed outside of Bollywood was composed of filth and squalor. A few years into my Bollywood obsession, I was able to separate fact from fantasy, but by then I was hooked.

I've acquired most of my Bollywood DVD collection through eBay. And my eBay habit was expensive. But there was just…something… about the combination of music, song, and dance. The idea that family was more important than the individual. The concept that love could be honorable. And controllable.

Most of the time, in Bollywood, the characters never even kiss.

That's my kind of love.

I closed the door and stood in front of the bulletin board it had hidden. The one Joe could not have seen. The bulletin board held a photo of my best friend: Andreas. We'd met each other in junior high. Hung out together through high school. Hung out, in fact, until he had died of AIDS three years before.

The bulletin board also held photos of the children I sponsor. Orphans, all. Though I grew up without a mother, they all have it ten times worse. I've always sponsored two from the same orphanage. I liked to imagine they could be friends. As I stood there, I said a prayer for Antonio and Jorge, hoping the Mexican sun would smile on them in the morning. For Nicolette and Adriana, that they would be protected from the diseases which run rampant in Haiti. For Maria and Gloria, that they would never be tempted by the corruption in Columbia. And for Carlos and Juan, that they would be inspired in their studies.

Then I sat down and wrote them each a letter.

The next morning the phone rang at 5:45.

I was up. The Academy class schedule started at 7:00 and so the work day on the hill, even during summer break, began at 6:45. But just because I was up didn't mean I wanted to talk on the phone.

But Joe didn't know that. If he had, I doubt he would have cared.

"Jackie? Hey, would you mind doing me a favor? Following me over to Motor City on the way to work? I have to drop the SUV off."

"For good?"

"For a headlight replacement."

Too bad. "Sure. What time?"

"Six thirty?"

"Fine. See you then."

At 6:30 exactly, Joe rolled down the street and pulled in front of my car, and then we proceeded down the hill, went up Manitou Avenue, and headed over to Motor City. At least it wasn't far away. Most of the dealerships in town had decided to display their products in one location. If you couldn't find a car in Motor City, you weren't looking hard enough. Or you'd given up out of sheer exhaustion.

I followed him to his dealership, turned off the car, and wondered if there wasn't any other way to attract business than multicolored pennant flags.

Joe jogged over to my car, opened the door, and slid inside. Bonked his head on the roof when he straightened in his seat. Tried to slouch, but his legs were too long. Felt for a lever to adjust it.

"On the side."

He found one. The seat collapsed behind him.

"The other one."

He pulled at it and the seat shot back. He folded his arms behind his head and crossed his feet. "Not so bad at the right angle. You might want to go through Garden of the Gods. The interstate's backed up."

"Can't. It's not open. Not until eight." I eyed the interstate that ran above us. No one was moving. At least not in the direction we wanted to go. "We'll go through town."

I backtracked. Drove under the interstate on Cimarron. Turned north onto Nevada. Passed tree-populated Acacia Park, rapidly approaching the statue of General Palmer that sat in the middle of the road. No one ever quite knew for certain how to drive around him.

General Palmer is the reason Colorado Springs maintains its small-town mentality. It has more than 500,000 people, but it cannot figure out what to do about General Palmer and his trusty horse. Local wisdom held that the founder of Colorado Springs deserved a lovely, unobstructed view of Pikes Peak. To place him anywhere else would diminish his stature.

Well, he was dead. His stature has been diminishing for nearly a hundred years.

The answer, of course, was obvious. Move him across the road to Acacia Park. Give him his own little square of concrete so he didn't have to take up ours. As it is, the general causes untold traffic accidents each year. Mostly caused by drivers who are unable to decide, until the last minute, how to navigate around him.

When the city finally does something about the general, when it deals with the unreasonable influence a long-absent person has wielded over the simple interchanges of daily life, then the city will be well and truly ready to deal with growth. As it is, it remains unwilling to address serious problems like water, traffic, and infrastructure. Until it does, it may grow like a weed, but it will never mature. Never offer to its citizens all it could.

I'd blog about it, but then I'd give myself away. If anyone were looking.

"Isn't Poor Richard's around here somewhere?"

"The bookstore? It's one corner over. Tejon and Platte."

"Does it still have the restaurant? And live music?"

"I'm not sure."

"I used to go there with a roommate. We had these great wigs. Blond, shoulder-length surfer-style. The girls from Colorado College would at least talk to us when we were wearing wigs."

"Versus…?"

"If we came as cadets."

No surprise there. By some twist of fate, one of the most liberal colleges in the country, Colorado College, shared the same location as the Air Force Academy, one of the most conservative. "Great guy, your roommate."

"Oh, yeah. We used to…we'd go to Garden of the Gods all the time. We'd climb to the top of South Gateway Rock, the first one you see as you drive into the park, early on Saturday mornings when nobody was around. We'd rappel halfway down, then when tourists started driving through, we'd dangle there and scream for help. When they'd started panicking, we'd climb back up and drop down the other side."

"I didn't think you could climb in the park."

"You can if you register."

"You probably gave someone a heart attack."

"It was all in fun."

"Maybe for you."

We drove through the Colorado College campus. Passed the east side of Shove Chapel. It would have looked more at home in a Crusader's village with its small narrow windows and austere facade.

Joe sat up. Partially. "I always loved this campus. It's pretty."

It was pretty. It had grace and elegance. Century-old trees. Almost everything the Academy lacked. Except, perhaps, moral fortitude.

We made it to the Academy by 7:30. Not that anyone cared. New instructor training would start on 10 July. And until then, everyone who wanted to take leave had been encouraged to do so.

I worked on a program for online test taking and homework. I was hoping to have it up and running so it could be beta tested before classes started. It was a simple multiple-choice format. The challenge lay in security issues. How to ensure Cadet A didn't sign in as Cadet B. How to ensure answers couldn't be changed.

This experiment would be the precursor to online essay test taking and term paper submission. Most of the department's tests, even at the lower levels, were taken in essay format. By having cadets submit their tests online, we were hoping to lessen the temptation for cheating. And the impact of hundreds of paper copies on the environment.

I worked on it through lunch, waving Joe off when he tried to convince me to go eat with him.

I fiddled with fonts and formats. Debated the error messages. Was it better to remind cadets to select from answers (a)–(e) or was it better just to ignore the smart alecks if they tried to enter answers like (?) or (#%$)? Should the program report the scores to the cadets immediately, or should it reveal the result to the instructors' eyes only?

I ran through the test at least 20 times that afternoon. Made note of the things I needed to rework or rethink, including whether or not to have music from Beethoven's Fifth play whenever someone chose the wrong answer. I could picture it: The text from the question slowly dissolving into granular nothingness while the chords of the symphony pounded with despair, the word "WRONG" accompanying each beat. For a right answer? The Hallelujah Chorus?

Maybe not.

"You almost done?" His voice came from above me.

Startled, I looked up.

I found him staring down at me from over the cubicle wall. He grinned. "I wish I had your concentration."

"Are you…standing on your desk?"

"Yeah. I would've rolled around and come to the front door, but the wheels of my chair always get stuck in the carpet. Anyway, I'd like to pick the SUV up before they close if you don't mind."

I glanced at the computer clock. It was already quarter to five. "What time do they close?"

"Five thirty."

"Let's go." I saved everything and then logged off the network. "Did you log off?"

"Nope. It'll do it for me in…what? Twenty minutes?"

"You can never be too careful."

"Or too anal. How about this? I'll do the lazy man's log off."

I walked around the cubicle wall just in time to see him turn off the power to his monitor.

"Positive points for energy conservation. Negative points for poor security."

"That's me. An all-around well-balanced kind of guy."

I could think of a couple of other descriptions for him.

Joe folded himself into my car and then turned on the radio. "What is this? NPR?" He sent the dial off in the other direction before I could respond. Tuned into a song wailing about some paradise city. Started singing along.

I glanced over at him.

He was concentrating on playing an air guitar; concentrating so hard his eyes were shut tight from the extraordinary effort it must have required. He popped an eye open. "Why aren't you singing? This is a classic."

"I don't know this one." Or any other "classic" song for that matter. How do you fit in with your peers when you don't have a mother? There's a whole generation of influence missing in your life. At home, there's not a generation gap, there's a chasm. A gaping canyon that can never be spanned. Classic rock to my friends had been '50s music. Classic rock to Grandmother was something that has yet to be invented. Swing is as down as she gets. Glenn Miller is her favorite.

We sped down the interstate, just ahead of rush hour traffic, and made it to the dealership in about 20 minutes.

Joe hopped out of the car and went inside to the office.

I turned the radio back to NPR.

A minute later he stepped out of the door and gave me a wave. My signal to leave.

I rolled up to the garage about 15 minutes later.

Got out to push up the door.

As I got in the car and shut the car door, I was assaulted by the scent of Joe. A familiar scent that immediately brought to mind our cubicle.

I recognized the slightest hint of lavender. A suggestion of fir. Something powerful and...masculine. And something else. Some underlying note. Of cleanliness.

Something clean.

And pure.

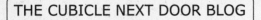

THE CUBICLE NEXT DOOR BLOG

What's wrong with me?

I'm worse than a shark.

I can smell your cologne from 100 yards away.

And it lingers in my senses, long after you are gone. Lingers in your cubicle like a forlorn ghost.

Posted on June 22 in **The Cubicle Next Door | Permalink**

Comments

Maybe you're allergic to colognes and perfumes.

Posted by: **justluvmyjob | June 23 at 01:52 AM**

Sounds like maybe those cubicle walls are blocking the circulation of air through the office. Is there a window you could open or something?

Posted by: **megluvsphysics | June 23 at 05:31 PM**

Are you sure it's not lingering in your heart?

Posted by: **philosophie | June 23 at 11:27 PM**

Eight

****

The next day Joe came into work with a request. "Can I ask you a question?"

"Maybe."

"Do you go to church?"

"Hypothetically."

There was silence, a rolling of wheels across his floor mat, and then a grunt as they hit the resistance of the carpet. Next, the sound of papers being shoved across a desk. A moment later his head appeared above the wall. "What's that supposed to mean?"

"I haven't found one yet."

"And you've been here…?"

"Ten years."

"I thought you'd lived here all your life."

"The church I went to before college was great. But when I came back, after Grandmother broke her hip, it had gone weirdo."

"Where'd you go to school?"

"East Coast. MIT."

"I had a roommate named Tim once who loved MIT T-shirts. Whenever he looked in a mirror, it said 'TIM.'"

"I suppose it's better than wearing a University of Portland T-shirt."

He snickered. "Computers?"

I nodded. "It wasn't fuzzy studies."

"Fuzzy?"

"In computers, things either work or they don't. And if they don't, there's a reason. It's because you, the person, have done something wrong. In fuzzy studies, from what I remember, almost anything can be right or wrong, depending on what sort of proof you can find."

"Or how well you can support your opinion. I guess you're right. But at least I could always bluff my way through papers. Bet you couldn't."

"I didn't have papers. At least not as many as you probably did. I had projects."

"Lucky you. So you haven't looked for another one?"

Another one what? I was starting to get confused. "Church? Oh, I've looked…"

"Well, I'm looking too, so let's look together."

"It's not—"

"I'll pick you up at 7:45 on Sunday."

I debated telling him to count me out. But he was so confident, so certain he would actually find one, I decided I wanted to be around when the disillusionment set in. "The early services usually start at eight thirty or nine."

"Not for church. For breakfast. We'll do church after."

"What if I had other plans?"

"At seven forty-five on Sunday?"

"Then I'll pick you up. We'll save at least a gallon of gas if I drive."

Grandmother came home that evening humming a Glenn Miller song. She paused when she saw me. "How was your day?"

"Fine. I'm going to church with Joe on Sunday, just in case I forget to tell you."

"Oh. Such a nice boy, that poor lieutenant colonel of yours."

"On his salary? Plus flight pay? He's not poor. And he's not my lieutenant colonel." He's not even that nice. Not really. "Why are you in such a good mood?"

She turned toward me, smiling. Her eyes were actually sparkling. "Guess."

"I have absolutely no idea."

"Someone looked at my Rossis."

A miracle. "Looked at them or asked about them and touched them?"

"Touched them and took them off the rack."

"Wow."

"He said he'd think about them. Come back tomorrow."

I lifted an eyebrow. We'd both worked in the shop long enough to realize if you let a customer leave without buying anything, they'd rarely come back. The chances of that happening bordered on never.

Grandmother looked at me with defiance glinting in her eyes. "I'm only telling you what he said."

I hoped he would. I really hoped so.

She was still humming as she washed the dishes.

Later that night, the ladies came over for poker. So did Joe.

I went upstairs and surfed the Internet. Hung out on the message boards for a while. Visited some chat rooms. Posted a blog.

On Sunday, I picked Joe up at 7:45. He tucked himself into the car. His head hit the roof whenever we went over a bump.

We ate breakfast at the Waffle House. And then we went to a church someone had told him about.

Here's the deal with me and God. My mother was so screwed up that in most cases I tried to do the exact opposite of what she did. I figured that strategy just might give me a fighting chance at Normal Life. Whatever that is. Assuming she'd converted to Hinduism, I took the opposite approach. She had many gods and goddesses; I chose just one. The one who said he was The One. Based on worldviews alone, there was no chance I would ever replicate her life.

At least not in my lifetime.

Joe gave me the thumbs-up that Sunday morning as the pastor began to preach.

I smiled back. No point in dimming his enthusiasm so early in the day.

He wasn't quite so chipper after it was all over. And I mean *all* of it.

The parade of singers and musicians. The loud music. The loud preaching.

"Think it would be...any different if we came again next week?"

"Do you?"

He grinned. Dimples flashed. "No. One down, tons left to go. We'll find one."

I just took a deep breath. Kept on driving.

Ignorance is the confidence of fools.

As we exited onto Highway 24, I saw Joe slouch farther down into his seat and lean forward to peer out the windshield. "Have you ever hiked the Incline?"

The giant stair stepper? "No." The Incline, a bald scar drawn straight up the side of Rocky Mountain, was due to an old railway that used to run a cable car up to its top for tourists. The severity of the incline ranged from about 40 to 70 percent. And from what I understood, the entire hike consisted of climbing railroad ties all the way to the top.

"Want to?"

"Let me think about that for a minute. No." Marathon runners jogged up the Incline for training. Military members hiked it for training. I'd never trained for anything in my life. Didn't intend to now.

"What else are you going to do today?"

"I could do nothing and have a better time."

"Come on. I bet the view is great from there."

"I'll bet it is too."

"Are you afraid of a little hike?"

"No. I hike all the time. Now and then. Sometimes."

"Where?"

"Mueller Park. The Black Bear Trail. When I can."

"Then the Incline would be easy."

I snorted.

"Really. It's straight up. No figuring out which way to go. Just onward and upward with a view at the top."

"I've lived here most of my life. I see mountains every day."

"But have you ever seen the mountains from above?"

"I've seen them from below."

"Totally different."

"And how would you know?"

"Flying. During flight screening as a cadet."

I'd walked right into that one.

"You've never flown over the mountains before? Ever?"

"I've flown, but it was always east. Over the plains."

"Come on. Just one little hike."

"One *big* hike. No thanks." I stopped at a light and looked over at him.

He was looking at me with determination in his eyes. He wasn't going to let it go.

I said the only thing I could think of. "So where did you fly?"

"Leadville. It's where all the cadets go to solo. They give you a certificate for landing there. It's the highest airport in the country, almost ten thousand feet."

"My grandparents met in Leadville."

"Was he a flier?"

I shook my head. "Grandmother lived there. Her father was a molybdenum miner."

"I never say that word if I can help it."

I felt my mouth twitch. Bit the inside of my lip to keep it from turning into a smile. "Grandfather was with the Tenth Mountain Division during WWII."

"The skiing soldiers."

"He joined up because he was a mountain climber, but he fell in love with skiing. After the war he came back, married Grandmother, and they helped run a ski resort."

"So how come you guys are in Manitou and not up there in Vail or Aspen?"

"After he died she got tired of the winters. Moved down. Met Betty and Thelma and Adele. They're all soldiers' widows too."

The light changed. I drove up the hill straight to Joe's house.

"Are you sure you don't want to hike it?"

"As sure as the last time you asked me."

He got out, started to shut the door, and then stopped. Bent over so he could see me. "Don't you get tired of viewing the world from the same angle all the time?"

"No. I never have."

THE CUBICLE NEXT DOOR BLOG

The view from here

What's wrong with the view from here?

Why do people always think they need something new or something different?

What if I'm happy just the way I am? What if I'm content?

What if I like my life just the way it is?

Posted on June 25, in **The Cubicle Next Door | Permalink**

Comments

Do you?

Posted by: **philosophie | June 25 at 12:04 PM**

Forget everyone else. Do what you want.

Posted by: **beetru2u | June 25 at 08:58 PM**

CLOSE

Nine

****

L et's go to the ramp." Joe's voice came from a spot somewhere above my head.

I looked up and saw him looking down at me over the top of the cubicle wall. "Would that be the Bring Me Men Ramp or the Core Values Ramp?" In a knee-jerk response to a sexual assault scandal, the Academy had removed the slogan "Bring Me Men..." from the ramp that led from the lower level of the complex to the terrazzo. The ramp was a key symbol for cadets. New basic cadets would march up the ramp to start their USAFA experience. Four years later they would march down as firsties, just before graduation.

Any feminist would only have had to read the following lines of the poem to understand the phrase was meant to be figurative, not literal. Even I could figure that out. But in politics, as in most things, it's much easier to defend the black or white than it is the gray.

Joe mumbled something. I couldn't hear what it was, but it almost sounded like a sneeze. He got off his desk and stalked down the hall.

I followed because I didn't have anything better to do. Watching the year's new basic cadets come in always made me think of the circuses in the old Roman Colosseum.

We took the stairs down several stories and surfaced on the second floor. Then we walked to the southern window-walled corridor and joined the crowd gathered at the western end.

We were late. Joe was tall enough to see over nearly everyone's head, but I didn't have that ability.

So I improvised.

I ducked into the Military Strategic Studies Department and went to chat with their systems administrator. I found him at his computer. "Hey, Dave."

He turned around and swept a handful of dark hair back from his forehead. "Jackie. What's the word?"

"In-Processing Day."

"Today? Already? Didn't they just do that last year?"

"Yes. But the gods of Harmon Hall demand new flesh every year."

He gave a salute to his computer screen. "Hail, superintendent. We who are about to die salute you." He closed out the program he was working on and spun in his chair to face me. "Should we have popcorn?"

I followed him down the hall to the MSS break room. He popped some popcorn while I pulled out my wallet and threw a buck in the coffee can for two cans of pop.

"Where should we watch? If the deputy weren't in town, we could use his office."

"Is the colonel in?"

"Watch the spectacle from the best office around? I like your style!"

The colonel, in fact, was in a meeting for the next hour, so we watched from his office.

The upperclassmen had spent the the previous week tidying up the pavement just in front of the ramp. At that corner of the cadet area, Vandenberg Hall stretches its arm out past the quadrangle of the terrazzo. At ground level, nestled up against the ramp, is the cadet post office. Out in front of the post office an area about half the length of the Vandenberg extension had been roped off.

It had also been delineated by a bold line of paint. And inside, forty pairs of footprints had also been painted. All of them facing Vandenberg Hall.

As we walked into the colonel's office, a bus pulled up. It was filled with brand-new basics. They'd been told to report to the Academy with a toothbrush and a razor.

And that's it.

Chipper upperclassmen in T-shirts, camouflage BDU pants, and berets moved toward the bus, whistling and smiling. Clapping. Waving. We could hear their noise from inside the office.

Dave rubbed his hands together in imitation of an evil genius. "Okay. First one on the bus to wave back. You call it."

"Girl in the blue shirt."

"Guy in the yellow baseball hat."

I won. And as soon as she waved, a few others tentatively joined her.

As we watched, the upperclassmen circled the bus, still rah-rah excited about all those brand-new basic cadets. They reached their hands up as if they were going to high-five all those happy, excited young men and women inside. And then they started beating on the sides of the bus.

So hard it began to sway.

And that's when the magnificent dream began to morph into reality.

Poor souls.

The upperclassmen marched onto the bus and began yelling. We could hear them clearly from where we were standing.

"First VBT. You call it." I was giving him the honor of calling the first Very Bad Thing. I had to give him half a chance; this was only his third In-Processing Day.

"Um…"

"Hurry! They're about to get off."

"Hair."

"Clothes."

The bus started rupturing people. Each basic was supposed to run to one of those painted sets of footprints and stand there at attention.

Except…oops. Someone had brought a suitcase. Dang. A draw. But we both winced when we saw that. Either there was a giant toothbrush and razor packed inside or…? Nope. Oh. Too bad. He got double-teamed. Now there was someone yelling in both his right and his left ear.

Another guy didn't quite get to his footprints fast enough. But then again, he'd decided to wear a Superman T-shirt. Oh, dear. Bad wardrobe choice. Now he was doing push-ups.

Ditto for the guy with the bleached Mohawk.

And the one with the Mickey Mouse tank.

It happened every year.

It was fun to watch, but normally I can't last for more than three busloads.

I crunched through the last of the popcorn kernels. "I'm off. Thanks for the popcorn."

Dave turned from the window and lifted his can of pop. "Thanks for the drink."

I caught up with Joe outside. He was standing with a group of other bag-clad officers. Ostensibly watching the show outside, but doing more talking than watching.

"Hey, Jackie! You headed back?"

"That's what they pay me for. To do my job."

"I'll go with you."

There was a piece of popcorn stuck between my teeth. I hate popcorn, but I never remember why until after I finish eating it. "How did you survive all that?"

"In-Processing? That was the easy part. You're so afraid the first day, you'll do anything they tell you to. You lose your identity. You don't have any of your stuff from home. They shave your head. Give everyone the same clothes. You totally disappear into the group. The group becomes your identity. It's best if the upperclassmen never notice you."

"You become a clone?"

"At first."

"Didn't that bother you?"

"Not really. You're too busy trying to survive. It's when you start to take back your identity as an upperclassman that this place really starts to bother you. Then you start to perceive the injustice."

"Cramped your style?"

He smiled. "You could say that."

"Come on, how bad could it have been? It was a free education with a guaranteed job at the end."

Joe snorted. "Free? Nothing's free. It was a $250,000 education we paid for one nickel at time. Clothes, computers, laundry, haircuts… everything was deducted straight out of our pay."

"See, the experience of most college kids centers around the word *poor,* not *pay.* And what about all the great camaraderie? Wasn't that worth it?"

"What? Bonding with roommates while you're getting ready for the SAMIs? The Saturday Morning Inspections? Yeah, that was really fun. We'd stay up until three in the morning cleaning the sinks and light fixtures and organizing our underwear and then some upperclassman would come in and find dust on the pipes underneath the sink."

"They'd look for dust on purpose?"

"They never found any by accident."

"They did it every week?"

"Sometimes they had Morale, Welfare, and Recreation inspections instead."

"Why? To catch you smiling?"

"To catch you drinking."

"They let you have alcohol in the dorms?"

"No…but then, you're not supposed to surf the Internet at work either, are you? There was one guy who hid peppermint schnapps in a mouthwash bottle. He added a little food coloring to make it green."

"Isn't that against the honor code? What is it? 'I will not lie, cheat, or steal'?"

"And I will not tolerate those who do. Of course it is. But you're not lying if they never ask the question, are you?"

"But what if they did?"

"You didn't answer. You told them to go ahead and search."

"Such a stellar example you all set for the freshmen."

"It's not like *they* were such innocent lambs. Try getting nuked once or twice. When we ate dinner, sometimes the freshmen would take milk cartons and fill them up with leftovers. Grease from the meat. Peas. Ketchup. Soup. Clam chowder was the best. Then they'd take it to their room and let it ferment. For days. Weeks. And then, on a special occasion, like an upperclassman's twenty-first birthday, the freshmen would come find you and drag you outside and dump the whole thing on top of you."

"And, of course, you never nuked anyone when you were a freshman."

"Only the upperclassmen you really liked. Or really hated. That was the worst of it. You got nuked, you puked, and you still weren't quite sure whether they liked you or hated you."

"But you came back. You're here. It couldn't have been all that bad."

He stopped climbing and leaned against the railing. "It was that bad. But not always. There was good mixed in. Good friends. Good laughs. Good times. But that's not why I'm here. The department sent me away to get my master's. Russian history, remember?"

I nodded. How could I forget with the sickle and hammer Soviet flag he'd tacked to his side of the cubicle wall?

"The idea was that eventually I'd pay them back by teaching. Of course, sponsoring a pilot is a risky prospect. It's hard to get away from flying."

"How'd you convince them to let you come?"

"I didn't. They made me, after the headaches started. Some days, during my worst assignments, I used to think it might be fun to come back. Do something with the cadets. But not anymore. Not now that I have what I wished for. I'm here because it's the only thing left I can do."

THE CUBICLE NEXT DOOR BLOG

Greener grass

How is it that we always seem to want what someone else has? Or has had? Kids who were only children always wish they had siblings. Kids from big families wish they had been the only child. We can acknowledge that circumstances have made us who we are, but then we wish that same person away in an instant. Who might we have been if we'd lived a different kind of life? Is it envy? Or just curiosity? What if I were the boss instead of just a cubicle worker? Would I still be me, or would I be someone different? Do wishes exist only in utopia? Does a wish granted diminish the wish itself?

Posted on June 29 in **The Cubicle Next Door | Permalink**

Comments

Utopia now!

Posted by: **justluvmyjob | June 29 at 10:05 PM**

Maybe the wish is also a part of who we are.

Posted by: **philosopie | June 30 at 11:51 AM**

Wish I may, wish I might...be the CEO of the company. Then I'd fire the current one. That would be sweet.

Posted by: **onlyagofer | June 30 at 04:13 PM**

(CLOSE)

Ten

****

Two weeks later, all the faculty had returned from vacation. And after that, the dreaded practice teaching sessions had begun. Or practice hazing, depending on your point of view. All the new instructors in the department taught a practice lesson. And the rest of the staff and faculty filled the classroom, pretending to be cadets. Afterward, we were supposed to give them feedback on how well they'd done.

It was kind of fun.

Our department taught in several permanently assigned rooms. It allowed the instructors to keep equipment in the closets and charts on the walls. The rooms were configured with long stretches of desks and swivel chairs attached to the floor.

The idea of practice teaching was to put some pressure on the new instructors so they could get a feel for classroom teaching. We all had assigned roles to play. The department deputy for personnel came in with his uniform on wrong. The colonel was carrying a cup of coffee. One of the civilian instructors was chewing gum. Another was reading a magazine.

Two of the military instructors were supposed to keep up a running conversation throughout the practice teaching session. Another would ask all kinds of stupid questions. Estelle even joined in, showing up late for class.

The trick was for the new instructors to notice and comment on all the bad behavior and still teach the lesson in the allotted time with good explanations and enough attention to detail and moderation in the voice to entice the class into paying attention. At least enough to keep them from falling asleep.

Military academy instructors don't just have all the normal disruptions to handle, they also have rules such as "No food or drink in the classroom." They have an "on time attendance or demerits" policy. Cadets must wear the uniform of the day properly or get a Form 10. Stuff like that.

As one of six new instructors, Joe was in the spotlight. And he was the instructor scheduled to teach first.

He ambled over to Colonel Webster, who was nursing his cup of coffee. "What's that you've got there, Cadet Webster?"

"Coffee, sir."

"Can I see that for a moment?"

"Yes, sir."

Joe took the mug from the colonel, walked to the door, opened it, and set the cup in the hall. Then he walked back to the front of the classroom. "You can pick it up on your way out."

He scanned the rows of cadets for a moment, and then he picked up the trash can and walked down the aisles. He took the magazine from the civilian instructor, dropped it in the trash can, and then he walked over to the other civilian, held the trash can up in front of her while he clapped her on the back. "No gum."

At that moment, Estelle walked into class late.

"Cadet Thompson, report in!"

Estelle shot him a confused glance and then turned and scurried right out the door.

Joe smiled. "Know why there are rules at this academy? Is there a purpose to all of this?"

There was complete silence in the room.

"Cadet Morris, what is the purpose of the fourth class system? Why are you condemned to life in purgatory when you're a freshman?"

"Sir, the purpose of the Fourth Class System at the United States Air Force Academy is to lay the foundation early in the cadet's career for the development of those qualities of character and discipline which will be expected of an officer. These qualities must be so deeply instilled in the individual's personality that no stress or strain will erase them, sir!"

Lt. Col. Miller raised his hand.

"Cadet Miller?"

"How do you spell character? Is it with a 'c' or a 'k'?"

"With a 'c' me after class."

I was supposed to be the "staring off into space" cadet. And I was. Only the space I was staring into happened to be right in front of Joe.

The topic was premodern civilizations. And the way he taught it was interesting. I wish I'd had a history teacher like him in high school. He filled up most of the time with his lecture. He seemed perfectly at ease using PowerPoint slides. He was so at ease, in fact, that the end of the lecture caught everyone off guard.

"That's all I've got. Any questions? Any comments?"

"Will any of this be on the exam?"

"Everything I say, everything in the book, and everything on the syllabus is exam fodder. Any other questions?" He glared around the room. Dared anyone to raise a hand.

No one did. His practice session was officially over. Joe walked over and slouched into a seat behind mine.

The only comment came from another new instructor. A civilian who used to teach at West Point. "In a situation where a cadet brings coffee into the classroom or chews gum, wouldn't a Form 10 be appropriate?"

"Leadership by Form 10?" Joe didn't bother to keep the scorn out of his voice. "That sure worked well when I was a cadet."

Colonel Webster stood up and cleared his throat. "Yes, a Form 10 *can be* given for violations like those, but we usually prefer to save them for gross violations of the rules. Skipping class, being out of uniform, belligerence, that sort of thing. Captain Finney? You're up."

Captain Finney stood up. Grabbed a sheaf of papers and walked to the front of the room. His eyes darted around the class. "Um…Colonel—Cadet Webster, what is the rule about food and drink in the classroom."

"I missed breakfast."

"That may be the case, but you're not allowed to drink coffee here."

"I stayed up all night working on a paper. If I don't have caffeine,

I'm going to fall asleep."

Captain Finney's eyes took another quick tour of the room, and then they suddenly fixated on a spot just behind my left shoulder.

I turned around and saw Joe making broad sweeps with his head toward the back of the room.

The captain's face brightened. "Oh, yeah. Sir, if you think you're going to fall asleep, then just stand up at the back of the room."

Poor kid.

He was so relieved to have taken care of the colonel he forgot to chasten the deputy about wearing his hat inside, or Estelle for coming in late. I think the chatterers felt sorry for him because they stopped talking. And I saw the bubble-blower swallow her gum.

The captain lurched through the PowerPoint slides, read verbatim through his notes, and otherwise gave a poor performance.

Next up was a major. He came down hard on everyone. But you could tell he'd put a lot of time into the presentation; he sounded as though he was reciting a speech.

Colonel Webster raised his hand.

"We'll save questions until the end of the period, Cadet Webster."

I had propped my head on my left hand and was staring off into space when I felt something wet ping my cheek. I saw it drop to the desk. I looked down.

A spit wad.

I was turning my head around to look over my shoulder when another one zinged off my nose.

I turned all the way around.

Joe was grinning at me.

"Cadet Harrison, is there a problem?"

I turned around to face the instructor. "No, sir." But there would be later.

The last person that morning was the new civilian instructor, the one who had taught at West Point. You'd think she would have known what to expect. But then, she'd never had Joe in her class before.

Halfway into her lecture, a crumpled ball of paper landed by my right elbow.

I'd been falling asleep, and I blinked.

Sat up.

Looked behind me.

Joe was gesturing with his hand for me to open it up.

So I did.

"Dear Jackie, do you like me? Check one." He'd drawn little check-boxes next to the choices. "No. Just as a friend. A little. Yes. Alot."

Hadn't he learned anything from spell-checker?

I heard a tap-tap-tap of shoes and looked up from the note to find Ms. West Point standing in front of me. She took the note from my hands.

"Why don't we share this with the rest of the class? 'Dear Jackie, do you like me?'" She faltered. Glanced at me. Frowned at Joe. Tried to figure out where to go from there.

I was blushing.

She was floundering.

Joe was grinning like a maniac.

The rest of the class was laughing.

It was as if I were reliving my worst junior high school memories. Even way back then, the people I had spent most of my day with had laughed at me. I'd been a target. But I had also learned to move with a purpose.

Moving with a purpose.

It became the story of my life. As long as I was doing something or going somewhere, I was a moving target and my peers at school were unlikely to focus on me. Unlikely to single me out from the crowd to pick on. I had found a group of kids as odd as I was. We sat together at lunch. Sat next to each other in classes. Tried to exert the minimum effort in phys. ed. We didn't experience life together as much as we experienced it alongside each other. We each did our own thing, in the same general area, at the same general time. Which was a very roundabout way of saying I was a geek.

Am a geek. Not just a technie, but a real nerd. With a geeky job. Wearing geeky clothes.

Thanks, Joe, for reminding me.

With Ms. West Point looking on, I slipped into my old habits, slid out of my chair, and left the room. Kept on walking.

"Jackie?"

I turned. Saw Joe standing in the doorway. "Thanks a lot! And by the way, it's spelled separately. A. Lot." I would have yelled more, but I was having logistical problems. It was hard to yell at someone you were trying to get away from.

He had one more thing to say before I turned the corner. "I was just kidding. Haven't you ever gotten a love note before?"

I would have laughed if I hadn't felt like crying.

I stalked down the hall and then climbed the stairs instead of waiting for the elevator. Took them two at a time. When I got to my desk I slouched into my seat and started running reports on the network.

Joe came in half an hour later. I heard him toss his bag into the corner. Then I heard him stand on his desk. Watched his head and shoulders emerge from his side of the cubicle. "I'm sorry. I was just trying to be funny."

"You weren't."

"I know. You've probably gotten notes that were much more romantic. I should have taken more time. Thought of something really good to say. Maybe…Roses are red, violets are blue…"

"Just…leave it. I'm fine. It's over."

"Okay. Roses are red, violets are blue, Jackie's a wet blanket and a spoilsport too." He stuck his lower lip out and blinked puppy dog eyes at me.

"Now *you're* sulking? Because *you* made fun of *me?*"

"No."

"You are."

"No, I'm not."

"Yes, you are."

"Am not."

"Are so! I can't believe this."

"I was just having fun."

"At my expense. It might have been nothing to you. You get laughed at every day. I don't."

"*I* laugh at you…"

I glared up at him.

He stared right back at me. "Because of you..." He grinned. "Lighten up. It's not every day you get a love note from someone like me!" He disappeared before I could respond.

But he wasn't too far off. It wasn't every day. It wasn't even every year. Joe's love note had been my first. And all I wished I could do was wad it into a ball and throw it at his head.

THE CUBICLE NEXT DOOR BLOG

Disregard

Casual disregard of other people has become endemic in America. It's practically the defining motif of our culture. Particularly in the workplace. Disregard of people's privacy has led to the proliferation of cubicle farms. Disregard of people's job descriptions has led to poor task distribution. Disregard of people's dignity has led to micromanagement. Disregard of people's feelings has led to emotional isolation. No wonder no one likes being at work anymore.

Posted on July 17 in **The Cubicle Next Door | Permalink**

Comments

Exactly why I choose to work for myself.

Posted by: **philosophie | July 18 at 01:19 PM**

I'm only working until I find a job I don't have to work at.

Posted by: **mustsurftolive | July 18 at 03:51 PM**

A little R-E-S-P-E-C-T would go a long way.

Posted by: **justluvmyjob | July 19 at 08:47 AM**

CLOSE

Eleven

****

Several weeks later I rolled out of bed, took a shower, pulled on a red T-shirt and jeans, and laced up the flaming low-tops.

Saturday was my day at the store and Grandmother's day to get things accomplished.

I had no idea what things there were to be accomplished and there was never much evidence of accomplishment, but she deserved every break I could give her.

I walked out the front door and headed for town. I passed a dozen turn-of-the-century houses, some built entirely of wood with curlicue trim and wide front porches. Others had been set atop foundations of the area's iron-stained stones. Some of them were painted in crazy color combinations of pinks, purples, and yellows. Others in more sober dark blue, spruce green, or gray.

Many had large expanses of lawn fronting them. Even the least and smallest had a few large hulking trees. From this vantage point, I might have been living in Ohio or Illinois.

But if I raised my eyes to the horizon, I could see the other side of Manitou Springs. The side that edged up to the Garden of the Gods. And it was a view of a completely different world. One where trees had been reduced to midget size. A world gone Martian red, where '70s-era dwellings had been strewn amid the house-sized boulders.

Manitou was only about eight blocks wide. Cottonwood-lined Fountain Creek divided it lengthwise into halves. From Manitou Avenue, the main street in town, the ground rose on either side at nearly a 15-degree angle. Lots had been gouged out of the cliffs. Houses with no backyards hung on for dear life. Down in town, some of the shops were only ten-feet wide—the exact amount of space available before butting up against a cliff.

I slipped down a side street filled with antique shops waving colorful flags and dangling artful signs, crossed Manitou Avenue in front of the clock tower, and then I ducked down Canyon Avenue and unlocked the door to the shop.

I opened the door and then switched the "Out Skiing" sign around to "Yes! We're Open!" After turning on the computer and the cash register, I walked to the small office in the back to get the packing lists for the new merchandise Grandmother said had come in. I skimmed the line items. It looked like a shipment of trekking poles. Grandmother was probably hoping summer tourists would scoop them up as souvenirs of their Colorado vacation.

The bell on the door rattled as it opened. Jingled as the door shut.

After folding the list in half and tucking it in my pocket, I shut the office door and went out onto the floor. A small group of people, cups of coffee in hand, were strolling in different directions. Picking up merchandise, turning it over, putting it back down. I knew what they were doing: killing time until the rest of the stores in Manitou Springs opened. They only had about an hour left to wait.

I plucked the list out of my pocket and took it to the counter. I smoothed it out and started entering the information into our database, one I had created for Grandmother when I was 12 years old. With only minor modifications it had survived intact for two decades.

The door opened again. A woman walked through it. She started toward the wall of ski accessories and tools but then was distracted by the glass display case of altimeters.

The coffee drinkers had all circled back past each other and now they were heading toward opposite corners of the store.

I kept on with the data entry.

The door opened again.

"Hey!"

Everyone in the store turned toward the voice.

Only Joe could have matched the cheery tone of our "Open!" sign at 8:15 on a Saturday morning. He came right up to the counter and leaned against it.

I flicked a glance up toward him and continued with my data entry. "Hi."

"Just out walking around."

"Good for you."

"Thought I'd buy some skis."

"We don't do downhill here."

"I already have a pair. I'm interested in cross-country."

I gestured to the inner aisles of the store where skis sprouted from the display racks. "Take your pick."

"Anything in particular I should be looking for?"

"Your favorite color maybe?" I interrupted our scintillating conversation to help a customer. A real one. She was interested in wax. Mostly because she was leaving for New Zealand on a ski trip later in the afternoon.

By the time I finished helping her, another customer had come in and Joe was talking to him. They had gravitated to the center of the store and were looking at Grandmother's Rossis.

I walked over to them. "Hello."

"Good morning. Lovely day, isn't it?" It took me a moment to decipher the customer's English because it had been spoken with a British accent. The man had twin dollops of gray fluff sticking out from either side of his head. He was wearing a button-down shirt with a buttoned-up sweater vest. And while he had been holding the Rossis close with one hand, the other had been skimming their glossy length.

I looked at Joe.

He winked at me. "This is Mr. Finley from England."

"Welcome. Are you thinking of buying those or marrying them?"

"Cheeky sort of girl, isn't she?"

Joe dimpled. "Part of her charm."

Mr. Finley pierced me with his gaze. "Then it must be in the eye of the beholder."

Something about him made me want to stick my tongue out, but I didn't because I'd figured out who he was. "You come in every day to look at these, don't you?" He was Grandmother's customer.

Mr. Finley sighed as he replaced them. "I do."

"Why don't you just buy them?"

"I might.".

"Today?"

"I don't think so. No. A purchase like this would be an extravagant luxury not to be indulged in with someone who is merely selling ski equipment. Skis like these must be purchased from someone who appreciates them as the fine work of a master craftsman."

"My grandmother will be here on Monday."

"Ah. Just so." He reached out to shake Joe's hand and nodded at me. "Well, goodbye then." He walked out of the store. The door closed behind him with a tinkle.

I turned to Joe. "How about you? Still interested in mere ski equipment?"

"Do you have something in neon green?"

"We just might. I don't suppose you're a groomed trail type of skier?"

"Why ski someone else's trail when you can make your own?"

"Just wanted to be sure. The first decision to make is whether you want a metal edge. It makes skis better for turning, but it also makes them harder for touring."

"So it's either one or the other? Turning or touring?"

"You could buy partial. Almost have the best of both."

"Good. That's what I'll take."

"I don't suppose you'd be interested in a pair of waxless, would you?"

"And take all the fun out of skiing? Nope."

"But do you plan to be truly faithful about waxing?"

He held two fingers up in the air. "Scout's honor."

"Because if you are, then you'd get better performance out of a sintered base ski. But if you aren't, then your skis will just collect a bunch of dirt and pine pitch and they'll end up being slower. Your choice. But you better not lie to yourself about how often you're willing to wax."

"Let me think about it."

"How much do you weigh?"

"Two twenty."

"How tall are you?"

"Six feet."

"And how much control do you want to have?"

"I'm totally out of control."

I couldn't help myself from smiling, but I tried very hard not to laugh. "Yes, I know. But because you're a novice, I'd recommend a wider ski. It's more stable. It would give you more control than a narrower one."

He shrugged. "Okay."

"Listen, are you serious about buying or are you just here to torment me?"

"Both. Seeing you six days a week isn't enough."

I felt my cheeks warm. I was being ridiculous. He was only flirting. "Then what about sidecut?"

"Who what?"

"The difference in the width of the ski, taken in three measurements." I pointed at the Rossis as an example, starting at the bottom. "At the tail, the waist, and the shovel."

"You're the expert. What would you recommend?"

"The more sidecut, the easier it is to turn. The less a ski is sidecut, the easier it is to ski straight. And fast."

"Can't I have it all?"

"In cross-country skiing? No. Sacrifices must be made."

"Well, that settles it. I have no idea what I want."

"Why don't you just rent a pair? Or two or three. Then you can try all the options and decide for yourself."

"You guys do rentals?"

"No."

"Bummer. Can I look at boots?"

"Sure." I turned away from the racks of skis and started toward the boots. "But there's no real standard for bindings, so you'll have to get both at the same time."

"Fine. Let's do it."

I walked him over to the display wall of boots. "We don't appear to have any in neon green, but I can check in the back."

"No need. What am I supposed to look for?"

"Well…there are control issues." I took a black boot from the display. "Cross-country boots are connected to the ski only at the toe. The wider the connection point, the more control you'll have over your ski."

"So why would anyone buy one of these?" He picked up a boot with a narrow connection point.

"For racing. Which you don't want to do."

"I don't?"

"No. You're tall. If you fell at high speed, you'd break your head." Not, of course, that it would make any difference to me.

"Then I could be the Headless Skier of Manitou. I could haunt my own house."

I decided to just ignore him. I took the boot from his hand, returned it to the shelf, and picked up a different one. "You'll want to check the torsion of the boot." I handed it to him.

He took it by the toe and the heel and twisted. Or tried to.

"A rigid boot will also give you more control."

"Then I'll try it."

"What size?"

"Twelve." He sat down on the bench and slid his feet out of their Birkenstocks. "Socks?"

"Under the bench." We kept a basket filled with them. No one in Manitou wore socks in the summer.

He tried them on. Stood up. Walked a few paces. "I don't know." He turned toward the display and grabbed another boot. Twisted. "How about this one? It's lightweight."

"It's injection molded, but it's not so good with metal edges. If you decide you want metal in your edges, try one of these." I took a box from the shelf and opened it. Handed him a stitch-soled purple-and-black boot.

He sat back down and tried it on. Stood. Walked a few steps. Then paced the length of the store. Came back. "These feel great."

"You'll want them to be a little big."

"They are. But not too big. I'll take them."

Once he'd taken them off, I took the box up to the counter. "Did you want the bindings now?"

"Might as well."

I went behind the counter and into the storeroom. I grabbed several bindings and walked back to Joe. "You'll have to make a choice. You'll definitely want a reinforced brace like this." I held one of the selections up. "But if you'll be doing a lot of off-trail exploring, then you'll probably want a riveted brace so you won't get stuck in the back country with a broken binding. It's an extra level of safety."

"Where do you ski?"

"Pardon me?"

"When you ski, do you ski trails or do you explore?"

"Grandmother and I skied trails. That we made up. Mostly."

He pushed the riveted brace bindings toward the box. "Then I'll take these."

"Not, of course, that I've skied in the last ten years. Or that I ever will again." Although if I ever did, it would be nice to do it with someone like Joe.

He just smiled. "You never know. So, what else do I need?"

"Besides skis? How about poles? Over there." I pointed toward a stand in the corner of the store.

He strode over and grabbed a set. "How about these?"

I shrugged. "Aluminum? They're sexy, but the fiberglass have better shock absorption."

While he looked at the poles, I gave directions to the Barr Trail to a different customer. "Turn left on Ruxton, drive past the Cog Railway. Take a right past the old steam plant. Park at the top of the hill in the gravel lot. They'll tow you if you park at the railway station." I've often thought about just posting the directions on the door to the store. And highlighting the part about being towed.

Eventually Joe came back with a set of poles in hand.

"Ah. The telescoping, jam-them-together-and-use-as-an-avalanche-probe poles. They're our best sellers."

"Really?"

"Psychology. No one wants to be in an avalanche, but everyone wants to imagine they're the kind of person who can ski into places where they could start one."

"Are you calling me a wannabe?"

"Are you?"

"No. I'm an am one."

I just looked at him.

"I am. You should ski downhill with me."

"No, thanks. Especially not now, Mr. Am One. I'd like to remain among the living for a couple more years."

"But I've got the poles. Even if I did start an avalanche, I could pull you out."

"Do you have a beacon? Or a shovel?"

"No."

"Then even if you did pull me out, I'd probably end up dying before you could ski for help."

"Nothing in life is safe. Living isn't safe. The risk is one hundred percent. We all die in the end."

"I'd at least like to arrive at death's door…"

"Safely?" His dimples flashed. Disappeared. Flashed again. He was trying really hard not to laugh.

I scowled at him. "How did you want to pay for these?"

"You kill me. You really do."

"Did you come in here just to flirt with me?"

Joe reached behind his back and brought his wallet out. Flipping it open, he pulled out a credit card and held it up like a badge. "*And* to buy boots and poles."

"I'm not interested."

"In what?"

I took the credit card from him and set it on the counter between us. "Listen to me. I'm only saying this one time. Leave me alone. I'm not interested. In anyone."

"I'm not just anyone. Come on, Jackie. It's me, Joe!"

"I'm not interested in you, Joe."

"Not even a little bit? Give a guy a break."

"I'm not."

"Then why are you blushing?"

"I'm *not*." I could feel my cheeks flush from pink to red before I finished speaking. I took his credit card and ran up the boots, poles, and bindings before I could make myself look even more foolish.

I handed the card to Joe. He took it from me, put it back in his wallet, grabbed the bags, and turned to go. But then he stopped. "You know, you're making this much more difficult than it has to be."

"You have no idea how difficult it already is."

Because if I really, truly weren't interested in Joe, then why was my heart racing? Why couldn't I seem to catch my breath whenever I looked into his eyes? Why did my fingers itch to reach up and run furrows through his wavy hair?

After closing up the shop in the evening, I walked back through town, passing an odd mix of architecture. Buildings styled from logs and stucco were suggestive of the Southwest. There were buildings sided with varnished planks, imitating an Alpine look, and hotels topped with onion domes. Looking at them individually, you could imagine yourself to be almost anywhere, but taken as a collective whole, you could only be in Manitou Springs.

Grandmother wasn't at home when I arrived.

I made enough dinner for two, assuming she would return at any moment. But by the time I'd finished my dinner, she still hadn't come. I put away the leftovers, washed the dishes, and then dried them, all the while contemplating calling Adele, Betty, and Thelma. I had to weigh the pros and the cons. I might find out where she was, but I might also cause needless worry. A sleepless night. Maybe even a heart attack. You never knew, at their age.

Deciding finally to make the calls, I had begun walking to the living room to the phone when I heard footsteps on the porch.

I pivoted and half-ran, half-walked to the back door. I pulled it open just as Grandmother put her hand out toward the knob. "Where have you been?"

She blinked and put a hand to her heart. "You scared me."

"I'm sorry." I let go of the door, took hold of her arm, led her over to the table, and pulled a chair out for her.

"Thanks." She bent over and then lifted a foot up onto her knee. Untying the laces, she slid the shoe off and put it down. "I haven't walked so far in..." She was smiling as she looked up toward the ceiling, contemplating just how long it had been. "Must have been years."

"You were out walking? By yourself? You could have broken your hip again!"

"Hmm?"

"You were all by yourself?"

"Of course not."

"Then with whom?"

"With Oliver. We walked the springs."

"You walked through town?"

"No. We each took a cup along and we toured the springs."

Springs. The nine springs from which Manitou derives its name. From Iron Springs, up by the Cog Railway, to Seven Minute Springs down by Memorial Park. "That's over three miles."

"Is it? It didn't seem like it. They all taste different. Did you know that?" She put her foot down. She bent to pick up her other one, placed it on her knee, and took off her other shoe.

"Who *is* Oliver?"

"Oliver? You've never met him?" She bent to return her shoe to the floor. Straightened. "But he said he met you just this morning."

"You mean that ill-tempered Englishman?"

"He has a lovely personality."

"It didn't seem like it to me."

"You've never been good at first impressions yourself. So you, of all people, ought to be a little more understanding."

"Do you know anything about him? Because he could be… anyone."

"I know he likes to cross-country ski." That was typical of Grandmother. She didn't trust downhill skiers more than was necessary. It was a sport that was too flashy in her opinion, involving people of dubious character going too fast on skis that were too short. Cross-country skiing, on the other hand, involved work. And work was always good. Therefore, cross-country skiers were also good people.

"Oh. Well, then he's golden! We might as well give him a halo."

"There's no need to be sarcastic. I'm so hungry, I could eat just about anything you placed in front of me."

That was as subtle as Grandmother ever gets. I rummaged for leftovers and heated them up. She ate them all.

Later in the evening, after Grandmother's snores had begun rumbling through the upstairs hallway, I sat down at my computer.

I checked out several message boards and a few systems administrator support groups. There are a very few people in the world who actually read computer software and hardware manuals. As far as I could tell, they were all systems administrators. I sent e-mails of encouragement to the posters of the day's worst horror stories.

Posted a blog.

Checked my e-mails. Received notification that my blog had received Readers Top Five status from the Weblog Review, based on the modifications I'd recently performed. Cool.

I hadn't looked at my blog statistics for at least a couple months, so I logged back onto the blogging website and brought up the reports. I felt my jaw drop. The last time I'd looked, I'd averaged ten visitors each week. And none of them had been new visitors. For the past month, I'd averaged two hundred visitors a week. Most of them new.

Strange.

I'd noticed a few new people posting aside from the stalwart "just-luvmyjob" and "philosophie." I thought they'd just been surfing by. Guess my modifications had been worth a sleepless night. Nothing else could explain the jump in traffic.

I logged out. Returned to my e-mail program and deleted the message.

Moved on to my next e-mail.

Mr. Please Deflate My Head

Have you ever met anyone who assumes he can do anything?
Assumes that just because he's good at one thing, he's good at
everything else? There's nothing about John Smith that bothers
me more than this. What kind of parents did he have that made
him so confident? The kind who did backflips whenever he accomplished the smallest little thing? The kind who went to every
single sports event he ever had? Parents like those are just plain
reckless. Don't they know they're creating monsters the rest of us
will have to deal with?

Posted on August 5 in **The Cubicle Next Door | Permalink**

Comments

God save us all from Supermen!

Posted by: **wurkerB | August 5 at 10:14 PM**

If we only had the hindsight to have some foresight.

Posted by: **philosophie | August 5 at 10:30 PM**

Is John Smith my boss? Because they sound a lot alike!

Posted by: **justluvmyjob | August 5 at 10:44 PM**

My condolences.

Posted by: **The Cubicle Next Door (TCND) | August 5 at 11:04 PM**

CLOSE

Twelve

****

I picked Joe up at 7:45 the next morning, Sunday, with some misgivings. He'd called me on my fascination with him. But while I could admit to myself I had one, it didn't mean I had to act on it.

We ate breakfast at the same Waffle House before heading up the interstate. Ordered the same meal, joked with the same waitresses.

We tried a church someone else in the department had recommended. By the time the service was over, we were just as satisfied with the experience as we'd been the Sunday before.

"Two down. Tons left to go."

"Do you want me to start marking up the phone book?"

Joe winked at me. "No. Next week's church will be the one. I can feel it."

Yeah. Just like I could feel winter coming.

The next morning Joe was hard at work by the time I walked into my cubicle. According to my nose, he'd already gotten himself a cup of coffee.

I peeked around the wall.

He was standing, hands on his hips, glaring at piles of paper stacked neatly across his desk. As I watched, he grabbed two stacks and switched the order. Stared at them again.

He didn't glance up at me. Didn't say hi.

I returned to my cubicle, shrugged off my bag, and then sat down. Logged onto the network and prepared to sync my Palm to my desktop.

"Wish me luck."

"Good luck." I gave my wheeled chair a push with my feet and tried to make it to the end of the cubicle divider so I could see what Joe was doing. I got stuck two inches off my plastic floor protector. Tried to push it back up onto the plastic, to no avail. It was mired in the carpet. I gave up, hopped onto my desk, and peered over the cubicle wall. "What's going on?"

"First day of class." He was standing now in the middle of his cubicle, briefcase slung over his shoulder. His eyes were darting toward every corner of the room, and he was patting the pockets on his bag. "I've forgotten something."

"What?"

He stopped and looked up at me with an impatient glance. "If I knew what it was, then I wouldn't have forgotten it, would I?"

I shrugged. "Do you have your PowerPoint slides?" The bureaucracy of the Air Force would screech to a grinding halt if it weren't for PowerPoint. None of the officers know how to make a presentation unless they can do it on computer-generated slides plastered with the department, organization, and Department of the Air Force logos. In fact, it's the only software program about which I voluntarily relinquish my expert status. Any airman has more knowledge on the topic than I could ever hope to accumulate.

"Slides! Thanks." He pulled the cords out of his laptop, slammed the screen shut, and took off down the hall.

"LCD! Shut Down! Barbarian!" Was all I could think to say before he was out of hearing range. I had just finished equipping the remaining people in the department with laptops. I was not about to start buying gratuitous machines just because *some* people didn't choose to treat their computers properly.

In fact, what I needed to do was start confiscating computers. And then give remedial training before reissuing them. I knew exactly who I'd start with.

When I was new at my job, Estelle used to farm out her correspondence to me. Not the important stuff that would eventually make its way to the one-star general, the dean of faculty, or the three-star general, the superintendent. Those documents were much too valuable to entrust to my shifty work habits. I got stuck with the inter or intrade-partmental memos. But only until Estelle realized I didn't double-space at the ends of my sentences.

After my second memo, she called me out to her office. "Jackie, thank you for typing this up, but I see you failed to double-space after your periods. Again. We need to remember *The Tongue and Quill.*"

I had no idea what she was talking about, and she must have seen the confusion on my face.

She pulled a slim softbound volume from the bookshelf beside her desk and clutched it to her chest. "This is my only copy, but I don't mind lending it to you if you want to read through it."

"No, thanks."

She held it out to me. "It's okay. Really. Just make sure you return it."

"I don't want it. Really."

"But it explains how to do everything. Like the two spaces at the end of each sentence."

"But I don't want to know how to do everything. I'm a systems administrator. If I need to communicate with someone, I'll send them an e-mail. I won't write a memo."

"Take it. Read it."

I had to take it. Her arm would have fallen off if I'd just left the book dangling from her outstretched hand. But I soon discovered that *The Tongue and Quill* was entirely outdated. The computer is not a typewriter, especially in word processing programs. There were a few formatting issues I didn't mind changing to revert to *The Tongue and Quill*'s standards, but I was not about to put in redundant spaces. Proportional fonts adjust proportionally to the characters you type. They automatically add the correct width of space after a period is typed.

But I reformatted some parts of the memo and e-mailed it to Estelle.

She called me.

"Did you read *The Tongue and Quill?*"

"Yes, I did."

"Then did you send me an earlier revision of the memo? Because this one still doesn't have the two spaces."

"No. That's the final."

"Where are the spaces?"

"They aren't there. *The Tongue and Quill* is outdated. I'm not going to teach myself bad habits just because whoever wrote it doesn't know what they're talking about."

"I wasn't asking for your opinion. I was asking you to format it to fit standard Air Force conventions."

"Sorry. I won't do that."

She hung up on me. But it was the last time she ever tried to farm her job out to me.

Maybe I wouldn't have to confiscate Estelle's computer after all. Maybe I could just consider her duly reformed. Under protest.

Joe returned to his cubicle two and a half hours later. He dropped into his chair. I heard him put his boots up on the desk.

"You survived?"

"*I* did. But I don't know if *they* did."

"What's your schedule tomorrow?"

"Nothing. I teach practically all day on M days, but I don't have anything on T days."

M days and T days. A unique Academy innovation. The cadets actually had two different schedules to keep track of, one for M day and one for T day. At first encounter, a person would logically assume one schedule held good for Monday, Wednesday, and Friday. The other for Tuesday and Thursday. However, despite the glamour of being a military academy, it was, after all, still military. M and T days alternated throughout the semester. One week, M days would be on Mondays, Wednesdays, and Fridays; the next, on Tuesdays and Thursdays. That way, each course on a cadet schedule would have an equal number of sessions. It allowed every cadet to carry an average of 17.5 semester hours instead of a meager 15. It also allowed a full portion of science classes. Enough that every cadet graduated with a bachelor of science degree, even if his actual field of study had been English. Or fine arts.

The next day it began: The parade of female cadets to Joe's office hours. From my chair, on that day, I could have assumed the entire cadet wing was made up of females. You couldn't blame them. It was just like high school—all the girls developed a crush on the cutest teacher.

Some of them were smart. They pled ignorance about the whole concept of premodern history. Made Joe repeat his lecture in entirety. Others asked a single question and were gone in five minutes.

There was a break of an hour around lunchtime, when Joe was all by himself, but then they were back.

Finally, at 4:30, after the last cadet had gone, I heard him lean back in his chair and sigh. "I thought the lecture was fairly basic. Maybe I just didn't explain it clearly enough."

"I think it's more a function of who you are. Until you have a sex-change operation, it looks like T days are going to be tough going."

There was silence for a moment. I heard his chair squeak. Heard him gulp a mouthful of coffee. Set his mug down on his desk. Far, far away from the keyboard, I hoped.

"Hadn't thought of that."

Well, everyone else had.

Even I had fallen under the spell of Joe.

That night, I made the rounds of message boards. Posted a message on one of them about people like Estelle. Got a flurry of responses.

I pulled up the traffic statistics on my blog. Viewership was up. Return visits were up. People were hanging out on the blog longer. Probably reading back through the archives.

I posted a blog and then checked my e-mails. Received notification that my blog had received Reviewers Top Five status from the Weblog Review. Cool. I was now on both the Readers and the Reviewers Top Five lists.

I deleted it.

Moved on to the next e-mail.

THE CUBICLE NEXT DOOR BLOG

I've got your back

John Smith doesn't know this, but I've got his back. He thinks I work just as long as he does, but I don't. Not really. I just stay until he goes home. In spite of considering himself the expert at everything, he doesn't know anything about the women here. Has no idea how many of them have paused at the cubicle and then kept on walking when they've seen me sitting at my desk.

He's too nice. Too patient.

And he doesn't need any drummed up sexual harassment charges just because it would be their word against his word.

He won't have to worry about that because I'll always be around just as long as they are.

Posted on August 8 in **The Cubicle Next Door | Permalink**

Comments

An interesting phrase, "I've got your back." Its origins may be lost in history, but it definitely has military roots. Similar to "I've got you covered," but more desperate. A pledge between two com-rades to remain loyal. Even until death.

Posted by: **NozAll | August 8 at 11:18 PM**

Very kind of you. Especially considering how much you dislike him.

Posted by: **philosophie | August 9 at 06:57 AM**

Sounds like you've won the cubicle mate lottery...or maybe he has.

Posted by: **justluvmyjob | August 9 at 01:40 PM**

(CLOSE)

Thirteen

****

The next week, it was back to work on the test-taking program. The accompanying sound effects had been officially deemed inappropriate. The colonel had wanted some standard reports added: average score and minimum and maximum scores. I'd thought of a few others, such as average score per period. I thought it might be an interesting statistic, even if I were the only one who ever knew—or cared—whether cadets scored better before or after lunch. In general, I preferred to build extraneous options into my programs rather than to try to add features after the fact. I also added a report for average score per instructor. Rumors were always floating around that some instructors liked to "teach the test."

I'd taken the test about 30 times to build a database of five fictional sections with six students each. Ran the reports.

Huh. Look at that. Maj NozAll appeared to be a very poor instructor. A programmer's revenge for having strayed too close to the truth on my last blog entry. I had tried hard not to leave any clues about my identity, including my place of work. Guess I hadn't tried hard enough.

Ms. Philosophie's sections had achieved the best scores. Well done!

Justluvmyjob's? Average.

Joe's voice recalled me from my fantasy world. "I was wondering if you could do me a favor…what are you doing?"

I minimized the window and then swiveled my chair to find him standing at the edge of the cubicle wall. "Nothing. What?"

"I'm doing the Pikes Peak Ascent on Saturday. Would you be able to meet me at the top?"

"Of the mountain?"

"Yeah. I could give you a change of clothes to carry for me."

"I work on Saturdays."

"Your grandmother told me. She said she'd work this one for you."

"You already have it arranged?"

"Can you?"

I looked up into his eyes. Then sighed. If they already had it figured out, there was no point in saying no. "Yes."

"Great!" He smiled before disappearing into his cubicle.

He brought a backpack over on Friday evening.

Grandmother made him sit in the kitchen with us and encouraged him to help himself to our dinner.

I passed him a plate of chicken breasts. His second serving. "What time will you be done?"

"I don't know. Ten? Ten thirty?"

"At the very latest or earliest?"

"Yes. And yes. I don't know."

I'd have to leave at 8:00 then, just in case he finished early. It wouldn't be any earlier than I was normally up on Saturdays.

The next morning I had to backtrack a half-dozen times before I was able to drive out of Manitou Springs. They had roads blocked off for the Ascent. I drove up Highway 24 and then turned off onto the Pikes Peak Highway. Paid my toll. Began the climb.

The first part of the drive was pretty. A typical mountain road, it wound through stands of thick trees, opening out now and then into a meadow or crossing a lake. Then the pavement stopped. Became dirt. The trees were sparser here. Thinner. The road swerved out occasionally into a hairpin, providing views back out over the valley and the broad plain east of Colorado Springs.

I could hear my motor strain. My little car didn't like the altitude, but it kept chugging up the mountain. I thought of turning off at the

Timberline Café, but decided a stop would just make it harder on the car.

The trees petered out and revealed the mountain to be a jumble of rocks and barren earth. A landscape doused in shades of brown. I rounded a corner and was directed onto a flat plateau. I parked the car, grabbed Joe's backpack, and waited for the race shuttle to take me to the top of the mountain.

I didn't have to wait long, which was good. The wind below had been filled with warmth, but the wind here had ice in its gusts. I fastened the top toggle of my coat, pulled the hood over my head, and sunk my hands into its deep pockets. I wished I'd thought to bring gloves.

I boarded the shuttle, sat next to a window, and enjoyed a series of thrills as my stomach tried to fall out of my body. The road clung to the mountain only through sheer force of will. And there were no guardrails.

Up at the top, I walked across the parking lot and into Summit House. I tried to walk past the donut vendor, but I couldn't resist buying one.

It was the altitude.

I wandered through racks of T-shirts, coffee mugs, and other souvenirs. Watched the Cog Railway train steam up the track and disgorge passengers.

I glanced at my watch. It was time to go outside. I bought a donut for Joe before I left. I wrapped it into a napkin and put it in my pocket.

The wind wasn't any warmer and the number of people at the top of the mountain had doubled since I'd been inside.

I walked back through the parking lot, around the Katherine Bates memorial, and over into the rocks. The finish line was at the end of a nearly invisible switchback trail that wound over and around large boulders.

Music was blaring from a monster-sized sound system. An announcer called out the runners' names as their numbers became visible. I couldn't see where they were coming from, so I picked my way over the finish line, in between runners, and clambered out toward the edge of the peak.

Far below me, a line of runners curved around the bottom of the mountain's face. Then they began to crawl up the contours of the mountain like ants.

Retreating from the edge, I picked a sturdy boulder and sat on top of it. Gazed in wonder at the view around me. An almost 360-degree view of the mountain range. Below me, the peaks of the surrounding mountains popped up from the horizon. Nestled in their valleys were sparkling alpine lakes. A thin strand of clouds was beginning to wrap around the farthest peaks and send exploratory fingers further east.

This was how life was meant to be lived. In appreciation of the earth.

After a dearth of runners, a new group pushed around the corner and into my view. They were halfway into their climb when I heard Joe's name over the loudspeaker.

I slid off the rock and scrambled over toward the finish line.

The heads of the group bobbed into view, disappeared behind a rock, surged forward into view again. Joe was in the lead, his number stuck on the front of his shirt. His yellow shorts were glaring against the rocks.

"Go, Joe!"

He didn't look up toward me, didn't look anywhere but straight ahead.

I pushed my hood away from my head and cupped hands to my mouth. "Joe! Go, Joe!"

He followed the trail, climbing vertically away from me until it switched back, sending him in my direction.

I took my hands from my mouth. Waved them over my head. "Joe!"

He looked up and started to grin. Stumbled. His face was flushed. His mouth hung open, gulping air. He pushed on, crossed the finish line, and grabbed my hand, pulling me past the crowd. Then he collapsed on the ground, knees up, and hung his head between them.

"I have a donut for you."

"If I eat a donut now, I'll throw up."

"Really?" If he were nauseous, it could mean he was suffering from altitude sickness. It was not uncommon, especially when you were above 14,000 feet. There was only one cure: Lose altitude. Fast.

"Could you get my water out of the backpack?"

I let the backpack slide from my shoulders, retrieved a water bottle, and passed it down to him.

He set it on the ground beside him and left it there for a minute before he lifted his head and had a drink.

"Are you okay?"

"I will be. Just give me a few minutes."

"Are you cold?"

"Yeah. But I don't want to change here." He held out a hand toward me. "Help me up?"

I grabbed his hand and tugged. Nothing happened. How was I supposed to get him down off the mountain when I couldn't even help him up? His face was still red and I could see rivulets of sweat beading up on his eyebrows, but he had to be getting cold. I could see my breath and he was still wearing a short-sleeve shirt and shorts. He could pass out and freeze to death before I'd be able to rally help for him.

"Joe! Come on!" I wrapped both my hands around his and began to pull hard. His fingers folded around mine as he pushed off the ground with his other hand.

He stood up straight while I put the water bottle in the backpack. He hobbled a few steps. Stopped. "I have to stretch." He placed one leg in front of the other. Bent down toward the ground.

"Can't you do that after you change?"

He turned his head away from the ground and looked up at me. "Why? You aren't worried about me, are you?"

"No."

"Just a minute. Let me stretch the other leg." He stood up. Shook out his legs. Crossed them the other way. And bent down again.

I counted to ten in my head and then grabbed him by the elbow. "Let's go."

"All right, all right."

"Do you still feel nauseous? Do you have a headache? Are you tired?"

"Yes. Yes. And yes."

"We have to get off the mountain. You could have altitude sickness."

"What are you going to do? Push me off? I could be nauseous because my stomach's been bouncing around for the last three hours. And I could have a headache because I'm dehydrated. And I could be tired because I just finished running thirteen miles straight up into the air. I'm okay. Trust me."

I paced in front of the restroom while he went in to change.

He came out, dressed in sweats. Still not warm enough for the weather, but warmer than what he had been wearing.

He smiled. "About that donut...?"

I could have hugged him. He was fine.

The next Saturday Joe came into the store. Leaned against the counter and propped his chin in his hand. "Hi."

"Can I help you?"

"I don't know. It's my birthday tomorrow. I was thinking of buying some skis."

"Thinking about it? Or wanting to do it?"

"Wanting to do it."

"What kind?"

"Partial metal, a little on the wide side."

"Waxless?"

"No."

"Sidecut?"

"Not too much."

I talked skis with Joe for the next hour before he finally settled on a pair. "You didn't bring your bindings with you, did you?"

He showed me his dimples before plopping his backpack on the counter. He unzipped it, brought out a bag, and spilled the contents onto the counter. The bindings.

"Great. I'll put them on for you."

I rung up his sale and gave him his credit card as he signed the receipt.

He turned away from the counter toward the door. Then he turned back. "Hey, about tomorrow? Help me celebrate."

"Happy birthday. If I had a horn, I'd toot it."

"I was thinking we could do something."

"What?"

"Whatever I wanted."

"When haven't we done what you wanted?"

"Well…fine. Since it's my birthday, and I'll be the Birthday King, we'll do whatever you want to do."

"Whatever *I* want to do?"

He shrugged. "Yeah. Whatever you do for fun."

"You can't back out."

"I won't."

"Promise?"

"I guarantee it."

The next day, two hours after attending yet another disappointing church service, we were dressed in bright colors and working our way down the grassy shoulders of I-25, picking up litter and putting it into large paper grocery bags. I wished I'd put my hair into ponytails. The wind was whipping it across my eyes.

I bent to pick up another cigarette butt.

Joe was bending part of a tire to fit it into the bag. "Why am I doing this again?"

"Because you said we could do whatever I wanted to do."

"I said something fun. Whatever you do for fun."

"This *is* fun."

"This is not fun."

"It'll get more fun."

"When?"

"When we look back on all the trash we've collected and see how clean it is back there."

"Jackie, that's not fun. That's work. How far do we have to go?"

"As far as we can."

"We could go forever."

"That's the point."

"What is?"

"Keeping the earth clean takes constant vigilance. If we don't do this, then who will? Fun is doing something unexpected just because you can."

He opened his mouth. Shut it. "You're unexpected. But that's not the point. The point is, who cares?"

"I do."

"You're probably the only one."

"So what if I am?"

"So if you are, then what's the point?"

"The point is that we're doing something because it's the right thing to do. Whether anyone else cares or not."

Joe just stood there, a fisted hand clad in a flowered gardening glove on his hip. He glared at me.

A van swerved across two lanes of traffic and rattled to a halt on the shoulder of the road, 50 yards away from us. We heard a door slam but couldn't see it through the swirling dust. As it settled, we saw a man walking toward us.

Joe closed the distance between us and then stepped in front of me.

The man stuck out a hand in Joe's direction. "Hi."

Joe took off his glove and clasped the hand. "Hi."

"I'm Gil Patterson with *Your News, Colorado Springs.* I film the Positive Choices segments."

Joe folded his arms across his chest. "Nice to meet you."

"Are you doing this cleanup as part of an organized group?"

Joe glanced down at me. "Yes and no. Today's my birthday, and Jackie organized the two of us to come out and do this. It's her idea of fun."

The man beamed. "Great! Fabulous. My other Positive Choice turned out to be high on drugs. What's your name?"

"Joe Gallagher."

"And?"

Joe replied for me. "Jackie Harrison."

"So how long have you been out here doing this?"

"Far too long."

"Okay. Stay right there, Joe and Jackie. I'll be back with the camera."

Gil jogged back toward his van. He opened the door and stuck his head inside. He returned several minutes later trailing a man holding a camera and various cords.

"All right. What I'd like to do is have you stand…" He looked out at the road, and then he looked across his shoulder toward the foothills. "Stand right here. We want to see some cars behind you." He grabbed my shoulder and stood me alongside Joe. "Okay. I'm just going to ask you some questions about cleaning up. Why you're doing this. The segment will air tonight. Afterward, if you give me your address, I'll send you a couple mugs with the station logo. Okay?"

He didn't wait for us to answer before turning his attention to the cameraman.

From behind the camera, an arm appeared, finger pointed up like a pistol. And then, suddenly, it swung down.

Gil smiled and then started to speak. "This is Gil Patterson with *Your News, Colorado Springs*. Today's Positive Choice award goes to Joe Gallagher and Jackie Harrison. Why are you out here today?"

Gil tilted the microphone toward Joe. "To celebrate my birthday, Gil."

"Do you celebrate this way every year?"

"No. This year's special."

"And why is that?"

Joe stepped closer toward me and put an arm around my shoulder. "Because of my friend Jackie. She thinks it's fun to do things like this for no other reason than it's the right thing to do. She doesn't care whether people think she's crazy or not. She's one of the most selfless, self-assured people I know."

"And how long will you be out here today. How far will you go?"

Joe looked down at me. "As far as we can."

We worked another couple hours after Gil left. We'd collected a half-dozen paper bags filled with trash by then. We hiked back to the car as the sun was setting behind the mountains. Threw the bags in the back.

Joe slouched into the car and stretched out. "You know, I've never been on TV before. That was fun. Thanks for spending my day with me. It was a birthday I'll never forget."

"Thanks for…the things you told Gil. About me."

"I meant every word."

THE CUBICLE NEXT DOOR BLOG

Mistaken identity

I think you've mistaken me for someone else. Someone stronger. Someone better. That's not who I am at all.

Posted on August 27 in **The Cubicle Next Door | Permalink**

Comments

Don't you hate that? It's like they think you're Superwoman. You can do everything. Yeah, right. She went out with the '70s.

Posted by: **justluvmyjob | August 27 at 09:53 PM**

But maybe it could be. If you wanted to be.

Posted by: **philopsophie | August 27 at 10:13 PM**

That may, in fact, be the image you are presenting to the outside world. Many successful people worry that people will discover they aren't really who everyone else thinks they are. That their success is a big hoax. It's called Imposter Syndrome. And the funny thing is, you become who you're desperately afraid to admit that you're not. The correct perception, in this case, is usually everyone else's.

Posted by: **NozAll | August 28 at 07:48 AM**

At least he thinks you are someone. That's better than being no one.

Posted by: **survivor | August 28 at 09:12 AM**

(CLOSE)

Fourteen

****

On Friday afternoon Estelle sent an e-mail around the department advertising ten free tickets to the football game the next day.

I deleted it as soon as I read the word "football" in the subject line.

Joe didn't. He raced down the hall and came back five minutes later holding two tickets in his hand. "I got the last two!"

"Great."

"Want to go?"

"I don't do football games."

"I'll have to add it to the list. Don't do lunch. Don't do dates. Don't do football games. What's wrong with you? Don't you know how to have a good time?"

A good time? No, in fact, I did not. Not in the normal sense of the word. If Good Time can be defined by playing bridge with your grandmother's closest friends, then maybe I did. If Good Time can be defined as terrorizing hapless waiters with superior wine knowledge along with three of your closest friends from MIT or trying to write a code to solve the unsolvable Hilbert's tenth problem, then maybe I did. But in the classical cow-tipping, football-game-attending sense of the word, no, I did not.

"You've never been to a game?"

"No."

"Never? Not even in high school?"

Especially not in high school. "No."

"I'm picking you up at nine."

"That's fine, but I'm not going. You know I work for Grandmother on Saturdays."

"I'll just tell her you can't."

Touché. Because the way Grandmother and her friends treated Joe, they'd gladly donate me as a virgin sacrifice if he ever asked.

"I'm not good in the sun."

"I'll bring sunscreen."

"If I have to go, then I'm driving."

"I don't think it would be a good idea because—"

"If you're going to make me go somewhere I don't want to go and do something I don't want to do, then the very least thing I ask is we not waste gas doing it. Okay?"

"Okay, okay. Fine."

At least he hadn't added, "I'm just telling you…" But he should have. Who would have known the huge field in front of the football stadium turned into a parking lot on Saturdays during football season?

Not me.

Because there actually was a parking lot up on top of the hill. And that's where I had been heading before I had been directed into the field lying west of the stadium.

"Why are they making me go this way?"

"Because this is where you're supposed to park."

"On the grass?"

"Everyone else is doing it."

"It has a hard enough time growing as it is."

"You'd better go, because there are about twenty cars lined up behind you."

While Joe put a forearm up to the roof to protect his head, I bumpity-bumpity-bumped over the ground, praying my carburetor or muffler or any other mysterious car part wouldn't fall off and get swallowed by a hole. I was directed into an invisible parking space by a kid wearing an orange safety vest about five sizes too big.

We got out. Joe reached into the backseat for a backpack that he slipped over one shoulder and two collapsible mini chairs decorated in the Academy's blue-and-gray colors.

"Want me to carry one?"

"I'm fine." He stood for a minute, looking in several different directions, and then he started off south, away from the stadium.

"Where are we going?"

"To the department tailgate. Over there."

"Over there" turned out to be at the opposite end of the field, across another road, and down a ways. We got to tramp through quite a few other tailgates. By the time we got to ours, I was hungry.

Joe dug a small blanket out of his backpack and spread it on the ground. He handed me a bottle of sunscreen and then went to fill two plates with hamburgers, chips, and chocolate chip cookies. He ended up eating all of my chips and two of my cookies.

We watched some of the kids run around. Partook in a discussion about the general caliber of Academy cadets and a downward trend in their level of respect toward instructors. Overheard a discussion between parent and small child about whether it was worth hiking to the porta-potties all the way over by the stadium to go to the bathroom, or whether it would be easier and less smelly to just go in the woods.

Then we finally decided to head to the stadium.

We walked all the way to the east side to take advantage of the speedier lines reserved for personnel, but they still wouldn't let me take in my bottle of water. And it wasn't even "bottled" water. It was filtered tap water from home because bottling water can make it up to 10,000 times more expensive than turning on your own faucet and consuming the exact same amount.

"It's just water."

"I'm sorry, ma'am."

"I'll drink it in front of you."

"If you'd like, ma'am."

I unscrewed the top. Took a swig. "See? Water."

"Yes, ma'am."

I screwed the top on and started to pass through.

"I'm sorry, ma'am, but you can't take the bottle in with you."

"Didn't we just do this? It's water. Remember? I haven't died yet."

"I'm sorry, ma'am."

At least it was only a 12-ounce bottle instead of a 16-ounce one.

Then people would have been even more upset when I stood there and drank it. All.

They finally let me through.

Joe slid a glance at me. "Was that really necessary?"

"Yes. I brought the water; I obviously wanted to drink it. Do you know how much water is wasted each year in El Paso County? Do you know in how many years our aquifers are going to run dry?"

"I don't know whether to be impressed with your knowledge, cheer your chutzpah, or strangle your cute little neck. So spare me the lecture."

"You probably leave the faucet running when you brush your teeth, don't you?"

"*And* I let the shower warm up for five minutes before I use it."

He only said that to irritate me.

I think.

We made our way to the south side of the stadium and found our seats just in time to see half of the cadet wing march onto the field. The rest of the cadets were already seated in the student section of the bleachers. After saluting, the playing of the national anthem, and a couple additional maneuvers, they broke formation and ran to join their fellow cadets in the stands.

I heard the sound of airplanes in the distance. A formation of planes flew overhead, followed by a B-1 Bomber. The most impressive thing was the roar it made when the pilot turned the afterburner on.

And then a plane began to circle, high above the stadium, and parachutists jumped out, trailing smoke. The Wings of Blue, the cadet parachute team, came down in formation, one carrying the senior class flag, another carrying the POW flag, still another the U.S. flag. The group landed in the center of the field.

After everyone had finished clapping and sat down, the football teams ran onto the field. The sports announcer started talking, although I don't think anyone could understand him.

It wasn't far into the game when everyone stood back up. I think it was because the ball was near one of the ends of the field. Then everyone groaned and sat back down. And then it started all over again. The gradual buildup of tension, the gradual rising from the seats, the intense concentration directed toward the field, and then, sudden relief.

This time, everyone cheered.

"So the object of the game is to…"

Joe looked down at me. "You've never watched a game before?"

"No."

"Well, it's like this…" He bent down toward me, looking all the while at the field. He must have realized I couldn't really see over the heads of the people in front of me. "Hop up here." He took my hand while I stepped up onto the bleacher. "Nobody will mind for just a minute."

This time, I bent down toward him so I could hear him talking.

"Notre Dame has the football now, right? And they're trying to get it into the end zone for a touchdown. They can either pass it—throw the ball—or they can run it. And during any given play they can use a combination of passing and throwing. Most of the time, only the quarterback can throw the ball. Anyone can run with it. Their turn is over when they either fumble the ball—drop it—or they get tackled. Each time the ball reverts to them, they're trying to move the ball ten yards. They get four tries to make it. And that's about it. The rest is technicalities."

That gave me enough information to follow the game. I stepped down off the bench. I still didn't understand why the whistle got blown or why people had to kick the ball. Joe had only talked about passing and running.

And I didn't understand the scoring at all.

But there were enough other things going on that it was…fun.

The first time Air Force scored, Joe grabbed my arm. "Look over there." He was pointing toward the cadet section.

I saw some of the cadets break away from the cadet area and run onto the field. They dropped to the ground and started doing push-ups.

"The fourth classmen run onto the field and do push-ups every time Air Force scores. One for each point in the accumulated score."

Heaven help them if the Academy team ever happened to run the score up.

After Air Force had scored for the third time, I saw their mascot run out onto the field with them. It was a big blue bird. He helped keep count, but didn't do the push-ups himself. During halftime, he rode around the edge of the field in a miniature airplane.

"I'd say the most fun is being had by that bird."

"The Bird? I guarantee it."

The way he said it made me dig a little further. "Is that a cadet in there?"

"Yep."

"Were you ever the cadet in there?"

"Can't tell. Bird's honor."

"So you were?"

"Maybe."

"Tell me."

"Or maybe not."

He was. No doubt in my mind. I could just picture him hopping all over the place, posing for pictures with little kids and mooning the opposing team like this bird had just done. It was my guess Joe had invented that particular move.

A fanfare sounded over the loudspeaker as a small group of cadets walked out onto the field. Unlike the cadets sitting in the bleachers, this group was lucky. Instead of wearing the full blue uniform, complete with hats and jackets, this bunch was wearing only polo shirts and track pants.

The announcer launched into a spiel about the group, members of the cadet Falconry Club. Apparently, the Air Force Academy had the NCAA's only performing mascot, a falcon. Cadet volunteers. They put it through its paces, urging it to wing its way around the stadium while stalking the "prey" they were swinging around at the end of a string.

It did what it was supposed to. It caught the swinging meat and landed on the football field before being picked up by a cadet. A hood was placed over its head and it was taken away.

Poor bird.

Maybe someday it would spot a real mouse out in the parking lot and swoop out of the stadium and into freedom, only to be run over by someone's SUV while it was trying to eat.

I'm all for the environment, but I'm also a realist.

The mood changed in a matter of seconds. Looking toward the field, I saw the teams filing back into the stadium.

A chant began from the cadet section. It sounded like...*You pay for our school! You pay for our school! You pay for our school!* I stood on tiptoe and leaned toward Joe. "You pay for our school?"

He grinned. "They do. We're taxpayer supported, remember?"

The second part of the game went along much like the first. During a time when the players weren't playing, music flared from the cadet band. I could hear the cadets singing.

Joe sang along too. As loud as he could. "You'll never fly, so..."

"Um. Excuse me. What did you just say?"

"'The Falcon Fight Song.'" He began to sing, repeating the words for me. "'Never say die, keep flying high, for the Air Force Academy!'" He smiled. All innocence. "Go, Air Force!"

"Uh-huh." I could almost guarantee I'd heard the word "die," but it hadn't been after the word "say."

After the game, the Notre Dame side began to empty. The people around us stood but remained in the stadium, staring at the field. The Air Force football team gathered together and faced the cadet section. The subdued melody of a song drifted up from the field.

Beside me, Joe sang along.

It was a hymn to those who had made the ultimate sacrifice. People like my father. As a cadet, he must have stood in this stadium more than once, singing that very same hymn.

I wondered if he'd ever imagined people might sing it about him. Or that he would have a daughter who would listen while it was sung.

We joined the crowd leaving the stadium and walked to the car.

I tried to shrug off a mantle of thoughts better left stored away. Tried to dodge the idea that, no matter how hard I tried, I was doomed to repeat my mother's mistakes. I could almost feel my reserve and self-control crumbling whenever I was around Joe. I was haunted by the idea that it was only a matter of time...but I couldn't make myself stay away from him. Aside from logistics and the nonavailability of office space, I just didn't want to.

Oh, how the mighty have fallen.

I was used to being able to control my thoughts and my feelings. I wasn't used to having someone pound on my heart, asking to be let in. But just because someone was knocking didn't mean I had to answer.

I concentrated my attention instead on the traffic free-for-all taking place around me. "You might have to get out and push me to the road."

"If I do, can I drive next time?"

"Let's see what happens."

We bumped through the field and reached the road 20 minutes later. We actually drove off the base an hour after the game had ended.

"So what did you think?"

"It was okay. Fun. It was fun." I merged onto the interstate. Colorado Springs must have some rule about entrance and exit ramps being no more than 30 feet long, left over from the days when cars could only go about ten miles an hour, tops. "Did it bring back good memories?"

"Some."

"Was it hot inside that bird suit?"

THE CUBICLE NEXT DOOR BLOG

Haunting thoughts

I am haunted, sometimes, by the thought that we are pro-
grammed to play certain roles. That we are destined to be certain
kinds of people. That our parents, no matter the size of the part
they played in our lives, place us on the chessboard of life in the
middle of some cosmic chess game. And the only instructions we
are given are "Do as I did," or worse, "Don't do as I have done." Is
it possible to escape ourselves? To become people entirely of our
own making?

Posted on September 2 in **The Cubicle Next Door | Permalink**

Comments

Maybe, if you lived in a world inhabited only by you.

Posted by: **philosophie | September 2 at 08:09 PM**

Ah—the classic question of predestination v. free will!

Posted by: **NozAll | September 3 at 10:24 AM**

I don't know about escaping myself, but I'd sure like to escape the
jerks around me!

Posted by: **justluvmyjob | September 3 at 01:39 PM**

It doesn't matter. You take your place on the board game of life
and you just do the best you can.

Posted by: **survivor | September 3 at 04:17 PM**

CLOSE

Fifteen

****

The following Tuesday Ms. West Point came in late in the afternoon with a cadet. A fourth classman. "Is Joe in?"

I gestured to the other side of the cubicle.

She leaned around the wall. "Cadet Prescott has some questions about the written assignment for 101. I have a meeting I need to go to…" she glanced at her watch. "Right now."

"First, let's have an altimeter check."

There was a sound of swift motion. The clicking together of heels. "Sir, my altitude is 7250 feet above sea level—far, far above that of West Point or Annapolis!"

"All right. Thanks. At ease."

Was that nice? The poor cadet! Just a pawn in the mind games between Joe and Ms. West Point.

After the cadet had left, I heard Joe climb up onto his desk.

"About Sunday…"

I started to smile and I looked up at him. "You giving up? Already?"

"No. Pick me up at the normal time."

"I was planning on it."

He stood there.

"Was there anything else?"

"No."

"Is your boundless optimism fraying?"

"No."

"Flagging?"

"No. Just because you've abandoned all hope doesn't mean I have to."

"You really don't know anything about me."

"I know some things."

"You don't know everything."

"I know enough."

"Enough to what?"

"Know you're weird in a cute sort of way."

"I am not…cute."

He gave me a long look. "No. You're right. You're not."

Funny how hearing the truth can feel like disappointment.

He flashed a grin. "You're fascinating, mysterious, and intriguing. Cute is too benign for you."

"You can't just—"

"Just what?"

"Just…"

"What?"

"Nothing."

"You know what the problem with you is?"

"Why don't you fill me in since you know so much about me."

"You won't trust anybody."

"Amazing. You've got me pegged. Now I feel complete. Thanks. How much do I owe you?"

"For you? Since you're so screwed up, it's free. You're my gift to humanity."

"I feel so unworthy."

"Exactly. It goes along with the not trusting anybody." His head disappeared and I heard him settle back into his chair.

"Jackie?"

"What?"

"I take referrals—tell all your friends."

Sunday's experience was a repeat of all the other churches we'd attended.

We'd been given a bulletin by a greeter who had smiled at a point somewhere above our heads, sat through another sermon with five points and two sub-points apiece. We'd taken our Visitors Forms out to the Welcome Center, which turned out to be an optimistically titled folding table laden with stacks of church events fliers.

The man beside the table took our forms, looked at them a moment, and then handed us each the ubiquitous goody bag filled with handy information on the church, their mission and vision statements, a booklet written by their pastor, and a coupon for a free espresso drink at the coffee cart in their lobby.

We thanked him and walked away.

"Do you want to?" Joe gestured toward the coffee cart with his chin.

"Not really."

As we stood there trying to decide whether to go or stay, clutching our bags that had "Welcome" stamped across the front in large, electric red letters, not one person stopped to talk to us. Traffic flowed right around us. Our only function in the church appeared to be as a median. As a barrier separating the people who flowed around us in both directions.

"This sucks." Joe strode toward the Welcome Center.

I had to dodge people to keep up with him. By the time I got to the table he had plunked the Welcome Bag down on top of it. "This is really nice, thanks very much, but I don't want a mission statement, a booklet, or coffee. What I'd really like is someone to look at me and talk to me and make me feel like I'm visible."

The man standing behind the table blinked. "What?"

Joe started to repeat himself and then stopped as he realized the man wasn't looking at him, but beyond him, over his shoulder. We both turned at the same time to follow the man's gaze toward a woman standing across the lobby, gesturing at her watch.

I started to smile.

Joe sent a stern look in my direction and then reached into several of the bags, removing free coffee coupons. We handed out six of them to random people on our way to the door.

"What is it about churches in this town?"

"They're full."

"No, they're not."

"Not jammed full. They just don't need more people. They have their little groups and committees. They've handed out the uniforms. They're busy. They've got people to talk to, plans to make, friends to eat lunch with." What else could I say? Colorado Springs may be church-friendly, but it wasn't people-friendly.

"There has to be at least one church…"

"You'd think."

"How long did you look for one? When you first came back?"

"About four months."

"A different church each Sunday?"

I nodded. "For a while. I went to a couple of them more than once."

"And you never found one?"

"No."

"Did you ever try to join a group? Bible study? Anything?"

"Sure. There were lots of sign-ups going on, but nothing ever seemed to get arranged. At one church I talked to a ministries coordinator. Tried to find a place to plug in."

"What happened?"

"A circular dialogue. I kept asking where the church needed help and he kept asking what I wanted to do."

Joe snorted. "We can't not go to church."

"It's not the preferred solution, but it doesn't make us any less Christian, does it?"

"We'll find one."

Life developed a predictable rhythm. Joe dodged in and out of his cubicle on M days. Stayed chained to his desk during office hours on T days. Came over to Grandmother's for poker night on Wednesdays. On Sundays, we went to church together.

Any kind of casual observer, and all of Grandmother's friends, had figured out by then that Joe and I were dating. In the non-dating sense of the term. Joe was smart. Smart enough to know I'd say no if he ever actually asked me out on a date. I'd told him so myself. It was on the official "Jackie doesn't do" list. So he didn't ask and I never had to say no. We just kept enjoying each other's company.

Oh, the dangerous games we play with ourselves.

I never imagined that being with Joe would make me want what I'd long ago decided I could never have.

One Monday, after a long T day filled with silly questions, I heard something thunk the wall. Heard a slap as it hit Joe's hands. Heard it thunk the wall again.

I watched the thumbtacks pop out of my apathy poster. Saw it drop to the floor. "Will you knock it off?" I scrambled under the desk to try and find the thumbtacks. Ended up planting my knee right on top of one. "Ow!" I hit my head as I tried to back out.

Thunk.

I climbed on top of my desk only to duck as a miniature basketball came flying up toward my head. It must have rebounded from the metal joint between cubicle sections because I heard Joe catch it.

"Half—no—*all* of the questions they're asking me are things they could figure out for themselves if they'd bother to read or even listen in class."

I tried again. Stuck my head up. Made sure he wasn't going to throw the ball. He was turning it over between his hands, examining the seams.

"So tell them to study for themselves. They need to learn to own their knowledge. Take responsibility for it."

"I would have been embarrassed to ask my instructors these kinds of questions. They would have thought I was an idiot." He threw the ball at the wall again.

I flinched. "Why don't you just go work out? Don't you have to exercise? Keep in shape?"

He paused. "Maybe I should."

"What's the worst that could happen? All those poor cadets would have to read the book for themselves?"

So the next T day, the first period before lunch, he worked out. And no less than ten cadets came to see him.

"Is Lt. Col. Gallagher here?"

"No."

"Do you know when Lt. Col. Gallagher will be back?"

"No."

"Can I wait here for Lt. Col. Gallagher?"

"In my office? No."

When he finally returned, his hair was damp, his cheeks were red, and he smelled like soap. He was practically glowing.

"Have a good workout?"

"Great! Thanks for the suggestion. I'm going to keep it up. Every T day."

"There were about fifty cadets who stopped in looking for you."

"Really?"

"It seemed like it."

"So did you help them? Or did you just tell them they needed to own their knowledge." He dimpled before he disappeared into his cubicle.

"I would have if I'd had the time, but I was supposed to be working in between keeping track of you on behalf of the cadets. Because we all know our only function in life is to make them happy."

Next T day, before Joe left to work out, he taped a sign to the end of the cubicle wall. "That should take care of anybody's questions."

"Should it? What does it say? Joe's dead, take a hike?"

"It says, PT eleven to twelve."

"Which would be short for...?"

"Physical training."

"And everyone knows that's what it means?"

"At the Academy? I guarantee it."

I wish he would have guaranteed everyone knew how to read. People still asked me questions about where he was, even after I told them to read the sign. I drew the line at taking messages for him.

Secretary.

Systems administrator.

Two separate job descriptions. And neither of them included being Joe's keeper.

THE CUBICLE NEXT DOOR BLOG

Treat me right

Here's something you don't know, John Smith. Everyone treats me like your secretary. I spend half the day not telling people where you are. Not telling them when you're expected back. Not taking messages for you. In fact, there's only one person who doesn't expect me to be your secretary: You.

Posted on September 11 in **The Cubicle Next Door | Permalink**

Comments

In fact, the word "secretary" was coined in the Middle Ages for someone who dealt in secrets or could be trusted in confidential business. Only later was the term applied to those who recorded business transactions. The word "secret" has the same root as "seclude" and "secure," all of them words identifying a person or thing set or kept apart from others.

Posted by: **NozAll | September 12 at 07:23 AM**

Doesn't treat you like his secretary? Then give him a break! He's a keeper.

Posted by: **justluvmyjob | September 14 at 08:17 AM**

(CLOSE)

Sixteen

****

So. I was sitting in a staff meeting, ostensibly taking notes about computer issues while in fact making a grocery list. I had then moved on to drawing a series of ocean waves. Embellished the scene with a beach. Palm trees. I was just starting on sand dollars when I heard my name taken in vain.

Estelle responded, pen poised over the tablet she used for taking the minutes of our meetings. "How many people in total?"

Joe answered. "Four, plus Jackie." He didn't usually attend the meetings; he was only sitting in for someone else.

Estelle scribbled down the information. She glanced at me over the top of her reading glasses. "Is that okay with you, Jackie?"

I glanced around the room.

Joe was giving me a thumbs-up.

"Yeah. Sure."

Being volunteered for assorted and sundry team and committee meetings was not uncommon, so I wasn't worried. I'd find out all the details when I read Estelle's minutes. Minutes were one thing she did quickly. Mostly because the colonel required an almost immediate report on the action items. The minutes would be broadcast to the entire department within the hour.

I returned to my sand dollars.

An hour later, I was staring at my computer screen.

"Um, Joe?"

"Yeah?"

"Have you read Estelle's minutes?"

"Reading them right now."

"This part about the Emma Crawford Coffin Race?"

"Yeah?"

"I think Estelle put my name into the wrong item...right?"

"Nope. She got it right. You volunteered to be Emma."

"Emma?"

"Emma Crawford. You know, sit in the coffin while the history department team pushes it down Manitou Avenue."

"No, no, no, no, no. I *never* agreed to do that."

Here's how I knew I hadn't agreed. The Emma Crawford Coffin Race was run in Manitou Springs every October, the Saturday before Halloween. It was in commemoration of Emma Crawford, who had come to Manitou Springs at the turn of the last century in search of a cure for tuberculosis. She met an engineer who was working on the Cog Railway, became engaged to him, but died before the wedding took place. Her fiancé buried her on top of Red Mountain, where she could commune with nature and the various spirits she insisted were waiting for her up there.

Many years later, after having been buffeted by Colorado weather, the peak disintegrated and let Emma and her coffin go. Nameplate and all. She took a ride down the mountain and was discovered by two local boys.

I was not going to be Emma Crawford.

And I was certainly not going to sit in a coffin while it was being raced down Manitou Avenue.

"Yep. I'm pretty sure you did. At least, that's what the colonel thinks."

Great.

Just great.

Because the colonel had this thing about responsibility and accountability. Whatever it was a person agreed to in a meeting was what that person absolutely had to do. You had to come through. Because, in his words, "If I tell you I'm dropping a bomb on Bolivia, I sure as #$!% better not drop it on Beirut."

Dang. Double dang. Dang, dang, dang.

He also had a thing about department togetherness. And if I was going to ride in a coffin race and four department members were going to push me, then at least half the department was going to be arm-twisted into watching us.

Mandatory department fun.

"I'm going to kill you."

"Could you at least wait until after the Coffin Race?"

Three weeks later I was wishing I *had* been responsible and kept accountable and followed through on my threat to kill Joe.

"Look dead." Joe was standing in front of me, scrutinizing my face.

"I'm trying."

"You don't look dead enough."

"Listen, do you want to wear this dress? And this hat? Because we could change costumes."

It was 10:30 AM on the day of the race. We were at Joe's house. The four mourner-runners and I. We were being dressed by the mourners' wives. They had gone all out. Joe and his cohorts would be running in tails and top hats. They were all sporting black armbands and walking sticks.

I had been being dressed for over an hour. Someone had put way too much work into my costume. There were bloomers and underskirts and petticoats. A camisole and corset. The dress was of gray satin with a low square neck edged by white lace that was attached at the shoulders with white roses. Fake ones. The sleeves looked like deflated puffs and hung down around my elbows. They were also edged in lace. The waist was gathered and then it dropped to the floor and trailed out behind me. A tripping hazard. I was required to wear a helmet during the race, so they had hidden it inside a hat. A decorated version of a top hat, it sprouted bows and feathers and all sorts of other things. It also had a gray veil draped across the front, conveniently located for maximum opacity for the coffin ride down Manitou Avenue.

The women were coating all my available skin with white clown paint. "Don't move your mouth," one of them cautioned "or the paint will crack."

They finished painting me. Fastened the helmet onto my head. Then it was time for pictures.

The other three mourners got up from the couch where they had been watching football. They put their jackets on, stuck their hats on their heads, and pulled the elastic bands down under their chins.

"Where should we take them?"

"Let's take some on the couch. Then we can take more outside with the coffin."

"Jackie," one of the wives grabbed me by the elbow and dragged me over to the couch. "Lie there and pretend you're dead."

There seemed to be a lot of that going around.

I fell onto the couch, trying hard not to move anything with paint on it. I clasped my hands on top of my chest. Joe shoved a bouquet of black roses into them.

The four guys knelt beside the couch in various poses of grief.

Joe looked the most stricken. Of course. He knew his time on earth was limited. By me.

Outside, Joe lifted me into the foam-padded, red-satin lined coffin. For the first photo, I lay down, reenacting the pose I'd struck inside. Then I sat up, the way I would during the race.

He grabbed my arm. "Look d—"

"Don't...say...it."

The guys smiled. I didn't.

After the pictures were taken, they wheeled me down Pawnee Avenue.

"Hey, want to practice, Jackie? We could let go. Race you to the bottom of the hill."

That's Joe. Always the joker. Because flying down the hill on Pawnee Avenue would send me whizzing across Manitou Avenue and dump me right into Fountain Creek.

They didn't let me go.

We arrived safely at Memorial Park and lined up with the other coffin contestants waiting to be checked in. We had our coffin inspected and measured. Received our race schedule. I stood beside the coffin while our team was judged. Then we joined the Parade of Coffins.

Joe and the other guys each carried a bag filled with slimy rubber eyeballs and globs of gook filled with maggots. From time to time they reached into their bags and threw their ghastly treasures out into the crowd. A chorus of shrieks accompanied our coffin on its way down the street.

I sat in the coffin and waved, but not too often. I didn't want to crack my paint.

Crowds lined the avenue, separated from the coffins by garlands of tape, in some cases looking suspiciously like the black-and-yellow tape used to rope off crime scenes.

All sorts of people watched us go by. Average families composed of Mom, Dad, and two kids. Groups of punked-out teens. Clusters of aging hippies.

After the parade we waited in Memorial Park until it was our turn to race.

The racing was done in pairs. Each coffin was responsible for keeping in its own lane.

The mourners wheeled me up to the starting line. They each grabbed hold of a regulation handle, attached firmly to the side of the coffin, projecting not more than ten inches from the sides.

I looked over at the other team. They were dressed as ghouls with gray-green faces and drooping black robes. The woman sitting inside was a skeleton, complete with white hair and black-rimmed eyes.

Creepy.

"On your mark!"

I grabbed onto the edges of the coffin.

"Get set!"

The guys bent forward, toward the finish line. Joe was on the left side, at the back.

"Go!"

We were off.

The crowd was cheering, I could tell by their faces, but the only sounds I heard were of shoes slapping the road and heavy breathing.

"This thing is a bear to push!" We weren't even 50 yards into the race and one of the guys on the right was already complaining.

I glanced over at the other team. They were catching up to us. "Just run!"

"Did anyone put oil on the wheels?"

A couple paces went by before anyone answered Joe. Then they all answered at once. "No."

"Stop talking. They're catching us!" Turning in my coffin seat, I could see the other team advancing with every step.

"Go faster!"

Joe tore his eyes from the finish line. Glanced up at me. "You're supposed to be dead!"

"Faster! They're passing us!'

"Be...dead!"

There were only 100 yards left. "Go, go, go, go, go!" My chants were interspersed with Joe's "be dead, be dead, be dead."

At ten yards we were coffin-to-coffin.

"Come on! Push it! Let's go!"

The guys exhausted the last of their energy and sprinted across the finish line. By the time they crossed, I was curled into a crouch, holding onto the sides of the coffin, screaming and yelling my head off.

I stood up, reached down, and high-fived everyone.

Then I realized what I was doing.

I was supposed to be dead. Boy, I'd really screwed that up.

But Joe whisked me off and gave me a hug before setting me on my feet.

The colonel was there, with his wife and about 15 other families from the department. They all congratulated us.

An hour later, it was our turn to race again in the first of two final heats.

Again, we won. Again, I wound up at the finish line on my knees, inside the coffin, cheering on the guys.

The winner of the next heat was faster than us by two seconds.

Oh, well.

Runner-up wasn't bad.

At the end of the day, we'd almost won, I'd almost lost my voice, and I'd almost decided to let Joe live.

THE CUBICLE NEXT DOOR BLOG

Surprise, surprise

I had the chance to work on a project with John Smith. On a project I would have vetoed out of hand had it been up to me. The results were of no importance to myself or anyone else. It was extracurricular in the way only mandatory office fun can be. But I found myself behaving in completely unexpected ways. Maybe even...enjoying...the experience. I still don't know what it means.

Posted on October 28 in **The Cubicle Next Door | Permalink**

Comments

Experiment. Experience is all there is to life.

Posted by: **philosophie | October 28 at 10:03 PM**

Yeah, 'cause once you finally get it all figured out, that's when you die.

Posted by: **survivor | October 29 at 11:28 AM**

Don't you just hate those "not required but highly encouraged" events?

Posted by: **justluvmyjob | October 30 at 08:02 AM**

Unexpected behavior reveals a disconnect between who you perceive yourself to be and who you really are. Hypothesis states you will resolve this conflict only by engaging in behaviors to eliminate the contradiction between the two perceptions.

Posted by: **NozAll | October 30 at 12:13 PM**

Otherwise known as Festinger's Theory of Cognitive Dissonance. Thank you, Mr. Fortune Cookie, for your scintillating analysis.

Posted by: **thatsmrtoyou | October 30 at 12:26 PM**

CLOSE

Seventeen

****

The next week I was watching ABC's news journal with Grandmother. They kept teasing viewers, just before cutting away to commercials, with an upcoming story on blogs. Reading tantalizing bits of blog entries. Talking up how they were cyber diaries just waiting for electronic eyes to read them.

I was marginally interested.

Mostly for security's sake.

Since I did, in fact, have a blog. And I didn't want anyone to know who I was.

So I suffered through an exposé on biomedical research. And another on customer service hotlines. Finally, the blog segment came up. It was the last story.

Of course.

The story started by flashing the logos of the most popular blogging sites. Had fade-outs of different blog titles. And then a voice-over started reading from a blog.

I'm worse than a shark. I can smell your cologne from 100 yards away. And it lingers in my senses, long after you are gone.

I swallowed my water down the wrong pipe and started to cough. Couldn't stop. But I could still hear the voice. It kept right on reading.

John Smith doesn't know this, but I've got his back. He thinks I work just as long as he does, but I don't. Not really. I just stay until he goes home. In spite of considering himself the expert at everything, he doesn't know anything about the women here. Has no idea how many of them have paused at the cubicle and then kept on walking when they've seen me sitting at my desk.

They were reading from my blog!

Grandmother snorted. "This is public television. They shouldn't be talking about things like that. What kind of person writes this sort of thing?"

I did.

I wrote that sort of thing. But I never though anyone would read it.

The voice went on say people blogged for many different reasons. That my blog, The Cubicle Next Door, was, at first glance, just a blog about modern life, but if read carefully, provided perhaps some shades of office romance. Of the modern girl next door. A diary filled with the angst of unrequited love.

Angst!

They actually called me the Ingenue of the Blogosphere.

I sat through the rest of the segment praying that at the end they would put someone else's URL up on the screen. Hoping that somewhere out in cyberspace I had a clone.

As it turns out, I did not.

On the way to work the next morning, I felt exposed. As if everyone in the world knew I was ABC's favorite ingenue. If only they could see me now: dark green sweater, lime green Converse. Hair pulled back with two rubber bands that had last been used to hold stalks of celery together. I had ceased to be anyone's ingenue at the age of three.

All the way down the interstate I lectured myself about the blog.

I had only ever started it for therapeutic reasons. To vent. To whine. To rage. And those reasons still held true. Especially after last night. I'd never asked for publicity. Didn't want it. In fact, it could hardly make a difference.

In anything.

The only person I really didn't want to know about the blog was Joe. And what were the chances he'd even watched TV the night before?

Football?

Maybe.

A news journal?

Never.

So I was safe.

Joe was already in his cubicle when I got there. Sipping coffee and leaning over his laptop.

"I could order you a cover for your keyboard. That way when you spill coffee on it, you can just wipe it off. No harm. No electrocution."

"Hey." He barely looked over at me.

"Don't let me disturb you."

"Hmm?"

I shrugged out of my coat, draped it over a stack of boxes. Logged on to the computer.

"Hey."

"You already said that."

"There was this blog on TV last night."

I broke out into a cold sweat right above my lip. "Really."

"Here. I'll send you the URL."

I opened the e-mail from him and read my very own address on the Internet. "I never read blogs. Waste of time."

"Never?"

"Ever."

"Because it seems like this one would interest you."

"Why?"

"I don't know. It just reminds me of you."

"What's it about?"

"Some girl. I'm reading backward to the beginning."

I brought up the blog and went into my archives. Brought up my very first entry, a little over a year ago. Scanned for anything at all that might give me away. Nothing.

Went to the next one.

"Huh."

"What?" What had he found?

"Nothing."

I worked my way through the first month, horrified by the number of things I'd blogged about. Why couldn't I keep my big mouth zipped? Or my hands hidden inside mittens. Something. Anything.

"Wow."

"What?" I kept bringing up entries. Skimming them for hints, clues, anything that would give me away. Heaping humiliation upon myself.

"Wow."

"What? What!"

"She must really like this guy."

"Who? Which guy?"

"The one she's blogging about."

"The blog's about a guy? I thought it was about a cubicle. The Cubicle Next Door."

"It's about the guy in the cubicle next to her."

"Oh. But maybe it's not. Maybe it's…symbolism."

"Symbolism?"

"Yeah, you know. Like…water equals life and winter equals death."

"Then what would this equal? *My little car doesn't stand a chance in a face-off against an SUV. It's the equivalent of modern day jousting. Or boxing without separating the athletes into weight classes. And that's what John Smith drives. Too bad. I might have been able to like him.*'"

"Oh. That's easy. SUVs are symbolic of man's inhumanity against man."

"For example…?"

"For example…it's always the little guy who gets crunched up. Her little car versus the guy's big car. Big box stores versus Mom and Pop stores."

"Oh. SUV as metaphor. The car as a literary vehicle. Tied in with jousting to lend a historical perspective to the plight of modern man. The image of the boxer, pummeling his opponent."

"Yeah. All that…stuff."

"Then you two have a lot in common."

"We do? We don't. I don't think we do."

"You both hate SUVs."

"Have I ever said that?"

"Frequently."

"I didn't mean *hate*. That's a rather strong word, don't you think?"

"Well, I don't think there's any way you could mistake this one: *'I'm worse than a shark. I can smell your cologne from 100 yards away. And it lingers in my senses, long after you are gone.'*"

I put my hands over my ears. Placed my forehead on the desk. Stop it. Stop!

You know how awful your voice sounds when you hear it on video? Being quoted to yourself is five times worse. What was I doing writing love letters on the Internet? It was almost like poetry. And I suck at poetry. I always have.

This is my personal hell: having Joe read my blog to me verbatim, from start to finish. Over and over and over again. "Maybe we shouldn't be reading it."

"Why not?"

"Maybe she didn't think anyone would see it."

"It's on the Internet in the public domain. Why would you blog if you didn't want people to read it?"

I didn't know. I really didn't.

Joe fell silent for about 15 minutes.

I sorted through my e-mails. Updated my Outlook calendar with various meetings. Cleaned out my Sent Items e-mail box. "Are you still reading?"

"Yes."

It took him about two more minutes. Then I heard his chair push away from the desk. "It's an M Day—I'm late!"

"See you later." I said it to his back as he went flying down the hall. I sighed. Slumped in my chair. Everything was okay.

I was still safe.

Later in the evening, after all the trick-or-treaters had gone to bed, I went into the blog. Went to the reports area where it listed how many people had visited.

My heart skipped a beat.

I blinked. Squinted at the figure. Blinked again. But there was no way to turn 20,000 into 2000. Or even 200. In the last 24 hours, I'd had 20,000 people visit my blog.

My life had been placed into a fishbowl. I had become an exotic species of Internet fauna. Twenty thousand people, whom I didn't know, now knew both the first and the last things about me. They were reading all my secrets. And recently, every single entry of the blog had to do with Joe.

What was I supposed to do?

I closed out the reports and returned to the blog site. Scrolled through the comments from my last entry. I looked for comments from my regulars first. It made me feel better to know there were still people out there who had been with me from the beginning. There were about 20 times more comments than normal. Some made me laugh. Others made me blush. Several I deleted.

What was I supposed to do?

The blog had always been available for anyone to see. Nothing about that had changed. Joe had read it, but he still didn't know it was me...blogging about him. Nothing about that had changed, either. There were thousands of people peering into my soul, but no one had the ability to assign that soul to me. So everything was okay. I didn't have to do anything differently. I only had to keep on doing what I was doing.

All I had to do was keep pouring out my thoughts and my feelings—my heart—onto the Internet.

That's all.

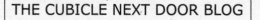

THE CUBICLE NEXT DOOR BLOG

Setting the blog straight

Okay.

The first thing I want to say is that this blog is not about John Smith. It's about life in a cubicle. The Cubicle Next Door. Get it?

It was originally established to vent my feelings about the life of a worker hidden away behind a tiny desk in a large bureaucracy.

And that's it.

If you personally feel some emotional connection to my thoughts or feelings, all I can say is it's entirely coincidental. If you mis-construe these posts to be from some virtual girl next door, then that's your mistake.

I just wanted to make sure we're all on the same page here.

Posted on October 31 in **The Cubicle Next Door | Permalink**

COMMENTS

You go, girl!

Posted by: **grrlpower | November 1 at 01:13 AM**

On the same page? Oh yes, we certainly are. ;) (Meet me in the supply closet tomorrow at 3:15.)

Posted by: **iknowubabe | November 2 at 06:05 AM**

Relax. We're with you. You've perfectly captured the essence of the modern human condition.

Posted by: **philosophie | November 2 at 08:34 AM**

Of course it's all about the job.

Posted by: **justluvmyjob | November 2 at 09:31 AM**

Methinks you protest too much.

Posted by: **theshrink | November 2 at 08:45 PM**

CLOSE

Eighteen

****

About the whole Internet blog thing? I just made one tiny miscalculation. I hadn't realized Joe would become a regular reader.

Or that he would read the entries aloud to me every morning.

I just made sure I drank my coffee after he was done. Because if I had actually been awake enough to hear him, I might have had to slit my wrists.

Why didn't I just stop blogging?

I couldn't.

No one knew about Joe except for me. And the 30,000 people who read my blog. The numbers increased daily. There was no one I could talk to about him. Not in real life, anyway. So the blog served some sort of purpose. I could imagine it was like talking to a friend.

Or a mother.

It made things a little trickier. I had to try not to quote myself. Online or off.

But people started connecting. I lost track of how many comments I received thanking me for giving a reader the courage to just tell Mary or Sue or Tina about their secret crush.

I *couldn't* stop blogging.

I was offering a benefit to humanity. I was running a do-it-yourself dating service.

I was stuck.

One morning Joe returned from his M day lectures at lunchtime.

He threw his bag into the far corner of the cubicle. I heard it hit the wall.

He walked around the wall dividing us and leaned against it.

I swiveled my chair to face him. "What's wrong?"

"Everything. I don't know if I can do this."

"Do what?"

He threw his hands out. "All of it. Everything. The whole cubicle desk job routine."

"You miss flying?"

"Yeah. I don't quite know what to do...aside from repainting my house, room by room." He rubbed his hands across his eyes. "It's not just about the flying. It was the chase and the hunt and the mission. It was the reason behind the flying I enjoyed. I guess I hadn't realized how much of me...how much of my life...was about being a pilot."

"Give yourself a chance. There's got to be something else you enjoy doing."

"I used to play football, but it's not like I can do anything with that. The football team already has a sponsor. I checked. The same colonel's been doing it for about fifteen years."

"You don't *like* teaching?"

"I do, but...I guess I just have to get used to this being what I do." He smiled. I'm sure he probably meant it to be cheery, but his smile didn't reach his eyes. "Hey, I've noticed *you're* having lots of not-so-good days lately too."

"Why do you say that?"

"You haven't been your normal snarky self this week."

"Shouldn't that be a compliment? Maybe I've become a reformed communist mercenary. Ever think of that?"

"No. I think it's something else."

I got a tingly feeling up and down my spine. He knew. Somehow he'd figured it out. This was it. "What do you think it is?"

"I think it's like that girl on the Internet says."

No question as to which girl he was talking about. "What does she say?"

"You find yourself behaving in completely unexpected ways...you think you might not even like being snarky. You're starting to have fun.

So you're trying to figure out which perception of yourself to reinforce. The snarky one or the nice one."

"That wasn't TCND. It was NozAll." As if he knew anything at all.

It was the dimples that gave me the warning. "I thought you didn't read that blog. I thought you said blogs were a waste of time."

Think fast.

"Um…"

Think faster!

"I don't. Really. It's just that…you're the one who reads it. To me. All the time."

The dimples disappeared. "Well…that's true."

"It is. Every morning." Every *single* morning.

"So, you have plans for tomorrow, for Veterans Day?"

"Always." At least this year, Veterans Day fell on a Saturday. Ironically, the past year when it fell on a Friday, it was just a normal school day at the U.S. Air Force Academy.

"What are you doing?"

"Visiting the cemetery."

"Which one?"

"The Academy's."

"By the roach clip?"

"The what?"

"The Polaris Memorial. That weird statue. It used to be by the chapel…we'd twist sheets to put in the middle of those metal tongs. Made it look like a giant roach clip. You know." He put two fingers up to his mouth. Pretended to smoke a joint. Crossed his eyes with the effort.

"I visit to put flowers on my father's grave."

His eyes uncrossed his eyes and sobered up. "He's buried there? You're kidding."

"No, I'm not kidding. He died in Vietnam."

"I'm sorry. A lot of people died in Vietnam. A lot of good people."

I nodded. Then I stood up and walked over to the coat tree where my jacket and scarf were hanging. Pulled the scarf off and wrapped it around my neck.

"Nice scarf."

"Thanks."

"It…uh…pretty much matches anything."

"Pretty much."

"You didn't pay for it, did you?"

"No. I made it."

"Why?"

"Because I needed a scarf. And I felt sorry for all the yarn at the Salvation Army." It had been sitting there in a giant plastic bag. All of it dyed in colors nobody wanted anymore: various shades of brown. Rust. Orange. Garish green. Startling purple.

"And now we can all feel sorry for you."

"It's just a scarf. And it's indestructible. Feel it."

Joe took hold of an end and rubbed it against his cheek. Dropped it. "It's scratchy."

I picked up the end he'd dropped and tucked it into the coil I'd wound around my neck. "It's acrylic. It'll last forever."

"Are you sure you want it to?"

"It keeps my neck warm. That's all it has to do." I pulled my green duffle coat on and fastened all toggles but the top one. Pulled the hood over my head.

I went down the stairs and out by the Aero Lab parking lot and sat on the wall. I had a prime view of a tangle of trees and bushes and frost-browned grasses in the valley below. I let the cold chill of November seep into my thighs and then into my bones.

I hunched my shoulders and felt the coat stretch taut against my back. I found that if I dropped my head just the slightest bit, my chin dropped down into the scarf. It was scratchy, but I could also smell the lingering scent of Joe.

The next day I removed some sprigs from a rosemary plant growing in a pot in the kitchen window. Then I put on my coat and scarf, got into my car, and drove up the interstate toward the Academy. Pulled into the cemetery and parked the car. Stayed inside until I was certain I was alone.

I'd told Joe I was going to put flowers on my father's grave, but, in truth, I never had. I'd always taken rosemary. It's the one thing I'd remembered from English class, that quote by Shakespeare about rosemary being for remembrance.

And I did remember.

I remembered things my father had never had the chance to know.

There were already flowers on top of his grave. A dignified ruffle of blue carnations, white daisies, and red roses interwoven with red, white, and blue ribbons. The same arrangement as the year before. And the year before that. As long as I'd been paying my annual visits, in fact. I assumed they were from my father's parents.

I knelt to tuck my sprigs of rosemary in between the flowers.

Because I remembered too.

"Hi, Dad. It's me."

I touched the marker. Read the words I had memorized years ago.

Michael Murray O'Flaherty. Captain, U.S. Air Force. His graduating class. The date of his birth and the date of his death. Four lines which encapsulated everything I knew about him.

I rose to my feet and stood beside his grave for a while. Watched an airplane trace an arc high above me, leaving white contrails stretched across the sky.

Joe called me later that afternoon. Wanted to talk about church.

"Are you ready to concede?"

"No. I just thought maybe we should change strategies."

"How?"

"Maybe we should consider proximity instead of—"

"Personal recommendations?"

"Yeah."

"The closest is just down the hill."

"Isn't that Catholic?"

"We don't have to take communion. We could actually walk. Save about—"

"A gallon of gas. I know. What time should I stop by?"

"Just a second." I searched the Internet for the name of the church.

Ended up having to specify "Manitou Springs." "Service...er...Mass starts at ten fifteen."

"So I'll pick you up at ten."

"Fine."

"We can do lunch after. Instead of breakfast."

He picked me up at 10:00 on Sunday. I wore my darkest jeans for the occasion. I had the feeling Catholics were probably dressier than Protestants.

We walked down the hill, turned the corner and came upon the church. Just walking into it was a magical experience.

Low stone walls enclosed the lot. We walked across a stone-and-brick bridge that breasted Fountain Creek. A grotto to our left offered a chilly haven. A statue of Mary, sheltered inside, implied infinite peace. A listening ear. A willingness to give you the benefit of doubt. God knew what he was doing when he gave Jesus a mother.

Would that I had been so lucky.

We walked through the iron gate, now pushed open, and toward a small white church. Its narrow windows were lined in blue. The roof over the door and the roof over the church were both topped by simple white crosses. But the best part was walking inside.

People noticed we were there. They validated our presence by smiling. Or simply by looking at us. Not in our direction or over our shoulders, but into our eyes.

We listened to a sermon. Homily. Whatever it's called.

There was a moment, when people went up for communion, when I thought I might feel awkward, but I bowed my head and began to pray instead. Let my mind revisit the beauty in my world.

A recent view of Pikes Peak, the wind fanning the snow off the top of the mountain. The solid, steady rhythm of the anniversary clock on the mantel in the living room. A clock that had marked the hours of my grandfather's days and the minutes of his grandfather's before him. The brilliant intricacy of a computer and its interlocking pieces. A machine made up of incredibly small parts that had the power to map out the universe.

I had just finished sampling that particular thought when a hum began to infiltrate my consciousness and lower my thoughts to more mundane levels. Like who was doing the humming and why.

As if I couldn't guess.

I opened my eyes and slid a glance toward Joe.

His elbows were propped on his knees, his head resting against clasped hands.

Maybe...maybe it wasn't him.

I glanced around. Didn't notice anyone being overtly odd. Resumed my prayer.

Heard that hum again.

Opened my eyes. Noticed Joe's feet.

They were tapping.

I nudged him.

He flinched. Straightened. Looked at me and mouthed, *What?*

I put a finger up to my mouth. *Shh.*

He looked around. Looked at me. *What?*

I leaned toward him. "You were..." He really didn't know he had been humming. Communion was over by that point, so I just dropped it.

Afterward, we walked out of the church and into bright sunshine. It warmed our faces even as our bodies hunched against a chill wind.

We walked over the bridge and up the hill toward home.

We were almost at Grandmother's before Joe remembered about eating. "Want to grab lunch somewhere?"

"You could...do you want to come in? I could fix us something."

"Sure. Thanks."

We turned at the house. Climbed the steps from the street.

Joe retrieved the key from under the mat. Opened the door and then stood aside to usher me in, his hand at my back.

We walked together into the kitchen. Found a note on the kitchen table. Grandmother was out with Oliver. Didn't say out where. Didn't say when she'd be back.

I sighed. It was her day. She could spend it with whomever she wanted to. I opened the refrigerator and took a mental inventory of the contents. "Do you want an omelet?"

"I'd love an omelet. I always burn them when I try and make one myself."

"You probably cook it too fast. You have to be more patient."

I gave him some mushrooms to slice while I grated the cheese. Then I started some butter melting in a pan and whisked the eggs while I waited. I knew Joe ate out for lunch when he was at work, but I had no idea what he usually did for dinner. "Do you cook? For yourself, ever?"

"I get by. Tacos are easy. And spaghetti. I grill. You want me to wash this for you?" He was holding up the cheese grater.

"Thanks."

He put the grater on top of the cutting board he'd been using and took everything to the sink. Turned the water on high. Squirted dish soap over it all.

I walked over and turned the faucet off to stop the water from going straight down the drain. "Most of the time, people don't need as much water as they think they do. You don't need any really until it's time to rinse."

"Yes, ma'am. Where's the sponge?"

I handed him a washcloth.

"And the problem with a sponge is…?"

"That most sponges aren't made of sponge. They're synthetic."

"Which is evil because…?"

"They aren't biodegradable."

"And smelly old washcloths?"

"Can be washed. Again and again and again."

He shook his head and started scrubbing. "When they start making washcloths with a scrubby side, that's when I'll make the switch."

While I put the remaining eggs and cheese away, Joe finished up the dishes and set them in the rack to dry.

I saw him glance at his watch. Look over in the direction of the living room. "Can we eat in front of the TV? Would you mind? The Seahawks are playing. They're my team."

I shrugged. It didn't matter to me.

When the omelets were done, we took our plates out into the living room. I handed Joe the remote and let him find the game.

After we had finished eating, I took our plates into the kitchen. Joe started to get up, but I motioned for him to stay. He smiled at me and then slouched into the corner of the couch and got comfortable.

On my return to the living room, as I passed in front of him, he reached out and grabbed my hand. He tugged me down to the space beside him and spread his arm along the back of the couch. "Are you afraid of me, Jackie?"

"No." I was telling the truth. I wasn't afraid of him…I was afraid of myself.

"Then lean back. Relax." He crooked his arm around my neck and pulled my head in toward his shoulder. "I won't bite. I promise."

"Will you let me out of this headlock?"

He released me immediately. "Of course."

I folded my arms across my chest and settled into the couch. Leaned against him. Just a little.

There were the rules in the game I was playing. I didn't have to acknowledge anything I didn't want to. That was one of them. And as long as I knew what was going on, I could pretend I didn't.

I only let myself play because something in me needed what Joe was offering, devoured the attention he gave me, and craved the warmth of even casual contact. But I trusted myself. I knew I wouldn't become tempted by him. Addicted to him. I knew I would recognize the moment I started to need him too much.

And when that happened, I planned to flip the game board over and walk away.

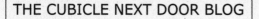

THE CUBICLE NEXT DOOR BLOG

Little things about you

I can tell what kind of day you're having before you figure it out yourself. I can tell by how high you fill your coffee mug. I can tell by how long it takes you to start typing. Some days, you even hum. Did you know that? But mostly, I can tell by your smile.

Posted on November 12 in **The Cubicle Next Door | Permalink**

Comments

There are some people known as chronic hummers. But they don't hum. They hear hums. Hums that appear to be at such low frequencies no one else can hear them.

Posted by: **NozAll | November 12 at 04:02 PM**

What? Like those people who transmit radio signals off their dental bridges?

Posted by: **justluvmyjob | November 12 at 07:49 PM**

I think smiles provide glimpses of the soul.

Posted by: **philosophie | November 12 at 08:36 PM**

So what does he hum if it's a good day? "In the Mood"?

Posted by: **theshrink | November 12 at 09:11 PM**

CLOSE

Nineteen

****

The next week blew in with a storm, a reminder of just how close we lived to America's endless, empty prairies. The fruited plain.

On Tuesday only essential personnel were required to report in to the Academy. After receiving the news via the department phone tree and passing the message on, I returned to bed and basked in the knowledge that I was considered nonessential. I got up about noon and then spent the rest of the day in chat rooms and on message boards.

By Tuesday evening the city had cleared the streets, leaving head-high snowbanks at the foot of everyone's driveway. Or in our case, garage. I had just about resigned myself to the fact the snowbank wasn't going to dissolve when the doorbell rang.

Grandmother had already settled into her chair to watch the news.

I unfolded myself from the couch and walked to the door.

I opened it to find Joe standing there with a shovel. He was wearing a striped neon green knitted hat with side flaps and a pom-pom on top.

"Nice hat."

He smiled. "My mom made it."

"You might want to consider finding a new mother."

"It keeps my ears warm."

"And probably makes four-year-olds jealous."

"Do you want your garage shoveled out or not?"

"Who is it?" Grandmother was curious, but not curious enough to get out of her chair.

"It's Joe."

"Who?"

"Joe!"

"What did you say?"

Joe dimpled and came through the door. He walked into the entry so Grandmother could see him. "It's me, Mrs. Harrison."

"Joe! Why didn't you say so, Jackie?"

I heard her release the lever on her chair.

"Please don't get up. I didn't mean to disturb you. I was wondering if you wanted me to shovel you out."

She came up to him, eyes shining. "How thoughtful! Thank you so much. Why don't you go out and help him, Jackie?"

"Yeah, Jackie. Why don't you?"

That's how I found myself out shoveling snow with Joe. He was a hard worker, I'll give him that. Since the snowbanks were high to begin with, we were soon throwing shovelfuls onto mounds higher than our heads.

I took a break. Stood straight to stretch my back. Started shoveling again. "So what did you do today?"

"Slept in."

"Then what?"

"Started stripping my kitchen cabinets until the fumes got to me. Went out and shoveled snow. And here I am. How about you?"

"Slept in. Played around on the Internet. Was about to come out and shovel snow. And here you were."

Joe paused and leaned against his shovel. "I can finish up the rest of this."

"I'm fine."

"Really."

"I'm...okay...really." I wasn't mad at him. It was just taking a while to catch my breath. I tossed a shovel full of snow up toward the snowbank to show him just how okay I was. I missed. It trickled back down.

"Drop the shovel, Jackie." He was holding his own shovel up in front of him like a sword.

"No." I held mine up too.

After three parries, he'd backed me up against the snowbank and wrenched the shovel from my hand. "I'm trying to be a gentleman, so just let me."

"Okay."

"Okay? That's all you're going to say?" He was looking at me suspiciously, as if he thought I might attack him at any moment.

"Okay." I was tired. There was too much snow and the snowbanks were too high. What else could I say? He was a godsend.

He gave my shovel back. And ten minutes later, he thumped his own against the ground. The remains of the snowbank slid off onto the street. He handed me his shovel. Then he stripped off his gloves, stuffed them into his pockets, and flexed his hands several times.

"You need a ride tomorrow? Because of the snow?"

"I'm fine."

"I know *you're* fine. I'm talking about your car."

"*It's* fine."

"Okay." He stepped toward me and held out his hand for the shovel.

I handed it back to him, but I didn't let it go.

"See you at work."

"See you."

He turned to leave.

I put a hand over his to stop him.

"Thanks for shoveling us out."

"You're welcome." He reached out a hand and tucked a lock of hair behind my ear. Then he rested his warm palm against my cheek for a moment before turning around and trudging off down the street. I went back inside the house.

Grandmother called out when she heard the door shut. "Jackie? Is Joe with you?"

"No."

"Why didn't you invite him in?"

"He had to leave."

"Oh. What a shame."

"It's no big deal. Tomorrow night is poker night."

"Why don't you play with us?"

"I don't know. Maybe."

My car *and* I made it in fine to work the next day. And the next. And the day after that: Friday.

By that time, Joe had been inspired by the white stuff. "Let's go cross-country skiing."

"Why?"

"Because I bought those skis and I've never used them."

"When? I'm at the store on Saturdays."

"Let's go tonight."

"Tonight?"

"After work. We'll get something to eat on the way back. In Divide."

I caught myself with my mouth flapping open and shut. Although I wanted to say no, I couldn't think of a reason why. But did that mean I had to say yes?

"I'm done teaching by three. Can you leave a little early?"

After years and years of staying late? "Yes."

I guess I was going.

We walked down through Fairchild Hall and then Joe gave me a ride down to the parking lot. "I'll pick you up at four fifteen."

"I'll—"

"No, I'll drive. I don't care how many extra gallons of gas we'll use. At least we're guaranteed to get there and back."

I spent the ride home trying to figure out where I'd stashed my skis. And boots. And all the other skiing paraphernalia I owned.

As soon as I parked the car in the garage, I jumped on top of the hood and stood there, peering into the rafters. I finally spied my skis and poles and pulled them down. So that was good.

Found my boots sitting in the corner. Swept the cobwebs away and knocked them on the floor to give notice to any homesteading spiders.

I ran into the house and tore through my drawers looking for my ski clothes.

Finally found them.

I pulled on my black synthetic material zip turtleneck and tights. Were they made from organic fibers? No. But would they keep me from freezing to death? Yes. If technology can improve quality of life, then I'm all for it. I threw a maroon-colored wool zipneck sweater and a navy windbreaker jacket and pants into a backpack. Rifled through a dresser drawer to find some sports socks. Grabbed a hat and gloves from the closet downstairs. Found a couple energy bars and threw them on top of the clothes. Filled a bottle with water. Grabbed another smaller bag that always held a compass, matches, thermal blanket, wax, and a cork. Got down to the road just in time for Joe.

"Are you sure you want to do this? It's a lot harder than it looks. You can change your mind. Right now. I won't hold it against you."

He just laughed, took my skis and fastened them onto the rack that was perched atop his SUV. "Ready?"

I climbed into the beast and slammed the door shut. Threw my boots and backpack into the backseat. They landed next to his.

We drove out of Manitou on Highway 24. Just past town, the trees disappeared and the road started snaking through a series of canyons. When we arrived at Mueller State Park, the sun had hidden behind the trees, but it had left bands of sunset colors in its place.

At the park, we tugged our boots on and cinched them up. I rummaged through the bag and pulled out my sweater. Put it on. Zipped my jacket on over it. Pulled on my hat.

Joe got our skies down from the rack. Planted them in a nearby snow bank. I fished out my sack and took out the cork and some wax. "Could you hand me one of the skis?"

"Which?"

"Any."

He brought a ski over to me. Reaching down to the ground, I grabbed a handful of snow. Tried to mold it into a snowball. When I opened my palms, it disintegrated. That's how I knew I'd need a cold wax. If it had stayed together, if the snow had been wet, then I would have used a warm wax.

I leaned the ski against my body and got to work. Most people think waxing skis is complicated, but it's really not. You just have to match the type of snow to the type of wax. The shovels and the tails are glide waxed so they won't grip the snow. The kick zone is grip waxed so it will. And that's all there is to it. People who make a big deal about wax use an iron to get it just right and melt the wax into the pores of the ski.

As my grandmother's granddaughter, I think elbow grease works just as well.

For the glide wax, I rubbed the wax on and then polished it into the ski. For the grip wax, I applied a different kind of wax and then used the cork to rub it in. Repeated the process about three times to build up layers.

While I had been applying the grip wax, Joe had grabbed another ski and had put on the glide wax. He handed his ski to me when I was done with mine and I finished it off with grip wax.

We finished preparing the two remaining skis together.

I gave Joe his pair of skis and then set my own on the ground in front of me. I stepped onto one and used my pole to close the binding over my boot. Then I stepped onto the other and stamped the skis to the ground to make sure everything was fastened.

Joe did the same and looked over toward me. "Ready?"

As much as I would ever be. I slipped my backpack on and turned my skis to the forest. "Let's go."

There was a sort of trail that led up through the snow drifts, off into the trees. I knew from experience that once we got into the trees, the whole wilderness would open up before us. We could go wherever we wanted.

I started off at a slight jog, positioning my skis in a herringbone pattern so I wouldn't slide backward. I made it up past the snow drifts and then turned around, panting, to wait for Joe.

He was still standing beside his SUV, looking up at me.

"Are you coming?"

"Just give me a minute. I've never jogged on skis before."

"It's easy."

He punched his poles into the snow, started forward, made it halfway up and then stalled. "What do I do from here?"

"How are your skis positioned?"

"Exactly where I want to go. Straight toward you."

"Then they only have two choices: sliding up or down. Put them together at the tails and pretend you're a duck. You'll be able to go wherever you want to."

"Quack, quack." In another minute, he'd made it to my side.

"You okay? Going to make it?"

"I'll be fine. Lead on."

I stuck a pole into the ground, shoved off, and skied through the trees. There wasn't a sound except the swish-swishing of our skis.

And an occasional exclamation from Joe.

After about 20 minutes I slowed to a stop. I plunged my poles into the snow, unzipped my jacket, and took it off. Peeled off my sweater and stuffed it into my backpack. Put the jacket back on.

Joe did the same.

We skied on through the darkening canopy of trees. Then we broke out into a clearing.

In front of us was a road. It wasn't plowed, but it was hard packed. A perfect surface for skating. It led toward Pikes Peak. I raised a pole and pointed in that direction. "What do you think?"

"Why not?"

I pushed my way through the hard snow that passing vehicles had thrown out toward the side of the road. Put a tentative ski on the hard surface and then pushed off with one foot. Pushed off with the other.

This was one of my favorite parts of skiing. Being able to "skate" over a hardpacked section. Working up a rhythm.

Pole. Push. Glide. Pole. Push. Glide.

Gaining momentum.

Feeling the wind buffet my cheeks.

Pole. Push. Glide.

I could see a pink sunset reflected off the snow on Pikes Peak in front of me. Imagined myself at the top. Nothing but the wind and me. Free from emotional entanglements. Free from any obligations.

Pole. Push. Glide. Pole. Push. Glide. And glide. And glide forever.

There was a rhythm to cross-country skiing I couldn't find in my ordinary life. Here in the snow, with no one around, I knew exactly what to do. Here, I was the expert. And the trees, the snow, the sunset, and the shining moon, they all loved me. And I loved them too.

I'd stayed away from this too long.

When the road suggested a decline, I stopped. I put my hands to my knees, poles sticking out to the side behind me. Took greedy gulps of air in through my nose and released them through my mouth. Felt, rather than saw, my curling breath.

After a while, I stood up straight.

Heard Joe's skis scrabbling along the road, his poles crunching holes in the snow.

I turned my skis to face him.

He'd figured it out and he was skating too. In fact, he skated right past me. I saw the flash of his teeth as he went by.

Turning my skis around, I put them together and bent in a classic skier's pose. Pushed off with my poles and started down the hill.

I picked my left foot up and leaned on the right one when the road curved right. Put the left foot down and picked up the right one when it curved left. Saw Joe standing still in the middle of the road.

Plowed right into him.

I threw my arms around his waist, leaving my poles to dangle from their wrist straps.

We leaned forward and then we leaned back, trying to achieve a balance. Finally we gave it up and collapsed with Joe sitting in my lap.

"You can't just stop in the middle of the road like that! What were you doing?" I was pushing at him, trying to get him to move.

He leaned to the side and tried to climb over my leg, but our skis got tangled.

I scooted back until my skis were clear of him. I crouched above them, getting ready to stand up.

But then he reached a hand back and took hold of one of mine. He slid me forward until I was sitting next to him. "Looking at the stars. Have you ever seen so many?" He ducked his head as if he thought he were obscuring my view.

I let go of his hand and planted it behind me in the snow. Leaning back, I tilted my head at the sky. The veneer of sunset had disappeared and abandoned the sky to the stars. Hundreds of them were glittering in the chill of the night.

Joe leaned back too, and when our arms became tired of propping us up, we lay back in the snow. Stars were zinging through the night air. Falling stars. Shooting stars. Dancing stars. And from that position, it felt as if the show were just for me.

For us.

We lay that way for a long while, on our backs in the snow, with our skis pointed up toward the sky.

In fact, we lay that way so long I fell asleep.

And woke myself up snoring.

Stayed absolutely still, trying to figure out if there is any way a snore can sound like something else. A bear? A rabbit? Some other sort of small furry animal? "Have I been snoring for a long time?"

"Not that long." I could sense a smile in Joe's voice, but at least he wasn't laughing.

"Why didn't you wake me up?"

"Because I figured if you had fallen asleep, you were probably tired."

"Well…I was. And now I'm hungry."

"I have an energy bar."

"So do I."

"Mine's Dutch chocolate."

"And you really truly believe that's healthy for you?"

"There's a picture of a dancing chocolate chip on the wrapper."

He sat up and gave me a hand to help me sit up too. We each ate a bar as we sat there watching the stars. And then we turned ourselves around and started for the car.

The hill hadn't seemed very big when we'd come down it, but it was steep going back up. I finally gave up on trying to jog it.

Joe did too.

We paused, gasping for air, slumped over our poles.

"See…the thing about downhill skiing is that it's only one way. They have lifts to take you back up the mountains."

"Because downhillers are lazy."

"Well, then your lazy is my smart."

"You never get to see shooting stars when you downhill."

"That's true."

We herringboned up the rest of the hill and then skated to where we'd broken out of the forest. Once we got to the SUV, we hopped out of the skis, fastened them to the ski rack, and then threw everything else in the back.

We stopped at Wines of Colorado, near the Pikes Peak Highway, for dinner. Dined in a room that perched above Fountain Creek.

As we gave our order, Joe glanced over at me. "We're not going to be kissing later or anything, are we?"

"I don't do—"

"Just checking. That's what I kind of figured." He looked back at the waiter. "I'll have the Whole Smoked Garlic to start and a Ribeye Steak Sandwich with...the red potatoes."

I ordered their Colorado Wine Burger with beans.

"Do you feel obligated to order potatoes? Since you're from Idaho and everything?"

Joe's dimples flickered. "I just don't particularly like coleslaw or beans."

"Where did you grow up?"

"Pocatello. Dad's a professor at Idaho State."

"What does he teach?"

"History. American history."

I began to smile.

"What?"

"Is that why you chose Russian history?"

I read amusement in Joe's smile. "Maybe."

"You don't get along with him?"

"We get along fine. I just didn't want to go to ISU. So we made a deal when I was in high school. I could go somewhere else, anywhere else I wanted, as long as I figured out how to fund it."

"What does your mom do?"

"She used to teach first grade. She retired last year. Now she knits. She's making sweaters for everyone in the family."

"And hats? Striped, with pom-poms?"

Joe laughed. "She's really into it. It drives my sisters crazy. When they go over to visit Mom and Dad, they have to keep their kids from unraveling her projects and playing with all those balls of string."

"Yarn."

"Whatever."

"How many sisters do you have?"

"Two. And one brother. How about you?"

"None."

"I always wished I didn't have any. Especially at Thanksgiving. I only got to do the wishbone every other year."

"Poor you."

"I know!"

The waiter came with Joe's garlic and set it on the table between us.

Joe picked up a cracker from the plate and offered it to me.

"No, thanks." It smelled good, but garlic and I weren't the best of friends. "Are you doing anything for Thanksgiving? You could come over. All the poker night ladies will be there."

"Will you be?"

I nodded.

"Then I'd love to come. Thanks for asking."

I couldn't stunt the pleasure that bloomed inside of me, so I concentrated on drinking my water instead.

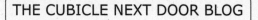

THE CUBICLE NEXT DOOR BLOG

How do you do that?

Half the time you make me want to scream. But the other half?

The other half of the time you're kind of...nice to be around. It's sort of...fun. More than fun. It's comfortable. Comforting.

How can you make me want to scream and make me feel like I've been wrapped in a big warm blanket? All at the same time?

Posted on November 17 in **The Cubicle Next Door | Permalink**

Comments

Blankets can very symbolic. Especially those woven by indig-enous peoples. Choices of colors, designs, and patterns convey deliberate messages about the weaver and his or her place in the world.

Posted by: **NozAll | November 17 at 11:05 PM**

She's not talking about blankets. She's talking about John Smith and the way he makes her feel. Our reactions to others reflect not their emotions, but ours.

Posted by: **philosophie | November 18 at 08:14 AM**

He's probably just trying to suck up to you. Are there any big projects due he'd want your help on?

Posted by: **justluvmyjob | November 18 at 08:49 AM**

As long as you have a blanket, you can live almost anywhere. I should know. I have.

Posted by: **survivor | November 18 at 9:01 AM**

He might be bipolar.

Posted by: **theshrink | November 18 at 09:37 AM**

CLOSE

Twenty

****

The following week, my thoughts turned toward Thanksgiving.

We usually had Adele, Betty, and Thelma join us for the day. They'd come over early for coffee and the Macy's parade. And then, afterward, they'd start working on the food. We had the same thing every year: a tray of jumbo olives, carrots, celery, and pickles; cranberries; Adele's homemade rolls; Thelma's rutabaga casserole; Grandmother's Log Cabin Jell-O salad; Betty's green bean casserole and pecan pie; my turkey and stuffing. Not because nobody else could make them, but because I didn't like my stuffing cooked inside the bird. Too many risks of food poisoning.

Everything seemed to be going as planned until Grandmother mentioned Oliver over dinner one night.

"Oliver?"

"I thought it might be a good idea."

"To invite him over? For Thanksgiving? Why?"

"He doesn't have anyone else to celebrate with."

"But he doesn't *have* anything to celebrate. He's English."

"He has things to be thankful for too."

"But—"

"I already asked him and he already agreed to come."

Fine.

Thanksgiving with an Englishman. I supposed it would be okay. I mean, we hadn't yet declared war on England when the Pilgrims came over.

I wondered how eager he'd be to help us celebrate the Fourth of July.

If Oliver had been the end of it, Thanksgiving would have been okay. But it wasn't just Oliver who was coming. I had begun to regret asking Joe to come. I liked the idea of Joe, of having him around, but celebrating holidays with him was just too familiar. Too personal. As if he was becoming a permanent part of my life. It just seemed…intimate…as if it was making too much out of our relationship. But I'd already asked him. He'd already accepted. I was stuck.

I'd just finished hanging Oliver's coat in the closet on Thanksgiving morning when the doorbell rang again.

It was Joe. He'd brought a box of donuts with him. And he was just in time for the parade.

"Hi."

"Joe? Is that you?" Grandmother was calling out from the living room.

Joe craned to see around me. "Yes, ma'am!"

"Aren't you coming in?"

"Just as soon as Jackie lets me in the door."

I stood aside to let him through.

He handed me the box and went to hang his coat in the closet. By the time I made it into the living room with a stack of napkins and the donuts, he was sitting on the couch in between Betty and Adele.

After I put the turkey in the oven, I dragged a chair in from the dining room and sat near the hall.

They all traded stories of past Thanksgiving Day parades for the next few hours. Recounted the story of Thanksgiving to Oliver. In detail. Down to the rationing of grains of corn that first cruel winter in the New World.

By the time the parade was over, the football games had started. Someone gave Joe the remote and he surfed the channels fast enough to make me dizzy. I went into the kitchen and started chopping onions and celery for the stuffing.

The ladies soon joined me, filling the kitchen with laughter and even more stories, taking over the counter space. In five minutes, I had been nudged out. I found myself exiled to the kitchen table.

I slid all the onions and celery into a stockpot and sprinkled them with seasoning salt, pepper, and sage. I took it, along with five loaves of white bread, out into the living room. Sat down at the end of the couch and starting tearing slices of bread, letting the pieces fall into the stockpot below.

The football game broke to a commercial.

Both Joe and Oliver stirred, looked away from the TV, and realized I was sitting there with them.

"Do you need help?"

I eyed Joe. Calculated how long it would take me to shred five loaves of bread. "Please."

He slid down the couch next to me. Put three of the loaves on the floor and kept one for himself.

I used my foot to position the pot between us.

He got through one loaf before the game came back on. After that, he was useless. He didn't even realize he'd stopped helping until the next commercial break. "Where's...you already finished?"

I nodded.

"I'm sorry."

"It's fine."

I picked up the pot and set it on the edge of the couch between my legs. I plunged my hands into the fluffy drift of bread, reached to the bottom, and slid my hands under the onions and celery. I brought them up to the top and started mixing the ingredients together. The sage-laced smell of Thanksgiving rose from the mixture.

Joe stuck his head over the pot and inhaled. "*This* is what women's perfume should be made of. Don't you think so, Oliver?"

"Either that or the scent of a summer's breeze."

Joe inhaled again. "Sage and celery?"

I nodded.

He took another big whiff. "The way to a man's heart. Although the perfume you wear isn't so bad, either."

"I don't wear any."

"You wear something."

The conversation was heading into dangerous territory. It was one thing to go to church with Joe or sit beside him on the couch. I went to church. I sat on couches. It wasn't personal unless I let it be. But the way I smelled? That was different.

I used soap. Apricot-scented organic soap that came wrapped in tree-free or recycled paper. And a shampoo I made myself from soapwort and lemon verbena. "Are you done?"

"Hmm?" He looked up at me with a blank stare and then turned toward the television. The football game had come back on.

I collected the bags from the loaves of bread, put them in the pot on top of the stuffing mix, and went into the kitchen. I had to elbow a place for myself at the stove, but I was able to set some previously frozen chicken stock in a saucepan to melt.

I helped Adele roll out her dough. Mixed up the bean casserole for Betty. Checked on my bird. Mixed the stuffing with chicken stock and put it in line for the oven. Wandered out into the entry hall. I considered going upstairs and seeing who was online, but I thought it might be rude with so many visitors in the house.

Joe saw me vacillating and waved me over.

I sat on the couch and tried to remember what he'd taught me about football. Ended up instead wondering how apricot and lemon verbena smelled together.

Eventually, Grandmother's voice intruded on my thoughts, calling us into the dining room.

We all sat down, Oliver waiting until the rest of us were seated before he seated himself.

But then Grandmother pushed her chair away from the table, muttering about the turkey. That caused Oliver to stand once more. "Could one of you men do the carving? It's still out in the kitchen. Jackie usually does it, but I'm sure she could use a break."

I could?

"Oliver can do it. My dad hasn't initiated me yet into the Brotherhood of the Carving Knife."

Oliver cleared his throat. "Well, come along then. We can both pay a visit to Old Tom. Have you got an apron, Helen?"

Apparently she did. Because when he walked into the dining room carrying the turkey, he had a pink-and-yellow floral apron draped around his neck, tied off neatly at the waist. Joe had one on too.

Oliver placed the turkey at Grandmother's end of the table while she hovered at his elbow. There was much quiet conversation between the two men. Much pointing with the knife and stabbing with the meat fork. But when it was done, there was an ample mound of meat stacked on the platter.

Grandmother repossessed the aprons and returned them to the kitchen.

Again, Oliver waited until Grandmother sat down before he seated himself.

It started me wondering.

After the first rotation of food, Betty realized the cranberries were missing.

"I'll get them." I pushed my chair away from the table and stood up.

Across from me, Oliver did the same.

"It's okay. Sit down. I've got them." I found the can of jellied cranberries in the refrigerator, cranked a can opener around the top, shoved a table knife down to the bottom of the can, and shook it out into a bowl. Perfect. It stood on its end, the metal corrugations from the can intact.

Oliver stood again when I reappeared from the kitchen, and remained standing until I not only put the bowl on the table, but also sat down in my chair.

"More water, Oliver?" Grandmother still had the eyes of an eagle.

He began to demur, but I decided to get the pitcher anyway. I rose.

He rose.

"Will you sit down? I've got it."

"If I sit down, then you will deprive me of the pleasure of standing to acknowledge your singular beauty."

"He means, he's standing because you're a lady." It might have come across more tactfully had Adele not shouted.

"Thank you, Adele." I caught Joe trying to smother a laugh out of the corner of my eye. "And thank you, Oliver."

He closed his eyes and inclined his head just exactly the way I'd seen actors do in medieval movies. Next, I'd probably start calling him Your Grace and kneel to kiss his hand.

Now that I knew what that was all about, I started an experiment. I waited until he was cutting a piece of meat, and then I stopped eating, put my fork down, and leaned slightly forward, as if I were about to get up. I wanted to see if leaping to his feet was some sort of instinct or whether it had more to do with how observant he was.

He put his fork down, placed his knife along the edge of his plate and leaned forward too.

I leaned back.

He picked up his fork and knife and resumed cutting.

Score one for Oliver.

The next time, I waited until his fork was halfway to his mouth. And I wasn't eating at that point, so I didn't put off any signals. I just leaned forward a little, tiny bit.

He put his fork down and leaned forward too.

Score two for Oliver.

So then I waited until he wasn't eating at all. I waited until he was involved in conversation. Until he had half-turned away from me and was talking to Thelma.

And I leaned forward even less than before.

So did he.

Score three for Oliver.

The next time I tried, I caught him while he was in the middle of passing the butter to Betty. And I actually stood all the way up.

And so did he, butter dish in hand, waiting for me to do something.

So I bent over and picked my napkin up off the floor. Sat back down.

The next time I tried, he was laughing, a full-blown laugh. Head thrown back. But the minute I leaned, his head snapped forward and he pierced me with a stare.

I leaned away.

He leaned away.

I leaned forward.

He leaned forward.

I rose. One inch.

He rose two.

I sat back down.

He didn't. He was on to me.

And so was Thelma. "Will you stop being so fidgety? You're making me nervous."

And that was the end of that.

Over pumpkin pie, the ladies got Joe talking about the Academy. From a cadet's perspective.

Betty mentioned her daughter had once attended a cadet ball.

"When I was there, each class had a ball. I don't know for sure what they do now, but I know they still have one at Christmas."

"That's the one she went to: the Christmas one. She said it was absolutely gorgeous. All those young men in uniform."

Joe winked at me. "The Christmas trees are pretty nice too."

Betty looked at Joe with narrowed eyes. Then she turned those eyes on me. "You said they're having one this year?"

"Yes, ma'am."

She smiled. "Then you should take Jackie. You've never been to a ball, have you, Jackie?"

Adele answered the question for me. "No, she hasn't. What fun you'll have! What day is it, Joe?"

"I don't know. I'll have to find out."

"It's a date! You find out and then Jackie will put it on her calendar."

It was *not* a date! It was a total setup.

After dinner, Joe and Oliver went into the living room while the rest of us cleaned up. Theoretically.

I stacked, scraped, and washed the dishes while the others reminisced yet again about Thanksgivings past. Who among their long-dead friends had made the best pumpkin pie. Who had tried to pass off canned gravy as homemade.

At last, dishes done and gossip exhausted, we made our way to the living room.

Joe was in a chair, watching football.

Oliver was sitting, stick straight on the couch, knees together, hands folded on his lap. His head had fallen to his chest and he was snoring softly.

Grandmother shook her head and then went and got a blanket from the closet. Began to tuck it around his legs. Glanced up at him. She looked as if she wanted to plant a kiss in her palm and press it to his forehead. But she refrained.

At that moment, the crowd on TV went wild. Joe whooped and leaped from his chair.

Oliver stopped mid-snore. Blinked. Saw Grandmother smoothing the blanket and the rest of the women standing. He scrambled to his own feet, undoing all the work she had just done.

Score one for me.

Just before Joe left, Grandmother went into the kitchen to make a plate of leftovers for him. She came into the entry hall carrying a foil-covered plate in one hand and what looked like a bone in the other. "Is this yours, Joe? Or Oliver's?"

Joe took it from her hand. "The wishbone! We set it aside."

He held it out to me. "Take the end. We'll see who gets to make a wish."

Everyone was watching, so I took the end and pulled. The bone stretched, and then cracked, leaving me with the larger piece.

Adele clapped her hands. "Make a wish!"

I looked at Joe.

He was looking at me.

I dropped my eyes to the wishbone. I wished I were normal, wished I could just fall into a relationship without a second thought. It might not have been the first time I'd wished it, but it was the first time I really understood what I was missing.

We went to the Catholic church on Sunday.

Again.

People were starting to notice we never took communion. Asked, in the most roundabout of ways, whether we were Catholics.

We told them we were not.

They asked if we wanted to become Catholics.

We said we did not.

They weren't quite sure what to make of us.

And we weren't either.

There was no praise band at the church. They played music I'd never heard before. Had rituals I was not familiar with. But they kept talking to us before and after service. Mass. They knew who we were. They knew where we lived and where we worked. So we kept going back.

That Sunday, when we heard they needed someone to serve coffee and donuts after Mass, Joe volunteered.

THE CUBICLE NEXT DOOR BLOG

Thanks

It seems appropriate, at this time of year, to say thanks. So, thank you, John Smith.

For being an okay kind of guy.

For being nice to the people who make up my little world. Not everyone would take the time to do the things you do.

It hasn't been nearly as bad as I expected, sharing a cubicle wall with you.

Posted on November 23 in **The Cubicle Next Door | Permalink**

Comments

It is interesting to note that although the idea of a day set aside for giving thanks began with the Pilgrims, it was not an annual event with those first colonists in the New World. It was not until more than a century later, in 1789, during the American Revolution, that George Washington suggested an official day of Thanksgiving. New York was the first state to turn it into an annual tradition, but not until 1817. And it was left to Abraham Lincoln to appoint the last Thursday in November as the official date of celebration. He did it in 1863, like George Washington before him, in the throes of war.

Posted by: **NozAll | November 23 at 09:09 PM**

And as the great Winston Churchill once said, "All the great things are simple, and many can be expressed in a single word: freedom, justice, honor, duty, mercy, hope."

Posted by: **survivor | November 24 at 08:10 AM**

I find most things in life aren't nearly as bad as I expected. The imagination is sometimes much worse than reality.

Posted by: **philosophie | November 24 at 08:12 AM**

To life on the cubicle farm! To us and those like us.

Posted by: **justluvmyjob | November 24 at 11:41 AM**

Exactly what sort of people make up your little world? And how many of you...er...them are there? Should we just call you Sybil?

Posted by: **theshrink | November 24 at 11:51 AM**

CLOSE

Twenty-One

****

An e-mail appeared, the first week in December, about the department Christmas party. A time for the faculty, staff, and their family members to invade the colonel's home, drink spiked eggnog, and talk about the same things we talked about at work.

Everyone was supposed to bring something. I signed up for an appetizer.

I'd signed up for an appetizer for the last ten years.

I had a great recipe for a pesto-and-goat-cheese mold with roasted red peppers. I served it with crackers. As long as I'd been bringing it to potlucks, I'd never had leftovers.

That Thursday, on the way home from work, I stopped by Manitou's taffy shop to see Adele. She'd owned it since the 1960s.

The taffy machine was turning, stretching out candy between its mechanical arms. I opened the door and was overcome by a wave of sugar-coated nostalgia. When I was younger, I had split my time between helping Grandmother in the ski shop and Adele in her shop.

"Jackie!" She flipped up a section of the spotless white counter, paused to sneeze, and came over to give me a hug. "When's the last time you came to see me?"

"It's been a long time." I kissed her cheek. "You usually come to see me."

"Here. Have a piece of taffy." She took a piece of orange candy from the display box.

I took it from her. Unwrapped it and popped it into my mouth.

Savored the smooth hard surface before it began to stick to my teeth.

"How's Joe?"

"I work with him. We share an office."

"And?"

"And that's it. You probably know more about him than I do. You're the one who plays poker with him every week."

"But you're dating, aren't you?"

I shook my head. Relented. "Sort of. But not really."

"But he's asked you out, hasn't he?"

I shook my head.

"Why not?"

I shrugged. "It's too complicated to explain. Grandmother told me you had a cold. I came over to see how you were doing, not to talk about Joe."

"Well, he's always talking about you."

The next day, as I was working, I heard Joe clear his throat. And soon after I heard him speak.

"You don't have to go to the Christmas Ball with me if you don't want to."

My fingers paused, hands poised above the keyboard. "I guess before I spent time and energy thinking about it, I'd want to actually be asked. Directly."

"Would you go to the Christmas Ball with me?"

Joe's voice came from high above my head. When I lifted my eyes toward the sound, I looked into his. His arms were folded on top of the cubicle wall, his chin resting on top of them.

I heard myself say yes before I remembered I couldn't dance. Had never danced. Before I remembered I didn't even own a dress. But I had to say yes. If I didn't, I knew Adele would never speak to me again. And neither would Thelma or Betty.

His dimples flashed before he disappeared behind the wall.

A dance.

I was going to a dance.

With Joe.

The next morning, after having endured a sleepless night, I decided to let Grandmother in on the news.

"I have…a situation."

Grandmother raised her eyes from the newspaper. "A situation? What sort of situation?"

"Joe asked me to a dance."

"I know, I was there. At Thanksgiving. It was about time."

"For what?"

"For him to take you on a real date."

"It's not a date. It's a dance. And it would be silly to go to a dance without a…date. It really is a date, isn't it?"

"It's a date."

"But I don't have a dress."

"Don't worry about the dress. I've been fantasizing about seeing you in a dress for years. Decades."

"I don't want one with any…stuff on it."

Grandmother lifted an eyebrow. "Frills and lace? Of course not. Don't be ridiculous. Betty will have just the thing."

Betty? I doubted it.

But then, I wasn't a wearer of dresses, was I?

We went over to Betty's house that evening after work. She brought dresses out of her closet by the armful. Among them was something simple in satin. Very plain. Very straight. It was strapless and had a high waist with the embellishment of a long thin horizontal bow. It was made of silvery-lavender material.

Betty shook her head as soon as she saw it. "You probably wouldn't want to try this one on. It's strapless. More of a spring dress, really."

I nodded. She was the expert, after all.

We went through the rest of the dresses. There were several that were the right size, but the wrong style.

Adele looked at the pile of rejected dresses on the bed and sighed as she patted my hand. "I don't know what to tell you. Guess you'll have to go shopping."

The other women looked stricken. They knew what that meant. While their definition of shopping meant boutique, mine started and ended with the local thrift store.

"There has to be something. Are you sure she tried them all on?" Grandmother wasn't about to let me leave without a dress.

"Yes." Betty surveyed the mound of discarded clothing on her bed. "Except for the strapless."

Thelma seized it from the pile. "She'll try it on."

"It will be much too cold." Adele barely squeezed out the words before sneezing.

"She can wear a coat." Thelma shoved it into my hands and pushed me toward the bathroom. "Try it."

I went into the bathroom and unzipped the dress. The material was heavy and slippery. Substantial. The color was slippery too. It wasn't really gray. It wasn't really lavender. It existed in the shades between them. I stepped into it, not bothering to take off my jeans or T-shirt. I had already decided that if I had to wear a dress, it wouldn't be strapless. But I looked in the mirror and changed my mind.

I unzipped it, tugged off my T-shirt, and slipped the straps of my bra off my shoulders. Brought the dress up to my chest and zipped it up again. Turned to see the view from the back.

I was still standing there, gazing at myself, when Adele knocked on the door and then pushed it open. She stood there for a long moment. "That's it. That's the one." She reached in to grab a tissue before she half-turned and then called over her shoulder to the others. "Come and see."

A moment later, they were crowding the doorway, trying to see over each other's heads. Only Thelma had a clear advantage.

"It's beautiful, but it's still strapless and it's still December." Propriety, at least in apparel, was Betty's motto.

Thelma, however, was much more practical. "She can wear a coat. You do have one, Jackie, don't you?"

"I have my duffle coat."

"She can't wear a duffle coat. Give me a minute." Betty relinquished her space and we could hear her padding down the hall. Several minutes later, she returned carrying a pile of sleek white fur.

"I can't wear that...whatever it is."

"It's a rabbit fur capelet." She held it out by the puffy round pom-poms.

"And how would you like it if someone made a capelet out of your skin?"

"Already been done. You know that movie? The one where there's a cannibal?"

"Hannibal something..."

"With the elephants?"

"No. With the guy who wears the mask."

"Jason."

"No. The other mask."

"Freddy."

"The other one."

I decided to put them out of their misery. *"Silence of the Lambs."* Thank you, Adele, for that vivid mental picture.

Betty held it out to me again. "Just try it."

"It's against my principles."

"Well, so is going to dances, if I'm not mistaken." She settled it across my shoulders and tied the strings, leaving them to dangle mid-chest. It looked exactly like the cape Priscilla Dillon had worn in the second grade. The cape I'd always admired, always secretly longed to pet, always craved to own. Hers even had a muff to match. "But what about my arms?" The cape only covered my shoulders and upper arms.

"We'll just have to find some gloves." Adele was busy patting the capelet. As if she thought by pressing it onto my skin, I'd change my mind about wearing it.

"I have a better idea!" Betty plodded back down the hall and returned a minute later. "There's a muff to match!"

A muff. "Can I...try it?" I pushed my hands into the satin-lined middle of the muff. And that was it. In an instant all my principles deserted me.

Betty beamed. "And if that's not warm enough, just remember Joe is a nice tall boy. I'm sure he wouldn't mind tucking you underneath his arm if you get too chilly."

They all smiled.

I scowled, trying to reconcile my traitorous feelings with my firmly held lifelong beliefs. I finally told myself the rabbits were long dead and I might as well redeem their deaths. Put them to good use.

Reduce, reuse, recycle, redeem.

Before I left with the dress, Betty loaded me up with shoes, gloves, and some sort of contraption she called a corselet that dangled straps. I just dumped them all into a bag and draped the dress over my arm.

The three of them waved from Betty's door as Grandmother and I left. "Don't forget!" Adele called behind us. "We'll come over next Saturday to help you get ready."

The first crisis took place long before Saturday. It was two days later, on Sunday, when I actually started listening to myself think. My thoughts were these: *I'm going to a dance with Joe. I'm going to a dance with Joe? I'm actually going to a dance. I'm going to dance?*

That was the first point at which I tried to back out.

"Do you know Joe's number?" I asked Grandmother at dinner.

"Of course. Don't you?"

"No." I had never called Joe. I never had to. I saw him practically every day. Why would I know his phone number?

"What do you need it for?"

"To call him."

"Why?" Grandmother may not have been *the* quintessential grandmother, but she still had a sixth sense about some things.

"Because I can't go to the dance with him."

"Why not?"

"Because I can't dance. It would defeat the purpose of the whole evening."

"I'll teach you."

She told all the others and the next night, after work, they congregated in the living room. They sat on the couch, all four of them, listening to a Glenn Miller record as I stood in the middle of the floor.

Adele finally took charge. "Thelma, you be the man."

"I can't. I've never led. I've always followed."

"Betty?"

"I wouldn't even know how to begin."

I stood there, staring at them. "So all of you know how to dance, but only if there's a man for a partner?"

Betty laughed. "What other reason is there for dancing?"

"I'll call Oliver." Grandmother pushed off from the couch and picked up the phone.

He showed up ten minutes later in a tweed sports coat pulled over a wool sweater and an ascot knotted at his throat.

"How may I be of service?"

Grandmother took over. "Jackie doesn't know how to dance."

"Do you have any music?"

Adele returned the needle to the record and the sounds of a waltz began floating into the air.

"My dear, may I have this dance?" Oliver had bowed at the waist and extended his hand. But it wasn't offered to me. He was talking to Grandmother.

"But…it's Jackie who doesn't know…"

"Of course it is, but one of the best methods of learning is by observing."

"Oh. Well then…" She placed her hand in his and he drew her into a sweeping turn and then proceeded to swirl her around the living room.

And just to be clear, my problem is not with observation. I could watch people dance all day. My problem is in application. In actually applying those same steps to my own clumsy feet.

By the time the song was over, there was color on Grandmother's cheeks and she was laughing. Oliver twirled her to the couch, where the other ladies were seated, and then he released her hand. "Thank you, my dear. That dance was lovely. Would any of you other ladies care to dance?"

That crafty old man danced with all of the women before he finally turned his attentions to me.

"Now then, Jackie, let us proceed." He extended his hand and I took it in mine. He had a surprisingly strong grip and a steady arm. He tried to spin me around as he took me to the middle of the living room, but I was taken by surprise and my arm refused to bend.

He released me and put his own hand up to the middle of his back.

"I'm sorry! I wasn't—"

"It's nothing. Just a wrenched muscle. There's no need to worry yourself about it." He grasped my hand again and waited several beats before catching up with the music.

This time, he didn't try to spin me, he just tried to turn me, but I didn't get the signal, I guess, because I ended up running into him. "I'm sorry!"

"Let's take a moment to converse. This may help: You must not be too stiff or too limp. There is tension required for dancing so that signals don't get missed. Dancers communicate with their bodies, not with words. We'll try again." He stood in place for several beats, simply rocking to the rhythm, and then he moved a foot forward and then back.

I tried to follow, tried to do the same.

"Marvelous. We'll just keep on for a moment."

True to his word, he let me get comfortable before trying any more tricks. And then I felt pressure underneath my shoulder blades. A pressure that made me think he wanted to turn to left.

And so I let him guide me around in a turn.

"Lovely."

And then I felt him press again and he guided me in a turn to the right.

"Splendid."

And then his hand lifted mine as his other hand guided me underneath the tunnel our arms had made. He'd spun me! And then he took me on a full circuit, turning and spinning me around the living room floor.

The ladies left soon after.

Oliver stayed, dancing with Grandmother. I watched them for a while. With her, at least, he relaxed. She seemed to soften his stiff English facade. As I crept up the stairs to go to bed, they were still dancing.

THE CUBICLE NEXT DOOR BLOG

What am I doing?

I've agreed to do...one, two, three...things I've never done before. And all because you asked me to. I used to be able to depend on the word "no." But it's as if I've forgotten how to pronounce it. What is it about you? What am I doing? And why?

Posted on December 3 in **The Cubicle Next Door** | **Permalink**

Comments

Although "no" is not a universal word, a surprising number of peoples have a negative response that sounds similar. In languages from Byelorussian to Kurdish to Saramaccan, your "no" would still probably be understood as "no."

Posted by: **NozAll** | December 3 at 09:03 PM

Sounds like you have the ability to be rude in almost any language. What talent!

Posted by: **theshrink** | December 3 at 09:14 PM

You sound like me. My initial responses are always no. Trains people to leave you alone.

Posted by: **survivor** | December 3 at 09:48 PM

Sometimes, special people unlock the hidden depths of our souls.

Posted by: **philosophie** | December 3 at 10:25 PM

What'd I tell you? He *was* trying to suck up to you, wasn't he?

Posted by: **justluvmyjob** | December 3 at 10:32 PM

This is a G-rated blog! I've just deleted three obscene comments! I'll do it again if I have to.

Posted by: **TCND** | December 3 at 10:41 PM

Grow up you guys! (Because that's what they are; girls wouldn't post stuff like that.)

Posted by: **justluvmyjob** | December 3 at 10:45 PM

Gentlemen don't use four-letter words.

Posted by: **theshrink | December 3 at 10:49 PM**

It's the lurkers. Can't trust them, the sneaky son of a guns.

Posted by: **survivor | December 3 at 10:53 PM**

Twenty-Two

****

Saturday dawned bright and clear. The day of the dance. The day Grandmother and her friends would help me get ready for the dance.

The doorbell started ringing at 6:00. Thelma was first. She'd brought a bag filled with biscuits. Betty was next. She came lugging a hard-sided cosmetic case that had seen better days. Adele brought an old-fashioned beauty parlor-style hair dryer, equipped with an articulated hose and an attached inflatable cap. They deposited their treasures in the middle of the kitchen table and then stood staring at me.

I was afraid to move. Afraid even to flinch. Afraid if I tensed even one muscle, they'd be all over me.

Thelma was the one who finally broke the silence. "Where are those shoes?"

"Shoes?"

She shuffled in the direction of the stairs as if she were going to climb up to my room and find them herself.

"Just…wait a minute. I'll go get them." But I didn't move. I was afraid to leave them alone. Afraid if Adele plugged her gadget in, it would short-circuit the wiring in the house. Afraid if I left, for even a few minutes, Betty would open her cosmetic case and the past-their-expiration-date cosmetics, when combined with oxygen, would combust in a minor explosion of talcum powder and shimmery baby blue eye shadow. I didn't want to have to clean up that mess.

But Thelma was still moving toward the stairs, so I turned her back around toward the kitchen table and went to find the shoes myself.

By the time I got back, the worst had happened. The table was now a garage sale jumble of odd-colored makeup. And from the acrid smell, I could tell someone had plugged the hair dryer in.

"It still works!" Adele was holding up the now-inflated cap.

Wonderful.

Thelma relieved me of the shoes, took them to the table, and sat down in a chair. Then she took a biscuit from her bag, split it open, and began to rub my shoe with one of the halves. "When I saw these shoes last Friday, I said to myself, 'Those shoes need a good biscuit shine.'"

A biscuit shine.

She polished away for a couple minutes, going through three biscuits in the process. Then she held them up for everyone to see.

They looked as if they were brand new.

I walked over and took them off her hands. "That's incredible! How did you know how to do that?"

She blushed. That's about as much pleasure as I'd ever seen her exhibit. Tanks aren't prone to full-blown displays of emotion.

They spent the morning going through Betty's cosmetics and talking about the good old days. At 1:00 they walked into the living room to watch a movie on the Sci-Fi Channel and promptly fell asleep.

I tiptoed upstairs and took a shower. I wrapped a towel around myself and took the dress from the closet, holding it out in front of me, not quite daring to touch the material.

Then I shrugged into a bathrobe and surfed the Internet for a while. Finally I wandered downstairs. I discovered them in the middle of a game of pinochle. They threw their hands into the middle of the card table as soon as they saw me and hustled me into the kitchen.

"Sit down right here." Betty pointed to a chair that had been pulled away from the table. She patted my arm then, as if I needed some sort of reassurance.

I sat. There was nothing else I could do. I was completely in their clutches.

Adele, clasping her hair dryer, elbowed Betty out of the way. "I'll need a comb and a bowl of water."

She unzipped a small pouch and dumped its contents onto a newly cleared space on the table. They were long thin strips of material. She turned to look at me with an appraising eye.

"You don't have to tie me up." I hadn't seen any scissors, razors, or other sharp objects, so at that point I figured the best thing to do was just get it over with. "I promise I'll stay."

"The only thing I plan on tying up is your hair."

At that, Betty looked up from the table. "You're doing rag curls?"

"Mm-hmm."

"And just how do you plan on drying them in time?"

She held up the hose attachment. "With this miracle of modern technology."

I understood her to be playing fast and loose with the definition of "modern."

"They don't stay as well if you don't sleep on them."

"And who was it that fixed your hair when you had your eye on Mayor Fitzhugh?"

Mayor Fitzhugh? He'd been long gone from office. And long married to Miss Maggie Sims. Their small intimate wedding of 600 people was still talked about by those in the know.

Betty shot a glance in my direction. "We don't really need to talk about that."

Adele pretended not to hear and began separating the strips, pulling them into long lengths.

Thelma set a bowl filled with water on the table.

Grandmother appeared with an assortment of combs. "Rattail, pintail, or flattop?"

"I'll start with the flattop and the rattail." She plucked the big one with the rounded handle and the one with the pointed end from Grandmother. Then she dunked the large comb into the bowl. She used the rattail to separate a large section of hair on the crown of my head. She fished the other comb out of the bowl and used it to wet the hair. Then she put it down and picked up a strip of cloth.

I felt my hair pulled taut and then a rolling sensation. Another tug and then a release of tension.

Adele turned toward the table to grab another strip.

I put a hand up to my head. Felt a small bundle of hair.

Adele had turned around. "I'm tying the rags around your hair and curling it up." She grabbed a mirror from the table. "Here. Watch how I do it."

She grabbed another length of hair and tied a strip around the very end of it. Then, grasping the sides of the strip and the hair, she rolled it all the way to my scalp and tied the strip around it in a knot.

By the time she was finished, tufts of cloth stuck out all over my head. I looked like a 1940s shrew. All I needed was a bathrobe and a cigarette. Oops. My mistake. I was already wearing the bathrobe.

"Now we'll set you up with the hair dryer."

We had to move my chair so it could be closer to the outlet. And then I had to pull the card table from the living room so the hairdryer could sit close to my head. Adele placed the cap on my head, pulled the drawstring tight and then turned the machine on. It whirred in my ears and inflated, making me feel as if I were a balloon. It began to warm. And then it got hot.

Desert hot.

My scalp began to bake.

My ears started to itch.

And then it became jungle hot because I had started to sweat from places I never knew had sweat glands. My temples. My eyebrows. The inside of my elbows.

I reached up a hand to my head to scratch it, and only succeeded in deflating the cap. I took my hand away and it reinflated. I did it again, because when it deflated, it stopped blowing for a microsecond. Just long enough to feel as if that millimeter of scalp had run away from my body and plunged itself into an ice-cold mountain lake.

"Stop that!" At least I think that's what Adele said. The hair dryer was so noisy I couldn't really hear her.

Betty pulled a chair away from the table and placed it in front of me. She sat down and gestured for my hands. I held them out toward her. She stared at my fingernails for a while. Then she got up, rummaged around her cosmetic case, and came back with a stick, some small scissors, and a bottle of lotion.

She squeezed the lotion onto my nails and rubbed them into my skin. She waited about five minutes and then picked up the stick and tried to shove it under my cuticles. At least that's what it felt like.

We had a tug of war with my hand.

I won.

I rose from my chair, as far as the hair dryer would let me, and then sat on top of my hand.

She kept talking to me, gesticulating wildly, but the problem was, I couldn't hear her. And I kept trying to tell her, but she wouldn't stop talking long enough to hear me.

Thelma finally pulled the dryer cord from the wall and I heard myself shouting, "...can't hear you!"

And Betty shouting back, "Stop shouting!"

The cap deflated and fell, flaccid, to my head. "Sorry. I couldn't hear you."

Adele had untied the cap and now she removed it. As soon as she turned her back, I planned to poke a hole in it so it could never be used again. At least not on my head.

"I need to trim your cuticles before I paint your nails." She was holding out her hand, asking for my own.

I was still sitting on it. "With that stick?"

"I have to push them back before I can trim them."

"With that stick?"

"Yes."

"Let me see it."

Betty held it out to me.

I brought out my hand and took it. Then I broke it in half. Gave it back to her. "Let's just skip that part and go straight to painting."

She narrowed her eyes and then rose, marched to the table, picked up something, and marched right back. It was another stick and she held it up in front of my eyes. "They come in packs of twelve."

We had a stare-off.

She won.

I gritted my teeth and suffered in silence.

When she was done pushing, shoving, and trimming the cuticles, she started on the nails themselves. Clipping them, filing them, and buffing them to a shine. And that's when she made her peace offering. She led me to the kitchen table, sat me down, and lined up four bottles of polish in front of me. Then she sighed and pulled a fifth one from her case. "You can even have clear if you want."

And that's when I made my peace offering. "No, thanks. Let's do pink."

"Fuchsia?"

"Bubblegum." Thirty years of slights still had to be made up for.

It took until after my nails were painted for my hair to cool down. Seriously. But when it did, Adele unknotted the strips and pulled them off. Then she ran her fingers through my hair.

"Oh, my." Such simple words, but coming from Thelma, they spoke volumes.

"Are you sure…?"

Something in Grandmother's voice made me grab the mirror from the table to take a look. If I had been expecting an afro, I might have been happy. Overjoyed. Might have even picked Thelma off her feet and twirled her around the room. As it was, I figured I just about had time to jump in the shower and wash all the curls out before Joe came to get me.

Unfortunately, Adele caught me by the elbow before I could start my dash to the stairs. "Don't you worry."

"She'd better worry. I'd be worrying." Betty would be worrying? That was a very bad sign.

"Oh, hush. Who used to have the biggest bouffant in town?"

This was not sounding good.

She stood on tiptoe to latch onto my shoulders and push me down into the chair. "Just give me fifteen minutes and you'll be looking like Miss America."

Miss America 1962.

Adele took a comb from the table, separated a section of hair, and then began trying to relieve me of my scalp. At least that's what it felt like. "I don't think bald was the image I had in mind."

"Your hair is limp. And fine. I did rag curls for body and now I'm teasing it to give it volume."

I glanced at the other women in the room. They looked as skeptical as I felt.

Adele teased for another five minutes before she stepped back and surveyed her work. She put the fingers of each hand up to her mouth.

Licked them. And leaning toward me, she spread her fingers across my bangs, pressing them toward my forehead.

Eww.

She combed through them, stepped away again. Licked her middle and pointer fingers and made some sort of sticky adjustment at the sides of my forehead. Then she grabbed an industrial-sized aluminum can and began shaking it so hard one of her clip-on earrings popped off.

"What is that?"

"Spray net."

"For my hair? Does it really need that? Won't your…saliva…just hold it in place?"

"Not for the next six hours. Close your eyes. Try not to breathe."

I could have used a gas mask. It smelled terrible, it tasted awful, and it was doing something funny to the insides of my nostrils as I breathed. I sneezed.

"I told you not to breathe."

"Sorry. At some point, survival instincts insist on keeping me alive." I put a hand up to my hair, feeling with my fingers.

Adele spot-sprayed me before I could close my eyes again. Placed her hands on her hips. "Shake your head."

I turned it from side to side.

"Faster."

I shook my head until I could hear it creaking.

"See? It doesn't even move."

I didn't think it would ever move again.

Adele returned the can to the table. "I almost forgot! The finishing touch." She approached me, a bow in hand.

"I don't do bows."

"And how would you know? Now be quiet and look down."

She practically had to drill a hole in my hair in order to make it stick. "Want to see?"

No, I didn't. Because if I didn't look, then I could pretend everything was still normal. But she so clearly wanted me to view her work I couldn't say no.

"Ta-da!" She held the mirror up before me.

Hmm. I looked…like something. Someone.

"Make your neck longer."

"We don't have time for plastic surgery."

"I mean, sit up straight and push your shoulders down."

I sat up straight. Tried to lengthen the distance between my head and my shoulders. Looked at the women in front of me. They were all nodding.

"What?"

"You look good."

"Perfect."

"Just like Audrey Hepburn."

Maybe. I had the short bangs. The dark hair. Maybe, if she had ever worn her hair slightly bouffant at the crown, with curls at the back and a bow in the front. Maybe.

While Adele packed her hair dryer away, Betty took over.

She reached into a pile of metal implements and brought out a pair of tweezers. Put her glasses on, leaned toward me, and squinted into my face.

"What are you planning to do with those?"

"Tweeze your eyebrows."

"Why?"

She stood up straight and put a hand to her hip. "Because the eyebrows are the window shade to your soul."

"Really."

"Yes, really. If you're expecting Joe to gaze soulfully into your eyes, you've got to roll up those shades! Be open for business! Now close your eyes."

I did. Only to feel them flying open seconds later. "Ow! Ow! Ow!"

"You're going to have to sit still if you expect me to do this right."

"I don't expect you to do this at all! Give me those tweezers."

Instead of putting them into my outstretched hand, she hid them behind her back. "No."

"Give them to me."

"I will not." She stared at me defiantly over the top of her reading glasses. "If there is one day in your life you are going to look beautiful, it's today. You were not meant to sit at home every Saturday night in front of a computer. Joe is the best thing that's happened around here since…since you were born! So if you think we're going to just let you go to the Christmas Ball looking like something a dog's been chewing on, then you have another think coming."

Adele lifted her head and looked at me.

I looked at Thelma.

She stared right back.

Since I was born? Really? Because I'd always assumed Grandmother was having the time of her life when I came along. Assumed it must have been quite a shock, going from being the widowed owner of a ski shop to being a widowed grandmother, raising a granddaughter, running a ski shop. I'd always understood she did what they do up in Leadville when winter starts coming: got out the gear, laid up extra provisions, and waited until the spring thaw.

Adele winked at me.

I closed my eyes, lifted my head, and sighed. "Then I'm going to need some ice."

Twenty-Three

****

A half hour later, Grandmother approached the couch in the living room, where I was reclining without ruining my hair, and lifted the sandwich bag of ice cubes from my brow. "How are we doing?"

"*We* are doing just fine. *I*, however, am not. I think I'll call Joe and tell him I'm not going."

"Oh no, you are not!"

They had to threaten to use physical force to carry me to the kitchen before I agreed to go under my own power. After pushing me into a chair, Betty began unscrewing caps of flesh-colored bottles. Poured tiny amounts onto the back of her hand and then ran a finger through them and drew a line on my cheek, near my neck.

"I'm going to a dance, not a war."

"It's foundation cream to even out your complexion. You do have nice skin, don't you?"

Was that a compliment? From Betty? For me?

She had taken off her glasses and let them dangle to her chest on their pearl chain. She backed away from me several steps. "Turn your head just a little."

I swiveled my head to the right.

"Mm-hmm. The other way."

I swiveled to the left.

"Mm-hmm. Okay. Now take this washcloth and scrub all of that off your face. You're lucky you have such lovely, long lashes."

Another compliment?

"Otherwise we'd have to use this."

At that moment, as she held up a metal torture device, squeezing it open and shut, I decided I'd much rather be lucky than good.

"The mascara's all dried out anyway." Grandmother was holding up a tube that refused to be opened.

Betty sighed and then picked up a wedge of spongy material and placed it on top of one of the beige-colored bottles and tipped it over. Then she rubbed it across my face.

"She looks kind of pale, doesn't she?" From the sound of her voice, Adele was hovering near my ear.

"She *is* pale." If Thelma had said it, then it was probably true.

"She's always been pale. Remember when she was born? You could practically see the blood pump through her veins." Betty stopped rubbing. "There. You can open your eyes now."

I opened my eyes.

"What color eye shadow are you going to use?" Thelma was surveying Betty's collection.

"Use blue. Blue goes with anything." But then again, Adele had carrot-red hair and her favorite color was purple.

"Only in the sixties. What color are your eyes?" Betty had put on her glasses again.

"Blue."

"Then we'll use purple."

"Use brown. It goes with blue." Since when had Thelma had an opinion about fashion?

Betty turned toward Thelma, one hand on her hip. "But her dress is lavender and brown is boring."

"That's what I always used."

Three heads swung to look in Thelma's direction.

"I didn't know you ever wore eye shadow."

"I did until 1979."

"Well, if we didn't know you were wearing brown eye shadow to go with your blue eyes, then I don't think we want to use brown eye shadow to go with Jackie's blue eyes either, do we?"

It was clearly a rhetorical question because Betty was so very clearly the expert on makeup.

She perched her reading glasses on her nose, looked down at the table with a piercing glance, and then grabbed a fat pencil. She held it up in front of her face as if she were a nurse, checking a syringe. "Pencil sharpener."

It took everyone a minute to realize she expected us to not only find a pencil sharpener, but also give it to her.

Adele located it and slapped it into the palm of her left hand.

She took it with her right hand, sharpened the plump pencil, hefted the weight, and then readjusted her grip. She leaned in and pulled at the skin beneath my left eye. "Look up."

I looked up.

Breathing heavily, and with a shaking hand, I could feel her draw a line below my lower lashes. Then she did the same on the other eye.

She stepped back. Took her glasses off, leaving them to dangle. "Good. That's good." She put her glasses back on, ordered me to look down and drew lines above my upper lashes. Then she snatched a combination set of four shades of purple eye shadow from the table. They ranged from pale lavender to a smoky plum. She squinted at me from behind those glasses and then squinted down at the eye shadows. She took a small applicator from the set and commanded me to look down. As I did, she drug it along the bottom half of my eyelids.

"Ouch!"

"Just one more side. It's my arthritis. Sorry."

She wasn't really sorry. I could tell. She was taking revenge for all the times in the last 30 years she'd wished I would wear a dress. Do something with my hair. Go out on dates. But I couldn't leave because I didn't know how to do any of it by myself.

She took the other applicator from the set, ground it into the pale lavender shadow and then spread it over the top of my eyelids. She put it back, took up the other applicator, and actually made a hole in the plum eye shadow as she loaded it up with shadow. That's how much force she was using. And then she pressed it onto my eyelids. I'm sure the imprint of the applicator is stamped into my brain. Forever.

After I stopped seeing stars, I realized she had said something to me. And now she was making faces at me. Was that really necessary?

"Like this."

"What?"

"Make fish lips."

"Fish lips?"

She sighed and held out a compact toward me. "For the blusher."

"So she knows where to put it." Adele was still hovering by my ear.

I looked around at all of them. They were all making fish lips and looking for all the world like a demented school of goldfish. Glub, glub, glub.

So I did it too.

Betty twirled a brush around the compact and then spread it across my cheeks.

Then she took her glasses off again, and searched through the supplies on the table, finally seizing on a lipstick. "Open your mouth."

I opened it.

"Not that much. Just a little. As if you were exhaling cigarette smoke."

As if I'd know exactly what that's like. But I pretended.

"That's it..." She'd opened her mouth too. And now the tip of her tongue was sticking out the side of it as she applied the color to my lips. "Okay. Now smudge your lips together."

I smudged.

"Oh, dear."

"What?"

"It looks as if your lips bleed."

"They do? Where?" Couldn't they have left well enough alone? Now my lips were bleeding?

"Here." Betty handed me a washcloth. "Wipe off the lipstick. We'll start over with a lip liner."

"Lip liner?"

"To stop the bleeding."

I half-rose from the chair. "Maybe I should get some ice instead."

"For what?"

"The blood."

"What blood?"

"From my lips."

"Your lips aren't bleeding."

"You just said they were."

"Your *lipstick* is bleeding. It's going outside your lip line. That's why we need lip liner."

"Oh." If I'd known Cosmetics was a foreign language, I would have studied harder for the test.

Betty sharpened another pencil and then drew lines around my lips. She colored them in with lipstick and had me smudge again. "Let's see." She smiled brightly.

I smiled.

"Perfect." She drew a tissue from the box and handed it to me. "Now use this to blot the lipstick."

"Why?"

"Because you want your lips to look stained, not painted."

I did?

All the ladies were nodding.

I guess I did.

Betty glanced at her watch and then clapped her hands together. "Quick! The dress. The gloves. He'll be here in ten minutes!"

They rushed me into my bedroom and stripped away my bathrobe, leaving me standing almost naked in the middle of the floor. Did they have no shame?

"You can't wear that bra!"

"I'll get your dress."

"Where are your pantyhose?"

"Do you have a purse?"

"Stop!"

They froze.

"Out!" I pointed at the door.

Call me crazy, but there are some things I just like to do myself. Getting dressed is one of them.

I tried to untangle the contraption I'd borrowed from Betty. The one I had assumed was a bra. Now I wasn't so sure. "Grandmother? Could you come help me?"

She pushed the door open. Paused when she saw what I was holding.

"What is this?"

"It's a corselet."

"And what's it for?"

"Everything. Here. Give it to me and turn around."

With some tugging and cinching, she finally had it fastened. She spun me around and handed me a pair of nylons. "Put these on. One on each leg."

"And how are they supposed to stay up?"

She sighed. She held one open while I stepped into it and then she shimmied it up my leg and attached it to two of the straps. Then she did the same for the other.

"I don't suppose you'll be wanting to know how to undo these…?"

"Won't you be awake when I get home?"

She sighed.

I took a slow step. Testing the contraption. The top of it certainly covered what it was supposed to, but it did it in a rather uncomfortable way. The bottom held my nylons up. In four places. But in between, they had already started to sag. "I don't like this."

Grandmother gave me a look. The Look. "Sometimes, Jackie, we have to do things we don't like."

"Beauty is pain? Is that what you're telling me?"

"Growth is pain. *That's* what I'm telling you." She held the dress for me while I stepped into it, and then she zipped it up. She picked up the rabbit fur and settled it on my shoulders. Then she took it off. "Why don't we let Joe have the full effect? You can put this on downstairs," She propelled me into the bathroom. "Take a look."

Remember before how I said I was intense looking? Well, this was the intense, exotic version of me.

Exotic?

Hard to believe, right?

But somehow true.

I heard the doorbell and then the sound of the front door opening and shutting. The sound of the floorboards wheezing in the living room.

"I don't want to go."

"Don't be silly."

"I really don't. I won't know what to do."

"Now you listen to me. All you have to do is put one foot in front of the other until you get to the bottom of the stairs. And then all you have to do is go into the living room and smile at Joe and thank him for inviting you. And then all you have to do is sit in his car until you get there. And then all you have to do is have fun. Do you think you can do that?"

I looked at her. Opened my mouth to speak.

"It was rhetorical. Don't answer. Hold out your hands."

I held them out while she shimmied the gloves up over them.

Then she stepped back and smiled. "Now go."

I went.

One foot in front of the other until I was at the bottom of the stairs.

And then I forgot what I was supposed to do because Joe was already there. He was waiting. For me.

Men in flight suits don't do much for me. Men in mess dress? Well, that's an entirely different uniform. A short-waisted dark blue tuxedo, complete with cummerbund and bow tie. And Joe, with his wide shoulders… well, let's just say he filled it out. Nicely.

I forgot what I was supposed to say, so I smiled like an idiot.

But then Joe did too, so we were even.

"You look absolutely…stunning."

If he'd called me beautiful, I would have known he was lying. As it was, he took the cape from Grandmother's hands, settled it across my shoulders, and tied the pom-poms. But not before bouncing them up into my face.

Then he held the muff for me while I put my hands inside. After that he held out his arm for me to take.

We both laughed when we realized it wouldn't work with my hands already inside the muff. So he just looped his arm through mine.

I'm not sure if we even said goodbye before we left.

I know I didn't wave.

Twenty-Four

****

The drive to the Academy was odd.

So different than driving during the day when it was light outside. And when I wasn't wearing a dress.

Joe concentrated on the road. Headlights bounced on and off his face, throwing his profile into relief. Once on base, he drove up onto the hill and took a tour of the Harmon Hall and Arnold Hall parking lots. They were full. More than full. He decided to park in his normal spot instead. He helped me climb down from the SUV. I almost forgot the muff, but he saw it on the floor and gave it to me.

I pushed a hand through it and wore it like a giant furry bracelet.

We took the elevator up into Fairchild Hall and walked through darkened halls to the north end of the building. We crossed the bridge by the library and walked onto the terrazzo.

It was clear. And cold.

Everything seemed more brittle. The stars. The wind. And my shoes. They weren't low-tops. And they were sliding.

"Need a hand?" Joe extended his toward me.

I looked at it. Looked up at him. His face was shadowed, his back toward the moon. I grasped it.

It held steady. Even as my heel skidded on the pavement and I started to go down, his arm remained stable, his hand keeping me upright. After I regained my balance, I was hesitant to let go.

It wasn't a difficult hand to hold onto. His grip wasn't too tight or too loose.

Stepping out from the protection of Fairchild Hall, we were hit with the full force of the wind. It lifted my pom-poms up and threw them behind my shoulder. I could feel them straining, beating against my back, trying to escape their tethers.

Joe's hand tightened on mine. He pulled me close to his side. "It's coming off the mountains." He pointed with his chin up to the foothills that rose behind the Academy, but I knew he was gesturing farther. Beyond what we could see. That wind was coming from the snow-drenched peaks of the Rocky Mountains, which hid behind those hills.

He stopped and turned toward the hill in the center of the terrazzo. The pull of his hand around mine turned me with him. "They say Spirit Hill was built to break up the wind. It would have peeled the roof off Mitchell Hall."

That sounded a little far-fetched.

I saw Joe's dimples. "That's the rumor, anyway."

"Sometimes I think this whole place is one big rumor."

"I know at least some things that are true."

"What kinds of things?"

"Well...forget it."

"You can't start telling me a story and then just stop."

He dropped my hand. Looked at me. I saw indecision in his eyes. Then he gestured toward Arnold Hall and started walking.

I stood there watching him walk. "What?"

He turned around and walked backward. "Just stupid cadet tricks."

"Like what?"

"Like...sledding down Spirit Hill on cardboard boxes. Putting bubbles and dye in the fountain. And moving the static displays."

"The planes?"

"Yeah."

"How?"

"If you have enough people, you can do just about anything."

"You moved the planes? Did you roll them?"

"No. We carried them. That's why they're tied down now."

"To where?"

"The middle of the terrazzo. So if you were marching, you'd have to march around them. Stupid things like that."

I shivered. Tried to make the fur spread farther down my arms, but the wind tunneled through it and blew it up in back.

Joe saw me shiver and came back to me. He put an arm around my shoulder and said, "Let's get inside."

There was nothing I could do but put my arm around his waist. I needed all the warmth I could get.

Once inside we followed the sound of music, checked my capelet and muff into the cloakroom, and then made our way toward the ballroom. There were two sets of wide spiral stairs at either end of the room that led down to the dance floor below. Joe led me toward the railing. Looking over it provided a view of the lower floor.

Tables were set up on the left side of the room, leaving the right side free for dancing. Music pulsated from speakers on a stage. A DJ, ears encased in headphones, was planted beside the windows along the outer wall of the room. There were several 20-foot-high Christmas trees. The food tables were decorated with ice sculptures and burbling fountains of punch.

"Shall we?" Joe crooked his elbow toward me. I wrapped a hand around his arm.

He walked me toward the stairs and then suddenly stopped, detached my hand, and drew me around in front of him, refixing my other hand to his other arm. He winked at me. "So you have smaller steps."

The stairway spiraled down to the ballroom. Joe was correct. His long legs could handle the wider steps along the outside of the spiral. Mine didn't need the challenge.

"Cadet training. Mrs. Merchant pounded stuff like that into our heads."

"Who was Mrs. Merchant?"

"The Cadet Wing Hostess and go-to gal on all sorts of things, from how to eat escargot to how to address the general's wife."

At the bottom of the stairs, he stopped and called out to another officer. "Hey, Todd! What are you doing here?"

A tall, stocky man in mess dress turned toward us. A grin lit his face. He came over and clapped Joe on the back. "Hey, bud! How're you doing?"

"I didn't know you were here. Are you instructing?"

"Nope. AOC. Someone's got to keep an eye on all those fine young cadets. How 'bout you? Instructing?"

"Yep. History."

"So why are you here?"

"I was hungry. There's free food, right? Anyway, Todd, this is Jackie."

I held out my hand to shake his.

"Todd and I were in the same squadron at Elmendorf, up in Alaska." He glanced at his friend. "Jackie and I work together."

"Nice to meet you. I was thinking I could do a touch and go, but it looks like I'm here for the night. Anyway, nice to see you." He punched Joe in the arm and took off toward the dance floor.

Joe led me over to one of the food tables.

"Would you like to translate?"

"What part?"

"Is Todd supposed to be flying tonight?"

"I don't think so."

"He was talking about touching and going somewhere."

"A touch and go. It's a maneuver. When you're flying, you power off, touch down on a runway, and then reignite the engines and go up again. At the start of things like this, there's always a receiving line. So as a cadet, if you were required to be at one of these but didn't want to stay, you could come down that staircase," he pointed toward the one we'd just come down, "shake all the hands, keep moving, go up the other one, and be on your way. A touch and go."

"Is that why he didn't expect you to be here?"

"No." He picked up a cracker and popped it into his mouth.

"Would you care to elaborate?"

"Not really. Want something to eat?" He was holding out a plate toward me. "Aren't you hungry?"

Now that he'd mentioned it, I was. I hadn't really eaten since… dinner the night before. How had that happened? I took the plate from him and watched him pick up one for himself. I waited for him to start piling it high with food.

But he had decided to wait for me. "Ladies first."

"No. Please, go ahead."

"If I go first, I guarantee Mrs. Merchant will materialize before us and bean me over the head with a candle snuffer."

"Really. Please."

"You first."

"I'm not hungry." Of course, that wasn't true. But all the food was booby-trapped with toothpicks and sauces and dips. And I wasn't good at…parties. Was I supposed to use the same toothpick for fruit that I used for olives? Or was I supposed to take a separate toothpick for each piece of food? Was the spoon in the dip for putting it directly on top of the cherry tomatoes and baby carrots, or was it for putting the dip onto my plate? Was I supposed to slather cheese spread directly onto my crackers?

Joe sent a glance in my direction, took my plate from me, and saved me from starvation. "Tell me what you want and I'll just put it on the plate for you. That way, you won't get those gloves dirty."

That sounded good. Great, in fact, but were you really supposed to eat at events like this?

When I failed to answer, Joe just started taking one of everything. "How about this—just tell me if you *don't* want something."

I nodded.

"Or better yet, why don't you get some punch and then find a table?"

Punch was something I could be good at.

At least I thought it was.

Several minutes later, Joe joined me at the table. By that time I'd managed to get two glasses of punch to the table, but not without spilling them over my gloves. So I'd taken them off and was trying to figure out what to do with them. If it hadn't been Betty who loaned them to me, I might have just thrown them away.

Joe set one of the plates in front of me. He picked up a cherry tomato that had rolled off the edge and popped it into his mouth. Apparently he assumed I had the appetite of a horse.

For this night, at least, he was right.

I'm glad I hadn't taken "Buffet Dining" as a graded course. I would have failed. At least by Mrs. Merchant's standards. There was a forest of toothpicks covering my plate. And a lake of dip and a puddle of cheese spread. Among which stood several islands of mini-quiches and chicken wings. "Thanks."

Joe was in the middle of a mouthful of food, so he just smiled.

After he'd finished his food he excused himself.

I watched him wind through the tables, stopping to talk to cadets. Clap several officers on the back. Eventually, he ended up talking to the DJ. I saw him glance at his watch. Shake the DJ's hand. Then he returned to me.

Joe cleared his throat. Then he picked up my gloves and stuffed them into the inside pockets of his jacket, one on each side. "Would you like to dance?"

"Um...the honest truth is I don't know how. Not really. Oliver tried to teach me last week, but..."

"That's okay. I don't know how, either. But that shouldn't stop us from trying."

"Mrs. Merchant didn't teach you?"

"There was a limit to what even the sainted Mrs. Merchant could accomplish."

He was holding out his hand, so I took it.

A doo-doo doo-doo '70s underbeat started. The crooning words were about some girl who had no money and dressed funny. Wild and free. Someone named Rosemary who had love growing all over the place.

Joe sang right along, doing some Egyptian walking, throwing his arms out and shouting "Hey!" along with the music, dancing circles around me. Catching my hand to pull me in close and dance several steps. Letting it go to dance around me again. Clearly he had no problem finding rhythm. Or finding a sub-beat. He was a one-person floor show.

Then the song segued into something slightly slower. Something lighter.

He grabbed my hand. Keeping it in his, he repositioned us so we could face each other. He put a hand to my back, underneath my shoulder blades. Began dancing, a sort of quickstep version of the dance Oliver had done. He was more limber than Oliver had been. He looped us crazily around the dance floor in a series of three quick steps and then a pause for a double-long beat. Warbled words into my ear. They were lyrics about "never finding another you."

I had put my hand on his upper arm, the way Oliver had showed me. I didn't have any problem with tension. Or interpreting signals. For just that one song, just that one night, I figured I could handle it.

So when Joe pulled me close, I followed his lead.

When he pushed me out and then spun me, I went along. But he didn't spin me back. He kept me close, my back against his chest, his arm across my waist, singing into my ear.

Then when he finally spun me back, his arm tightened, pulling me to his chest, and I laid my head on his shoulder.

When his cheek grazed my head, I closed my eyes.

But when the song ended, I wasn't quite sure what to do. What was the right thing to do? He'd asked me to dance, but was the offer only good for a few dances or for all of them? Were we supposed to go sit down now? Or were we supposed to stay and dance the next?

Before I could decide what to do, the music started up with a tropical tempo. Joe began dancing again. And so did everyone else. I mean *everyone*. The song started with a bunch of "Ole's." The tables emptied and everyone bounced out onto the dance floor. The main theme of the song seemed to be about feeling hot-hot-hot.

And I was not-not-not.

Everyone else seemed to know you were supposed to shout hot-hot-hot with your arms up in the air. And that you were supposed to rumba around like the Chiquita banana girl. Fortunately, the floor was so crowded, I don't think anyone noticed I wasn't dancing.

Except for Joe.

He slid an arm around my waist. Had me swaying with him to the beat, letting me go only to chant the hot-hot-hots.

When the next song began, it was clear it was going to be another fast one. Joe grabbed my hand and drew me toward the closest set of stairs. We climbed them and found a span of unoccupied railing. We braced our forearms on it and leaned forward, watching the pulsating crowd below.

It provided a chance to recover from the dancing.

A chance to get a grip on my heart.

Twenty-Five

****

T hanks, Joe."

He turned his head toward me. "For what?"

"Dancing with me."

"Ah. Well, technically, I should be thanking you for wasting your dance time on a guy with limited moves and even less talent."

"I've never danced with anyone before. Except Oliver."

"Why not?"

"No one ever asked me."

"What else haven't you ever done?"

"I've never..." held hands with anyone, kissed anyone, slept in anyone else's bed but my own. *Stop it!* "I've never been downhill skiing."

"Ever? And you grew up in Colorado?"

"It was against Grandmother's policy."

"So you guys never went up to the mountains on vacation?"

"We never went anywhere on vacation. Except one time when I was little. We went to the beach. Have you ever been before?"

Joe nodded, his eyes roaming my face.

"I've always wanted to go back."

"Where'd you go?"

"Somewhere in Oregon. We drove. But I'd go anywhere. Did you know every seventh wave is a big one? I'd read it somewhere, so when we reached the ocean, I sat down in the sand and I counted. It's true."

"Why didn't you go back?"

"I don't know. I guess I could have visited the Atlantic while I was at MIT, but there was never enough time. And then Grandmother had her accident."

"The one with her hip? She seems to get around fine."

"She does. But I wouldn't feel right about leaving her alone."

We stood there for a while, watching the cadets dancing below. And then I got a call I couldn't ignore. "Do you know where the restroom is?"

He turned around and offered his arm. "It's just down the hall."

A cadet from one of Joe's classes saw him and stopped us to ask if we could take a picture. There were four couples, the girls fresh and dewy-eyed in glittery eye shadow, glossy lips, and upswept hair. They lined up for the picture. Smiled. Smiled again for the backup picture.

Then their little party broke up so the girls could go to the restroom.

I trailed them.

The restroom was filled with girls, but the stalls were empty. Lots of giggles. Lots of laughter. No flushing of toilets.

They were all facing the mirrors, but observation revealed they were actually talking to each other in the course of reapplying lip gloss or rearranging pins in their hair.

I did what I needed to.

They were all still there when I was done.

I gave myself an extra glance in the mirror. My hair looked fine. It hadn't moved. Neither had my eye shadow or lipstick.

I smiled at myself like I had seen the other girls do. Ended up feeling silly.

Left.

Joe was loitering in the hall outside. We walked back the way we'd come, but instead of returning to the dance floor, we went the opposite direction, into an alcove in the wall, opposite the railing.

"How would you feel about a game of foosball?"

"How would you feel about getting your butt kicked?"

Joe was digging the ball out of the slot, but he glanced up at me from underneath his brows. "I don't think I'll have to worry about that."

I grabbed two handles and leaned over the table. "Bring it on."

As it turned out, Joe did have to worry about being beaten.

Three times.

Merry Christmas, Lt. Col. Gallagher!

After the third game, we took a break and stepped away from the table, only to find ourselves surrounded by cadets.

We ended up playing doubles. And we beat every couple willing to challenge us.

"Just call us the King and Queen of Foos." Joe and I high-fived after the last game. Joe glanced at his watch. Looked around the room and out into the hall.

I realized the music had stopped. And so had the buzz of voices.

"The dances ends at midnight. We're about to turn into pumpkins." He spun a handle. "Let's go."

I didn't know what to say on the ride home, so I settled on asking him about Christmas.

"I'm going home. I mean, back to Idaho. My mom really gets into the holidays."

"And you'll have a sweater waiting for you."

"Probably."

"When do you leave?"

"In a week and half. Day after the cadets go on break. What are your plans?"

I shrugged. "Just the normal."

"Decorate a tree? Make eggnog? Go to church?"

"I'll probably go to church. Now that I have one."

"No tree?"

"You mean why don't I chop one down and kill it for my own pleasure? Americans chop down twenty-five million trees a year just so we can haul them inside and enjoy them for four weeks at our leisure." I hadn't decorated a tree since third grade, when the thought of cutting one down became too cruel to contemplate. Grandmother had been happy to agree. Less fuss.

Joe was giving me a strange look. "There is such a thing as an artificial tree."

"It's not like Christmas tree equals Christmas. A third of Americans don't even put up a tree. And think of people in Africa and South America. Where would they get a tree? Or ornaments? That doesn't mean they can't celebrate."

"So how do you celebrate?"

"By taking the thought of Christmas and extending it out through the year."

"And the thought of Christmas is?"

"John 3:16."

"For God so loved the world that—"

"Exactly."

"I didn't finish."

"You already said the most important part."

"No...that would be 'gave his only begotten Son.'"

"But he wouldn't have done that if he hadn't 'so loved the world' first."

Joe took his eyes from the road, turned his head, and looked at me.

"He loved the *world*. Not just the people in it, but the entire thing. The ground, the trees, the animals, the air...he created all of it. With the same care he created us. We're so egotistical that we put ourselves and our own conveniences first, ahead of all the other thousands of things God made. And the ironic thing is he put us in charge of all this. We were supposed to protect it. And keep it. And all we've done is ruin it. There's no way we'll be able to get around *that* on Judgment Day."

"Yeah, well, I think most people are more concerned about explaining why they lied to their mothers or cheated on their science tests. So the Bible according to Jackie is...?"

"God with us. Emmanuel. Jesus left the place where he was loved and everything he had and chose to spend the day with us in his perfect world that we had messed up. He saw beauty in things that were broken and people who were discarded. He redeemed us. And then he taught us how to reduce ourselves for others. Reuse the mess we had created to redeem each other. Recycle his words and share them with everybody."

"I can't decide whether you're weird or just plain different."

"I'm me."

He laughed. "That's the only thing I'm sure of." The SUV slowed as he downshifted and turned off onto the exit. "Reduce. Reuse. Recycle. Redeem. So what do you give for gifts?"

"I give trees."

"But you just said—"

"Trees and geese, although with avian flu I might give something else this year..."

"Well, do me a favor and leave me off the geese list, okay?"

"There's only Grandmother and me, and we have everything we need. So I give gifts to people who don't have *anything* they need. Did you know an acre and a half of rain forest disappear every second? And when trees vanish, then erosion and pollution show up. Sixty dollars to Heifer International buys a bunch of trees. I used to buy flocks of geese...you know, six geese a-laying..."

"I never thought of you as the sentimental type."

I scowled at him. "And FARMS International sponsors a pedal-powered van rickshaw project in Bangladesh."

"That sounds right up your alley."

"You asked, so I'm telling. It's a micro-loan project. All the loans have to be repaid and then recipients have to tithe. Which in turn helps support a church, which can then start reaching out into the community."

"So you give gifts to people you don't even know."

"I give gifts to people who need them." And every year I made one big gift. Last year, it had been a Gift Ark through Heifer International. It had cost five thousand dollars.

"Then maybe you could give a little my way."

"What do you really need that you don't already have?"

Joe fluttered his eyelashes at me.

"If you really want to do something for someone, go in with me on a women's development project."

"Which is?"

"Training women in livestock development. Most of those who live in poverty are women. They produce the majority of the third world's food, but they own less than one percent of the land. Does that sound fair?"

"So what are you doing? Agitating for revolution?"

"Soliciting for education."

"How much is it?"

"Ten thousand."

"Dollars?"

"Dollars." And I was almost there.

"You just plan to give away ten thousand dollars?"

"What use do I have for it?"

"Okay. I decided. You're weird. You must be the only person in the world who thinks that way."

When we reached Manitou, I decided to make things easy on him. "You can just go straight to your house. I can walk home from there."

"Not while I'm driving."

"It's only a couple blocks."

"And I only asked you to a dance. So only I get to decide where I drop you off. And I'm dropping you off at your house."

He did better than that. He parked the car and came around to my side to open the door. Took my hand and helped me out. Only he didn't let it go. He walked right up to the front door with me.

Thankfully, Grandmother had left the porch light on. It made it easier to find the key under the corner of the doormat.

Joe retrieved it and unlocked the door himself. Pushed it open. "Thanks for coming with me. Technically, we shouldn't have been there, but I had a great time."

"What do you mean we shouldn't have been there?"

"It was the *cadet* Christmas Ball."

"Then what was Todd doing there?"

"He's an AOC."

An Air Officer Commanding. He was in charge of a squadron of a hundred cadets.

"We shouldn't have been there?"

"It doesn't matter. Who knew? And we had fun."

The whole evening I'd felt out of place. As if I hadn't belonged. And

I'd just discovered how true that was. I hadn't.

"Well…" Joe leaned forward, his arms out.

I walked into them.

He gave me a hug and then he patted me on the back. "Thanks."

I smiled at him, walked inside, and shut the door.

But on the way upstairs, I felt like crying. And I didn't know why.

I found myself standing in front of Grandmother's room, so I pushed her door open. "When you're at a buffet and there are things to be picked up with toothpicks, do you use the same one for everything?"

She closed her book and took her glasses off. "You use a different one for each thing."

"What about dip? If there's a spoon, do you put dip on the vegetables or on your plate first?"

"Your plate."

"And cheese spread…?"

"Goes on the plate first."

"And when you go into the bathroom and girls are standing there smiling at themselves in the mirror?"

"They're checking to see if there's something stuck between their teeth."

"You knew? All those things? How come you never taught me?"

"I—"

"The world is full of rules and I don't know any of them. None of them. Not one. And Joe knows them all."

THE CUBICLE NEXT DOOR BLOG

Why?

What did I ever do to you?

Why do you think you can just crash into my world and drag me out into yours? Why do you think I'd even want to go? Who do you think you are? Why can't you just leave me alone? Why do I even care?

Posted on December 9 in **The Cubicle Next Door | Permalink**

Comments

Are you just being rhetorical? Because I don't know.

Posted by: **NozAll | December 9 at 11:58 PM**

You care because he's there.

Posted by: **philosophie | December 10 at 06:19 AM**

What did he do? What happened? I don't get it.

Posted by: **survivor | December 10 at 08:37 AM**

It could be anything. Maybe you make him laugh. Maybe you help him see the world in a different way. Maybe it's because you're pretty. Maybe he admires you because you're fearless. Maybe there's just something about you that sets his heart on fire.

Posted by: **theshrink | December 10 at 2:30 PM**

I still think it's because he wants something from you.

Posted by: **justluvmyjob | December 10 at 3:12 PM**

Twenty-Six

****

Most of the people who commented on the blog I'd posted on the ninth wanted to know what the big deal was. And I couldn't tell them. Because I didn't know.

But I did feel foolish. As though I had enjoyed something I had no right to. The ball. The dances. Joe.

I'd finally stumped NozAll. That had been worth it. And the-shrink's comment had made me laugh.

Fearless? Obviously he didn't know me at all.

The whole ball experience had made me self-conscious. Self-aware in the worst sort of paranoid way.

Joe must have sensed my mood because he didn't say much when we walked to church the next morning. And there was lots he could have said. Like, "My, your hair looks…different." It would probably look different for the rest of my life. No thanks to Adele. Whatever she'd done when she was trying to scalp me had created a hundred tiny knots on the top of my head and a permanent pouf. And when I'd tried to wash all the makeup off my face earlier in the morning, the soap had left my eyes red-rimmed and dry. I sat on my hands during the service so I wouldn't scratch my eyes out or tear my hair up by the roots.

We lingered for coffee after, chatting with some of the members… parishioners?…the nice people who filled up the pews.

On the way up the hill toward home, Joe asked me a question I had to stop and think about. "Want to go to the Christmas party with me?"

I did. And I didn't. "Are you asking me on a date?" Another one?

"I'm asking you on a carpool. There's not much point in driving separately. Especially out to Larkspur."

That was true. Larkspur was in the hills between Colorado Springs and Castle Rock, but it felt as though it was in the middle of nowhere. Especially in the winter. At night.

"Oh. Then sure. But I'm driving." And I'm not wearing makeup or letting anyone touch my hair ever again.

"Do you think that's wise?"

"I think it's better for the environment. I'll pick you up at five thirty." I'd signed up to bring an appetizer, so theoretically I needed to be on the early side of late.

"And...can I ask you a favor?"

"Just as long as it doesn't involve a felony, like going to a ball you're not invited to."

"Nope. Just driving me to the airport. In Denver."

"When?"

"The next morning. Sunday."

"Just as long as I'm—"

"You can drive."

The next Saturday evening we carpooled up to Larkspur. When we reached our destination, we weren't so early that we were able to park in the driveway. We settled for a precarious spot on the winding road that led up to the house. Joe carried a six-pack of beer in one hand and a duffel bag in the other. But they still didn't stop him from somehow managing to open the front door for me.

I plowed my way through the crowd. A couple people saw the cheese mold I was carrying and followed along behind me. When I arrived at the kitchen, the countertops, island, and table were already overflowing with food. I did a little tidying up, mixed baskets of various shaped pretzels, and emptied several plates by placing stuffed mushrooms, mini quiches, and wedges of summer sausage on the same platter. I collected used cups and threw them away against my better judgment. By the time I was finished, there was plenty of room for my small platter, but half the mold had already been eaten. I confiscated the box of crackers from someone and arranged what was left of them around the cheese.

In the process I spied a familiar toxic mix of homemade punch disguised in a gallon-sized milk container sporting a hand-drawn skull and cross bones. Stayed well enough away.

I grabbed a bottle of water, filched a few mushrooms, and went out into the living room. I sat down on the fireplace hearth and waited for the festivities to begin.

I didn't have to wait long.

Fifteen minutes of polite conversation later, Joe came stomping down the stairs. But it wasn't the Joe I'd come with. This Joe was a malign elf chomping on a cigar. Dressed in a green turtleneck and tights with a red tunic over the top. An elfin hat. Long pointed ears and curly-toed shoes completed the picture. He had slung a garbage bag over his shoulder.

Someone dragged a chair into the living room for him. He sat down and began calling names. Ms. West Point was first.

She tried to just stand there quietly beside him, but he yanked her down on his knee.

"That West Point's tough. I heard a story once about a cadet who was having a hard time staying awake. The instructor told him to stand up along the wall. So he did. He stood in front of a window, figuring the fresh air would help him stay awake. But he fell asleep anyway. And he fell right out the window. Woke up when he hit the ground. Got up, ran back to class. And you know what the instructor did? Gave him a Form 10 for leaving without permission."

Everyone roared.

Ms. West Point just smiled.

Joe Elf handed her a brand new package of Form 10s, wrapped in a cheery red bow.

He went through about half the department.

And then he called my name.

I got up. Went over. Wasn't about to sit on his lap.

But he smiled around the cigar at me and winked. And when he put a hand to my waist, I suddenly felt myself perched on his knee.

"A little bird told me you're very belligerent...er...*diligent* about your job. That you treat computers like treasured children and coworkers like common criminals. So here's a little something to help you keep the ruffians in line."

Ruffians. Only Joe would utter a word that had gone out of use a century ago.

He handed me a pair of brass knuckles.

Everybody laughed.

I didn't think it was very funny.

The next morning brought snow with it. And it had started sticking to the roads.

About ten minutes before I was supposed to pick Joe up, he knocked on our door.

"I thought I was supposed to pick you up at your house."

"You were. But I changed my mind. We're taking the SUV."

"That would involve me driving it back from the airport, and I don't do SUVs. I don't even normally sit in them. I'm making a big exception in your case."

"Then make it a gigantic exception."

"My car is fine."

"Your car is made out of a shoebox. I wouldn't be surprised if the engine was held together by rubber bands and clothespins."

Now that was not nice. And he must have known it.

"It's just that I don't want to be flying over Utah worried about whether or not you made it home alive. Okay?"

He wasn't really asking a question. In fact, he could have substituted the phrase "Got it?" because he was clearly not going to let me drive my car. Not that morning.

I grabbed my wallet and shoved it into my pocket. Felt the doormat with my foot before I shut the door to make sure the key was still there. It was.

Joe opened the SUV door for me and shut it after I got in.

I felt the SUV slide for a fraction of a second as we turned onto Manitou Avenue. Joe drove at 25 mph down to the interstate. And compared to other vehicles, he was going fast.

At the stoplight I glanced around, surveying the traffic. It wasn't too heavy. Hopefully it would remain as light until after I got home. I trusted my own driving in bad weather, but I wasn't so sure I trusted anyone else's. In looking over into the other lane, I saw a single duffel bag on the backseat. And that was it.

"Aren't you staying for the week?"

"Christmas through New Year's. There's lots of celebrating to do. Lots of nieces and nephews to play with." He saw me looking at the bag. "They teach you how to pack light in Boy Scouts. How to make one pair of underwear last four days. Things like that."

"By washing it in a stream?"

"By wearing it right side out, frontward and backward. Inside out, frontward and backward. Four days."

"With the added benefit of being able to scare away bears with your foul scent."

Cars had already begun to slide off the interstate. I saw Joe look at them as we passed by, and then he slid a look at me.

He had been right about the weather. "You were right. We needed the SUV. Are you happy now?"

"Ecstatic."

My car was not the most stalwart of vehicles. I have never pretended it was or wanted it to be. Because most of the time in Colorado when snow falls, it's gone by the next day. Sometimes by the same afternoon. So most of the time, I don't need a Driving Machine. The environmentalist's dilemma: Stay at home the two days in the year when the snow is really bad or waste gas for the remaining 363 days?

Easy choice.

North of town, at Monument, the shoulders of the road looked like a game of bumper cars. The altitude was just enough different, the wind had just enough bite, that the road turned into an ice rink under certain conditions. Like the ones we were having. Looked like the early birds had gotten more than they'd bargained for that morning.

Joe downshifted and steered around a three-car collision. "When you come back this way, try not to step on the gas or the brake unless you really need to. Just go slow. No quick movements."

"You might not believe this, but I've been driving in Colorado most of my life. If you tell me next how the roads become slippery right after it starts to rain, I'll have to throw something at you."

"It's really slippery out here."

"I know."

"Just warning you."

"I'll be fine."

"Maybe you could call me when you get home. I'll probably still be waiting at the gate."

"Right. I'll hurry home so I can do that."

"Don't hurry, but would you call? Please."

"I'll call."

He made me write his cell number down on a napkin I fished out of the glove box.

We finally made it to the airport and climbed out. He grabbed his duffel bag. I walked around to the driver's side, trying to avoid the biggest piles of slush.

"Thanks. See you next year." He lifted a hand as he walked backward toward the curb. "Merry Christmas."

"Wait."

He stopped.

I walked up to him, took a small paper bag from the pocket of my coat, and gave it to him. "Some cookies. For the flight."

His smile encompassed his whole face. "Thanks." He leaned down and kissed me on the cheek. "A pretty woman to see me off. Food to take with me. What could be better? You're not going to cry, are you?"

"No." Not on the outside.

"Well…I've got to…" He shrugged. "Have to go."

"Bye."

"Bye."

I watched him walk into the terminal.

He'd left the monster running, so all I had to do was get in and drive.

I made it out of the airport without sliding around too much and merged onto the interstate. It was slippery. More than I had realized.

But driving the SUV was kind of…nice. It was. It was nice to be so far off the ground. It was nice to be able to see around and over the tops of other cars while I was driving. It was nice to think of those thick tires biting into the snow, cutting through the slush. Nice to know that if I got in an accident, I'd probably come out of it just fine.

And I began to understand the right of all Americans to own an SUV, even when they don't need one.

I pointed the beast south and let it rumble down the road.

In the last decade, there had been an explosion of growth from South Denver toward Colorado Springs. Castle Rock, the midpoint, was a slash of tidy middle-class suburban sprawl. Rows of new developments were strung across the two sides of the interstate, their white frames gathered like a flock of seagulls against the lee side of the mesa.

When I got to Monument Hill I downshifted. Many vehicles in the Colorado Springs area sported bumper stickers saying "Ski Monument Hill." They weren't just being facetious. Monument is notorious. It's the most treacherous place between Colorado Springs and Denver in the winter.

I crept past the fake tree cellular tower near the County Line Road exit. Saw the chapel in the distance. From my vantage point, coming down the decline, the foothills looked likely to sweep the northern parts of the county up in their undercurrent and deposit them on the other side of the hills.

But as I drew parallel to the Academy, I could see the illusion. The movement was halted by a plateau, a brief pause in the march of land up to the Continental Divide.

By the time I reached Manitou, the sun had banished the snow-storm and driven the clouds into hiding. The snow had begun to melt off the streets.

I parked the monster in Joe's driveway. I'd walked halfway home before I realized I hadn't locked it. I never lock my own, but I figured I owed Joe's vehicle that courtesy. Went back.

I beeped the key chain at it.

Turned around and started home again.

I picked up my pace when I remembered I was supposed to call Joe to tell him I'd made it home okay.

THE CUBICLE NEXT DOOR BLOG

Gone

The department is a wasteland of empty chairs and abandoned desks. I feel like a forlorn, forgotten child. It's strange—I used to love this week every year. I could actually get things done. No meetings. No e-mails interrupting my work. And now I'm counting the days. Dropping paperclips into the mug on my desk one-by-one. Why has your absence made my week so bleak?

Posted on December 27 in **The Cubicle Next Door | Permalink**

Comments

If you're converting the Christmas holidays into a personal affront, you might suffer from abandonment issues. Rejection is an instinctive fear, one of the first we ever experience. But the biggest tragedy of abandonment is that the victim often copes by blaming and then abandoning themselves. Many victims of aban- donment go through life sabotaging all their close relationships.

Posted by: **NozAll | December 27 at 08:09 PM**

Don't pay any attention to him. I feel the same way about my officemate. Most of the time I want to kill him, but when he's gone...well...I guess I kind of miss him.

Posted by: **justluvmyjob | December 28 at 08:10 AM**

I hate to say it, but it might be true. Maybe absence really does make the heart grow fonder.

Posted by: **philosophie | December 28 at 08:12 AM**

Get over him. People come and go. In fact, mostly they just go.

Posted by: **survivor | December 28 at 11:41 AM**

Twenty-Seven

****

The ladies reverted to bridge that Wednesday night. They didn't need me as a substitute, but I lounged in the living room anyway, eating a slice of applesauce cake and sipping tea. That's when Adele had her great idea. "Let's go up to Cripple Creek!"

Cripple Creek. An old gold mining town in the mountains, southwest of Pikes Peak. Though the population of the district has shrunk by at least half in a little over a century, Cripple Creek still draws people up to where the air is rare. But these days, the sound of commerce is the ka-ching of slot machines instead of the chug and grind of mining gear.

Betty laid her cards carefully on the table, facedown. "I haven't been there in years."

"We deserve a break. And it's Christmas." Adele, herself, looked like Christmas. She was wearing a ruby-colored satin shirt and had an emerald green bow pinned to her hair.

"Who's going to drive?" That's Thelma. The straightest point from A to B. No use in talking about it if they couldn't do it.

They all turned toward me. I felt pinned to the couch by their expectations. "You can't all possibly fit into my car."

"I wasn't thinking of *your* car." Adele's eyes were twinkling.

"Whose? Thelma's? Betty's?"

"I was thinking of Joe's."

Which is how I came to be driving Grandmother and her three closest friends up to Cripple Creek at 6:00 Friday morning in Joe's

SUV. I took the day off work. There was no one around the department to even care. I tried to convince the ladies to stay overnight, but they wouldn't hear of it.

"And pack a suitcase?" Adele had frowned at the thought.

Thelma was frowning too. "I don't think I even own one anymore."

"I never sleep well if it's not in my own bed." Betty would know.

We wound our way up through the canyons between Manitou Springs and Divide, and emerged at Florissant. I pulled into the Fossil Beds National Monument and did a quick oxygen check. At altitudes like these, with women like those, you never knew what might happen.

"Everyone still breathing? Anyone feel faint? Speak now and I'll turn around. Otherwise, the next stop is Cripple Creek."

They all said they were fine, even though Adele looked a little blue in the lips. She swore it was her lipstick.

Half an hour later, we crested the hill that looked down into the town. Normally, Cripple Creek sat at the bottom of a well-scoured bowl. But today it almost looked pretty. The barren ground and the assorted rubble of abandoned mine shafts and homesteads had been covered by the grace of new-fallen snow.

The mining district is one gigantic object lesson about littering. Know what happened when the gold petered out? People left. Left behind all sorts of things. From houses to bicycles. From scaffold-like headframes and hoists to pails. Piles of rubble still marked the entrances to unprofitable mines—and there were five *hundred* mines at the height of the gold rush. Guess what? All that trash was still there. And at this altitude, it probably would be for another 200 years. The earth mends slowly, if ever. A gouge in the landscape at 10,000 feet will stay raw and ugly without urgent and regular care.

We parked at Womacks Casino because, well, it was paved. And it was free, as long as you played for a while inside. So we did. And then we wandered into the connected Legends Casino.

We paused for lunch at the Gold Rush Hotel and Casino and then gambled some more. I thought about an idea I'd been toying with all week—getting a gift for Joe.

I wasn't going to of course. Because that would be admitting I thought about him…cared about him…more than I was supposed to. Which brought up another thought. Maybe the time had come to put a stop to our relationship.

But that wasn't very practical, was it? We worked together.

So maybe it was time to just stop doing so much with him. Stop seeing him socially.

Maybe.

By 2:00, everyone's eyes were droopy. Even mine. No one had hit a jackpot or scored big at blackjack, but they all insisted they'd had fun. As much fun as they'd wanted. So we piled into Joe's SUV and drove home.

They slept all the way while I yawned.

I drove back to Denver on Sunday to pick Joe up.

He bounded up to the SUV when he saw it.

I got out and changed sides. Let him drive it home. Because I'd driven it enough.

He tossed his duffle bag in the back, put the SUV in gear, and pulled away from the terminal building.

I saw him scan the dashboard. Saw his eyes return to the odometer.

"You didn't *drive* the SUV while I was gone, did you?"

"Um…"

"Because I know you don't do SUVs."

"Well…"

"And you certainly wouldn't have driven it a hundred miles or so…?"

"I filled your tank up."

He just smiled.

I have to admit, I had missed those dimples.

On Monday, a paper plane sailed over the wall of the cubicle and landed on the floor behind my chair. I spun around to retrieve it.

Written on one of the wings was this question: *Have plans this Saturday? Besides work? Which I can get you out of…*

"Well…"

"Because I signed us up for something."

"How? I don't remember lending you my signature."

"Well, if you can find someone's signature, which I did…and you put a piece of paper, like an entry form on top of it, which I did…and you hold it up against a window…"

"The last time you signed me up for something, I ended up racing down Manitou Avenue in a coffin."

"And you had a lot of fun. Admit it."

"Maybe. Okay. I did."

"Very good, Jackie! Now, maybe you can say, 'Thank you, Joe.'"

"Thank you, Joe."

"Meet me at my place on Saturday."

This was it. A good time to act on my resolve. To tell Joe I wasn't going out with him anymore. I climbed up onto the desk, airplane in hand; but as soon as I saw him, my resolve crumbled as if I'd never had any to begin with. I threw it down at him. "At what time?"

"Make that Friday after work. You throw like a girl. We'll have to practice."

"I throw like a girl?"

"Yep."

"Is that supposed to be some kind of an insult? Because I *am* a girl."

"I know. But you don't have to throw like one. I'll teach you. Hey. Do you guys have any fruitcake?"

"Fruitcake? No. Oh no, no, no. You signed me up for the Great Fruitcake Toss, didn't you?"

"Did I?"

"Didn't you?"

"I did. Do you have any?"

"No." Grandmother and I didn't believe in fruitcake.

"Then we'll have to rent some."

On Friday evening I knocked on his door.

Joe answered it, wearing his ridiculous knit cap—with flaps—and holding a fruitcake. He looked cute. So cute I wanted to reach out and…hug him, kiss him, do something.

So I made myself stand there and do nothing. "I thought you were going to rent some."

"I was. But we have to practice. Might as well do it with the real thing." He shut the door and jogged down his front steps. Paused at the bottom. "Are you coming?"

"I'm leaving the wrapper on."

"Fine. Great. Here." He slapped the brick of fruitcake into my hand.

"Couldn't you find a lightweight version?"

"Hey, at least I didn't get the round kind with the hole in the middle. Let's see you throw it."

I tossed it.

Joe leaned over to pick it up. "I didn't say 'toss.' I said 'throw.'"

"It's a *toss,* Joe. The Great Fruitcake *Toss.*"

"You're not going to win any prizes by tossing. You've got to throw it. Like this." He leaned back and then launched it into the front lawn of the neighbors, two houses down. Then he had to jog over and get it. Jog back. "Put some oomph into it this time."

Our oomph-o-meters must have been calibrated differently, because my throw yielded only slightly better results than the toss had.

He walked two steps, picked it up and brought it back. "Okay. Don't push the fruitcake. Try to throw it. Launch it." He picked up my forearm with both hands. Shook it, causing my wrist to flap. "Don't be going all limp-wristed on me. Repeat after me: I am Woman! See me throw!"

"Repeat after me: Let go of my arm, or I'm going to hit you with it."

He dropped it. "Okay. Good. Just channel all that negative energy into the fruitcake. Ready. Throw."

Negative energy? All my energy that evening was positive. So positively focused on Joe that I was going to have to figure out how to moderate my feelings. And fast.

I threw it.

Basically, I pretended it was Joe's head and I flung it. Far, far away from me. It landed in the yard next door.

"I knew you could do it!"

It snowed that evening. Hard. But by morning the skies were clear, the drifts were sparkling. If tradition held, the sun would melt it and in two days the snow would be just a fond memory. Today, however, it was cold. And Converse low-tops do not a pair of boots make.

I pulled on a T-shirt and two sweaters. Who knew how long we'd be standing around Memorial Park, waiting to toss our fruitcake?

I looped the scarf around my neck for good measure. About five times. It was ten feet long. Pulled on mittens. Toggled my coat up over everything.

Joe showed up right on time. Figured. He probably couldn't wait to start throwing fruitcake.

He held a thin square box in one hand and a fruitcake in the other.

"Ready?"

"In a minute. This is for you." He held out the box. "Merry Christmas."

I took it from him, sat on the stairs, took off the lid, and lifted out the present. It was an oblong scarf, at least six feet long. It was wool, of the finest weight. And it hadn't been subjected to shrinking in any sort of dryer. It was striped in sage, burgundy, and midnight blue. The borders were decorated with a fantastical riot of paisleys.

It was the nicest thing I'd ever owned.

"I bought it at a vintage store when I was in Idaho. They said it was from India. Originally. And I thought...I mean...I know you like Indian movies...so, anyway..."

"Thank you. Very much." I unbuttoned my coat, unwound my own scarf from my neck, and draped it around the banister. "Guess you won't have to feel sorry for me anymore, wearing this scarf."

I went to the mirror in the hall and put Joe's scarf on. "Am I up to your standards now?"

"You were always up to my standards. It reminded me of you; I thought it was pretty."

It *was* pretty. And I felt like a chameleon, changing my spots. Because even though it had come from a vintage store, it was a better kind of vintage than I had ever bought. Draped around my neck, it made me feel like a kinder, gentler sort of Jackie.

This was a whole different experience than the Christmas Ball. Then, my finery had been borrowed. No one had pretended it was anything but temporary. And I had, admittedly, looked very nice. Quite nice. Stunning, in Joe's own words. I could be that way for one night. And it didn't matter, because I knew in the morning I would go back to being me. The real me.

This scarf was also real. But it was not me. Definitely not the me that I am. But it did represent a me that I could be. All the time, if I cared to.

And I did. As I was looking in the mirror, I wanted that reflection to be me. All the time. My traitorous soul was doing backflips that Joe had bought me a scarf and that he seemed to want me to look nice. And the worst part was I wanted to look nice for him.

Me.

Miss Shrunken Sweater Converse.

Me.

I was not supposed to care about things like this. I was not supposed to care about Joe.

But what could I do? I couldn't not wear it.

So I fastened my coat, shoved on my mittens, and walked with Joe down to the park.

It was strange, wearing something Joe had gotten me. It was intimate. Sort of like having him wrapped around my neck. We stood on the sidewalk, waiting for a gap in the traffic so we could cross the street. I caught a glimpse of myself in a storefront window. Caught myself liking the way the scarf looked.

We watched some preliminary events while we waited for the actual toss to begin. And all the while the scarf sat there wrapped around my neck, twisting itself into my thoughts. Warping them. Making me see myself differently. Making me think different things.

I didn't like it.

I was living inside a vortex. Everything was spinning out of control.

By the time my turn to toss came, I think I might have actually hated Joe. Hated him for being thoughtful. And kind. And including me in all his stupid schemes. I hated him for making me laugh. For making me scream. For making me blog. But most of all, I hated him for making me care what I looked like.

I took all that negative energy and channeled it into the fruitcake. In fact, I was the fruitcake. I became the fruitcake: A vile mix of ingredients nobody ever really wanted.

When it came time to toss, I hurled. I threw it so hard I won first prize. In the women's category.

"Fantastic! I knew you could do it!" Joe high-fived me. "You know why you won, right?"

"Because I threw it. With oomph."

"Nope. Because all the other women threw like girls."

Of course they did. Because they *were* girls.

And I didn't want to be. Couldn't be. Had no right to long for things I couldn't have.

THE CUBICLE NEXT DOOR BLOG

Me

All I ever wanted to be was me. It's the only thing I was ever good at. And then you came along. It's not as if you want me to be someone else. It's more like you want me to be...more of myself. Is that possible? It's as if you see more in me than I do. But, the thing is, when I'm with you, I do too. But I don't know if I want to. There are certain things I told myself I wasn't interested in being or doing. But since there's been you, I find I am.

Posted on January 6 in **The Cubicle Next Door | Permalink**

Comments

It sounds as if you need to make a decision. Decision-making theory is a fascinating field of study. Most people satisfice when they make decision—that is, they make a decision that is "good enough." One which will satisfy them. However, psychologists also realize that other factors come into play: conflict resolution and avoidance theory. Which brings me back to the theory of cognitive dissonance. Eventually you will have to resolve the contradictions of your perceptions of yourself.

Posted by: **NozAll | January 6 at 08:09 PM**

Will somebody stick a cork in him please?

Posted by: **justluvmyjob | January 7 at 07:03 AM**

Listen, if John Smith makes you unhappy, then he's not worth it.

Posted by: **survivor | January 7 at 08:45 AM**

All you ever wanted to be was you? Maybe that's the only thing he ever wanted you to be too.

Posted by: **theshrink | January 7 at 09:16 AM**

Don't you guys get it? John Smith is making her realize how unhappy she has been, not how unhappy she is right now. He makes her happy. Or at least he has the ability to.

Posted by: **philosophie | January 7 at 09:52 AM**

CLOSE

Twenty-Eight

****

The next week Joe was at it again. He caught me off guard as I was getting ready to go home.

"Let's go skiing."

"We already went skiing."

"Downhill."

"No."

"Come on. We tried cross-country. Now it's my turn."

"We're not taking turns. Don't you have any other friends?"

"No. Don't you?"

"Of course."

"Who?"

I started naming people from my online groups. "Byteboy. CybrGrl. MuthrBrd."

"ByteBoy? What kind of a mother would name her son ByteBoy? Is he an android or a person?"

"They're online names. From message boards."

"Have you ever met any of these people? In real life?"

"No."

"But they're your friends?"

"I talk to them every day."

"Have you ever thought you might be screwed up?"

"Have you ever thought you might be a pain in the butt? Listen, are you trying to make me feel sorry for you? Guilt me into going skiing?"

"Yes."

"It's not working."

"What if I started whining?"

"No. You've been monopolizing all my free time. At first, I was just trying to be nice to you. But now you're annoying. I have things I need to do."

"Like what?"

"Like…lots of things."

"List five and I'll leave you alone."

"I am not a cruise director. I'm not responsible for you having a good time. I don't even normally like having fun."

"So that means you *do* have fun when you're with me."

"It means you're on your own."

That worked for a couple of days. But then he was back, hounding me, harassing me, bullying me into skiing with him. It wouldn't have worked except I'd become addicted to him. My will was gone. Both my spirit and my flesh were weak. I began to flirt with the idea, even though I knew it could ruin my life. Forever.

And the next time he asked, I said yes.

"Great. We'll go on Monday since it's a holiday. I'm driving. I'll pick you up at seven."

I would have said something else to him, but all I saw was his back as he walked down the hall.

On Monday I woke to brilliant sunshine streaming through my windows. With any kind of luck, all the snow in the mountains would have melted. Maybe it would be too warm to ski.

I decided to call Joe. Just to check.

"Morning, Jackie."

"How did you know it was me?"

"Who else would be calling to try to weasel out of going skiing?"

"But have you looked outside yet? The sun is shining. The snow's probably melting. Who wants to ski in slush?"

He just laughed. "Seven o'clock. And remember to bring sunglasses." After saying that, he hung up on me.

I jumped into the shower and nearly scrubbed all my skin off.

I was that mad.

I didn't like the thought of downhill skiing. It just made it possible to fall faster down the side of a mountain. I didn't like the odds of downhill skiing. Falling faster just provided more opportunities to break a bone. I didn't even like the concept of downhill skiing. Being out in the snow sharing a private glimpse of nature with hundreds of other people I wouldn't know.

Except for Joe.

Was it worth it? Really, truly worth it?

Maybe.

And that thought just made me more mad. What was wrong with me? Over the past six months I'd done at least a dozen things I'd never done before. At least!

I pulled on layers of clothing. Filled a backpack with waterproof outer layers, gloves, a hat. And sunglasses.

I didn't usually wear them. I preferred to see the landscape around me in its natural colors. But for rare occasions like this one, I'd bought the biggest pair of sunglasses in the thrift store. Betty had seen them once and referred to them as "Jackie O's." Personally, I thought they looked more like a bug's eyes. The important thing was they protected both of mine and kept me from squinting.

Joe picked me up at 7:00. On the proverbial dot.

He got out of the SUV before he saw me coming out the door. He caught my backpack as I threw it at him and tossed in onto the backseat before shutting my door. Then he got into his own seat. Had the nerve to dimple at me. "You only have to try it once. If you hate it, you can stay in the lodge and I'll buy you as much tea as you want."

"Who says I should even try it at all? I'd never be doing this if it weren't for you."

"You can thank me later."

"You don't get it, do you?"

"Get what?"

"It! You're always making me do things I don't want to do."

"It's called having fun."

"I already know how to have fun."

"Oh? Then what would you be doing right now if you weren't here with me?"

I shrugged.

"Sleeping in? Helping your grandmother? Blogging?"

"Blogging?"

"I assume all you computer geeks have blogs."

"Oh. Yes. Blogs. They're the way we geeks coordinate our plans to take over the world. Except we write them in code with invisible text fonts so only those in the geekhood can read them. Better be careful… that's all I have to say."

Joe grinned. "Maybe I'll take you hostage. That way I'll have something to bargain with. I could be the….Geek Consort in the new world order."

"Ha-ha. So where are we actually going?"

"A-basin."

"As opposed to C- or D-basin?"

"Arapahoe Basin. One of the first ski areas in Colorado. Ask me why I picked it."

"Okay. Tell me, Joe, why did you pick Arapahoe Basin as the place we'll be skiing today?"

"Well, Jackie, I'm glad you asked! Arapahoe Basin sits right on the Continental Divide. It has the highest skiable terrain in North America with breathtaking mountain views. The management company has also undertaken a corporate commitment to care for the environment. They view the Basin as a priceless treasure and intend to preserve it, both environmentally and visually, for generations to come."

"And we'll really be able to tell what they think about the environment when we go into the cafeteria and see whether they serve coffee in Styrofoam cups, won't we?"

Joe shrugged and turned up the radio. It was a country music station.

Close to Loveland Pass, west of Denver, was an adopt-a-road sign. Arapahoe Basin had sponsored ten miles of roadway. Now anyone can adopt a road. But not everyone can manage to keep it clean.

A-Basin had.

Joe didn't say anything, but I could tell he'd noticed that I'd noticed.

Twenty minutes later, we finally arrived. I put on the rest of my layers and tucked my sunglasses into the pocket of my jacket.

We went to the ski rental shop near the lift where I got outfitted for a reasonable price. Outside, walking around, I couldn't get used to the boots. Or the idea that once I put on the skis, I would be connected to them at both my toe *and* my heel. It seemed like too much of a commitment. Especially in a sport which involved going down hills at high speeds.

"But if anything happens, if your foot starts to twist at a strange angle, then the binding releases and you're free."

"Can you guarantee that?"

"It's always worked for me."

Somehow, that didn't reassure me.

But Joe had been right about the breathtaking views. And I had been right about the sun. But it wasn't melting any snow. The wind was arctic. I fished the sunglasses out of my pocket and put them on.

"You're stylin'!"

"Don't make fun of me."

"I'm not. Look. Those are what everybody who's anybody is sporting."

What could I say? He was right. Slim chic women wearing coordinated outfits of powder blue and soft pink were wearing the same style of sunglasses I was. For once I was fashionable.

We stood in line for lift tickets. Joe graciously pointed out they reduced prices for carpools of four or more. He also decided I should be confined to the Molly Hogan beginner hill. I was sort of wishing I could be confined to the café.

Lift tickets purchased, we stood in line at the lift.

And I started reading the signs.

"Joe?"

"What?" He'd been squinting off into the distance, but he turned his head to look down at me.

"This sign says that under state law I'm not supposed to ride a lift until I can load, ride, and unload safely. That in case of emergency, the ski patrol will *evacuate* us. Was there some course I was supposed to take before riding this? Maybe I'd better just stay here."

"Hmm. Yeah. Maybe you're right. I'm sure you won't be able to stand up there and wait for the chair and then just sit down on it like those six-year-olds ahead of us. Wow. That requires tons of practice. They probably had to go to school to learn how to do that. Want to duck out?" He was holding his arm out toward the parking lot; his dimples were mocking me.

"No."

"Good! It's our turn."

He shuffled me into place so my back was facing the fast-approaching chair, and then he slipped an arm around my waist and began to speak quietly. "Here's what's going to happen. The chair is going to nudge you behind the knees and pause. At that point just sit down on it. Pretend it's your chair at work."

I thought about making a run for it, but then I realized I still had my skis on. And then I felt a pressure behind my knees and Joe was tugging me down onto the chair. And we sat there for half a second. I was just starting to relax when it jerked forward. Swayed.

My skis were still touching the ground. I still had time to bolt.

Joe grabbed my hand. "Good job. That wasn't so bad, was it?" He reached up and pulled a bar down over and in front of us.

By the time I was able to nod, my skis were no longer earth-bound.

I tried to do what he had said. Closed my eyes and imagined myself at work, but when I opened them, there was no desk in front of me. No computer screen. In fact, there was nothing at all but air. And we were sitting in a chair that was basically open to the ground below. There was nothing to stop me from standing up and jumping out but common sense. Nothing to stop me from falling should I suddenly go weak-boned and slide right out of my seat.

I dropped Joe's hand and pressed close to him.

"Scared?"

"No." Maybe. I was counting on him to just shove me off into the snow when we got to the end because I wasn't sure I'd be able to get off by myself.

I felt his arm come around me, pull me close, and then release me. "I won't let you fall off. Don't worry. Look at the scenery. It's gorgeous. Isn't this great?"

Great? I had other words for describing this special type of life-threatening insanity.

His shoulder was pushing my face out into the world. I opened one eye. The tops of the trees were at eye-level now. How high up did that mean we were?

There were skiers whizzing by beneath us. There were boys and girls playing follow-the-leader, skiing in giant S-curves down the slope. There were myriad sparkles dancing in the snow.

He took my hand and pushed the bar up with his other. "Ready?"

"For what?"

"To get off."

"Can't we just go around again? Get off down at the bottom?"

"No. On the count of three. One—two—"

At three, he pulled me off the chair with him and straight out into the snow ahead of us. Looking back, my chair rounded the corner of the lift and disappeared. I'd probably never see it again. "If I die up here, remind Grandmother I want to be cremated. There's no point in taking up space after I'm dead. Much less risk of communicable disease if there's no flesh left to rot."

"You can remind her yourself. This is the beginner's slope. No one has ever died here."

"Yet."

"Turn around so at least you'll be headed in the right direction."

I tramped my skis around in a circle so I was staring down the beginner's slope. "Are you sure they call this a slope? Because it looks pretty steep to me."

"Not down at the bottom. See how it tapers off?"

"Is that the reward for surviving?"

"Okay. There are some rules for downhill skiing. First of all, you generally move in the direction your skis are pointed."

"Got it."

"Whenever you're starting out onto a new slope, always look uphill and yield to others."

"Right."

"Never ski out of control."

"That might be a problem."

"Okay. Ready?"

"For what?"

"To ski."

"How?"

"You just push off and go. Gravity takes care of the rest."

That didn't sound very reliable.

"One—two—three—"

If I'd have known he would push me on "three," I might have just sat down in the snow right there at the top of the so-called slope. As it was, I screamed my head off all the way down the mountain. Mostly to warn people to get out of my way. I heard it ringing through the air, but the echo sounded suspiciously like Joe's laughter.

He plowed to a stop right beside me.

"That wasn't so bad, was it?"

"I didn't give you permission to push me."

"But you wouldn't have gone down on your own, would you?"

"I might have. And you didn't have to laugh."

"I'm sorry." He really wasn't. His dimples told me that. "I just couldn't believe you're a screamer. I'd never have guessed."

I stuck my poles into the ground. Looked around for the café.

"Let's go back up." He was already sliding away toward the chair-lift.

"Again?"

He stopped. "Think about it. You went down the mountain totally unprepared. There's no way you can't do better this time."

"What kind of warped logic is that?"

"The kind you use all the time. Come on, Jackie. The line's getting longer."

That time, I kept both of my eyes open all the way to the top of the slope.

By lunchtime, we'd made six runs. And I was starting to add a little swish to my skiing. On the fifth run, Joe had tried to show me the basics of using my edges and planting my poles to make "C-turns" so I could learn to do some "carving."

"I'm not a turkey."

"It's not like you're a never-ever. You're an expert at cross-country. It's just a matter of time before you'll be up on the black diamonds."

"A never-ever what?"

"It's not like you've never ever skied before."

"And black diamonds are?"

"The hardest, steepest runs."

"Oh. Well, I'll just tell you now I'll never be up on the black diamonds. In fact, that's *my* definition of a never-ever."

"We'll see."

"We'll see what? What is there to see?"

"From up there? At the top of the world? Everything. And it's a thrill you wouldn't believe to do something your eyes and your mind insist can't be done."

"And what if it can't be?"

"You just have to have faith in yourself. Confidence in your ability to survive...or you die in the attempt. That's my motto, you know."

"What? 'Die trying'?"

"No. 'Live recklessly. Die young. Have a good-looking corpse.'"

"Very noble, Joe."

He winked. "I know. That's me: A Noble Man." He tipped his chin up and turned so I could see his profile.

After lunch, we made three more runs and then I pleaded exhaustion. It was frigid, the wind was howling, and I was tired.

"If I get on the chairlift one more time, I won't be able to get off. I'm not kidding."

"Could you give me just a little more time? To ski Pallavicini?"

"Would you like extra cheese with that?"

"Seriously. It's one of the longest, steepest runs in the state."

"Go. I'll be fine."

"Thanks."

An hour later, we were returning my skis and boots.

We drove home, stopping in Castle Rock for dinner at a fast-food restaurant. Not my choice, of course, but I had been sleeping when we'd pulled into the parking lot.

I was still feeling dazed as I looked at the menu.

"Just order the super meal. You'll get fries and end up getting the drink for free."

"But I don't want fries and I don't need a four-liter drink."

"It's a better deal."

"Not if I won't eat it. Do you know how much food gets thrown away every day? And do you know how many people in the world would love to go dumpster-diving in America?"

"It's not like you can mail four extra fries to the Congo."

"But I'm making a deliberate choice about what I consume and I'm thinking about other people when I do it. What if everyone started to do that? I know it's unrealistic, but I can start making the world a better place if I start with me."

Joe just grunted. And he ordered a super meal anyway.

But at least he didn't order one for me.

And he didn't use a straw.

THE CUBICLE NEXT DOOR BLOG

The way I see it

Have you ever been 100 percent sure about something? Something that defined who you are? I have been. And today, I found out I wasn't the person I thought I was. It's embarrassing. Because if I'm not that person, then who am I? If I was so certain about a thing like that, a thing that turned out not to be true, then what other things have I been wrong about?

Posted on January 15 in **The Cubicle Next Door | Permalink**

Comments

Statistically speaking, 100 percent is an impossibility.

Posted by: **NozAll | January 15 at 08:19 PM**

Who you are is who you will be. Life is in the becoming.

Posted by: **philosophie | January 15 at 08:24 PM**

It's like you work hard your whole life to figure out who you are and then you realize that's not you at all.

Posted by: **justluvmyjob | January 15 at 08:28 PM**

Keep a narrow mind. Things seem to work out better that way.

Posted by: **survivor | January 15 at 08:33 PM**

If you're not that person, could you be Julia Roberts instead? There doesn't seem to be enough of her to go around.

Posted by: **theshrink | January 15 at 08:35 PM**

...oops. I meant an open mind.

Posted by: **survivor | January 15 at 08: 36 PM**

Twenty-Nine

****

Tuesday evening, as we were watching the news, Grandmother looked at her watch and then rose to her feet.

"Where are you going?"

"To get ready."

"For what?"

"I'm going out."

"At this time of night? By yourself?"

"I'm going out with Oliver."

"Where?"

"I don't know."

"Is this a date?"

She sighed and sat down next to me on the couch. "I suppose it is."

"But...then...why didn't everyone come over and help you get ready?"

"Good heavens. It's just a simple date. There's no need to create a big fuss."

"Whereas, there was with me?"

"Of course there was." She smiled. Kissed her palm and pressed it to my forehead. Left me to wonder why as she walked up the stairs.

About half an hour later, the doorbell rang.

I looked toward the stairs. No sign of Grandmother.

Clicking the TV off, I walked to the door, opened it, and let Oliver come in. "Why are you here?"

"To take your grandmother to see a movie."

"No. I mean why are you here? In Manitou."

"Because I want to be."

"Don't you have family somewhere?"

"I don't. Not anymore."

I waited to for him to say something that would make me feel sorry for him, but he didn't. "So you just...?"

"I travel. Ostensibly, to ski. I'm just an old gypsy whose wanderings have made him unsuited to life in England." He cleared his throat. "There's no snow there, you understand."

"And no mountains."

"Exactly."

"So what will you do in the spring?"

"Sorry?"

"When the snow melts?"

"Oh. Er..." His train of thought must have been interrupted by Grandmother coming down the stairs because he never answered.

"Right. You look lovely, Helen. Shall we go then?" He offered Grandmother his arm and they walked out the door without a backward glance, leaving me to wonder about the purpose of dating at the age of 85. By the age of 80, everyone was living past their life expectancy anyway, right? So what was the point? Grandmother was usually so practical. Logical.

I was still pondering the puzzle of Grandmother and Oliver at work the next day. I ran a statistical analysis on a hypothetical relationship between the two of them. Every way I ran it, the numbers were clear. Oliver should be dead. And if he weren't, he would be soon. There was one variable, however, that I had no way of computing. It was possible those who lived past their life expectancies had a different standard deviation in their expected life spans than those who did not. But there was no way of knowing for sure.

I graphed the expected lengths of the rest of their lives, just out of curiosity, and then graphed my own. Imagined what it would be like to be 85 and look back on my life. What things would I be proud of? The van-rickshaw project? No, not proud. Just glad I had helped.

I'd be proud of Antonio and Jorge, Nicolette and Adriana, Maria and Gloria, Carlos and Juan. But I would still be alone. I knew I couldn't trust myself to be with someone, but I wasn't happy with the alternative either.

"So this is where you've been hiding!" A feminine voice with hints of laughter startled me and made me look up from the computer. I turned toward the hall and saw a petite blonde in blues standing with a hand on her hip, grinning into Joe's cubicle.

"Kate!"

I watched as Joe came out of his cubicle, enveloped her in a hug, and then let her go. "You working here?"

"Yep."

"Since when?"

"Just this month. It took that long to sort out the craziness at the Personnel Center. Join Spouse assignments are never easy."

"How are the kids?"

"Fine. Doing great. How's Harry?"

"Not so good. Dead."

"Harry's dead? When? Why didn't you tell me?"

I saw Joe shrug.

"When did he die? How did it happen?"

"Last summer. Cancer."

"I'm sorry." She put a hand up to his arm. "I know he meant a lot to you."

Joe shrugged again. Crossed his arms. "So you're teaching where?"

"Pysch. Back in the department. Seems like old times. Almost."

"Steve here too?"

"No. He's at Pete Field, east of town."

"That's right. I'd forgotten he was a space guy."

"I was just passing through. I have to get back for office hours. E-mail me sometime. We'll have you over for dinner."

Joe smiled at her. "I'd like that."

She returned the smile and then turned to leave. It seemed to occur to her then that I had watched the whole encounter. "Hi. I'm sorry. I didn't mean to disturb you."

Joe now turned toward me too. "Kate, this is Jackie. We...work together."

"Hi." Her eyes swung toward Joe. Swung back toward me. "Work together, huh? Watch out for this guy."

I glanced at Joe. "I am well aware of his coffee-drinking habits. Believe me."

"Coffee-drinking? Well, that's a new term for it! Anyway," she turned away from me back toward Joe, "see you later."

By the time she had disappeared, Joe had vanished. I heard him typing. Heard him stop. The chair squeaked and I could imagine him leaning back for a stretch.

I started typing myself, labeling my charts, but I kept having to stop and delete misspelled words. I finally gave up and pushed my chair away from the computer. Decided to do something about the piles of cable on the floor. I seized the end of a narrow cable and started looping it around my hand. That done, I tethered it with a twisty and dropped it.

Pulled at the end of another one and looped it around my elbow and palm.

Secured it.

Who was Kate?

Dropped it to the floor.

A former coworker?

Chose another.

So it would appear.

Wound it.

But that didn't explain about her being back in her department and it seeming like old times.

Secured it.

Maybe she was in his class at the Academy.

Dropped it to the floor.

That would fit. But then, who was Harry and why would she know about him?

Chose another.

Maybe...had she been his girlfriend?

I stood there a full minute before I realized I hadn't done anything with the cable.

Maybe she had been his girlfriend.

A girlfriend. Why should that have been so surprising? A guy like Joe with a Super Smile. And dimples. Just because I'd never had a boyfriend didn't mean he'd never had a girlfriend. In fact, the more I thought about it, the more I realized I was probably right.

But the only way to know if I was right would be to ask Joe. So I did. But I wound the cable first and dropped it onto the pile I'd made. Then I kicked the other cables into the corner.

"Joe?"

He was typing. Didn't stop. "Hmm?"

"Who is Kate?"

"Kate?"

"Who was just here."

"Oh." He stopped typing. "She's my ex-wife."

Ex-wife.

Funny. No matter how many times I repeated those words to myself, I couldn't quite turn them into "girlfriend." Although, to be fair, I'm sure she once was his girlfriend. Ex-girlfriend. Because I assume in order to become a wife, you cease to be a girlfriend.

Wife?

Joe had been married?

"Did you...do you...have kids?"

"Kids? Yeah. We had Harry."

Harry? Harry had been their child? And Kate hadn't even known he had died? No wonder they'd gotten divorced! What a witch!

"He was our hairy child." Joe's voice came from above. He was standing on his desk.

"Harry child?" Something wasn't making sense, but I couldn't figure out what it was.

He must have seen my confusion. "Hairy. H-a-i-r-y. He was a dog." The faintest smile urged his lips upward.

"Oh. Well. I'm sorry."

"That's okay. He was old. Fifteen. We got him the first year we were married. That's ancient for a boxer."

"And you called him Hairy?"

"A joke. Like calling a bald guy Curly. You know."

"Oh. Yeah." But I didn't. Not really. I didn't know what to think about a Joe who had been married, who was still on speaking terms with his ex-wife, who had once owned a dog—a boxer—named Hairy. I didn't know what to think at all. "So will you go?"

"Where?"

"To dinner. At Kate's house."

"Probably. Maybe. She's a great cook."

"And her husband won't mind?"

"Why would he?"

"Wouldn't he think it's a little strange to have his wife invite her ex-husband over for dinner?"

"We were only married for two years. Kate and Steve have been married for...at least ten."

"And possession is nine-tenths of the law?"

He scowled down at me. "It isn't like that. Kate and I never should have gotten married in the first place. The wedding was during June Week, right after we graduated, and eighty percent of June Week weddings don't survive. Real life was nothing like the Academy. I was in pilot training at Williams near Phoenix. She was doing intelligence training at Goodfellow in Texas. We saw each other for about four weeks, total, during our first year of marriage. And we realized we got along better when we were apart. That we were better friends than we were lovers. And even then, we weren't great friends. We had shared an experience: The Academy. But we had never really shared our lives."

My cheeks flamed. I glanced down at my computer. Poised my hands above the keyboard.

"She and Steve are a perfect match. Why shouldn't she be happy? She's still a great person. Always has been." His head disappeared behind the cubicle wall. I heard the thump of him jumping from his desk.

Later that evening, I found myself staring at my blank blog screen, not knowing what to write.

My whole idea of Joe had been turned upside down. And inside out. He'd been married. He had an ex-wife. With whom he was still friends. He'd owned a dog.

There was nothing inherently wrong with any of those facts. The only problem I had with them is that they didn't fit the image of Joe I'd constructed in my head.

I already knew he was kind. I already knew he was gracious. I knew he was forgiving and loyal. I just didn't like to think someone else had benefited from his finer traits.

Someone else who had shared a part of his life I hadn't.

But that wasn't quite the entire truth. I had nothing against Todd and all of the other pilots who'd flown with him. Nothing against his academy roommates, for instance. Or against his high school friends.

But I had everything against a woman named Kate.

Why? Because I envied her.

I was jealous.

I could never remember being jealous before.

Seeing the world through green-colored glasses?

Sure. Especially when other kids had liverwurst sandwiches in their lunch boxes and I had beef tongue salad.

But turning into a green monster?

No.

I never thought I'd break one of the Ten Commandments. Not one of the major ones. But I found myself, that evening, coveting a neighbor's husband. Ex-husband.

And it was not a redemptive experience.

I hadn't realized before just how dangerous jealousy was. But as I thought about Kate, a person I didn't even know, jealousy began to grow and wrap green stalks of greed and anger and malice around my heart.

I didn't know her, but I hated her.

Without reason. Without provocation.

I hated her in the worst way. I hated her on principle.

She had everything I was discovering I wanted: Joe's respect, Joe's friendship, Joe's loyalty, Joe's life. That was the main thing. She had life in common with Joe.

I just had life beside him.

And it didn't look as if that would change.

The saddest, most tragic part about my feelings was that they were completely irrational. I didn't own Joe. Didn't even hold his heart.

And how could I blame him?

My heart wasn't worth holding.

I'd have to be some kind of a moron not to think the past hadn't left marks on my life. I'd like to think if my father had known about me, and if he hadn't have been killed, he would have come back for me. My father is my favorite parent. And I never even got to meet him.

My mother, on the other hand? What can you say about someone who abandons a baby?

Too much.

I've had so many thoughts on the topic, ranging from empathy to self-pity, that I decided several years ago to disassociate myself from her. It might not be healthy, but it's stopped me from picking my scabs. I was in danger of becoming an emotional self-mutilator. Like Robbie, the creepy guy I sat next to in second grade. People assumed we were friends. Not because we ever talked to each other, but because we didn't talk to anybody else.

Those scabs I picked just kept bleeding. Kept getting deeper. Besides, if you leave them alone for long enough, don't scabs eventually heal on their own?

I do have Grandmother. I take care of her and she takes care of me, in her own way. She was never touchy-feely, and I realized long ago that words are not the only way to say "I love you." But that's never stopped me from dreaming and wishing for a pair of arms that belonged just to me. And for a voice that would, as many times as I wanted to hear it, say, *I love you, Jackie.*

Which doesn't mean I'm emotionally impaired. I'm still functional.

There's just always been this question for which I'll never have an answer: What if my mother had stayed around long enough to get to know me? Would she still have left? I know it has everything to do with her and nothing to do with me, but I have always been afraid the answer would have been yes.

Any sane person might wonder whether I even acknowledged the parallels between my life and my mother's. She, having been the epitome of all things liberal. Me, being the epitome of all things environmental. Which people assumed meant liberal, even though it didn't.

She, falling in love with an Air Force officer who instructed at the Air Force Academy. Me, having feelings for an Air Force officer who instructed at the Air Force Academy.

I used to despise her because she didn't "just say no." But now I know better. I understand now that she couldn't. Not if my father were anything like Joe. Not if he refused to leave her alone. Kept enticing her, entangling her, throwing up a giant detour sign that kept all her thoughts turning in his direction.

Acknowledge the parallels?

Of course I did.

I felt as if I were being drawn into her past. Felt her presence wrapping its fingers around my neck. As if she were trying to pull me back in order to gain a second chance at her own life.

I felt as if I were a hiker, scrambling for a foothold on a steep slope filled with scree. No matter how hard I tried to progress up and out, with every step I was drawn back, doomed to have to recover territory I thought I'd already gained. With every step, I hoped for a progression, but instead was rewarded with regression. To remain still was to be trapped forever on a barren slope. But to take a step, to try to leave, was to risk a slide.

What if it wasn't her?

What if it was me?

What if I was just like her?

You're supposed to learn about history to stop it from repeating itself. But I don't know the first thing about her. Don't know. Don't want to know.

I'm exactly the sort of person I always make fun of.

But it's not really that funny, is it?

THE CUBICLE NEXT DOOR BLOG

A plea

Help me.

Posted on January 17 in **The Cubicle Next Door | Permalink**

Comments

A two-word entry? This is weird. Do you think she's all right?

Posted by: **survivor | January 17 at 08:23 PM**

I don't know. TCND, if you're there, can you let us know if you're okay?

Posted by: **philosophie | January 17 at 08:24 PM**

Where is NozAll when we need him?

Posted by: **justluvmyjob | January 17 at 08:25 PM**

What do you want me to do? I'm only 15 years old!

Posted by: **NozAll | January 17 at 08:26 PM**

Maybe she got called away from the computer before she could finish?

Posted by: **theshrink | January 17 at 08:27 PM**

I heard about this guy once in China who was chatting with someone online when he started to have a heart attack or something. The other guy ended up calling all the way to China to get an ambulance for him.

Posted by: **thatsmrtoyou | January 17 at 08:28 PM**

I doubt she's having a heart attack "or something." Wild speculation doesn't help. It will only cause panic. Everybody just stay calm.

Posted by: **theshrink | January 17 at 08:29 PM**

How do you know? Does anyone know who she is? Do you think the blogging company does?

Posted by: **justluvmyjob | January 17 at 08:30 PM**

Thirty

******

I didn't post a blog for the next three days. An eternity for someone who normally posts daily.

Joe talked to me about the blog, just the way he talked to me about every blog entry.

"So what do you think she needs help with?"

"Who knows. Printer problems? Laundry? Opening a new jar of jam?"

"Think there's something wrong?"

"With her?" With me? Definitely.

"Who else?"

"Maybe there's something wrong with John Smith. Maybe he just won't leave her alone."

"Why would there be anything wrong with that? She obviously likes him."

"Obviously."

"So why should he leave her alone? That seems counterintuitive."

"Maybe love just isn't something she's prepared to do."

"You don't prepare for love. It's not brain surgery. That's why they call it 'falling.' Falling in love."

"Maybe she has osteoporosis. Maybe a fall isn't just a fall. Break a hip and you end up spending the rest of your life in a nursing home regretting it."

"I don't get it."

"I was speaking symbolically."

"I know. But she's not eighty-seven years old and I don't understand the symbols."

"I practically failed English in high school."

"So explain it to me using computers or math or something."

"Okay...maybe it's the difference between multiplying something by three and cubing it."

"Still not getting it."

"What's twenty times three?"

"Sixty."

"Now what's twenty cubed?"

"Twenty times twenty times twenty."

"Exactly."

"You're killing me here."

"It's eight thousand."

"Yeah? So?"

"Sixty is manageable. Eight thousand is totally out of control. Get it?"

"No."

Of course he didn't. That was the whole entire problem. He didn't get it. And I couldn't think of any way to be more plain.

Except, of course, to tell the truth.

But I was not prepared to do that.

"Jackie?"

"What?"

"Help me out."

Help him out? I was the one who needed help.

Joe's head appeared above the cubicle wall. He looked frustrated. "She likes him, but half the time it sounds like she hates him. Why?"

"I don't know. Maybe she doesn't know. Why do you care?"

"Because I don't get it. And she has to know. She's stopping herself from doing something she wants to do. She's holding herself back from him. There must be a reason."

"Maybe she's in control of her life right now and she's afraid if she lets herself like him, she won't be anymore."

"She's afraid of being out of control?"

"Maybe."

"She's *afraid?* But he seems like a nice guy. A normal guy. People fall in love all the time. It doesn't have to be the end of the world."

"But maybe it is. Love doesn't make everyone's world go around. Maybe love destroyed hers once."

"Love that destroys isn't love. It can't be."

Maybe not for him. But it had been for me.

Two days later, I was watching the evening news. Mostly to see what the weather was going to be the next day. The lite-news lady came on for her five-minute stint. She started with coverage of a county commission meeting. Then the camera panned away from her and zoomed in on a TV screen behind her shoulder.

"And now we go to Trevor Montero in San Francisco for an update on the status of the Cyber-Sweetheart Blogger. What's the latest information, Trevor?"

"Good evening. The latest information is that, as of yet, we have no information. For viewers who have just tuned in, America's Cyber-Sweetheart, known to the blogosphere as TCND, the initials of her blog, The Cubicle Next Door, posted an ominous two-word blog three nights ago. Those two words were 'Help me.' And there have been no posts from her since."

The camera angle slowly widened to take in the building behind him.

"Blog readers, who feared perhaps TCND was having a heart attack or some other medical emergency, immediately flooded the blogging service with e-mails, urging them to send medical care to TCND's address of record. The blogging company has continually stated that, although the cyber address of TCND is a matter of public record, the physical street address of the blogger is not. This evening, they are again stating they have no responsibility in this matter and they have no authorization to send someone to TCND's address nor to release that information."

Trevor turned toward the building that had been his backdrop and the camera zoomed past him to focus on a podium that had been set up on the front steps. A woman was speaking.

"As we have consistently stated since the events of January

seventeenth, we have no corporate responsibility in this matter. Access to personal information is on a need-to-know basis and only for the purpose of operating or improving our product. Any employee or contractor who comes into contact with such information is bound by confidentiality agreements and subject to prosecution if they do not choose to abide by them. Are there any questions?"

"Do you maintain the home address information of your clients?"

"As a matter of course, we do not."

"But is there not some way you could back door the information? From e-mail addresses or credit card billing information? Something?"

Of course they could, if they wanted to.

"That is not within the purview of our company's mission."

"But what if TCND is lying on the floor of her home having a heart attack?"

Then I'd already be dead, wouldn't I?

"To post a blog entry takes several steps. If TCND were having a medical emergency, it is highly unlikely she could have performed the steps in the correct sequence necessary to post a blog."

The camera zoomed out and panned the crowd. It was filled with a diverse demographic of people. Some of them were carrying signs. One was shaped like a heart and had "TCND + John Smith" scrawled on it. Another said "SAVE TCND!" And right next to it was one which said "SAVE OUR PRIVACY!"

The screen's view switched to Trevor and then split to reveal the local newscaster. "Why has there been such keen national interest over an anonymous blog, Trevor?"

"It's because this blog has pulled the heartstrings of America, Becky. This blogger, because she is anonymous, could be the girl working in the cubicle right next door to me. Her very anonymity has given credence to the all-American myth of the girl next door. It's not the fantasy of falling in love with a model or a movie star, because most of us don't work next to people like that. It's the fantasy of falling in love with a woman you admire but are too afraid to tell. The fantasy of hoping against hope that this woman actually admires you too."

"So you're saying it could be anyone?"

"It could be anyone."

It could be me.

I ran up the stairs and logged on to my computer. Logged onto the blogging site. Brought up a new post. Stared at it, not quite knowing what to type. In the end, I settled for this.

"I'm okay."

I was about to post it when I thought about all those people who had called the blogging company. All those people who had tried to save my life. And I decided they deserved something more. Something as close to the truth as I could tell them.

THE CUBICLE NEXT DOOR BLOG

I'm okay

I'm okay. I was just overcome—overwhelmed—with information about John Smith I never expected or anticipated. And it uncovered information about me I hadn't known before...almost wish I didn't know now.

I'm not used to feeling. I didn't think I had any right to feel. I would almost rather have a root canal than feel this way. But it doesn't matter what I tell my head. I can't control the things I dream in my sleep. Is it even possible that you dream of me too?

Posted on January 20 in **The Cubicle Next Door | Permalink**

Comments

You really scared me. Actually root canals don't have to be painful. They only fail about five percent of the time.
Posted by: **NozAll | January 20 at 06:23 PM**

You're missing the point. She's saying that the things she's thinking are excruciating. That she'd rather inflict bodily pain on herself than subject herself to emotional pain. TCND, I'm just glad you're okay.
Posted by: **philosophie | January 20 at 06:25 PM**

I had to redo every project I did over the last few days. I wasn't concentrating. Anyway, I can never remember my dreams.
Posted by: **justluvmyjob | January 20 at 06:26 PM**

There are a lot of people here who care about you. Hope you have the same support in your real life. Maybe he is dreaming of you. You should ask him. But if he starts telling you he's having that dream where he walks into a bunch of talking spiders and gets caught in their web and then they bite him and he takes a pair of scissors and cuts all their legs off...run away. Fast!
Posted by: **theshrink | January 20 at 06:30 PM**

You're a survivor too. It takes one to know one. (Hey, shrink—I have that dream all the time!)
Posted by: **survivor | January 20 at 06:37 PM**

Thirty-One

****

Hmm."

For Joe to talk to himself while he worked was not unusual, but there was something in the way he said "Hmm" that sounded dire. I waited for nearly five minutes before I asked. "Care to share?"

"Kumbaya and that sort of thing?" He began humming "It only takes a spark…"

I rolled my eyes and returned my attention to the keyboard.

"New e-mail. The department's looking for someone to deploy."

My hands froze. "When?"

"Next month."

"Where?"

"Iraq. Think they'll send me?"

"Why?"

"Jimmy's getting married next month. Pete's wife is having a baby."

"What's getting married and having babies got to do with deployment?"

"I'm single."

"You know, you ought to talk to them about marital status discrimination. It's not fair to make you go just because you're unattached! There's got to be something in the…" In the what? Employment contract? Labor laws? Joe was military. They could make him do whatever they wanted. "There's got to be something. You just got here."

"In June. Technically, they can deploy me anywhere they want, whenever they want."

"But everyone else has been here longer. One of them should have to go."

"Yep. That's what I'll say to Colonel Webster. It's not fair, sir. I haven't been here long enough yet."

"You *want* to go?" What was the tone I was hearing in my voice? Desperation?

"Join the military, see the world. What's not to like in Iraq? I could be the hero in my own movie. People shooting at me. Taking a bullet. Sounds exciting, doesn't it?"

I could imagine it all. Vividly. I'd been doing it for years. Every time I thought of my father.

"Oh—wait."

"What?'

"Hmm."

"What!"

"They only want pilots."

"And?"

"I'm not."

"What do you mean you're not?"

"I used to be, but I'm not anymore. Remember those headaches?"

I didn't know whether to throttle him or whether to hug him.

"Let's grab lunch."

"I already have mine. It's in the refrigerator."

"Is there enough for me?"

"No."

"Then we have to go out. Because I didn't bring any lunch and it would be rude for you to eat in front of me when I don't have any food."

"You could just stay on your side of the cubicle and you'd never know."

"Except that when you heat up the stuff you bring in, it always smells really good and it makes me really hungry."

"If you'd bring something in to work besides a bag of Doritos, then maybe you wouldn't be starving all the time."

"Come on." He had appeared at the end of the cubicle. Grabbed my hand from the keyboard and started tugging. "Come on, come on.

You know you want to."

And that was just the problem. I did.

I wound Joe's scarf around my neck. Pulled my coat on and fastened it up.

We decided to go to Arnold Hall. Joe was in the mood for Taco Bell. And Subway had salads.

It was a T day, so we were able to leave ahead of the crowd, before the cadets broke for lunch and left the instructors free for an hour. But Joe still saluted his way across the terrazzo.

"Did you see that punk's boots? They weren't even shined. They don't do any of the good stuff anymore. No more Smoker's Nights, no more SERE."

"What's that?"

"Survival, Evasion, Resistance, and Escape training. SERE."

"How would they teach you that?"

"Take you out to Jack's Valley and up into Mueller State Park, make you run around in the woods until you're caught and then simulate a POW Camp."

"By torturing you?"

"No. Just basic stuff. Sleep deprivation. Interrogation. Sensory deprivation."

"And how did you resist?"

"All sorts of ways."

"Was there a point to all of that?"

"Yeah. It made you understand how you react to pressure. You find out if you're one of those guys who'll blab at the first opportunity or whether you start to hallucinate when you're deprived of sleep or placed in solitary confinement. There were guys who started seeing bugs all over the place."

"And you were one of the guys who…?"

"I was an instigator. I kept the guards busy with stupid stuff so the escape could be planned."

"So basically, you were just annoying."

"Extremely so."

"And you probably consider that a positive trait."

"It's a life skill."

"You don't take anything seriously, do you?"

"And you take everything seriously, don't you?"

"No, I don't."

"Yes, you do, Miss Let-me-just-take-that-straw-and-plunge-it-into-your-heart."

I shoved my hands into my pockets and just kept walking.

"Okay. Sorry. But don't you think you take things…some things…just a little too much to heart?"

I stopped walking and turned toward him. "Well, if people like me don't, then people like you won't have any gas left to drive your monster SUVs around town!"

Joe held out his arms in a "see what I mean?" gesture.

I opened my mouth to respond, but nothing came out.

"Okay. Cease-fire. Different topic." He began walking again. "Let's be nice to each other for a few minutes."

I felt ashamed of myself. Decided to try. "Are you doing better? With instructing?"

"Yeah. I actually like it." He laughed. "Who would have thought it, right? I wonder what my pilot buddies would think about that."

"Who cares what *they* think. The important thing is what you think."

He sent me a look I couldn't interpret.

"What?"

"You have no idea how…fearless you are, do you?"

"I'm not fearless."

"Yes, you are. You don't care what anyone else thinks. You just go right ahead, doing what you want to do, being yourself."

I shrugged. Who else could I be?

"Hey. I was thinking about that blog. You know, John Smith seems to have a lot in common with me."

I had to run a few steps to catch up with him. "He does, doesn't he?"

He looked straight into my eyes. "Don't you think that's kind of strange?"

I looked straight back into his. "Not really. I've always suspected Estelle has a crush on you. I just didn't want to say anything."

He laughed. Quieted. "Seriously, though, don't you think it's strange he drives an SUV and makes her do things she doesn't want to do and...everything else?"

"He who?"

"John Smith."

"Not really. Half the population of the country drives an SUV."

"Around here they do."

"What are the chances it's about you? What do you do? Read that blog trying to find all the ways it could be about you? Because it's not." Half the time, it was about me. We were two halves of a confused morass of a blog.

We got to Arnold Hall, ordered our food, and took it out into the dining area.

"So how do you think she'd feel if John Smith happened to have an ex?"

"You're still thinking it's about you?"

"What if it were? Humor me."

I shrugged.

"Do you think it would bother her?"

I shrugged again. I was trying to buy time.

"Well, what would *you* think?"

What would I think? In some ways, that was safer than talking about what TCND would think. "I would think that you can't always have what you want in life. If it were me, it wouldn't make any difference. I'd feel the way I'd always felt: that some things in life just weren't meant for me."

"What do you mean? You wouldn't marry someone who's been divorced?"

"I wouldn't—won't—marry anyone at all. Ever."

"Why not?"

"I can't."

"Because...?"

"Because I just can't."

"So you don't have a problem with divorce, but you do have a problem with marriage? That's unusual. But then, why should I be surprised!"

"Look, my parents never got married."

"It's not uncommon."

"They met each other and it was cataclysmic. And afterward, my mother went crazy."

"I'm sorry...but I still don't understand what this has to do with you."

"Don't you get it? I'm her daughter. I will never do what she did to me. I will not do it."

"Who's to say you would?"

"Who's to say I wouldn't? I'd rather stay on the safe side of things."

"Safe side. You seem to want that to be the theme of your life. But I don't think it can be. I think you have a wild thing hiding inside."

"Exactly. That's exactly it. I think so too. And I'm not going to let it out."

THE CUBICLE NEXT DOOR BLOG

The lie

I told you a lie today.

It's not the first lie I've ever told you, but it's the first one I've done with the intention of deceiving you. (Instead of myself.) I wish, I wish, I wish I could tell you the truth. But saying a thing three times doesn't always make it true. And if I told you the truth, then you would know me. And I might not be the me you thought I was.

Dream girls are always perfect.

Dream girls are always pretty.

Dream girls don't pick their noses or wear holey underwear or drool in their sleep.

So dream of me tonight the way I wish I was.
Posted on January 26 in **The Cubicle Next Door | Permalink**

Comments

During the day we swallow our saliva, but during the night, the swallowing reflex becomes muted and drool collects in your mouth. Try sleeping on your back. Or try breathing through your nose instead of your mouth, unless you have a deviated septum. Drooling only creates problems if it becomes excessive. In that case, it's called sialorrhea and you may need treatment.
Posted by: **NozAll | January 26 at 09:15 PM**

Only in dreaming can you alter your reality.
Posted by: **philosophie | January 26 at 09:22 PM**

You can pick your nose and you can pick your friends, but you can't pick your friend's nose.
Posted by: **theshrink | January 26 at 10:08 PM**

Don't worry about it. I lie all the time.
Posted by: **justluvmyjob | January 26 at 10:41 PM**

Not me. I can't stand the guilt.
Posted by: **survivor | January 26 at 10:59 PM**

CLOSE

Thirty-Two

****

February began with a bang. And an ominous thump.

Grandmother had gotten up in the night and fallen down the stairs.

By the time I reached her, she was lying in the entry hall beneath the bottom step. Her eyes were closed and I couldn't get her to open them. Couldn't get her to say anything. Couldn't get her to respond at all.

I called 9-1-1.

And then I called Joe.

He arrived first and insisted we didn't move her. He got a blanket from the hall closet and spread it across her.

I knelt down beside her and reached a hand out to grasp hers.

"Don't."

I looked up at him.

"Her arm or...something else...could be broken. Don't touch her. Just in case."

I sat on the floor beside her.

We heard a siren in the distance. Heard it get loud and louder and then cut off mid-wail as footsteps came thudding up the walk.

Joe opened the door.

They placed an oxygen mask over Grandmother's mouth and nose. Brought in a backboard. Placed a collar around her neck. Took her out to the ambulance.

I climbed in beside her. One of the paramedics started to shut the door. "But, Joe—"

He poked his head in just before the door shut. "I'll meet you there."

The ambulance moved from the curb, siren screaming, carrying us off into the night.

At the hospital they took Grandmother from the ambulance and wheeled her inside. It took me a minute to jump out, and by that time she had disappeared. I went in through the doors marked EMER-GENCY and wandered through a maze of halls. Returned to where I'd started and walked in the other direction. Came to a waiting room. Everyone looked away from the nurse at the counter and stared at me with blank eyes. I stood in front of the counter, waiting for the nurse on duty to acknowledge me.

But the phone kept ringing and she kept on answering it. She kept one finger held up in the air, asking me to hang on for just a minute. But "just a minute" soon turned into five.

Finally, she set down the phone.

"Excuse me. I just wanted to know—"

It rang again.

"Can you wait just one minute?" The nurse picked up the phone before I could respond.

No. I really couldn't. Because by that point, I'd been at the hospital for more than ten minutes. And somewhere back there was Grand-mother. So I left the counter and walked through the doors I'd come in, determined to wander the halls until I found someone who could show me where to go.

But that was easier imagined than accomplished.

One long hall led into another and another. And although there were many doors that lined the halls, all of them were closed. And, I soon discovered, locked. I never came across another living soul. Although I had the idea somewhere in the bowels of the building were lots of dead ones.

For all I knew, Grandmother could be among them.

At the intersection of hallways, signs pointed to places like oncology, gynecology, and radiology. All of them places I didn't want to visit. Eventually, I walked out into a vast lobby. Deserted at that hour, in the morning the coffee cart would probably open and maybe a person would staff the window marked INFORMATION. But at 2:30 it was empty.

I put my face up to the glass window, turned it sideways, pressing my cheek against the glass, longing for a glimpse of a map. Finally I just gave up. I considered returning to the waiting room, but as I thought about my long sinuous journey to the lobby, I realized I didn't know anymore where I'd come from.

So I took the only course of action I could.

I went out the lobby doors, into the frigid night, and walked around the outside of the hospital until I came, once more, to the door marked EMERGENCY.

My plan was to take the phone from the nurse and strangle her with the cord until she told me where Grandmother was. But fate intervened. An ambulance was still parked out in front. Several paramedics were hanging out by the door. They were *my* paramedics. Grandmother's.

"Excuse me."

They stopped talking and looked toward me.

"Do you know where they've taken my grandmother?"

"Yeah, sure." One of them held the door open. "I'll show you."

He directed me to a sitting room. And seated there, side by side, were Joe and Oliver.

Joe stood as I approached.

So did Oliver.

"Where were you?" It was a relief to see Joe. I hadn't realized before that moment that I had been counting on his presence.

"Where were *you*?"

"Trying to find Grandmother."

"I assumed you were in there." He tipped his head in the direction of a door. "With her."

"She's in there?" I went to the door, tried to peer in the high window. I wasn't tall enough. I tried to push it open, but Joe stopped me.

He took me by the hand and led me to a chair. "When they're done, they'll come out."

"Did they tell you that? Do you know for sure she's still in there?"

"Yes."

"How?"

"They told me."

"But...but how did you get here?"

"The nurse in the waiting room brought me here."

"*Brought* you here? She wouldn't even hang up her phone for me. Grandmother could be dying for all I know and I couldn't even find her! Or you! I needed you! Where *were* you?"

"I was getting clothes for you." He took a bag from a chair and held it out to me. "And shoes."

I took the bag from him and sat down. As he and Oliver watched, I pulled a sweater on over my T-shirt. And a pair of Converse on over my socks. At least I slept in my socks. If that hadn't been my habit, I probably would have walked out of the house in my bare feet. Joe had also brought me a pair of jeans, but I wasn't about to pull them on over my pajama bottoms.

Now that I had clothes on, I began to shiver.

Shudder.

Heard my teeth actually bang together. Nonstop. Like a possessed keyboard.

I rubbed my hands up and down my thighs, trying to ignite some warmth. It didn't seem to help, so I folded my arms around my abdomen. Rocked back and forth, trying to disguise my shivers.

"Jackie?"

"Hmm." I didn't trust myself to speak, sure if I opened my mouth, my teeth would click themselves right out of my head.

"It will be okay."

"Mm-hmm." I agreed with him. It would be. Because it had to be. Grandmother had to be okay. And when I took her home from the hospital, we were going to sell her house and buy a new one. A one-story ranch. And I was going to convince her to sell the store. Making her walk down the hill into town every day was just begging her to twist an ankle or fall and break another hip. If she hadn't done that already. Why hadn't I realized how old she was getting?

The door suddenly swung open. A man in scrubs was standing there.

I tried to unfold myself and get to my feet, but they didn't seem to be working. And neither did my ears. I collapsed into my chair. I could see Joe's lips moving, but I couldn't hear what he was saying.

I saw his arm move out from his body. Felt it attach itself to the back of my neck. It was warm, and its steady pressure guided my head down toward my knees.

I let it float there for a while. I didn't have any strength to resist.

Joe's hand moved from my neck to my back. Started making furrows in my sweatshirt which reached right down into my skin. And I began to comprehend the conversation he was having with the doctor.

"So we can see her?"

I sat upright and Joe's hand fell from my back.

"In just a few minutes. Let us get her situated in the room first. I'll send someone out for you."

I stood up, ready to follow the man, but Joe pulled me down into the seat.

"In a few minutes."

And then another voice joined the conversation. "Terribly lucky, she was."

Joe grunted.

I leaned forward to see around him. And my eyes came to rest on Oliver.

"Why is *he* here?"

That question brought flames to Oliver's cheeks.

"Because I called him."

"But everything's fine."

"Of course it is. But I knew Oliver would want to be here."

"She's fine. It's okay." I wasn't talking to Joe anymore. I was talking directly to Oliver.

He nodded.

"*This* is why I came back from Boston. She's too old. She can't be trusted to take care of herself."

At that moment, a nurse appeared. She led me to Grandmother's room.

When I got there, I saw Grandmother lying in bed. Her eyes were open and her left arm had been wrapped in a sling. She held her other hand out toward me.

I grasped it.

"Don't worry. It's just my shoulder. I'm sorry. I was thirsty. I just wanted something to drink."

"Then why didn't you go into the bathroom?"

"Because I wanted some tea."

"Then you should have woken me up. I would have gotten it for you."

She patted my hand. "You aren't my servant. Or my nanny."

"I came back from Boston to take care of you."

"I don't need taking care of."

"It sure looks as if you do."

"I'm not your responsibility."

"That's not for you to decide. I was thinking we could sell your house and get something smaller. Something that's all on one level. And maybe you could even sell the store. So you wouldn't have to be walking all over town."

"I'm not selling the house. Or the store."

"What if you fall down the stairs again? Or trip while you're walking into town? You're old. Don't you see what could happen?"

"Don't you? You're talking about my house and my store."

"But I have a job. I can take care of both of us."

"I don't want to be taken care of. I'm not a child. And neither are you."

"What's that supposed to mean?"

She closed her eyes. Sighed. "No more talking."

I leaned over and kissed her cheek. "I'm sorry. We can talk later. Let me go tell Joe and Oliver you're all right."

"Oliver is here?"

"Joe called him."

"Send Oliver in."

And that's the way it was for the rest of the month, after Grandmother came home from the hospital. Oliver was in. And I was out.

Just like that.

But I'd never been more popular among the cyber community. Even people on my computer administrators' message boards were talking about The Cubicle Next Door. Not only was I talking about my blogs with Joe, but I was also talking about myself on the Internet—apart from my blogs. I couldn't get away from myself.

And then someone started a rumor that I was going to reveal my identity. On Valentine's Day, no less.

THE CUBICLE NEXT DOOR BLOG

Valentine's reveal

Okay, I don't know who started this vicious rumor, but I am not going to reveal my identity on Valentine's Day. Repeat, am not. Got it? For one, Valentine's Day is a holiday made up by greeting card companies for greeting card companies. I haven't sent anyone a valentine since third grade, when I was made to. Second, could there be a more obvious day to choose to reveal myself?

I'm not doing it.

Posted on February 8 in **The Cubicle Next Door | Permalink**

Comments

Actually, Valentine's Day was not made up by greeting card companies. It has a long and noble tradition in the Western world. February 14 was officially made a feast day by Pope Gelasius I in 496 to preempt the pagan revelries of Lupercalia on February 15. The feast's affiliation with romance began during the Middle Ages.
Posted by: **NozAll | February 08 at 08:15 PM**

Shut up, NozAll.
Posted by: **justluvmyjob | February 08 at 08:16 PM**

Shut your cakehole, NozAll.
Posted by: **survivor | February 08 at 08:17 PM**

Just because NozAll combats his feelings of inferiority (and at 15, I'm sure he has many of them) by supposed superiority doesn't mean we have to jump all over his back.
Posted by: **philosophie | February 08 at 08:18 PM**

Roses are red, violets are blue, I'm in the cubicle next door, right next to you.
Posted by: **theshrink | February 08 at 08:19 PM**

Eee-eee. Eee-eee. Psycho! Are you sure you're a shrink? Better be careful in the shower, TCND!
Posted by: **justluvmyjob | February 08 at 08:20 PM**

CLOSE

Thirty-Three

****

Joe came into work on Valentine's Day holding a bag of conversation hearts, those small pastel-colored sugar hearts that have cute little messages stamped on one side. "I love these." He poured a handful into his palm, shook them around for a minute, and then handed me one.

I took it. Read it. "BE MY ICON. I didn't know you were such a romantic."

He shrugged. Handed me another.

LET'S KISS.

He held out the bag.

I took a handful. Popped one into my mouth. Lined the others up on the desk in front of me. Took one from the lineup and handed it to him.

He took it. Read it. "DREAM ON. Ouch." He popped it into his mouth. "These are supposed to be conversation *hearts,* not conversation stoppers." He came over to stand beside me and surveyed my collection. Grabbed WHATEVER and GET REAL and ate them too. "Let's go somewhere for lunch."

I was all set to say no, but he kept on talking.

"Because, let's face it, you and I are about the only two people in the department who don't have significant others, so we might as well commiserate together."

I handed him another heart.

WHY NOT.

Joe wanted to go "somewhere new" for lunch. To Noodles and

Company down on Academy Boulevard. So we left a little earlier than normal to get there before the noon rush. But something happened when Joe got out of the car. He saw the Cold Stone Creamery right next door.

"We should save room. Get ice cream after lunch."

"That place is overhyped."

"Have you ever been before?"

"No."

He had been reaching for the Noodles and Company door to open it for me, but he changed his mind, put his hand at the small of my back, and propelled me to the next door down.

"We can't just have ice cream for lunch."

"Why not? Who will ever know?"

He wouldn't take no for an answer. Why didn't that surprise me?

"Okay. So here's what you do. You pick a flavor of ice cream and then as many things as you want to go with it and they mix it all up for you on that cold stone behind the counter. Get it?"

"Got it."

"If you want help, they have recipes listed on that wall." He pointed to the wall beside the counter.

"What do you usually get?"

"As much chocolate as they'll give me."

I wasn't in the mood for chocolate. I wasn't in the mood for strawberries, cherries, or anything else associated with Valentine's Day. I wasn't really in the mood for love. In fact, what I really wanted was to be in a place far, far away. I ordered something specializing in tropical fruits and coconut.

Our creations were pounded and mixed with two metal paddles and then plopped into huge waffle bowls. Joe's was dipped in chocolate. With sprinkles.

Mine, plain.

We sat down at a small round table pushed against a wall.

"So. Why aren't you married? Aside from all that stuff you told me the other day."

My eyes lifted my bowl of ice cream. "Why aren't you?"

"I was."

"And it was such a horrible experience you don't want to do it again?"

"No."

"You would do it again."

"Maybe."

"You haven't ever done it again, have you? There aren't any second or third ex-wives, are there?"

"You mean like, am I a serial divorced person? Is there some incurable flaw that keeps me from having deep, meaningful relationships? And is there some hidden idiot inside me that keeps trying?"

"Well...yeah."

"No. Actually...I keep hoping, but I've only been married once. Maybe I'm not a full-fledged idiot; maybe I'm just an optimist. If I were an idiot, I would have gotten married again while I was flying. That's what caused the problems in the first place. Not being together."

"Oh."

"Do you have a problem with divorce?"

"As a child of parents who weren't married? Am I even allowed to?"

Joe shrugged.

"You couldn't...there was no way you could work it out?"

"We tried. We saw a counselor. But it seemed pretty clear after a while that the thing we thought we had was just sex. And after we were married, we didn't even really have that anymore."

"At least it was something."

Joe looked at me then. "No. It really wasn't. It was nothing. Trust me."

He would know. "So you guys just said, 'Oops. Big mistake.' Shook hands and walked away?"

"Pretty much."

"What happened to marriage being sacred?"

"You mean, like so sacred I should spend the rest of my life monopolizing a person I had no right to marry in the first place? How does that do anyone any good?"

"It just seems that when you say you're going to do something, like spend the rest of your life with someone, then you should do it."

"I made a mistake. We both did. We were grown-ups, so we admitted it. We both took equal share of the blame."

"But the fact remains that you made a promise to God and everyone else that you were going to stay married. And then you didn't."

"So God's supposed to nail my butt to the wall every time I do something wrong. Is that what you're saying?"

"Am I?"

"Are you? That I should pay for that mistake for the rest of my life?"

"It just seems that it was awfully easy for you to walk away from a marriage. And if it was that easy the first time, why wouldn't it be even easier the second or third time?"

"Every time I've thought about being married to someone else, I've talked myself out of it. Done such a good job of it I've hardly even dated since the divorce. Because I was so sure of Kate, and it turned out to be the biggest mistake of my life. And that mistake didn't just impact me. It impacted her too."

"Doesn't look like she spent too many sleepless nights over it."

Joe looked at me. In his eyes was a warning. "Let me tell you about guilt. It's the idea that the reason we got married was because our relationship was based on all the wrong things in the first place. Would I do the same thing again? Of course not. But the thing is, it's already done. Could we have made it if we'd worked longer at it? Maybe. Who knows? God does. And thankfully, he isn't telling. Because that would be more guilt than I could bear."

"I hear what you're saying about guilt, but you're not hearing what I'm saying about staying. Not everything in life is engineered for your personal happiness."

"Don't you think I don't know that?"

"No, I don't. Because the last time you were unhappy, when you were inconvenienced, you just left. People need to be able to count on you. Some things need to be forever. Why should I, or anybody else, trust you to stay?"

He bashed in one side of his waffle bowl with his spoon. "Because I'm not the same person anymore." He picked a piece up by a jagged edge and dipped it into his ice cream. "Anyway. Let's talk about you. Tell me about your sordid past."

"I don't have one."

"Oh, come on. There must be something you've never told your grandmother."

"There really isn't."

"Forget high school. What about college?"

"Nothing."

"Boyfriends?"

"I've never had one."

"Why not?"

"Do you remember where I went to school?"

"Sure. MIT."

"Exactly."

"And? Tons of guys there!"

"I majored in computer science."

"Even better."

"It was a social nightmare. Every single guy was determined to lose his virginity, if he already hadn't, as soon as possible. I turned every guy in my major down at least once."

"So the old, 'Hey, baby, read my code'...?"

"Didn't work for me. Until I was a senior, and that's actually what they wanted me to do. I made friends with the guys, of course, but I never wanted them to get the wrong idea. I never wanted them to get too friendly."

"So you've never had a boyfriend?"

"After graduation I almost did."

"Now you're talking. So what happened?"

"With Rick?"

"With Tom, Dick, or Harry. Whoever."

"Nothing."

"Okay. You've got to give me more information or...I'm not going to help you finish the rest of that."

I looked down into my bowl. A casual observer would not have been able to tell I'd even touched it. But Joe had me figured out. He knew the guilt of not finishing what I ordered would be unbearable.

Because the only reason Americans were so fat and wasted so much food is because they kept consuming more than they needed and bought more than they could ever use. I gave in. "Nothing happened because that's about the same time Grandmother broke her hip."

"Define the word 'happen.'"

"To take place."

He frowned. "Try again."

"To cause to be."

"So what you're saying is, you didn't *marry* Rick because your grandmother broke her hip?"

"What!"

"You didn't *move in with* Rick because your grandmother broke her hip?"

"It wasn't like *that!*"

"You decided not to *bear his children* because your grandmother broke her hip? You could stop my speculation by just telling me the rest of the story."

"Okay. Stop. I didn't go out on a date with Rick because grandmother broke her hip."

"And how long did you know this guy?"

"A year."

"So if you'd been able to stay in Boston another five years, then maybe you would have kissed him? Is that what you're saying?"

"I'm not saying anything. You're the one who's doing all the talking."

"Sorry."

We ate in silence for a minute.

"Rick. That's it?"

"That's it."

"There's never been anyone else you've been interested in?"

"Not enough to lose my head over."

"Heart."

"I meant head. That's what my mother did. She had this…fling… a summer of love, with my father. He was a pilot, teaching at the Academy. Got sent to Vietnam. Died. He never even knew there would be a me."

"I'm sorry."

"And my mother flipped out. After I was born, she left."

"When?"

"Hours after I was born. She walked out of the hospital that same day and never came back."

"Where did she go?"

"India."

"Why?"

"She'd always been into the groovy stuff. Make love, not war. All that."

"Fill in this blank for me: My mother freaked out when my father died, therefore…?"

"Therefore, love isn't worth it, is it? Because what she called love ruined three people's lives: Grandmother's, mine, and hers. I am a love child. And let me tell you, there is no love. How can there be love when your mother dumps you the second you're born?"

"And therefore, love is…?"

"Overrated."

"Really?"

"Really."

"Hmm. Mind if I have some?" He'd finished his ice cream and now he was eyeballing mine.

"Go for it." I slid the bowl to his side of the table.

"You sure you don't want any more?"

"I'm fine."

"How'd you like it?"

"It was really good. Fabulous." It had been.

"Not so overrated then?" His eyes locked onto mine. And I knew he wasn't talking about ice cream. Not anymore.

"No."

"See? Sometimes it's worth taking a risk. Trying something new."

If only he knew. "Here's the thing, Joe. What kind of mother abandons a baby? The only souvenir of a man she loved? What kind of insanity is that? If it's love, then I can live without it, thank you very much."

"I don't think it was love, Jackie. Love doesn't make you run away.

Love makes you come back."

"Then what's the opposite of love? Hate? Are you saying she hated me? Because frankly, after thirty-two years of thinking she just didn't want me, learning she hated me would just about…"

"I don't think it was love that made her flip out. I don't think it was hate that made her leave you. I think it was fear that made her run away."

"Fear."

"I think she was a coward."

If he had been hoping that statement could get a rise out of me, he was mistaken. He could call my mother anything he wanted. "A coward. Well, maybe you've just helped me out. I've lived my life being everything my mother wasn't. Surely I can not be a coward too."

"Can you?"

"Of course I can."

"Then you might just have to learn how to love."

THE CUBICLE NEXT DOOR BLOG

You don't get it

Thanks for all your guesses of my identity. I'm glad you're having a great party here online. But you just don't get it. I'm not revealing myself.

John Smith doesn't get it, either.

Have you ever taken the basic stuff that makes you who you are and laid it out on the table in front of someone? And then had that person look it over and say, "That's not what you think it is"?

What do you say to that?

Especially when you think they meant to provoke you into looking at your life differently?

Here's what I did. I packed it all up again and put it away.

Posted on February 14 in **The Cubicle Next Door | Permalink**

Comments

Unpacking the psyche is a noble effort and not to be treated lightly.

Posted by: **NozAll | February 14 at 06:52 PM**

So what's wrong with that? Maybe he called it like it is. Sometimes a cigar is just a cigar.

Posted by: **theshrink | February 14 at 06:53 PM**

Are you speaking literally or figuratively?

Posted by: **docsin | February 14 at 06:54 PM**

Give him another chance. He's just a guy. Like every other guy.

Posted by: **philosophie | February 14 at 06:55 PM**

He's either with you or he's against you. You don't need the extra weight if he's not pulling in your direction.

Posted by: **survivor | February 14 at 06:56 PM**

CLOSE

Thirty-Four

****

I was working one afternoon in mid-March, running tests on the system when Kate suddenly materialized.

"Hey." She cast a glance behind her and then edged toward my cubicle.

"Hi."

"Can we talk for a minute?" Her voice was so low I had trouble hearing her. "I just wanted to stop by and…you know…"

Not really. "Were you looking for Joe? He should be here after sixth period."

"No. I wasn't looking for him. I was looking for you." She placed her hands on her hips. Took them away and crossed her arms in front of her instead. "The thing is, Joe is a really nice guy."

I felt my eyebrows lift.

"I mean, beyond all the jokiness and the flyboy stuff…"

"Yeah?"

"So I just wanted to know if…"

Clearly, the subject of Joe was making her uncomfortable. Was she thinking about having an affair with him?

"Well…he likes you. You know that, right?" She rolled her eyes. "I can't believe I'm saying this. It's not like we're in junior high. But he deserves to be taken seriously. That's all I wanted to say."

"Taken seriously? Then he should try *being* serious for a change."

She cocked her head. A line appeared between her eyebrows. "But…it's like they always told us when we were little. Boys wouldn't tease you if they didn't like you."

Nobody had ever told me that. "So Joe's been talking to you about me?"

"Yeah. Nothing bad, obviously. He's just...confused. So I was trying to help him see things from your point of view."

"Which is?"

"I know it probably seems strange to you, being friends with your ex-wife."

"It doesn't particularly bother me."

"We shouldn't have gotten married in the first place. I just...we thought if I told you we really were just friends..."

"We who?"

"Joe and Steve and I."

Oh, so now I was a group project?

"Joe's different since he's stopped flying. He's changed. He's much more serious."

"I don't know what he was like before. He's fine now. It's not him, it's me."

She frowned. Then shrugged. "I just wanted you to know."

Half an hour later, my tests were done, but I was still staring at the computer monitor. At the same frame I'd been staring at for the previous ten minutes.

Joe liked me.

It was unavoidable now, because the words had been spoken out loud. And now he would know—for certain—that I knew, because Kate would probably tell him she told me.

How had I gotten myself into this mess?

By being tempted?

No. By letting myself hang out around the temptation. By setting up a lawn chair and parking myself down right beside it. What a fool I'd been. You can't play with fire and not get burned. You can't hang around Joe and not fall in love.

I'd known it would end like this. I'd reconciled myself to going through life alone. And I was still going to go through life alone. Only now I'd have to do it with an ache in my heart.

I'd just have to hope it wouldn't be chronic.

The next Tuesday, I was sitting in my cubicle, minding my own business, when Joe returned from class, dumped his bag on the floor, and then came to stand in front of my cubicle door.

I flicked a glance at him.

"Hey. There's one of those movies you like playing at Twin Peaks."

"Which movies?"

"The Indian ones."

"Thanks for letting me know." I'd never seen one in a theater. Maybe I'd have to go.

"Want to go?"

"Where?"

"To see the movie."

I turned my chair so I could look at him. See if he was kidding. "You want to see a Bollywood movie?"

He shrugged. "I've never seen one before."

I was on the verge of saying no. But as I looked at him, I just couldn't do it. So I made a deal with myself. I'd say yes. I'd give myself one last chance to be with him before I started saying no again. For the rest of my life.

That's how we ended up in the center of the Kimball's Twin Peaks Theater, perched on the first seats in the upper section, legs propped up on the railings. We were halfway into it when Joe started talking.

"Have any more popcorn?"

I handed him the container.

He fished out a few un-popped kernels and started crunching. Shifted in his seat. Crossed his legs. Uncrossed them. "Okay. Enough dancing around the subject. Just kiss her already."

"Shh!"

"This is torture. Why does it keep showing them dancing in Paris and Tahiti and Saudi Arabia? They live in India. And they're both dirt-poor."

"It's beautiful."

"They love each other, right?"

"Yes."

"Then why don't they do something about it? Hold hands. Anything."

"It's not like they have to fall into bed every time they meet. There's something to be said for self-control and physical restraint."

"There's also something to be said for not looking like a dancing marionette."

"If you can't watch nicely, then please leave."

"Okay, okay."

He was quiet for a few minutes, and then he leaned toward my ear again. "How can you watch this without understanding the words? Why aren't there subtitles?"

"Are you blind?"

"No."

"Then use your eyes. Can't you see what they're feeling?"

"Maybe. I can guess. But it would be nice if it were backed up with words. Then I'd know for sure. I mean, she could be crying because she has something in her eye. How am I supposed to know for certain it's because of something he said? Give me a break. I'm a guy!"

"Just…shut…up."

He was good for about two minutes, and then he leaned toward me again.

I took the popcorn container from him, hunched over, and shifted down three seats.

He followed me.

I shifted down two more.

He did the same.

"If you don't stop talking I'm going to stand up—right now—and scream."

"You wouldn't."

"Oh yes, I would."

"If you stand up, then I'm going to stand up—right now—and kiss you."

"You wouldn't."

"Oh yes, I would." He was serious.

I plunged my hand to the bottom of the popcorn container.

There was nothing there but a few kernels Joe had left behind. I grabbed them and shoved them into my mouth. Started crunching.

He didn't say another word. Not for a long time. Not until one of the more elaborate song-and-dance sequences at the end. Then he leaned over and looked me straight in the eye. "If they sing one more song…"

The images from the movie screen cast kaleidoscope shadows on his face. His eyes were sweeping back and forth across my face.

"Aren't you going to stand up and scream?"

My scalp began to tingle. My mouth had suddenly gone dry. "Why?"

"I talk. You scream. We kiss. That was the deal." He stretched his arm across the backs of our seats. "You're not going to back out on me now, are you?"

I could not look away from his eyes. I wanted to, but I couldn't. It was a physical impossibility. I had no control over my body. Because before I could even register his question in my brain, my head began to jerk back and forth.

"Good." He smiled. I saw those dimples. Then I felt his hand caress my neck.

I must have closed my eyes because the next thing I knew, they were flying open as his lips touched mine.

He brought his other hand up to my neck.

And I must have closed my eyes again because all I can remember was being in a world devoid of any sensation but touch. And taste. And a feeling in the pit of my stomach as if I were driving down a mountain road way too fast. Careening out of control. And the only way to get out, to get through, was to hang onto Joe.

Literally.

When I next opened my eyes, I found I was clutching fistfuls of his sweater. And I meant to push him away, but then he started kissing my neck, and I decided it would actually be better if he were closer.

Slowly, I became aware of a sort of change around us. I tried to open my eyes, but it felt as if I were attempting to lift the garage door with just one finger. I put a hand to Joe's chest and tried to push myself away from it.

He put a hand up to cover mine and then brought it up to his face. He broke away from my lips.

I watched as he kissed my open palm and then released my hand.

And then we both blinked.

Because in between when our kisses had started and when they had ended, the movie had also ended, the theater had emptied, and the lights had been turned on.

Joe smiled. He gave me a last, quick kiss and then stood up and held out his hand for mine.

I just sat there, looking up at him. "Were we just making out? In public? In a movie theater?"

"Which question do you want me to answer first?"

"Were we making out!"

He sat back down. "We were kissing." He put his hands up to my face.

I batted them away.

"Jackie. We were just kissing. I didn't even...touch you anywhere."

"Well, it felt like you touched me everywhere!"

"Shh." He put out a hand to smooth my hair away from my face.

"Stop touching me!"

"Whoa! It's okay."

"It's not okay. It is not okay that I become just like my mother."

"You're not."

"How would you know?"

"You're not—"

"All I have to do is the opposite of what she did and *then* everything will be okay." I could feel tears coursing down my cheeks, but I could not stop them. "I am not my mother."

"You're not."

"I am not my mother. I will not be out of control. I can't see you anymore. I can't kiss you anymore."

"Okay. That's fine."

"I can't."

"All right."

"I won't."

He took me by the hand and pulled me onto his lap. He wrapped his arms around me and began to rock, forward and back. Forward and back. Forward and back.

"I can't see you anymore."

THE CUBICLE NEXT DOOR BLOG

The worst that can happen

It's happened. The worst thing I can imagine has happened. I've spent my entire life trying to guarantee it wouldn't, and it has.

Posted on March 21 in **The Cubicle Next Door | Permalink**

Comments

Technically speaking, you don't really know yet what the worst thing that could happen is because you haven't lived your life in its entirety. Something worse than what happened today could happen tomorrow.

Posted by: **NozAll | March 21 at 11:03 PM**

Like that's really going to cheer her up, you stupid fool!

Posted by: **justluvmyjob | March 21 at 11:36 PM**

Maybe it was the worst thing, but you're still alive to talk about it, right?

Posted by: **philosophie | March 22 at 07:25 AM**

Hey—you lived to tell about it. It can only get better from here.

Posted by: **survivor | March 22 at 07:41 AM**

CLOSE

Thirty-Five

****

I woke the next morning with a migraine. I stumbled out of my bedroom and down the hall to tell Grandmother.

She helped me back to bed. Made sure the shades blocked as much light as they could. I felt her press her palm to my forehead.

I grabbed it and held on.

She pushed my hair away from my forehead with her hand. Exquisite torture for a person with a migraine.

"I haven't had one of these since…college."

"Your mother used to get migraines."

I let go of her hand and raced down the hall. I made it into the bathroom before I threw up.

My mother had migraines. It figured. There was no use denying it anymore. I had become my mother. A woman given over to passionate emotions and ferocious headaches.

I asked Grandmother to call Estelle and then gave myself over to an aura of flashing lights and zigzag lines. The worst sinus headache imaginable. And the pounding of sledgehammers in my head.

And later, I slept.

Right until the doorbell rang at 2:30.

I rose from bed with a hand clamped to the side of my head, trying to keep my brains from falling out, and hobbled down the stairs.

Opened the door.

Squinted against the bright afternoon sun at the silhouette standing in the doorway.

It was Oliver.

"Hullo."

"Hi."

"May I come in?"

I stood there for a moment, trying to find the strength to resist him. Failed. I backed away, leaving the door undefended.

"I know a few things about pain."

I wasn't in the mood. I moved past him, into the living room, and collapsed on the couch. I pulled a pillow over my head and closed my eyes.

Sweet darkness.

He had followed along right behind me. I heard him help himself to a chair.

"We English are a curious people. We treat our dogs like children and our children like dogs, did you know that?"

I didn't. But I didn't find it relevant—at all—to the way my head kept pounding.

"Open the door and gesture the dogs into the house. Open that same door and push the children out into boarding school. Some children do well at that sort of thing, of course. I was not one of them. All I dreamt of while I was at school was coming home. Cried myself to sleep. Didn't mix with the others. But when I came home, all I could do was push my parents away. I was a very nasty child."

"You've aged well."

"Ha. Nice of you to say."

There was silence for a good long while. All I heard was the anniversary clock, ticking away on the mantel. All I felt was the heat from rays of afternoon sun that had slanted through the window.

He cleared his throat. "So you understand then, do you?"

"No."

He sighed. I heard him shift in the chair. "Even though what I wanted, more than anything, was to stay with my parents, I sabotaged myself at every turn. Made myself so nasty I knew they'd never ask me to stay. And why do you think that was?"

"Because you *were* nasty, Oliver."

"Because I was afraid, of course, that if I put the question to them quite baldly, they would have said no. That they would have said they didn't want me."

"So what, exactly, are you saying?"

"That perhaps I would have done better to just ask them at the first instance. To give them a chance to say yes.

"You think they would have?"

"I'll never know, will I?"

"I guess you won't. Was it worth it? Staying away at school?"

"I learned some things. Made the required connections. But I did it all alone, you see."

"You were lonely."

"Yes. I believe I was. And the danger in learning to live by yourself is that if you wait too long, it becomes much easier than the alternative."

"Which is?"

"To learn how to live with someone else."

"I know."

"Ah. See there? It might be easier, but is it better? People like you and I aren't afraid of a little work, are we?"

"No." We were just afraid of other people. And the possibility that they might not want us.

"Well, just keep in mind that you don't earn any medals for dying alone."

I thought about that for a while.

"Were you in the war?"

"Several of them."

"My grandfather was too. Did you earn any medals?"

"Several."

"What for?"

"Oh…well…for saving others…other people. It was so very long ago."

"Did you have to?"

"Do I understand you to mean, Was it my job? No. I wasn't a medic. No."

"So why did you do it?"

"Because I was in a position to. I had information that they didn't. Saw things they couldn't see. Of course, had I been able to, I might have just dashed off a note and left them to maneuver themselves. But sometimes, there is no time. And when you see someone in peril…and you know that you can help them, well, one does what one must."

"I see."

"I hope you do."

We sat there, together, for a long time. Our silence measured by the ticking of the clock.

And then the doorbell rang again.

I started. Began to remove the pillow from my head. A few small particles of light convinced me I shouldn't.

I heard Oliver clamber to his feet. Walk to the door. Heard him talking to someone. Heard him return to me.

There was a pressure on the couch beside me. I lifted the pillow enough to see he had sat down. He patted the hand that was clutching the pillow to my head. "Joe's come to call and I'll be off."

"But—"

"Remember, no medals. There's a good girl."

"Oliver?"

"Yes?"

"Thanks."

I heard his footsteps take him away from the living room. Heard the front door shut. Heard Joe cough.

"Um. Can I come in?"

I lifted the pillow. Sat up. Slowly. Squinted. "Sure."

"Are you okay?"

"Migraine."

"Maybe I could—should I close the curtains?" He was already on his way toward the windows. As he pulled them shut, the violence of the pounding in my head diminished. Instant relief.

"Thanks. How did you know?"

"I get…used to get migraines, remember? It's the only reason I'm here."

He chose to sit in the chair Oliver had just vacated.

"About last night…"

"I can't kiss you anymore."

He held up his hands. "I know. I know that's what you said. I'd just like to know why."

"Because I can't…" *No medals.* "I just can't handle it."

"Can't handle what? Is there something I can do to help?"

"I can't handle what this is. I don't have any kind of role model for relationships. I have a disaster model. I figure all I have to do is the opposite of what my mother did. So I'm not planning on…falling in love…with anyone."

"I'm not anyone."

"I know…" My glance dipped down to the pillow at my side. I just wanted to clamp it over my head and dissolve into sleep. I didn't want to be accountable anymore for the things I felt. "Why can't we just go back to the way things were?"

"You mean why can't you have it all? The dating without dating?"

"Well…yeah."

"You can't have it all. Sacrifices must be made. Isn't that what you told me once?"

"About cross-country skis. And sidecuts."

"Well, those sidecuts have been making furrows across my heart. I'm tired of skiing oblique turns. I want to ski straight and fast."

I did too. But I was afraid.

"I want more. And there can be more. Last night had to have convinced you of that."

"I can't do it."

"Why not?"

"Because I don't know how."

"Because you're afraid?"

I nodded.

"Of becoming your mother."

I nodded again.

"And what if that did happen? Would that really be so bad?"

I felt my mouth drop open.

"I mean—" He sighed. Got up from the chair and walked over to me. Eyed the space beside me. I didn't do anything to keep him from sitting, so he sat down.

"I'm not asking you to sleep with me or anything."

I felt a blush creep up my face.

"I'm not asking you to marry me. Or have a child with me. Or anything at all. I'd just like to be more…serious…about getting to know you. That's it." He gathered me into his arms and shifted me over onto his lap.

I sat there, head against his chest, basking in his warmth. In the luxury of being in what I'd just discovered was my favorite place.

"I'm not Superman, Jackie. You can't ask me to be near you without touching you or kissing you or thinking about the future."

"But you just said—"

"I know what I told you just now. But I lied. And I knew I was lying to you when I said it. I don't want to lie to you anymore. I think about a future with you all the time. I want to be more serious. I already *am* more serious. Can you meet me halfway here? So I can stop torturing myself."

His nose was nuzzling through my hair. It was making my stomach do handsprings. And the longing I had to kiss him was almost overwhelming. Almost unbearable. I could practically feel his lips on mine. And that's when I knew what I had to tell him.

"I can't."

He went still. Absolutely still. And then he rested his cheek on top of my head. "Are you sure? Are you positive it isn't the migraine speaking? I know how it feels afterward…like everything in your head has been disconnected."

I nodded.

"If I walk out that door, I'm not coming back."

"I know."

"Is this really what you want? Because I don't think it is. I love you. I think you know that…hope you know that…but I have to say it anyway. Even if you don't want to hear it."

I did want to hear it. Longed to hear it.

"That's it, then?"

I nodded because I couldn't trust myself to speak.

Joe kissed the top of my head and then slid me off his lap.

The problem was I loved him too, even though I knew he deserved someone far better than me. As he walked out the door, I even said it. "I love you too."

But he didn't hear it because he'd already gone.

THE CUBICLE NEXT DOOR BLOG

Help me

Help me say yes.

Posted on March 22 in **The Cubicle Next Door | Permalink**

Comments

Sometimes, when I have something important to say, I practice saying it in front of a mirror.

Posted by: **NozAll | March 22 at 07:19 PM**

Visualize yourself saying yes and then imagine it changing your entire destiny.

Posted by: **philosophie | March 22 at 09:37 PM**

Just do it. Say yes. You can always say no later.

Posted by: **justluvmyjob | March 22 at 10:05 PM**

If you need help saying it, then you probably aren't ready to say it.

Posted by: **survivor | March 22 at 10:51 PM**

Thirty-Six

****

You'd think God would have approved of what I'd told Joe. Approved I'd chosen deliberate, clearheaded decision making over passion. But I kept feeling incredible guilt. Incredible remorse. As if I'd made the wrong decision. Said the wrong thing. As if I'd broken Joe's heart for no good reason.

But God knew how awful I would have made life for him...so why wasn't God making me feel any better about it?

Mercifully, spring break was the next week. And Joe was off escorting cadets to Russia. I didn't have to see him or hear him for a whole week.

But it didn't stop me from thinking about him.

All the time.

He was torturing me from afar. Stretching me on a rack or pulling out my fingernails or whatever the KGB used to do at Dzerzhinsky Square would have been kinder.

All I could do was tell myself I'd made the right decision. That *I* would never find myself abandoning a child and running away to someplace like India. That *I* would never give myself a chance to be unrespectable. But a voice inside kept shrieking maybe it wanted to make that decision all by itself. And couldn't I leave well enough alone!

On Tuesday, I walked down to Estelle's area to check out the department's printers. I wanted to make sure we had enough print cartridges in stock for the cadet projects that would be due in mid-April.

When I rounded the corner and Estelle's desk came into view, I saw her dabbing at her eyes with a tissue. Dab again. And again. Saw her finally give up, fold her hands in her lap, and let tears cascade down her cheeks.

"Estelle?"

She looked up toward me, not bothering to wipe the tears away.

"Is there something I can do?"

She shook her head.

"Something I can say?"

She shook her head again.

I stood there for a moment, knowing that now was not the time to test the printers or count the cartridges, but not knowing what I should do. What are you supposed to do when someone cries?

What did I want when I felt like crying?

The firm grip of Grandmother's hand. Company as I listened to the ticktock of the anniversary clock in the living room. I had wanted to know I wasn't alone. I had wanted to know somebody had cared enough about me to stay when I needed them.

So I took a chair from its place by the wall and dragged it around Estelle's desk. I set it right next to hers and sat down on it. And I stayed there for a long while.

"My son just died."

I'm sorry didn't sound quite sorry enough, so I didn't say anything at all.

"He was supposed to have another two months. I was supposed to fly up next week. I was getting everything ready while everyone here was gone. Getting everything in order."

I handed her another tissue.

"We knew he was going to die. There wasn't anything they could do anymore. I just didn't think he'd die without me there." She turned toward me, her chin trembling. "I was his mother and I wasn't there."

"It's not your fault."

"But he needed me. And for the hardest thing in his life I wasn't there."

"All he had to do to die was wake up this morning. That wasn't hard. Death is easy. Living is the hard part. And you were there for that."

"I just…wanted to say goodbye. One more time. I didn't want him to go off without knowing I loved him."

"He knows. Because you spent your whole life telling him, right?"

She looked at me then, mute with tears. But she nodded. Then she grimaced. Swallowed. "Right." She took an unsteady breath. Then another. Dabbed at her eyes and cheeks. "Right." Took another breath and stood up. "I have to leave now. I don't know how the colonel will survive…"

"I'll take care of him. I can do it."

She smiled beneath watery eyes and then laughed. "But you can't even write a memo to the dean."

I reached down to the tissue box and plucked another from the top. "One more for the road."

She took it and pressed it to her nose. And then she disappeared down the hall.

I called the colonel's cell number and left a message.

He called back later in the afternoon and asked me to send flowers for the funeral.

I spent the next two days at Estelle's desk, answering phones, answering e-mails, and trying to make sense of her filing system. Both electronic and hard copy. But shifting in and out of my consciousness, like sunbeams through the ocean's waves, were thoughts of Joe.

I tried not to think about him, but that didn't stop me from feeling things about him and my mind from questioning me about him.

What if?

The fact remained that 15 minutes in a movie theater had left me clutching at his clothing and running my fingers through his hair. I shuddered to think what would happen if I actually started dating him on the record. Became serious about getting to know him.

Maybe the whole episode had been good. Maybe I did need someone in my life. But if that were true, then what I needed was someone with decorum. Someone with restraint. Someone with whom I would have no fear of losing my head. I needed…an Indian-style relationship. A relationship in which I could still keep my virtue.

I did not need a relationship with Joe.

But everything in me longed for him. I harbored longings for him in places I didn't even know had feelings. I wasn't used to feelings, outside of impatience, exasperation, and irritation. The spectrum of myself was growing exponentially. And it was so tightly strung, so wire thin, I could feel my heart begin to pound at the thought of Joe, my palms begin to sweat at the memory of his eyes. His hair. His lips. I was becoming completely unlike my normal self. And I didn't know if I could ever find that original person again.

Frankly, didn't know if I wanted to.

When that thought crossed my mind, when I actually heard it passing and saw its tracks, followed it to see where it was going, I was floored.

Grandmother and all her friends wanted me to be with Joe. Oliver wanted me to be with Joe. Kate wanted me to be with Joe.

Joe wanted to me to be with Joe.

It appeared the only person who didn't want me to be with Joe was me. And even then, my body, my thoughts, and my emotions had already gone over to his side. And they had taken both my heart and my head with them.

THE CUBICLE NEXT DOOR BLOG

Love?

Do I like the way your hair waves? The way your eyes glint? The way you smile? The way you laugh? Do I like them? Do I like all of the dozens of things that are you? Those questions are immaterial.

I'm far beyond like or dislike.

I'm in love.

Posted on March 30 in **The Cubicle Next Door | Permalink**

Comments

You mean you just now figured that out? Even I knew that.

Posted by: **NozAll | March 31 at 07:15 AM**

Bravo. Only in knowing your heart can you know the future.

Posted by: **philosophie | March 31 at 08:23 AM**

You're not going to get all mushy on us, are you?

Posted by: **justluvmyjob | March 31 at 08:48 AM**

Is this supposed to be some sort of epiphany?

Posted by: **survivor | March 31 at 09:06 AM**

CLOSE

Thirty-Seven

****

Joe returned to school the next week.

I was looking forward to seeing him, but I had no idea what I would say to him. His eyes had haunted me over spring break. He had stared at me long and hard right before he'd walked out the door. And I hadn't talked to him again before he left for Russia. Didn't know if I'd ever talk to him again. If he'd ever talk to me. I'd made it very clear what I wanted, and it wasn't him.

Too bad I hadn't made it clear how I *felt* about him, because that was a whole different story.

I was taking a break from Estelle's desk and had returned to my own when he finally came in. The sight of him, after a week's break, was almost too much to bear. I wanted to laugh. I wanted to cry. To…touch him. Something.

He didn't say anything.

I listened as he booted up his computer. Listened as his mouse began clicking.

When I couldn't stand the silence any longer, I climbed up on my desk. "So how was it? The trip to Russia?"

He glanced up from his computer, still typing. Glanced back down. "It was fine."

"Glad to be back?"

"Yeah."

I waited for him to elaborate, but he didn't.

"Estelle's son died last week. She's on leave. For the funeral and everything. I'm filling in for her."

Joe's hands had stilled. "When did it happen?"

"Tuesday morning."

"Was she there?"

"No. She was here."

"Alone in the department?"

"I was here."

"But was she okay?"

"No, she wasn't."

"Did anyone send flowers?

"The colonel asked me to. From the department."

"Does she know when she'll be back?"

"She didn't say. I'm sitting in for her until she gets back."

Joe grunted. "Good luck." Then his eyes dropped to his keyboard.

No point in sticking around when there's nothing to talk about. When you're not wanted. I dove into my cubicle. Finished up my work there.

Ended up eating lunch by myself.

The next day was about the same. I wished I could make things better between us, but that would have required...too much.

Oliver's words kept ringing through my mind. *No medals.*

The long afternoon hours, a time when we would normally alternate conversation with work, were excruciating. When I was visiting my desk, I finally brought up the one topic that had never failed to solicit a comment from him.

"Have you read the blog lately?"

Joe stopped typing. "No. Too much work to do."

"Oh. Because she asked for help. Again. She actually admitted she was in love with the guy."

"Well, good for her." He started typing again but then stopped mid-cadence. "In love? Are you sure that's what she said?"

"'Do I like the way your hair waves? The way your eyes glint? The way you smile? The way you laugh? Do I like them? Do I like all of the dozens of things that make up you? Those questions are immaterial. I'm far beyond like or dislike. I'm in love.'" As I listened to me quote myself, I had the feeling there was much more emotion in my words than I had intended. But I didn't need to worry. Joe wasn't listening.

By the time I'd finished talking, he had picked up the phone and started dialing. The only word I caught was "Kate."

And when he put the phone down, he walked out of the cubicle without saying a word.

THE CUBICLE NEXT DOOR BLOG

I'm sorry

But I don't know how to tell you that.

Fear made me say things I didn't want to say. Love wants me to take those words back. But my love has no voice. I've never heard it speak out loud before, and I don't know what it sounds like. It's whispering to me, telling me to say the craziest things, but I don't know if I can trust it. Don't know how those words will sound once they're said. Don't quite understand what they will mean.

I'm trying, I really am, but I don't know what to do. Maybe I'm too late. Maybe what we had is already gone.

Posted on April 03 in **The Cubicle Next Door | Permalink**

Comments

Gone? Faint heart never won fair maiden. What is this guy, a big wuss?

Posted by: **theshrink | April 03 at 07:43 PM**

There are only two possible responses to "I'm sorry."

Posted by: **NozAll | April 03 at 08:09 PM**

Just say you're sorry as soon as possible and get it over with.

Posted by: **justluvmyjob | April 03 at 08:10 AM**

Try. And keep trying. Love's voice is the softest, but it's also the strongest.

Posted by: **philosophie | April 03 at 08:12 PM**

Always do the hardest thing first. If it doesn't kill you, then the rest is cake.

Posted by: **survivor | April 03 at 8:36 PM**

CLOSE

Thirty-Eight

****

It came on the last Saturday in April. Grandmother had stopped by the store to do some end-of-season markdowns, so I'd gone home for lunch.

It didn't even look important. Aside from the foreign stamp. From India.

When I saw the stamp, I set the letter aside. Went through the other mail without reading it. Threw away the phone bill and had to retrieve it. I hoped Qwest wouldn't mind a little olive oil on their bill.

I pawed through the rest of the garbage to make sure I hadn't thrown anything else away. And when I looked back at the table, the letter was still there.

And it was not from my mother.

At least, it hadn't been addressed by her. I'd only received one letter from her in my entire life, but I knew her handwriting like I knew my own.

I got up from the table and poured a glass of milk. Turned around and drank it with my back pressed against the counter. I put the glass down, chewed on a fingernail.

The letter was still there.

It's a lot easier to pretend someone doesn't exist when they don't contact you. Not, of course, that the letter was from my mother. I had already determined it wasn't. But was that a good or a bad sign?

I turned around and rifled through the cupboards. I really wanted something crunchy. Like potato chips. The best I could come up with was rice cakes.

I crunched through half a bag.

And then I was thirsty again.

I poured another glass of milk.

The letter was still there.

And I was still hungry. For something sweet and gooey.

I opened the fridge, drew out a loaf of bread, a brick of sharp cheddar and a jar of apple butter. I popped two slices of bread in the toaster, unwrapped the cheese, set it on a plate, and concentrated on cutting it. There is an art to the perfect toasted cheese sandwich. The bread has to be toasted just to brown, but not dark brown or black. And the cheese has to be sliced thin enough so that it melts on contact with the toast. That's the tricky part. I cut three slices that were too thick before I cut one thin enough to use. Three more bad ones before another good one. My rhythm was all wrong.

I glanced toward the table and almost sliced my finger off.

The toast jumped.

I tossed it onto the plate. Contemplated cutting another slice of cheese, but decided it would take too long. I laid the cheese slices on top of one piece of bread, slathered apple butter across the other. Waited for the cheese to absorb the last of the warmth of the toast and then pressed the slices together and cut it at a diagonal.

I ate it.

The letter was still there.

I returned the bread, the cheese, and the apple butter to the fridge. Washed and dried the plate. Ran a washcloth across the counter to pick up loose crumbs. Picked up the toaster and shook it out over the sink. Shook it some more. Put it back.

I fiddled with the knobs on the stove. Grimy gook had built up along the dial faces and along their undersides. Why didn't anyone ever clean under there?

I went to the bathroom and came back armed with a handful of Q-tips. I dug under the sink for the container of Goo-B-Gone.

Half an hour later, the dials were clean. They were so clean they were glinting.

And then I walked over to the table, sat down, and opened the letter.

A bracelet tumbled out. The plastic-coated kind they wrap around your wrist at the hospital.

The letter wasn't very long.

Two sentences.

Signed by someone whose name I couldn't read.

It was dated 23 February.

The first sentence said my mother was dead.

The second sentence said the bracelet was the only thing she had in her possession and they had cut it from her arm after she died. I picked it up and looked at it. It was the bracelet she must have worn when she was in the hospital giving birth to me.

Fifteen minutes later, I was in my car on the way to the mountains.

I've never understood people who would rather drive through the wilderness than hike it.

Seriously.

Are they scared? Are they lazy? Do they just not know how?

I've hiked since I was little. Grandmother would fill a pack and we'd set out on Sundays, after I'd gone to church. Her pack always contained a compass and a handkerchief. A map and a knife. Food, water, and one of those little packs of tissues; they're easier to carry than a roll of toilet paper. And since we lived and hiked in Colorado, we always, always, carried rain gear.

All it took to spend time in the wilderness was a little common sense.

I ran the car off the highway at Mueller Park. Got out, slammed the door shut, and started hiking. Without a compass. Without a handkerchief. Without a map, a knife, water, or common sense. At least I had some food. A single energy bar.

I walked. Nibbled at the energy bar. Walked some more. But I wasn't really into it. My feet hurt. My head hurt.

My heart hurt.

I'd just sat down on a rock, taken the energy bar out of my pocket, and decided to finish it off when I heard something. Something that was rustling through the brush. I hoped it wasn't a bear. But what else could you expect on Black Bear Trail? As many times as I'd hiked in Mueller, as many miles as I'd ranged, I'd never actually seen one, although I'd seen evidence of them.

It rustled again.

If it was a bear, there was nothing I could do to save myself. Except fall on the ground and pretend to be dead. That's the advice everyone always hands out, but as I thought about it, I couldn't remember hearing about anyone who had actually done it.

Twigs snapped.

How many wild animals can snap a twig? They'd have to be pretty heavy to be able to do that, right? So…bears? An elk? A cougar?

Maybe not a cougar. They're supposed to be stealthy stalkers. I can't imagine they'd walk around snapping twigs. And if it were an elk, I'd just wave my arms around until it went away. Worst case scenario?

Still a bear.

Couldn't get much worse than that.

I had taken no precautions with my food. I hadn't buried my energy bar, tied it up in a tree or kept it in an odor-proof container. I could eat it, but then the scent would still be in my pocket. All of a sudden, I didn't want the scent of food anywhere near me. I threw the bar into the brush.

The sounds stopped. Maybe that was good.

They started again. That was bad.

I closed my eyes. I'm one of those people who never watch the scary parts in movies. But then I lifted an eyelid, just a little. It would be nice to know if the bear really were 20 feet long. What else would make so much noise moving through the forest?

Joe.

He burst into my clearing, cheeks ablaze and eyes aflame. "Just how many kinds of stupid are you?"

I scrambled to my feet as my knees liquefied in sheer relief.

"Out here in the middle of nowhere by yourself? What would have happened if you'd gotten lost? Or broken a leg?"

"Then I would have been finished off by a bear and haunted Mueller Park forever."

"I'm serious!"

"So am I. I thought you were a bear."

"Is that why you threw this at me?" He walked toward me, holding out my half-eaten energy bar.

I glared at him. "Why are you here?"

"Because your grandmother called me."

"And?"

"And we were both worried about you."

"I'm fine."

"Obviously you're not, or you wouldn't be wandering around the wilderness throwing food at people."

"You've found me. Congratulations. Now you can tell Grandmother I'm fine."

"But you're not."

"Yes. I am."

"Then why are you crying?"

"I wasn't. Not until you showed up. Everything would have been just f-fine if it hadn't been for you."

Joe stalked over and grabbed me by the shoulders. Then he sighed and enveloped me in his arms, tucking my head underneath his chin.

"More than anything else, I didn't want to be like her."

"I know."

"And now I'll never know what she was like."

"I know. Come on. I'll drive you home."

"I have my car."

"We'll pick it up tomorrow."

It was on the tip of my tongue to tell Joe on the drive home. I wanted to tell him everything. About the blog. About myself. But I fell asleep before I could say anything at all.

The next day, I vacillated between anger and grief.

My mother was dead.

How could I even begin to understand her? How could I forgive her? I'd never be able to talk to her. I'd never be able to ask her why. Ask her if she'd ever regretted it. Ask her if she'd ever thought of me at all.

But I kept coming back to that bracelet. She'd never taken it off.

But then she'd never come home, either.

Why not?

If she wore me next to her skin, then why hadn't she just come home?

Unworthy. Could that have been how she'd felt?

Because I felt the same way.

In trying to be the exact opposite of my mother, had I spun so far around the circle that I'd come to the place she'd vacated? Was I so certain I didn't deserve love that I did everything I could to stay away from it? I was living my life in self-imposed isolation. Just like she had. Only not in India. But was that really truly what I wanted? Regardless, I was trying hard to make sure it stayed that way.

Poor Joe.

Poor me.

I'd broadcast loud and clear I didn't deserve him. I'd given him a hundred reasons why. But he hadn't cared, had he?

Why should I have been surprised? He'd never listened to me anyway.

But that wasn't true, was it?

He'd always been listening. Since the very beginning. To the other hundred things I was too afraid to say.

Grandmother and I sat in the living room the entire morning before we said one word to each other. I was the one who began the conversation.

"Does it change anything?"

"Her being dead? No. I suppose it doesn't."

"But it feels different."

"Because there's no hope. Not anymore."

"I didn't ever really think I *would* see her."

"I know. I didn't either. But now the opportunity has been taken away."

"So am I mourning her or am I mourning the loss of an opportunity?"

Grandmother looked at me then, a sad smile on her face. "I don't know. You tell me."

"I don't know."

Grandmother shuddered. Put her hands to her face and began to weep. "I'm so, so sorry."

I got up from the chair and sat beside her on the couch. Put an arm around her and rested my head on her shoulder. "It's okay."

"It's not okay. None of it is okay."

"She made her choices."

"The same way I made mine. I spoiled her. Indulged her. Your grandfather and I both. We gave her everything she ever wanted. She had you. And then she ran away. I was determined you wouldn't turn out like her. I told myself I wouldn't let you. I'd been given a second chance and I was going to do it right. I was going to be the perfect mother."

"I would have settled for any kind of mother."

"I didn't want to drive you away too. I tried not to get too close. Tried to compensate for my weaknesses. I did the opposite with you. Because I wanted you to stay."

"And I did."

"But what kind of life have you had? Every time I wanted to reach out and touch your hand, kiss your cheek, I stopped myself. Because I didn't want to ruin you."

"I knew you loved me."

"You did?"

"Of course I did."

"But did I ever tell you? I never told you, did I? I've been foolish twice over. But I love you so very much. I love you, Jackie." She raised her head and kissed me on the cheek. Then she wrapped her arms around my neck and held on while she cried.

That afternoon, I drove out to the Academy. Went to the cemetery. Went to tell my father about my mother. I suppose it was foolish, because he probably already knew. Had already known for several months. But I needed to tell him myself. To feel as though I had finished something they'd started.

I wonder if they would have done anything differently had they known the day they met that there would be a moment like that one. A moment where I would stumble to the ground, lay my head on a cool stone, and water their memory with my tears. A moment where I would be unable to say "I love you" to a man I had never met and unwilling to say it to the woman who gave me birth.

But I cried.

For the third time I could remember, I cried.

I didn't know what was happening. Somewhere, deep inside, a floodgate had released an onslaught of emotions. I was swimming with them, struggling against them, trying to find a foothold in a self I hardly knew.

They could be a riptide from which I might never recover.

But my hope was that they would soon recede. Wash me up and then retreat with an ebbing tide. Leaving me high and dry, the emotions trickling away beneath me.

Leaving me stranded, but setting me free.

THE CUBICLE NEXT DOOR BLOG

Someone

Has there ever been someone in your life who has impacted you dramatically even though you've never really met them before?

There has been in my life. Up until now. The thing is, I never really liked or understood this person, but they were always in my thoughts. And now that they're gone, I'm not quite sure what to feel about them. Am I supposed to mourn this loss? Can you mourn a person you've never had charitable thoughts toward?

I don't know what to think. Or feel.

Posted on April 25 in **The Cubicle Next Door | Permalink**

Comments

To mourn is to express grief or sorrow. I suppose you could feel sorrow because the other person has died, for the expiration of their life, even though you might never have loved or might never miss them in your life.

Posted by: **NozAll | April 25 at 08:09 PM**

They had their chance at life. Let it go.

Posted by: **survivor | April 25 at 08:31 PM**

You're not responsible for other people's choices.

Posted by: **theshrink | April 25 at 09:17 PM**

It's like buyer's remorse. Right now, you're thinking of all the things you might have said or done while they were alive, right? But now you can't change anything you did or didn't do. It's a phase. Don't worry. You'll be liking life again soon.

Posted by: **justluvmyjob | April 25 at 09:52 PM**

Feel what you feel and think what you think.

vPosted by: **philosophie | April 25 at 10:58 PM**

Thirty-Nine

****

A week later Grandmother dropped a bombshell. It was conveniently timed to coincide with breakfast on Sunday. I hadn't been to church in two weeks. I'd fallen into the habit of sleeping in late on Sunday. And, consequently, eating late. A brief interlude before returning to bed.

"I have something to tell you."

"Is Oliver going to come in?"

"I don't think so."

"Because he looks like he wants to." I could see him peering through the window in the back door.

"He's waiting for me."

"Where are you going?"

"Out to lunch. To plan our wedding."

The cereal dribbled from my spoon onto the table. "I'm sorry, your *what?*"

"Wedding."

"Are you out of your mind?"

"Well…I might be. I'm 85. Maybe I am."

"You can't just wake up, get out of bed, and get married."

"No. That's true. You have to get a marriage license."

"There. See?"

"So we did. Yesterday. It lasts for thirty days."

"You mean this is premeditated? You've been talking about this?"

"Only for a week or so."

"But what about your shoulder?"

"What does that have to do with getting married?"

"Everything. Who's going to take care of you? Or are you planning on living here together?"

"I don't know yet. We're planning to go to London first. For our honeymoon."

"You're going to London on your honeymoon."

"Yes. Well…not really to London. We'll fly into London, but then go out into the countryside. Where Oliver grew up."

"But you've never been to London before. You've never been outside the country before! And what about your hip?"

She gave me a stern look. "That happened over ten years ago. And that's why I had it replaced."

"What about the store?"

"I'm thinking of selling it."

"Just like that! To whom?"

"I don't know. I thought I'd advertise in the newspaper. The house is paid off and you can cover the utilities, can't you? If we don't come back for a while?"

"Yes. But—how long will you be gone? And what about me?"

"We're not taking you. It's a honeymoon…"

"I get that. It just…I mean…what happens to me now?"

She leaned close to kiss me on the cheek. "Anything you want."

I sat at the table for at least an hour after she left, my cereal growing mushier by the minute. Grandmother and Oliver were getting married.

Married! At her age!

How had this happened? And why hadn't I seen it coming?

I decided to talk to Adele. I threw on some clothes and walked down to the taffy shop.

She started to smile when she saw me but then stopped. Slipped a furtive glance over my shoulder.

"Grandmother and Oliver are getting married."

"I know. She told me."

"When?"

"Yesterday."

"And it doesn't bother you? Just a little?"

"Why should it bother me?"

"That she's leaving. That she's going on without you. She's leaving you behind."

"She's not leaving me anywhere I don't want to be."

What was happening? Why was everybody acting strange? Had I woken up that morning in some sort of parallel universe?

I strode out of the store and hit the pavement at a brisk walk. There had to be someone who would understand.

Betty?

No. She'd be fixated on the honeymoon part of the whole event.

Thelma?

Why *not* Thelma?

I crossed the street and climbed the hill. Arrived at her doorstep out of breath.

"Jackie?" She peered beyond me. "Did you walk here? What's the matter?"

I held up one hand and placed the other on my chest. I took several deep breaths to stop my heart from racing. Finally had enough breath to speak. "Grandmother is getting married."

"I know. She told me."

"Does everybody know?"

"Would you...like to come in?"

"Thanks." I pushed past her and into her sitting room. Plopped into an overstuffed chair. "What's going on?"

Thelma sighed. She moved to the edge of the couch and sat down. "Your grandmother found a good, decent man who loves her and they're getting married. That's what happened."

"But...how can she just walk out on all of us?"

"She's not."

"She is. She's getting married and going to England for her honeymoon."

"And where's the problem in that?"

"She should be more responsible!"

"She's one of the most responsible people I know."

"See? And this is completely out of character!"

"I think it's completely *in* character."

"You don't just get married and leave. Someone could get hurt!"

Thelma looked at me, compassion radiating from her eyes. That wasn't fair. Tanks are supposed to be impervious to emotion. "Who? Your grandmother?"

"No. Me." I swiped at a traitorous tear that was sliding down my cheek.

"But that's just it. Her decision isn't about you. It's about her. And Oliver. And what makes them happy. So if you're feeling unhappy, make some decisions of your own."

On Monday, I let Joe have a couple minutes to sip his coffee and boot up his computer. Then, when I couldn't keep it to myself any longer, I scrambled up onto my desk. "Grandmother's getting married."

"Really? When?" His head jerked up, his eyes locked on mine.

"I don't know. They haven't decided yet."

"To...Oliver?"

I nodded.

He grinned. "That sly old fox." He looked away from me toward his computer and clicked his mouse. Then he looked up at me. "You seem...upset. Why aren't you happy for her?"

"I'm not her responsibility anymore. She can do whatever she wants."

"Did she say that?"

"No."

"You used to be her whole life, but now you have your own life. Part of growing up is letting people change."

"What?"

"In five minutes you can stop feeling sorry for yourself and start being happy for her."

"Is that all you have to say?"

"Yep. Pretty much."

I climbed down off my desk and slumped into my chair. Rubbed away hot tears of fury. "Well, why don't you try having a mother who abandons you at birth, and a father who dies before he even knows about you, and a grandmother who gets married on you, and then we'll see what you have to say!"

There was a long moment of silence. And then he answered. "It's not about you, Jackie."

I couldn't stop a sob from escaping my throat.

Grandmother and Oliver got married that Friday. A small ceremony at the courthouse. I was her maid of honor. For the second time that year, I found myself wearing a dress. It was getting to be a bad habit.

Joe was Oliver's best man. They both wore black pin-striped suits.

Thelma, Adele, and Betty were there. All dressed up. They clapped and cheered when Oliver and Grandmother were pronounced husband and wife.

And I did too.

By that point, after two weeks of thinking things through, I could truly wish them well.

Oliver took me aside after the ceremony. "I'm stepping into the role of grandfather for just this one minute. I'll step right back out if you don't want me. I thought you understood what I told you that day. About dying alone. I was talking about you and Joe."

"I know. And I do want you." I kissed him on the cheek. "It just didn't work out."

He grabbed my hand. "Only because you didn't want it to. Just remember this: Stupidity is only considered a virtue in fools."

"If I didn't think you were one of the kindest people I've ever met, then you could really start to get on my nerves, Oliver."

THE CUBICLE NEXT DOOR BLOG

New chapter

Someone else has left my life. For the moment. But this time, it's a good thing. And I'm happy about it. But this person is the only person who has ever really belonged to me.

Sometimes, it's just...hard.

Posted on May 18 in **The Cubicle Next Door | Permalink**

Comments

I don't think a person can ever really belong to someone else. They can be a part of you, but you can't really own them, like you can an Xbox.

Posted by: **NozAll | May 18 at 05:47 PM**

I couldn't have said it better myself.

Posted by: **philosophie | May 18 at 06:29 PM**

When something is good, you might as well be as happy as you can. Because you never know when things might get bad again.

Posted by: **survivor | May 18 at 07:42 PM**

I know it's probably hard. But you're also very brave.

Posted by: **theshrink | May 18 at 09:03 PM**

When the going gets tough, the tough eat ice cream. Indulge. It'll make you feel better.

Posted by: **justluvmyjob | May 18 at 11:39 PM**

Forty

****

I moped around the house over Memorial Day weekend. I cleaned, but I didn't make enough mess to require the recleaning of anything. The flower beds outside virtually ran themselves. I might have driven up to Mueller for a hike, but the sun was too sunny.

Finally, I walked out of the house and walked over to Joe's.

Rang the doorbell.

He wasn't home.

So I sat on his front step and waited.

Two hours later, he drove up. Parked his SUV. Got out.

"Hey. If I'd have known you were sitting here waiting for me, I might have stayed out longer."

I stood up. "Ha-ha. Where were you?"

He gestured toward the SUV. "Getting my oil changed."

"And?"

"Running errands. Who are you? Miss Marple?"

I felt my hands dig into my front pockets, lifting my shoulders. "The thing is, you were right."

"I was what? Could you say that again? A little louder so everyone can hear?"

My shoulders collapsed and I looked him straight in the eye. "You were right. I was feeling sorry for myself."

He moved past me and sat on a porch step. "Have you heard from your grandmother?"

I sat down beside him. "She called last week. She wanted me to box up some of her clothes and forward them to England. It cost about thirty dollars."

"Are they having fun?"

I nodded. "Having a fabulous time."

Joe grinned. "Imagine that."

We watched a car pass. Listened to some birds sing. Bees buzz. Joe stretched his legs out. Crossed them at the ankles and let his knees drop open. Began to whistle.

I pushed off from the porch and stood up. "Right. Well. Guess I'll go then."

"You came by just to tell me I was right?"

"Pretty much." And to see if there would ever be any hope of kissing you again.

"You might as well stay for lunch." He extended a hand. "Help me up."

I put my hand in his and hauled him off the step.

He kept hold of mine and pulled me up the stairs.

We walked together into his house.

He cleared off a corner of his kitchen table, closing half a dozen books and then stacking them into a tower. He topped them with the last three days' editions of the *Gazette* newspaper, but he left a three-ring binder splayed open, a lined tablet beside it.

"Homework?"

He looked at it and then winked. "I just have to stay one lesson ahead of the cadets, right? Have a seat."

I did. And watched as he took a loaf of bread, some bologna, and slices of processed cheese from the refrigerator. He set a bottle of mustard and a bottle of pickle relish on the counter beside them. Then he dumped some salad-in-a-bag into a bowl and threw some cherry tomatoes on top.

He began to assemble a sandwich. "My mom used to make me tuna fish and egg salad sandwiches for lunch. Said they were brain food. I hated them—they always got soggy."

"Lucky you."

"What did you get? Liverwurst?"

"I wish. Beef tongue salad. Or a Thermos full of oxtail soup."

"I got SpaghettiOs once in a while. Does anyone even own an ox in America anymore?"

"I had Twinkies. Sometimes."

"Well, Twinkies are tradable. Do you want mustard?"

"Please."

"Pickles?"

"Don't you mean relish?"

"Do you want any or not?"

"No, thanks."

"Lettuce? Tomatoes?"

"Both."

He took some chunks of lettuce and a handful of tomatoes and placed them on top of one side of the sandwich. Placed the second slice of bread over them and smashed it down. There were six bumps protruding from the bread when he delivered it to me.

"You could just buy big tomatoes and cut them into slices."

"I like these. They taste better. Want something to drink?"

"Water. Please."

He filled two glasses with water and brought them to the table. And then he made his sandwich. Sat down beside me and began to eat.

"Do you know what your grandmother's going to do with the house?"

"No."

"Are they planning on coming back?"

"I have no idea."

"Would you live there by yourself? If they decided to live somewhere else?"

"Sure. I guess. If she didn't sell it."

"What if she did?"

I put my sandwich down. "I'm still getting used to the idea that she's married. It's going to take me a while to get used to the fact that I might not be living in the house anymore."

"Sorry. Didn't mean to pry."

"It's fine." I picked the sandwich up again. A tomato bobbled out. I popped it into my mouth and felt a satisfying squirt. "It really is fine."

He cocked his head and took a long look at me. "Good. I'm glad it is. Fine, I mean."

"It is. It's fine."

"Any plans for the summer? Now that you're on your own. For a while, anyway."

I put my sandwich down again. "No. Why? Do you have a suggestion?"

"You could go to the ocean."

"I don't know…"

"It's not like you have your grandmother to worry about anymore."

"Listen, I said you were right, but I didn't say I wanted to wallow in it, okay?"

"Okay. Just making conversation."

The problem was, I didn't want to make conversation. What I really wanted was for him to put his arms around me and make the world go away. I wondered what he'd do if I were to lay my sandwich aside and claim his lap as my own.

I picked my sandwich up again just in case my body started getting any ideas.

"Anything wrong?"

"No." Yes. Almost everything was wrong. And I didn't know how to fix any of it.

We went to church together on Sunday. Everyone seemed pleased to see me. Told me how sorry they were that my mother had died. How happy they were that my grandmother had gotten married. Even the priest came up to give me a hug. I threw a look at Joe afterward. He just shrugged.

Monday morning began normally enough.

Joe brought a huge cup of coffee into his cubicle.

I tried to convince him not to set it down near his keyboard.

He laughed at me.

I ignored him.

But then he asked for my help. "Hey. You over there?"

"I'm here."

"Could you give me a hand?"

I got to my feet and scrambled onto the desk. "What's up?"

Joe was standing in the corner of his office near his coat tree. He had unzipped the top of his flight suit and shrugged out of the arms. Now he was in the process of tugging at his blue shirt.

"There are easier ways to bring it into submission."

He paused and glanced in my direction.

"I could find a match. The threat of annihilation might work. It's only polyester, right? Total meltdown."

"It's not the shirt. It's the wings. And the jump wings. I want to make sure they're lined up before I go to the bother of completely changing uniforms." He turned around to face me, buttoning the shirt. "I can never get them on straight. Help me out?"

I jumped off the desk and went over to his side. "What do you want me to do?"

"Are they straight?" He took a deep breath, planted his feet and stood at attention.

And I stood there looking at that broad expanse of chest. Those wide shoulders. The closely shaved neck that had one nick just beside the Adam's apple. The smooth stretch of skin from his chin toward his cheek. Those clear blue eyes.

I blinked. Blushed. "Um?"

"Are they straight? Are they lined up?"

"Are what lined up?"

His shoulders slumped. "The wings!" He straightened up again as I reined my eyes in.

"No."

He muttered something, started tearing at the buttons on his shirt. "I knew I should have done this at home."

My hands flew toward his. He was going to pop those buttons if he wasn't careful. "Let me."

His hands stopped as mine covered them.

I looked up into his eyes. Saw them staring down at mine. He'd never seemed quite as tall before.

He moved his hands, fell back into attention.

"Okay. Now what do you want me to do?"

"I don't know. I can't see the stupid things. I don't know which way to tell you to move them. But both the tops and bottoms have to line up."

I stepped back. Took a look. Figured out which set of wings to move in which direction and then peeled that side of the shirt away from his body. It left his standard white V-necked T-shirt exposed, stretched tight across his chest. I swallowed. Tried to concentrate on what I was supposed to be doing.

And it needed concentration. Both sets of wings were attached to the shirt by a series of prongs and frogs. I pulled the frogs off and looked around for someplace to put them.

Joe was looking down the tip of his nose at me. He was still standing at attention. But he was smiling. I could see his dimples.

"Can you make yourself useful?" I held the frogs up so he could see them.

He held out a hand I could drop them into.

I looked again at the outside of his shirt. The trick would be to shift the wings about one millimeter in a single direction without rotating or otherwise skewing them. "Do they teach classes on this? Tactical Dressing 101?"

Joe snorted.

"Why don't you just set these up and leave them on the shirt? It's not like you're ever in blues."

"I did. I washed this shirt last week. First time in two years."

I looked up into his eyes. He was laughing at me.

"Ouch." I'd stabbed myself with one of those fiddly prongs. I held out my finger to take a look at how deep the puncture was, to suck the blood if there was going to be any. The last thing Joe needed was a nice blood stain on his shirt. The wings popped out of Joe's shirt and bounced on the carpet.

We both reached down to pick up the wings and bonked heads in the process. Straightened up.

"Ow. You have a hard head!"

"Sorry. Here." He held out his hand. "Want me to do it myself?"

"No." I put a hand to his chest. "Stop fidgeting."

He stilled in an instant.

I could see the previous holes in the fabric. If I could match those prongs up with the holes, and then pull them out and move them ever so slightly… But without being able to see underneath the wings while I was doing it, the task was impossible. "You're going to have to take it off."

"What?"

I held out a hand. "Take the shirt off."

He grabbed the plackets of the shirt and held them together. "I don't think so."

"Come on, Joe. I can do it in two seconds if I can do it from the other side."

"Nope. Not without some music." He began humming a striptease and gyrating his hips.

"Joe, cut it out. Just give me the shirt."

He slipped a shoulder out of the shirt, rotated it, and slid it back beneath the material. He turned around and did a cute little shimmy with his butt, holding up his shirttails so I'd have an optimal view.

As if I didn't already have it memorized. And I didn't need to be taunted. I grabbed a shirttail. "Nice act. Save it for Broadway. Give me the shirt."

He two-stepped away from me, still humming. Still tugging that shirt back and forth.

I let go of the shirt.

He bent forward. Bent back. There wasn't an extra ounce of fat on his body. And the way he was twisting and turning showcased the effect of those T day workouts.

"Give me the shirt. Now."

He stopped. Grinned. "No. Catch me." He dashed around the cubicle wall and into my side of the office.

I'll never know why I did what I did. Chalk it up to momentary insanity. I rounded the corner, hopped onto my desk, took a flying leap, and landed on Joe's back, clasping him around the torso with my arms and legs.

"Hey!"

I turned my hands and reached them up over his shoulders. Leaned close so I could talk directly into his ear. The man's head was so thick, I wasn't surprised he hadn't understood me earlier. "Give me the shirt.

Give it to me now!"

"No!"

I reached an arm across his chest and tried to tickle him in the ribs.

He clasped my forearm and held it just off his body. "That's not playing fair."

"Well, neither are you!"

"You're the one who jumped on my back." He gave my forearm a tug and pulled me forward.

But I wasn't about to be dropped onto the floor. I locked my legs around his waist. Ha. I wasn't going anywhere.

And then, quick as a snake, he dropped his shoulder and pulled me around so I was facing him, my legs still locked around his waist. His arms were around me, clasped at my back. "You caught me. Guess I have to give you the shirt now."

The thing was, he wasn't laughing anymore. And he wasn't smiling. He was serious.

And while Dimple Joe is cute, Serious Joe is devastating.

I stayed there, looking into his eyes. I was so close I could count the flecks of white in them.

Then it happened. His gaze dropped from my eyes down to my lips. When he looked back, there was a question for me to answer.

And I just couldn't do it.

I unhooked my legs and slid down his chest. He enfolded me in his arms and held me close for a moment. He took a deep breath and then he let me go.

I pressed the wings into his hand. "Do it yourself." I turned on my heel without looking at him and walked out into the hall. I didn't stop until I'd achieved the safety of the women's restroom. It was only then that I discovered how tightly I'd been gripping the wings.

I had four puncture wounds in my hand.

They were all bleeding.

THE CUBICLE NEXT DOOR BLOG

One bird v. two

A bird in the hand is worth two in the bush.

That's what I've always believed.

I'm a low-risk kind of person. I have a job working with equipment. It never has opinions. It always does exactly what I ask it to do. I wake up every morning facing a day that is completely predictable. And I like it.

And then you came along. And now I have to work with you. You always have opinions. You never do what I tell you to. Just seeing you does the strangest things to my heart. And I have no idea what will become of you. Or me. Or us.

You have put the entire universe of my life into question and you're asking me to risk it all.

I want to. How I want to. But I can't.

Not yet.

Posted on May 29 in **The Cubicle Next Door | Permalink**

Comments

Classic psychology told us individuals seek to minimize risk in their environment. But psychologists have now identified a new breed of thrill seekers who, in fact, thrive on risk. Although not everyone fits this new identity, it can be said that taking risks is the only thing which allows you to define yourself.

Posted by: **NozAll | May 29 at 07:27 PM**

Only by risking much can much be gained.

Posted by: **philosophie | May 29 at 08:01 PM**

I'm the opposite, TCND. I always went into hyperspace when I played asteroids.

Posted by: **justluvmyjob | May 29 at 09:46 PM**

Here's what you can do: keep the one bird in your hand and buy a BB gun. With any kind of practice, it won't be long until you can have all three.

Posted by: **theshrink | May 29 at 10:23 PM**

Maniac. That's how serial killers get started! Does PETA have a hotline?

Posted by: **survivor | May 29 at 10:37 PM**

CLOSE

Forty-One

****

In my vast experience with men, my emotions had always been manageable. Sure, I had been attracted to Rick, but I had never jumped on top of him.

I needed to talk to someone. I chose Adele. I went to her house after work and asked my question as soon as she let me in the door.

"How do you fall in love with someone?"

"Well...it's a little difficult to say. Because no one ever plans on falling—over love or anything else. It just happens. If you knew how it happened, then you could avoid it. But you don't. So you do. Here, try one of these cookies." She reached into a cookie tin and fished out a neon blue cookie in the shape of a star.

I took it from her and nibbled at one of the edges. "But it seems that if you were going to do something so...out of control, you'd want to make sure you were...kind of...in control about it."

"There's lots of 'in control' about love, but that usually comes later. When you find out he's a stubborn old man who won't pick up his socks no matter how many times you ask him to or leave the toilet seat down or fold the newspaper up when he's through. But the falling in love is different. Falling is a feeling. Loving is a decision. Of course, you can fall in love with lots of people, but you don't have to make the commitment to love them. To marry them. That's the part you can be in control about."

"So how would you know if you *weren't* ready for a relationship with someone?"

"*Weren't* ready?"

"Just to be safe. I mean, you wouldn't want to be in a relationship if you weren't ready for one. Right?"

"Well…I don't know about that." She took a cookie for herself. Ate the whole thing before she resumed talking. "Would you like some milk?" She was already halfway to the refrigerator, so I didn't tell her no.

She took two jelly jar glasses from the cupboard, poured a glass for herself and one for me, put the milk away, brought the glasses to the table, and sat down again.

"Now, what was it you'd asked me?"

"About being ready for a relationship."

"That's right. Well. It seems to me that although you have to be the right person for a relationship, that being in a relationship with the right person will also change you. For the better."

"So you're saying I don't have to be ready?"

"I'm saying you don't have to be perfect. We're talking about Joe, right?"

I nodded as I picked up another cookie.

"Do you want to be ready?"

"Yes."

"Then you will be. And when you are, you will feel it."

"Could you be a little more specific? I don't want to feel, I want to know. When?" What I really wanted was a crystal ball kind of prediction. Dates and times. I was sure there was someplace in this town I could get one.

"This is life, Jackie. Think about how many things we know. And then think about how many things we don't. Sometimes you have to give up what you know in order to have what you can feel."

I was already shaking my head. "That doesn't work for me. I'm a 'bird in the hand is worth two in the bush' kind of girl."

"That's how you know that you're not ready for a relationship with someone."

"So what you're saying is, when I become a 'two in the bush is worth one in the hand' kind of girl, I'll be ready?"

She nodded.

"Well, thanks for nothing." I leaned over and kissed her on the cheek.

"What did you think of those cookies?"

"They were good."

"Can you guess the secret ingredient?"

Joe was pleasant the next week. Not distant. But very polite.

And I didn't like it.

I wanted the irreverent, impolite Joe back. The one who didn't give a rip what I thought about anything and always dragged me along on his misadventures.

And to lunch.

I was tired of eating dried up old chicken breasts. And carrots. And hummus. Hummus was for camels. That's what I'd decided.

I wanted poker night back.

Let's be honest. I wanted Joe. *Really* wanted him. Thankfully, my imagination could lead me no further down that merry lane.

But he was a perfect gentleman. As far as he knew, I'd blown him off. Twice.

I couldn't really count on him coming around again. I wouldn't if I were him.

What I needed was a way to commit myself to admitting my feelings without being able to back out. Because when it came right down to it, I was a big weenie.

I'd never asked God for anything before. Never figured I had the right to. There were so many people who had so much less than I did. But at that moment I couldn't keep myself from thinking the words, *God help me. Please!*

And he did.

I may have been a big weenie, but I was also a geek.

A geek who could do anything with computers.

And as I thought about it, I began to see a way.

THE CUBICLE NEXT DOOR BLOG

This gig is over

Okay, I can't stand it anymore. Here's the deal. John Smith reads this blog every single day. And he talks to me about it all the time. I've almost told him who I am twice.

I appreciate everyone's comments. (Most everyone's comments.) I appreciate the interest and the support. But I never did this for publicity. And I never wanted to be anyone's cyber-sweetheart. So here's what I'm going to do. On June 8 at noon, mountain time, I'm going to post my name in the comments section of this entry. If you want to guess who I am, be my guest. Just post it as a comment. If you're right, you win...a kiss.

But I can pretty much guarantee I'm not who you think I am.

Posted on June 04 in **The Cubicle Next Door | Permalink**

Comments

Please, please, please tell me you're Amy Wilson.

Posted by: **wurkerB | June 04 at 09:50 PM**

Don't be Amy Wilson. Be Maria Lopez.

Posted by: **onlyagofer | June 04 at 09:51 PM**

Be who you are.

Posted by: **philosophie | June 04 at 09:52 PM**

I'm taking bets on what state she lives in.

Posted by: **thatsmrtoyou | June 04 at 09:53 PM**

Hey—just heard this from someone who knows. "She" is actually a guy!

Posted by: **theshrink | June 04 at 09:54 PM**

I AM NOT A GUY, YOU PSYCHO!

Posted by: **TCND | June 04 at 09:55 PM**

CLOSE

Forty-Two

****

The frenzy of guessing began almost as soon as I posted the blog entry. The regulars, the ones whose comments I looked forward to reading, were pushed aside by the comments of hundreds of lurkers we'd never even heard from before.

The next day Joe practically tackled me as he came into work. "Hey! Did you see the blog?"

"No. Not lately."

"She's going to reveal her identity. Who do you think she is?"

"Who cares?"

"I bet she's some supermodel."

"On what basis?"

"I don't know. Just a hunch. She's smart, but she's not intelligent. Know what I mean?"

"No, I don't." I followed him around to his side of the cubicle. "What *do* you mean?"

"How smart do you have to be when you earn a million bucks just by smiling? I bet she's a babe. A blonde."

I went back and plopped into my seat. A blonde!

That afternoon Joe interrupted his typing with an exclamation. "Hey!"

"What?"

"I was wrong. I think I've figured it out!"

"What?"

"The blog."

"What about it?"

"I think it's actually a group of women."

"What?"

"Think about it. It's the only thing that makes sense. Otherwise she'd be schizophrenic."

"Schizophrenic?"

The next day he had a different theory. "You know, I was rereading all those blogs and I think I picked something up."

"What?"

"I think she's from Boston."

"Why?"

"I don't know. There's just an…accent…about the way she words things."

"There is?"

"Boston. I'm betting on it."

When he went off to teach, I looked through all my posts, wondering how I'd acquired a Boston accent from just four short years at MIT. And how it had exhibited itself in my writing.

But that afternoon when he came back, he leaned against the cubicle wall and made a pronouncement. "I was wrong about the Boston thing. I think the accent is actually Southern. I think she's a gorgeous, statuesque, redheaded Southern belle."

"Really."

I read the comments on my blog that evening. I counted more than one hundred new guesses before I stopped counting.

The next morning, when I got to the cubicle, Joe was already hard at work. But he looked up from his computer when I walked in. "Hey."

"Hi."

"You look tired. Long night?"

"Interminable."

"I stayed up too. Because I was thinking about the blog. And the thing is—"

"You know what? I don't want to know. I have work to do. And I have other things to think about. And it's a waste of time talking about a stupid, juvenile blog and some idiot woman who writes it."

"I didn't know you had such strong feelings about it. Sorry."

Just call it self-loathing.

I only had one more day.

And then I could call it done.

When I got out of bed the next morning, doom descended upon my shoulders. I took a shower. Stood in front of my closet. It didn't matter what I wore. The outcome would still be the same. Joe would still laugh. He'd probably flash me his dimples. And then he'd vanish into his cubicle and go back to work.

That's why I chose my flame low-tops. The symbolism was just too good to pass up, even to a computer geek like me. Going down in flames.

There was another Internet party.

Even bigger than the one in February.

I logged into the program and checked my statistics. I'd had a record day for unique visitors to the blog. A record day for total number of visits and number of comments.

If I were going down, then it looked like I was going to do it in front of the whole world. As noon approached, I got ready.

I opened a new entry.

Typed my name.

"Hey. You there?"

"Just a minute."

"You watching?"

"Yes."

"What do you think she looks like? Think she's a blonde?"

I made some sort of unintelligible noise.

"How do you spell pert?"

Pert? As in Kate? Blond, bouncy, cheerleader? Maybe I could beg the colonel to let me move my office to the supply room. If I threatened to crash his computer, I'm sure he'd do it. Nobody ever remembers the backup disks. "P-e-r-t."

"Thanks."

I did a last-minute scroll through the comments. One last effort to avoid baring my neck for the guillotine. As I scrolled toward the bottom, one last comment was registered. And it was addressed to me.

Jackie Pert Harrison.

Posted by: **theshrink | June 08 at 11:59 AM**

I went numb. I couldn't move. Couldn't think. My finger still hovered over the mouse which hovered over the send button on the computer monitor.

He knew.

He knew!

I pushed my chair back. Climbed on top of my desk.

He was waiting there for me.

"You knew."

He was staring down at me. A stare that was mesmerizing in its intensity. "I knew."

"For how long?"

"Since the first day I started reading it. If it hadn't been for that blog, I would have given up on you."

"But how did you know?"

"Read the post from 5 June."

I climbed down. Heard him climb down on his side. With shaking hands, I bent over the keyboard. Retrieved 5 June from the archives. The answer had been staring at me the whole time. "Che Guevara."

"Yep. I'd find him and kiss him if he were still alive!" Joe took my hands from the keyboard, pulled me out of my chair, and then drew my arms around his waist. Released my hands. His fingers pressed into the small of my back, pulling me closer, tight against that splendid chest.

"Maybe you could kiss me instead."

He smiled that million-dollar smile just before he did.

THE CUBICLE NEXT DOOR BLOG

Who I am

John Smith guessed. He knew the whole time. I'm Jackie Pert Harrison. And I sit right beside him, all day, every day, in the cubicle next door.

Posted on June 08 in **The Cubicle Next Door | Permalink**

Comments

Jackie Pert Harrison? But that's what theshrink guessed. How did he know?

Posted by: **NozAll | June 08 at 12:16 PM**

He knew because he *is* John Smith, you moron!

Posted by: **justluvmyjob | June 08 at 12:17 PM**

And? What did he say? What did you say?

Posted by: **survivor | June 08 at 12:18 PM**

Not very much. We were too busy kissing.

Posted by: **TCND | June 08 at 12:32 PM**

The best dreams are always the ones that come true.

Posted by: **philosophie | June 08 at 12:33 PM**

CLOSE

Epilogue

****

They call our cubicle Courtship Corner. People throw quizzical glances at it as they walk by, as if they're wondering just exactly what we did back there.

Nothing. And everything.

You know what they say about subdivisions. When your space gets divided, it's best if you can just make peace with the neighbors.

Did we get married, Joe and I? Of course we did. We had a military wedding at the Academy Chapel. Joe's father and mother, brother, sisters, nieces and nephews all showed up; they wasted no time in making me feel like part of the family. His mom had even made me a sweater.

Betty did my makeup. Adele did my hair. Grandmother was my maid of honor. Oliver the best man. All our friends from church were there. Even the priest. People say we had the longest saber arch in Academy history. All the history majors wanted to be part of it because Joe is their favorite instructor.

And I'm growing on them.

Joe took me to the ocean for our honeymoon. To Goa and the magnificent Indian Ocean that changes from sapphire to azure and back again with every wave. And there, after I said goodbye to my mother, I was finally able to say hello to the rest of my life.

And, by the way, the "rest of my life" included skiing some of those black diamond runs the winter after we were married. I even "took the hill" and skied Pallavicini. But please don't worry. I'm very much alive. And if you're ever in Colorado Springs on a Thursday night, and happen to catch a movie at the Twin Peaks, don't look too closely at the back row...or at least have the decency to wait until the lights come back on.

Other Books by Siri L. Mitchell

Kissing Adrien

"The French are always up for romance,
so when the crowd saw Adrien striding through the Paris airport
toward me, I'm sure they were hoping for a good kiss...
I was too."

Claire Le Noyer, 29, wants a do-over. She wants the life where she majors in history, not accounting. Where she takes two-hour lunches, not ten minutes in front of her computer. Where her pastor boyfriend treats her like an attractive woman he's deeply in love with, not like a nice pet dog.

But for now she's a Seattle numbers-cruncher with a wardrobe from REI sent to fashionable Paris to check out an apartment left to her parents by a mysterious cousin. When her childhood crush—handsome, pleasure-loving, and very French Adrien—introduces Claire to the City of Lights, béarnaise sauce, and kisses in very public places, Claire cautiously begins to embrace another way of living.

Who would have guessed Adrien would also introduce her to the bigger questions she must answer...Who is her one true love? And will she ever learn to enjoy the life God has placed right in front of her?

*A fresh, funny novel of faith and joie de vivre—
and what happens when they meet.*

"A sheer delight! Smart, funny, romantic, and intelligent. Loved it! *C'est magnifique!*"
—Laura Jensen Walker, author of *Dreaming in Black & White*

"Enchanting! Siri Mitchell weaves an irresistible tale. *Merci beaucoup!*"
—Ginger Garrett, author of *Chosen: The Lost Diaries of Queen Esther*

Something Beyond the Sky

Who knows when you'll meet your new best friend?
She might be just around the corner.

"We came from different states, different backgrounds, and different religions. But we soon learned that first impressions are often wrong, and that, when given a chance, the most unlikely people can become friends..."

Can one woman engage in life-changing friendship with someone she's just met? Can four? That's life on an Air Force base, where four very different women share only the common bond of being military wives:

Anne, newly married and with a university diploma in hand, finds herself unprepared for the realities of marriage, her limited job prospects, and people's strange response to her.

Rachel married beneath herself in terms of money but discovers she is bankrupt in relational skills. She'll give anything to keep her shaky marriage intact.

Beth resigned her commission to stay at home with her twins. How can she tell her husband that she thinks she made a mistake?

Karen battles an eating disorder while she tries to ward off questions about her husband's love, her lack of children, and her personal journey of faith.

In this compelling story of love, friendship, forgiveness, and truth, each woman discovers that with a little faith she can believe that yesterday's heartaches and today's troubles are nothing compared to what lies beyond the sky.

"Mitchell, a military spouse, looks at the lives of military wives through the eyes of four diverse women...Mitchell is at her strongest portraying the frustrations of women coming to grips with careers and motherhood (or infertility or pregnancy) and the challenges of military life. She is adept with flashbacks and withholds certain key bits of information until the right moment, which adds punch to the narrative."
—Publishers Weekly

"A profoundly moving book..."
—Joyce Erwin, Senior Protestant Chaplain's wife, Elmendorf Air Force Base

About the Author

Siri Mitchell graduated from the University of Washington with a business degree and has worked in all levels of government. As a military spouse, she has lived all over the world, including Paris and Tokyo. With her husband and their little girl, Siri enjoys observing and learning from different cultures. She is fluent in French and currently mastering the skill of sushi making.

If you are interested in contacting Siri, please check out her website at sirimitchell.com.